LIGIA DE WIT

BRADAÍS PLEDGE

BURDEN
OF
FAETE

Cursed Dragon Ship Publishing, LLC

6046 FM 2920 Rd, #231, Spring, TX 77379

captwyvern@curseddragonship.com

This books is a work of fiction fresh from the author's imagination. Any resemblance to actual persons or places is mere coincidence.

Cover © 2024 by MiblArt

Developmental Edit by Kelly Lynn Colby

Proofread by S.G. George

ISBN 978-1-951445-60-7

ISBN 978-1-951445-61-4 (ebook)

To those who dare to dream about pirates and faeries, no matter the age, and who set sail into the Sea of Reading with unwavering hearts, may your journeys be filled with endless adventures and your imagination forever unfurled.
For you, dear reader, is this book dedicated to.

Part One

ONE

Ryanne

If someone had told me I'd be floating beneath the crashing waves like a fish with human legs as sharks swam nearby while being hand in hand with the most dangerous foe of my beloved fae mentors, I would have thought them cuckoo as a pooka.

Swimming underwater was never my specialty. Water and I fared as well as the Erlking dancing with a gnome.

Having a bradaí in the mix had changed everything.

Titus and I witnessed a fascinating whale-feeding technique. The humpbacks plunged deep beneath a school of fish, then they blasted bubbles from their blowholes to stun the prey. It kinda reminded me of bradaís when they hunt innocent human seers like myself; though instead of bubbles they used their charm to stun us.

And yet here I was, fingers entwined with a bradaí while we were suspended in the water, he dressed in only his boxers and me in my bra and underwear—my makeshift bathing suit.

Shafts of light filtered down, chasing shadows away, exactly what I'd hoped for when I'd practically dragged him into the ocean with a silly pretext. His short raven hair floated undisturbed in the water. But the peace he'd reflected in the previous submersion wasn't present, and a slight crease settled in his brow.

Not what I was looking for.

With a kick, he returned to the surface, dragging me alongside. Damn. Once above, he let go of my hand, and I took a long gulp of fresh air, my lungs requiring it as soon as we breached the surface.

We were in open ocean, bobbing like buoys and, apart from his ship, nothing but water all around. Water! Something I'd avoided until recently. The bradaí floating not a foot away cured me of my fear, a bradaí with wavy hair plastered to his head and droplets of water stuck to an aquiline nose, heavy-stubble beard, and his golden earring, his eyes the exact shade as the dark green water.

I opened my mouth, and he pressed a finger against it faster than a gnome stealing mushrooms.

"No."

My lips quivered in protest. The feel of cold water clung to my skin, and salt invaded my mouth.

"Whatever questions you have, woman, will have to wait."

"I wasn't . . . Just one. Please?"

Titus swam backward.

"What are you doing?" I shrieked as the gaping span of water between us increased—he *mostly* cured me of my fear.

With mischievous laughter, he kept ahead of me.

"Don't do that," I said in a too high-pitched tone, shame coloring my cheeks. I shouldn't act like such a baby, but it was one thing to know his power would push predators away from me and another to swim by myself. Something touched my leg. "Nymphs!"

"There are none here," Titus said, refraining from an obvious chuckle.

The nymphs' chant sounded in my ears, echoes from a distant past.

Down, down you go.
Sleep with us below the surface.
Your eyes will widen and your lungs explode.
Come join us,
Down, down you go.

"Maybe," I said, finally grabbing his arm, "but you never know with those wackos."

My aquaphobia had been tamed—somewhat—but my nymphphobia was far from gone. Titus wasn't a merman, but his connection with the water was powerful.

No, not a merman, but a shark. A great white shark. I had to remind myself not to forget that part of him.

"You've never told me what happened between you and the nymphs," he said.

"How about we talk about this on the ship?"

"Let's get you back then," Titus said, nodding his head toward the nearby bradaí warship. "There's another storm brewing."

I glanced at where he was looking. Far away, light gray clouds gathered in one spot, like bullies in a huddle, and further away, darkness.

I held on to his neck, my body stuck to his. "Oh God, I hate storms."

"You hated ships, and yet, here you are."

"But storms . . ." My teeth clattered together.

"And you hated water. And yet, here you are."

"Just shut up and take me to the cabin."

He laughed. By Cuidi, how much I loved the way he laughed and how his shoulders shook while at it.

"The sea crashes and sweeps, but there's peace within," he said.

"Tennyson?"

"Me. You'll get it."

Yeah. No.

Once near the blast-to-the past ship, Titus grabbed a rope that hung at its side, and he easily climbed with me clung to his neck, my legs wrapped around his waist. His crew barely looked at us as we climbed onto the deck. One of the crew handed me a plush robe and water to rinse out the salty taste. Titus? He liked to dry on deck, no matter the weather. He just pulled on his discarded black trousers and white shirt, his favorite combination, along with his knee-high black boots and red jacket. A true pirate's life for him.

A dark, *immortal* pirate life for him.

As soon as we were settled, his crew worked to deploy the sails. The *Scáil Dragún*—similar to the USS *Constitution* marooned in Boston but a bit smaller at about a hundred and fifty feet long—was a barque encased in dragonwood to make it undetectable to humans. The sails, woven by sea nymphs to enhance the speed, were attached to three masts.

The poop deck rose at the stern, below which a couple of electric wall lamps framed a door. On the deck itself, the sturdy forty-year-old redhead Stephen maneuvered a gigantic helm. A black flag with a dragon instead of the Jolly Roger billowed on the mainmast.

It was cute, now that I wasn't a prisoner but a guest. I gave Titus a warm smile. A lost one, since he was staring at the ocean as if expecting the mighty waves to answer an unspoken inquiry.

Yeah, he was troubled for some reason.

The sails whispered that odd word, *feihnum,* and my touch of fae stirred—it was a feeling like a cold eel slithering inside me, wanting to be petted. That power had been growing, more so when engaging with Titus's own power.

Aine, I'd called it. My heart longed for the taigh, my second home, for its winding paths and buildings. Aine stirred and shapeshifted into brownies, gnomes, and pixies in a blur, all creatures I'd interacted with. When my touch of fae activated, everything happened inside me but my mind *felt* how the power transformed or acted. It was like knowing what my right hand was doing without looking.

But it hadn't been me prompting the images this time. I pressed a hand to my chest, commanding Aine to stand still.

The power shapeshifted into the taigh, sending me a message. I sucked in a breath.

Return to the taigh. Was that a fae's command?

"I have to say, I'm surprised you wanted to get in the ocean so soon," Titus said, taking me out of my inner mumblings.

I feigned a nonchalant shrug. "I wanted to see if I would fear it again."

"Not that successful, aye?" A quick wink took the bite away. "How old? When the nymphs got to you."

"Ten. They're scarier to me than any horror movie—they left me with a scar, the scaly bastards."

We stood near the railing, though I was a bit separated from it. Conquering one's fears wasn't easy, and I had lots of respect for any body of water.

Baby steps, as I'd said to Peter, my fae mentor, back in the taigh where Titus had been held prisoner.

The flag snapped with the wind, and chants from his crew mixed with the constant splashing of the water against the hull. A wave rose like a small mountain in the distance, the foam crowning it like snow.

Swimming in the ocean had always been a nightmare, or it used to be before I took this strange path, a task my fae mentors offered me, a simple human.

A human with a touch of fae.

The wind chilled me and messed my wet, chestnut hair. Titus had promised we'd buy more clothes in Paris.

Paris.

"You promised me Paris in three days," I said, keeping an eye on the dark, faraway clouds. "It's been two."

"Aren't you enjoying the sailing?"

"Ah, actually, I am. Where exactly are we?" It was impossible to tell. Nothing but water had been our companion since I returned to the ship after the traumatic experience in Wataru's lab, back in Japan. Had it been only two days?

"We're near the Panama coast, in the Pacific Ocean."

"And we'll get to Paris tomorrow."

"Aye."

"Paris doesn't have a port."

Finally, he smiled. "We're not sailing through the Seine, don't worry. But I promised you'd love the Dragon Portal, and I know you will."

"I used to watch dragons from Cuidi's taigh. Is there an actual dragon here?" My skin tingled, whether from excitement or fear, I couldn't tell. Probably both.

"Have patience, woman."

Patience wasn't a virtue of mine, but I'd been practicing in this new gig. You couldn't be otherwise when dealing with immortals. He was finally starting to open up, though I'd barely scratched the surface.

"I was wondering—" I started.

"This isn't the time, *ashtore*. I want to deviate the ship to avoid the storm, so you can sleep better."

Ashtore was an Irish endearment that meant *treasure*, something that could be taken in many ways in my case.

"It's about Aghna and why you can't kill fae."

"I *can*. All bradaís do; it's our main command. I choose not to, which is different."

"Okay, so—"

"Later."

"How about your friends? Kara and Sergei?"

"Later." His frown darkened.

Was that what was troubling him? The lost friendship with his kin? "By Cuidi, are we back to evading me?"

He leaned on the rail. "You swear by her a lot."

"Well, she's like my second mother."

"I've never heard you swearing by your mother's name."

"'By Harriet' doesn't have the same effect. Oh, and speaking of my family, I want to talk to them."

"The fae." He scowled.

"Not my fae family, silly. Tír D'aois doesn't get Wi-Fi. My human family."

"You're quite close to the fae," he said softly, a look on his face I couldn't pinpoint. Wistful? Longing? No, that was wrong.

"I've been with them since I was eight. They've taken good care of me, and they're so great, really. I love them, though they can be mysterious and . . ." My enthusiasm withered at that odd look again.

There was something unreadable in his expression, something that made me shiver, and I caught myself before taking a step back. Darkness. He was darkness, and I was here to study him by order of the fae. He could never find out.

He suddenly closed the distance and framed my face with his

tanned hands, his eyes the shade of the steely ocean. "I'm so glad I found someone like you. You're genuine. I can't tell you how important that is to me, to find someone who's not trying to manipulate me or lie to my face. It's refreshing."

I quickly hid my face in his chest so he wouldn't see my lying eyes.

Aine swirled inside me and shapeshifted again into one of the taigh's buildings, then coiled, expectant. The instruction was clear; I had to return.

I hoped fae wouldn't be expecting us in Paris, because as sure as hell I wouldn't go back.

Not yet.

TWO

Ryanne

The roll of the ship was a comfortable sensation beneath my feet. Salt sprayed us while the *Scáil Dragún* danced across the choppy waves like a dryad jumping over fountains back at the taigh. Some of the crew worked on deck, whistling, chanting, and treating the dragonwood with a special concoction.

Dark clouds covered the sky. Titus was inside the captain's mess with Homkar, his first mate. Bricius, my pixie guardian, was in his usual spot, flying among the sails in the mizzen mast, right above the poop deck.

Bricius had thought poop deck had a different meaning, but Titus explained it's the deck that forms the roof of a cabin built in the rear. Bricius still giggled every time it was mentioned.

I leaned my forearms over the rail, my gaze set on the sea. It felt like it'd been so long since I met Titus in that Starbucks back in Seattle. Then, I hadn't had a clue of what my fae power meant, except for my ridiculous visions; it was mind-blowing to think not even a month ago I'd been worried about them.

Carriers of my wishes, Cuidi had said.

Those visions used to show snippets of the guys I dated with the women they were meant to be with, because that was what I'd wanted, a relationship. What an idiot I'd been. Now, closer to my twenty-third birthday, I was certainly wiser. Only a tad, but I'd take anything.

Wiser, except about my quest. I'd been so certain I'd found the spark the first time I'd submerged with Titus, that bright light that connected all beings with Ard-Bheith, the Supreme Being. All beings but the bradaís.

Finding this spark was proof that Anord had created the bradaís with the same guidelines used by Ard-Bheith. If found and activated, it could sever the tight hold Anord had on the bradaís.

And here I was, back at square one on the big Bradaí board.

I waved at Bricius, and he zoomed toward me. We headed to the captain's cabin at the stern, four steps down from the main deck. How strange was it to be so open about my pixie guardian, even as the crew —all human but Homkar—couldn't see him. But they were used to strange things around Titus.

Titus's cabin was spacious and well-lit, with rectangular windows on the side wall. Like Titus, the ship was deceiving: modern when needed but old-fashioned at its core.

Bricius zoomed around like a seven-inch fly, dizzying me with his flapping gossamer wings. His wild orange hair was tousled by the wind, and his pale cheeks reddened. But his bright eyes, also orange, showed his excitement. Somehow he'd managed to procure himself a velvet vest and a puffy white shirt: a pixie-pirate. Considering how frequently he tried to eradicate pirates when he guarded me all those years, it was a seismic change in him.

His happy expression changed to concern. "What is it, Ryanne?"

"The spark, Bug. I was so certain when Titus and I were in the ocean the first time that I'd felt it. It wasn't there this morning." I rubbed my arms.

"You have to find it, yes, yes, yes. When I touched him myself, all I felt was some light breaking through the darkness."

"Cuidi said the spark is a bright orb of energy, and that I'd feel joy deep in my soul. It wasn't like that—what I saw was more of a pinpoint of energy, not an orb. And it was weak, elusive."

We kept quiet, each one lost in our thoughts. Bradaís were created by Anord, a dark god-like being from another dimension who wanted to control the fae, and who already controlled the bradaís like a master puppeteer. Cuidi, the Lady of the taigh, believed there was a way to cut that connection to Anord if we were to find the spark of creation within them.

That was where I came in. A human infused with a touch of fae power, a bridge, connecting both bradaís and fae. Fé Erie, the spirit of Tír D'aois, had shown me the fae path, and I'd taken it. I'd be the one to find a way to cut those strings, just as soon I found that elusive spark.

The touch of fae inside me provoked visions since we humans were way too concerned with the future, so the fae energy woke that part of us. Well, to us humans with a touch of fae. It also made us humans touched by fae slow to mature since fae weren't considered adults until they were a hundred years old. I was *cailín* to them, a child.

If that connection with Anord could be severed, then bradaís would be their own creature and might not be compelled to kill fae as they did now.

But Titus wouldn't . . . "Bricius! Titus won't kill fae."

"Are you certain? Because all the rest can and do, I assure you." His usually bright eyes darkened. "And they do it with glee."

"He doesn't *want* to. He said that in our first sea submersion but has been evasive since."

"Then he lied." Bricius nodded. "That's what they do."

"I felt the truth in his words." I paced around. "So it's not fae energy they have but something similar." I pressed a hand to my chest and felt Aine ready to jump at my command. "Cuidi said Anord used basic concepts of creation with them, so maybe bradaís aren't that different from fae?"

Bricius shot upward and gasped. "No, no, no! They aren't like us."

"Are you sure?"

He stroked his pointy chin for a moment, then sighed. "Perhaps you might be right. Bradaís aren't as we thought they were. At least not your pirate, no, no, no."

"Something's different with Titus, yes. He was vulnerable those times I felt that cold power of his: that first time here in his cabin, then underwater when he opened up. I need him to be vulnerable again to see if I can feel the spark."

"And how do you plan to do that?"

"We'll arrive to Paris tomorrow and . . . Paris! Bug, wouldn't Peter find us easily while on land?" I wriggled my hands. "I can't have him around!"

"The Lady would not let that happen, no, no, no."

My fae mentor, one I named Peter since I thought he was *the* Peter Pan when I first met him, hated bradaís with all his being. His hatred blinded him, and he would attack first and not ask questions later. He was *that* stubborn.

"What if Cuidi believes my task is finished?" I resumed my pacing. "She said I only needed to *feel* the spark, and Aine is pushing me to the taigh."

"What do you mean, pushing?"

I pressed a hand to my chest. "It sent me images of the taigh."

"But you're not done!"

"Not for a mile, so I don't get it. And I'm not ready to go. I gotta make Titus trust me enough for him to open up. To be vulnerable."

Trust. Something not quite happening between us yet.

Yeah, he might have kidnapped me from Cuidi's taigh, but it'd been my choice of taking Fé Erie's path that put me near him. A prisoner of my own making.

Admitting the truth to Titus, that the fae had sent me to him to discover a possible way for bradaís to get rid of the connection with Anord, well, that had to wait. Not to mention I had no idea how he'd react. Or even if he wanted to break that connection.

But that power of his bewildered me. Why would a bradaí, the fae's worse foe, created only to destroy fae, have a power so similar to my own?

I needed to know more, even if I had to do it behind his back—the fae's quest was now my own.

Were he to know I'd been sent by the fae to study him, that could make the shark in him snap.

THREE

Titus

A magnificent opus displayed for me to enjoy: a hissing gale galloping over towering waves, lightening radiated across the ragged ocean, while the *Scáil Dragún* dared them all. By the Morrigan, can anything be more beautiful than a storm in full?

A daring wave swept the deck, but no one was there to be swept out to sea. No one but Homkar, securely strapped to the helm, and I, Titus Aodhán Doyle.

Aodhán. A Name no one knew but myself and my creator.

The tempestuous ocean taunted me, my bare feet planted firmly over the planks. I stood near the bowsprit to feel the full rage of the storm, my waist tied by a rope. To the untrained human ear, sails would be silent—beyond their flapping in the wind. But I could hear their tune as a humming, connecting my ship with the ocean. Never had a storm beaten me or sent a ship of ours to Davy Jones's locker. The sea nymphs knew their trade, and the ship was well protected with their hand-woven sails.

I grinned, satisfied and feeling light for the first time in a long time. No dark sensation, no voice inside my mind. Instead, my chest filled with something different, as powerful as what made me yearn for the peace I usually found inside the water.

It was a matter now to prove my theory and see if Ryanne could really inhibit the beast inside me.

Would she be able to dim the gold lure too? Anord's balls, I hoped so. If I failed again, she would never forgive me.

And I couldn't lose her, not now that I felt at peace.

The beast was quiet, but whether because of Ryanne or due to the recent submersion in the ocean, I couldn't tell.

Time would.

Préachta, that alien cold energy dormant until Ryanne stepped into my life, exploded in my chest, and traveled down my legs, to my feet, connecting me with the dragonwood. I'd always known I could connect with it, though now it was evident why.

There is no cold, my beast roared, a voice inside me I could not dim by myself.

The bloody beast had denied the alien energy since I'd gained consciousness. Though I couldn't deny its presence, not anymore.

Rough waves lashed hard on the hull like a bully punching a child, and I pushed away any concerns about the beast for the moment. I could hear the laughter of the waves and the response of the dragonwood like a low roar inside the boards.

I shook a fist at the stormy sky, guffawing like a maniac. Something about storms stoked me, lighting a fire within like adrenaline to the danger-seeking humans. I opened my arms while the gale hit me and messed my hair. Rain mixed with seawater covered me.

My nature was this.

You are a bradai.

I was. A pirate who belonged in the sea. And I was bloody proud.

The air shimmered at the tip of the bowsprit.

The ghostly figure of a fae-woman took form, the same one who had been haunting me. Her long dress wasn't affected by the wind, yet her fire-red curls rattled around her. Smiling, she offered me her hand.

"Come to me," she said in a loud voice that pierced the hissing gale, even though her lips remained closed.

My beast held me back like an energy wall separating us, chaining me to my spot.

"What do you want from me? Why do you keep appearing?"

The beast roared. *Do not go. Stay away.*

The woman cocked her head, and a look of sadness covered her as she vanished into the howling wind.

Anguish pierced my chest, like a blind man who wishes to see the sun for the first time just to witness dusk. I stretched my hand to where she was, wishing she'd appear again.

No. You do not belong with them. You are a bradai.

Venom ran through my veins like an avalanche ripping my guts. I stumbled against the rails. Another wave swept over deck, and I lost my balance.

I fell into the water. The ocean embraced me as a mother would a son.

Morrigan's crow, what in Anord's hell?

But I let myself plunge, let the freezing waters numb me, for the beast to shrink into a corner, cowed by the water as it usually was. The beast, my connection to Anord and how he controlled me, disliked the ocean. Disliked anything that sang of joy.

I kicked back to the surface. Homkar leaned over the rail and pulled the rope tied to my waist. I took over and climbed effortlessly back aboard.

"Everything all right?" His tone was concerned, and there was a small wrinkle in his otherwise smooth forehead.

I knew why. This was the first time I'd fallen like that.

"Perfect. You think you can control the ship by yourself?"

"The sails are doing their job, sir. Really not much to do but ride out the storm."

"Call me if necessary."

His dark brow smoothed. "Do we really need that pest here, sir? I'm fine with the girl but not her pet."

"The pixie's brave; I'll give him that."

Homkar grunted. "Still to Paris then?"

"Paris, aye."

He laughed quietly. "Dragons' balls, sir. Can't believe my ears. Will you need a bodyguard?"

"No. I want to hide for some time."

He stared into my eyes and gave a slow nod of recognition. As if on cue, we both looked back at the irate ocean. The ocean that was my home yet a dangerous place for her.

"Miyuki." He clucked his tongue.

I gripped the rail. Miyuki, a lover of mine back in 1910, had also had a touch of fae, albeit not as strong as Ryanne's. And then, Edward came around—the powerful gobshite who led the bradaí per Anord's will. I scoffed. He was no leader but a bully who obeyed Anord blindly, like the good puppet he was.

My fist clenched tight. Weren't all of us puppets?

"Is Edward nearby?" I asked. Perhaps some of my kin had been attacked at this point.

"The bradaí network is silent."

"We'll take the Dragon Portal tomorrow. I want to show it to Ryanne after breakfast, so make sure the crew is below decks by then."

Land presented another problem: fae. I had to make sure Ryanne would stick to my side and not run back to them. I was, yet again, between the devil and the deep blue sea. The lesser danger were the fae, all in all.

"'Break, break, break, at the foot of thy crags,'" I recited one of my favorite Tennyson poems, my voice thundering over the hissing gale. "'O Sea! But the tender grace of a day that is dead, will never come back to me.'"

Ryanne's question when we submerged in the ocean together for the first time popped into my mind: "What makes your face darken when you're alone?"

The loss of Sergei's friendship and Kara's respect. What had happened between us. A chasm no one had wanted to cross.

The memory of the murder that drifted my so-called family apart surfaced like a corpse in the water.

What an irony. So many had I killed and yet the only murder I didn't do, was the one that broke my family apart. Kara, our former self-appointed leader, now worked by herself. Sergei? I had no idea, nor did I care.

The trust in each other had vanished like a bradaí's promise. Trust. Something I should gain with Ryanne.

FOUR

Ryanne

Titus yelled my name, blood tainting his pristine white shirt and seeping through his fingers. Too much blood. His eyes glazed, and he gasped, holding my hand between his sticky ones.

I wiped his blood, tears in my eyes, but the blood kept pouring. This didn't make sense—bradaís were immortal and couldn't die.

My eyes flew open to the darkness. A nightmare. It'd been vivid and nothing like my visions, not to mention I wouldn't have visions with a bradaí, since they weren't connected to humans or fae.

Titus was pressed against my back, his arm lazily draped over my waist. All was well, and I took a moment to relax my shaking breath. A delicious warmth spread through my body. The fire in my cheeks tangoed to every corner of my body as I realized I didn't want to remove his arm. My heartbeat and my breathing sprinted in a race to see which was faster. It was a tie.

But I couldn't give in. If I did, I'd never be able to return to be fully human, and I wanted to have that option open. Messing up with bradaís was okay if I kept my distance.

My fingertips slid over his bare arm, then I twisted a bit, sensing his tempting lips so near mine. I could reach out and taste them in his sleep. I stroked the line of his stubbled jaw and slid over the softer, slightly parted lips. So close . . .

Titus's eyes flew open to the night. He grinned.

Bricius snored, nestled as he was at the bottom of the bed, and Titus glared at him. Since Japan, Bricius slept here instead of the bathroom, which had been a real issue for Titus and for me.

But the bug was asleep.

I turned in full and stuck my body to Titus. He responded with quick hands that stroked my bare back, my nightgown riding up my thighs. My breath hitched, wanting more of him.

Screw the No Return to Human card.

"What, what?" Bricius said, sleepy.

I grunted, Titus growled, and I lifted my head to see if Bricius would fall asleep again.

But the darned pixie was a light sleeper.

"Are you two trying to—?"

"Bricius!" I sat up and pulled the covers to my chest. "Can't you go fly to deck or something?"

"That's a good idea," Titus said and waved a hand toward the door. "Go and play with the sails."

"It's dark, pirate." Bricius took flight and hovered between us, his butterfly wings catching the moonlight. "You and your pirate are getting too close, yes, yes, yes."

"Go to deck, pixie." Titus growled.

"No, no, no." He puffed his chest. "I've always slept with Ryanne." He yawned and settled between us.

Between. Our. Frigging. Bodies.

Titus looked at me. "Is there any way—?"

"No," I grumbled. "It's the story of my life." I let my head fall onto the pillow and sighed.

Bricius snored. Quite loudly, if you ask me.

"Let's get rid of him in Paris, shall we?" Titus mumbled.

I couldn't agree more.

"No, no, no," Bricius mumbled in his sleep. "I'll never be apart from Ryanne, no, no, no."

Titus turned his back to me, his body stiff.

Fé Erie had warned me to be clear of heart and mind, otherwise the quest would be a failure. And for that, I should push Titus's advances away. Not to mention I was just a cleansing agent for Titus to balance his energy. There was no *us*.

And yet, I wanted nothing more than to get lost in his arms, seize the moment and all of that.

But how to make Bricius disappear for a while?

Moonlight illuminated the cabin in bright silvery tones. Too intense. I looked up, squinting at the light. I clapped a hand to my mouth, stifling a cry of surprise.

Fé Erie stood beside the bed. Her big orange eyes looked at me without blinking. The intense silver light bathed her except for her fire-red curls, swirling around her—a flash of color in a mercury sea.

Fae couldn't find bradaís ships since water drains energies. But then, she was Fé Erie, the Queen-Knight of the fae and a spirit to boot.

She signaled me to follow her through the open door.

The moon shone with ghostly light upon the three masts and the furled sails. She stopped in the middle of the ship and gestured at the ocean. The intense salty smell reached me, and I could feel the ship gently bobbing.

This space felt like an alternate dimension of sorts, like the ones back in the taigh when Fé Erie showed herself to me, so maybe she wasn't really *here*.

The reflection of the full moon painted the ocean in the same silvery tones. A whale broke the placid surface, releasing a jet of water. Fé Erie pointed at the stern where the captain's cabin was.

"Oh, right! Titus. I found out he has a cold power not unlike mine."

The corners of her lips twitched upward.

"You knew that. Check." I wouldn't have minded a little head's up, but I guess you couldn't ask much from spirits. "Is that connected to the spark you want me to find out about?"

She stared at me with those big eyes reflecting eons of wisdom.

"Is that power of his the same as mine? Is it fae related?"

Not even a blink. *Great. I suck at charades. Should I ask how many words?* Though maybe it wasn't a good idea to joke with supernatural beings.

"Do all bradaís have that? I haven't met any other than him and—"

With a frown that creased her lovely features, Fé Erie signaled again toward the stern, not in the direction of the cabin but beyond where there was only silvery water.

"Titus can't kill fae. Okay, won't, but isn't that the whole point?"

She placed her open palm on my chest, and Aine responded like a kitten wanting to be petted. It vibrated like a tuning fork, but stronger than ever, so strong my body felt like a flimsy vessel.

"Be clear of mind, be clear of heart," she seemed to say inside my head.

Or maybe it was a whisper of a past time.

Her eyes held a warning while Aine kept purring inside.

And then, she was gone.

I closed my eyes for a moment, only to open them and find myself laying on the bed, daylight entering the empty cabin.

A warning. About what? About my Return to Human card? Somehow it was connected to my fae power.

But then, she signaled toward the stern. Maybe someone was coming.

Another bradaí.

FIVE

Ryanne

I flung the covers aside. Bricius hovered next to me.

"Fé Erie! She came here! What did she tell you?"

"Later, Bug," I said while I left the cabin.

Titus stood with his back to me at the top of the stairs, hands crossed behind his back. I climbed to the second-to-last step. Bricius grumbled something about seers being too mysterious, then zoomed to the sails, his favorite place.

Sunrise colors painted the sky before us; we were certainly heading east.

"Up so early?" he said without turning. "I have a surprise for you."

"I had a premonitory dream," I said. It wouldn't do to explain it was an alternate dimension. I climbed the last step and placed myself right behind him.

He looked over his shoulder, then turned to me, brows furrowed. "Why aren't you dressed? Go change."

"Don't be bossy, it's bad for PR. Besides, I have to tell you something." I crossed my arms over the nightgown he'd given me the first day on the ship.

He sighed and shook off his jacket, then placed it on my shoulders. "What's so urgent that it can't wait for you to dress decently?"

"You gave me this nightgown."

"For me. Not for my crew."

I rolled my eyes then climbed the last step onto the deck. Titus had bought me clothes when he took me from Cuidi's taigh, but his taste was on par with his own pirate clothing: long conservative dresses that reminded me a bit of the clothing I wore back at the taigh, including this nightgown.

I looked past him. The crew was busy on deck, some scrubbing and others mending the ropes damaged in the storm, but kept glancing at where we were without any discretion. I tightened his jacket over the silky nightgown.

"I dreamed of a fae." Cuidi always warned about not giving names lightly, so I opted to omit Fé Erie's.

"Who was he?" Titus all but spat.

"*She.*"

In a sudden movement, he squeezed my arms. "Long tresses? Red like they're on fire?"

His aquamarine eyes looked as if they wanted to see beyond my own. Why did they keep changing color like that? Did all bradaís have those strange eyes?

"Yes. Do you know her?"

He sucked in a breath. "Was the dream vivid?"

"Yes. She warned me about something at the stern." I gestured to where she'd pointed. "Another of your kin, maybe."

"Homkar!"

I winced at his yell, then slipped my arms into the jacket's sleeves and closed it around me.

The first mate walked briskly to us. Homkar was a tower of a man, with powerful biceps like a Seahawks player and skin the hue of mahogany with an undertone of berry. He wore his usual rough fabric vest and loose pants. Two golden rings adorned each of his ears.

"Captain," he said respectfully, nodding his bald pate.

"Place a lookout to observe aft for any of the bradaí fleet."

Homkar turned and shouted, "All hands on deck!"

Moments after, around fifteen sailors were on deck, working on the sails and ropes.

Sails flapped and timber squealed. Waves crashed against the hull, splashing a few drops of salty water over me.

"Now, what else did the fae say? Give me details."

"She didn't speak. Just pointed out beyond the ship. But it was night, and I couldn't see a thing. Have you seen her before?"

"You should have warned me immediately."

"What do you think I'm *doing*?"

Titus took a spyglass from one of the sailor's hands and watched the horizon behind us.

"A sail! A sail!" the lookout shouted.

"What color?"

"It's blue, sir. I can barely see it."

"Bloody hell. It's *him*."

"Captain, it's the *Thunder*!" the lookout shouted again.

Titus glanced aft and scowled. I knew he really disliked his kind. It took me some time to spot the vessel, advancing uncommonly fast, even to my untrained eyes.

He grunted something to Homkar, who in turn shouted to the crew. Some sailors then worked on the ropes—the rigging, as Titus had explained to me.

"Hammocks up and chests down," Homkar bellowed to the crew who weren't working on the sails.

"Hammocks?" I asked Titus. I hadn't seen any.

"We use the order to stow away anything that could get in the way of a fight, although technically it's out of date."

"Wait a minute," I said. "Why don't you use motors?"

"It's a bradaí thing. We ought to use sails in any pursuit."

"That's quite silly, if you ask me," I mumbled since they weren't asking me at all.

Homkar said, "We won't be able to outrun her, sir."

"Anord piss on that whore from hell. And it's too bloody late to call it. He'll *know*."

"Aye, sir. Too close."

"Call what? Who'll know?" I might as well be painted with invisible ink.

Both men frowned at the oncoming ship.

Titus swiveled to face me. "What are you doing here? Get inside the cabin."

He made as if to grab my arm, but I took a step back, glowering. He waved to his cabin, and I headed there, my chin up.

"I need you to listen," he said after closing the door. "Stay here. In fact, hide inside the head."

"Do you have any idea how crazy that sounds? Hide inside a *head*? What am I, a passing thought?"

"Just stay there."

"What'll happen?" I shimmied off his jacket and handed it to him.

He put it on and lowered his voice. "Edward's about to kick my arse. Just do what I say, and everything will be fine."

I gasped. "Your Alpha? Is he going to hurt you?" Fragments of my nightmare came to me. Blood.

"Are you worried about me?" he asked with the tone of someone who never had someone caring about him.

"Of course I'm worried. I don't want to see you hurt."

Titus cradled my cheek, his eyes a clear sky blue. Tingles covered my cheek, my neck, my whole body. With him giving me space and Bricius present all the time, we hadn't kissed in full since that time in the ocean three days ago.

But Bricius wasn't here now.

I pulled him to me. At his demanding lips, I opened mine, allowing the invasion of his tongue, the sweet taste of his kiss. Salt tang and musky lotion clung to him, and shivers roamed over me like foam over sand.

He broke the kiss too quickly, and the corner of his lips tightened, his gaze darkening, reminding me of the pursuit. "Hopefully, this will be over soon. Hopefully."

"Why not use your portal?"

Titus shook his head. "He has an uncanny way to sense us when we're at sea. He'll notice something odd, and I care not to have him know about my portal."

"I mean for me and Bricius."

His body tensed. "So you can leave with the fae?"

"No, silly, to hide *us* if you're so worried."

"I won't have that," Titus said, jaw locked. "The fae will be able to find you quickly with Bricius, and there should be no need for such drastic measures."

He held my hands and rubbed his thumb over my palms.

"You're not going to mark me again, are you?" Dear Cuidi, I'd been so adamant about finding the spark, I'd forgotten about the mark that acted like a *Find the Seer* app.

"I want to make sure there is nothing left, but you did a good job. It's gone."

"Why just the hand? Why not the arm or skin in general?"

"There's a center of energy in humans touched by fae. The hand is where it's most concentrated due to the constant arm movement."

"Like a battery of sorts?"

"Aye. While your power is inside you, the only way we can sense it in a human is through the hand. And not merely a brush. It must be a firm and focused hold."

Same as my visions before: they were triggered when someone I liked squeezed my hand.

Bricius zoomed inside the cabin and, for the way he was flying, he was upset. "The big man told me to hide here! And not with those words, no, no, no."

"Aye," Titus said, pointing at the bug, "and don't come out for any reason, do you understand?"

Bricius furrowed his little brow and opened his mouth to protest, surely.

"If the Alpha sees you, he'll know she has a touch of fae, and you'll both be dead. So keep hidden," Titus all but growled.

Then he left the cabin.

"He marked you *again?*" Bricius flew around the cabin to prove he was upset.

"No, he wanted to make sure it was gone."

It didn't take long for the first shouts to come through. I picked the first thing I found in the armoire, a long-sleeved blue dress. If I was going to hide, at least I'd change inside.

"Come, Bug," I whispered even though the noises outside the cabin would mask any conversation of ours.

Bricius followed me as I hid in the bathroom and closed the door after him, then closed the porthole window to avoid any of our conversation leaking out, but mostly to prevent Bricius from flying outside out of curiosity.

Bricius asked me again about Fé Erie's appearance since pixies felt her presence. So I told him about the dream-slash-alternate-dimension while I changed into the dress.

Shouts filtered down, making it hard to understand who was talking or what they discussed.

After some time, I whispered, "What's happening outside?"

"Do you want me to look?"

"No!" I lowered my voice. "No, they can't know you're here." I drummed my fingers over my arm. "But I can have a peek. I came here for the bradaís, after all, and here I am, hiding like a little gnome scared of the big, bad troll."

"They're worse than trolls, yes, yes, yes."

"But you yourself said Titus isn't that bad. Maybe—"

"No!" Bricius flew right in front of my face and held his palm toward me. "Remember that evil man in Japan."

I could still feel the gun that had pressed against my forehead. The impotence I felt then. *You're a wuss,* my friend Sam had said when I didn't want to hear details of violence.

"I'm a Certified Wuss," I whispered.

Bricius looked thoughtful. "Who said that?"

"Sam. But she's right."

"She is, yes, yes, yes."

"I can't be one anymore. I called an ogre." Well not called it, but my fae power had turned into one making Haru release me, enough for Titus to defeat him. "I'm not totally powerless."

Bricius let his hand fall. "Erlking creatures shouldn't be called. Too dangerous."

"But it helped!"

"I do not like that look on your face, no, no, no."

I clenched my fists. "I need information, Bug, and I won't get it here. What if Fé Erie didn't give me a warning, but a heads up for the next bradaí?"

Hair bristled on my arms and nape, and I hugged myself tightly, staring at the door with my mouth and throat dry.

"Titus won't kill fae. What if he's not the only one? Maybe Titus holds only one piece of the puzzle and Edward the other. Isn't that why I'm here? To find anything I can about bradaís and help the fae."

"Ryanne," Bricius warned. "Your pirate said all would be lost if—"

"*If* they see *you*. Titus only knew I was a seer because he saw *you* first. He only confirmed it when he shook my hand and sensed my touch of fae. They won't."

Bricius's wings flapped while he stroked his chin, what he did when he was thoughtful. At least he seemed to understand me.

"Titus won't be at peace until he settles those issues with his friends. That's why I couldn't feel the spark yesterday, if that was what I initially felt. I need more information and, by Cuidi, I'm going to get it. You stay put, Bug. Don't show yourself or we're both doomed." I stood up, my legs wobbling.

"Be careful, yes, yes yes."

"I've got to do this. For Cuidi."

My answers weren't here, hidden in this bathroom, but outside.

On deck.

Titus

T he Morrigan screw Edward. Why did he have to come now of all times? The fae's warning helped me to hide Ryanne before he spotted her . . . or so luck would have it.

The *Thunder* was about to catch up. She was magnificent, a fast British clipper with three masts, built like the *Cutty Sark*.

Homkar and I stood on the bridge, watching the maneuvers of the ship as it pulled alongside the *Scáil Dragún*. I grimaced. Edward insisted on boarding us, and, unfortunately, no one had been able to stop him from doing so.

No one could.

"'Cannon to right of them, cannon to left of them, cannon behind them. When can their glory fade?'" Tennyson felt appropriate. "I must make him mad, Homkar. Don't intervene; no matter how dire the outcome."

Homkar shuffled beside me. I could sense his uneasiness.

"Because of the girl," he said.

"Aye. He can't find her."

Homkar reluctantly nodded. "This is absurd, sir, if I may say so."

"If the Alpha wants to have his fun, I would not say nay."

If I thwarted his entertainment, instead of putting his nose in every nook of my ship, he'd be angry enough to focus on me and leave the ship alone. An image of him finding her made my stomach flip.

I felt something.

You do not feel.

While the *Thunder* approached, I cast a glance at the bowsprit. That fae woman had appeared to me before. What the hell did she want? And most importantly, who in Anord's hell was she? Not an ordinary fae, that was clear, but then my kin had only encountered fae, not their spirits.

She is no one.

Not surprisingly, with Ryanne away in my cabin, the beast intruded in my thoughts again. I gritted my teeth.

Edward leaned on the rail of his ship. "Heave to, Irish," he called from his ship while grappling hooks arched toward the *Scáil Dragún.*

"Overjoyed," I called.

There was no need to try to remove the hooks. Edward would keep trying, and the sooner this sham was over, the better. There was no need for the hooks, either, but Edward liked to keep the practice as it was when he came into existence, back in the 1600s. Except jumping from ship to ship. While he was accomplished in that, we'd lost many good men with that playacting back in the day, so instead we used modern boats and ladders.

Two boats circled the *Scáil Dragun* round to the offside and half a dozen or so men from the *Thunder* climbed onboard.

Edward kept his boarding crew young and fit, and yet it was a miracle they didn't fall into the sea. My lips twitched in disgust. Most likely the idiots thought they were about to fight like *real* pirates in a Hollywood movie. The code prohibited us from killing other bradaí, but the law didn't forbid fighting among humans, so occasionally a brawl broke out between our crews, and some ended up dead.

"This is degrading," Homkar said, echoing my thoughts. "You should return to the councils, sir, and advocate for this to stop."

The idea of going to another meaningless bradaí council made me grit my teeth, especially when at the last one Edward had marked me as Ivan's murderer, thus causing the rift between me and those who used to be my family.

You have no family. Remember your path.

The real reason for this cheesy comedy jumped over the railing, followed closely by Minho. At least they knew how to properly board a ship. Dressed in Helly Hansen mid-layer jackets and Sperry sailing shoes, both seemed like fancy yacht owners instead of ruthless bradaís.

Edward advanced with the confidence of someone who'd never been defeated, his once-stocky frame now brawny. Walnut brown hair swept his shoulders with the same careless attitude he wore.

Minho lifted his angular dark eyes and stared right at me, coal-black hair tied behind his cap. Echoes of the past slammed into me. While Edward was the one I hated the most, what had happened between Minho and I was an unsurpassable chasm.

His hatred hadn't dimmed in centuries. A hatred I was starting to understand.

Yes, hate is good.

I slid a hand through the air to retrieve my sword from my bradaí pocket—a dimensional space big enough for a few things—and trudged toward them.

"You look good," I said, loudly. "Have you lost weight?"

Edward patted his flat stomach. "The wonders of the modern world. Now I do Pilates and have turned vegan. Even Minho has tried it. Fascinating, is it not?"

"Yah, Captain," Minho said in a flat voice.

Homkar stood in front of Minho, who stepped back, the coward.

"Let's finish this, Edward." I gripped my sword with my left hand. Edward was left-handed, so I'd practiced with both hands to be on a level field.

Edward gave a dry bark of laughter. "That's why I've always liked you, Irish." His usual cruel grin disfigured his face. "Despite knowing the outcome, you're the only one who faces me with that challenge in his eyes."

"The Norwegian gal just did that, Captain," Minho said, deadpan.

"Whatever." Edward drew his sword.

Norwegian gal? Had Kara been hit? How did she fare? Nothing of consequence; she'd heal. And yet, I loathed the idea of knowing Edward had gotten to her. But then, that was him, always hitting all bradaís one after the other with the excuse of overseeing our business. A mindless thug obeying Anord's orders like the good puppet he was.

That was our grand leader.

He opened his arms wide. "Let the games begin!"

Minho choked. He and I had one thing in common—a profound dislike for Edward's love of cheesy phrases.

I lunged. Edward parried the blow without even trying.

"This is fantastic," he said. "You're still in shape. The other bradaís should take you as a model—they're spoiled. And look at you, you still keep that red jacket, like days of yore."

"You won't find me dead wearing that stupid cap you're wearing." I twirled to avoid his counterattack.

He touched his white cap. "Makes me look handsome, yes?" He placed a hand on his chest and raised his sword. "All the world's my stage, and all the other bradaís merely players."

He blocked my attack like swatting a pixie. Bloody Edward, he kept getting better and better.

"You're not even original," I said.

I threw myself to the floor, swiping my sword under him. He jumped in time and tried to skewer me. I rolled and rose to my feet.

I ducked barely in time, his blade swooshing above me. Morrigan's crow, he was fast.

"Have you made more changes to the ship?" he asked. "I've always been fascinated with the things you implement. We'll make sure to take a good look afterward, yes?"

Anord be damned. Time to get him mad.

I let Edward come forward. The crew had been acting like seagulls at the upcoming tide, giving us ample space.

"It's such a joy to have you here, Edward."

I stepped back, blocking his attacks. I groped the space behind me until my foot hit the mast.

"Always curious about me," I said. "Always wanting to know why I'm different."

Edward's lips twitched in a repressed snarl, his long hair messed up. The blade of his sword flashed, and I slid aside. His sword stuck in the wood.

"And you can't figure it out. However hard you've tried."

With a guttural growl, Edward pulled his sword to release it from the mast.

I retreated to a safe distance. "It doesn't bother you? You're the Alpha." I opened my arms, giving him my best smile. "The most powerful. The only one able to kill bradaís." I lifted two fingers.

Edward's smile dissipated from his face. His next onslaught tore my vest and scratched my skin. I grunted.

"And never."

His sword swept near my throat.

"Ever."

With a flick of the wrist, I parried his thrust and stepped back to make a move, metal against metal, striking sparks. Blades clashed, and I leaned toward him, grinning.

"Have you known—"

"Enough!" Edward stuck his sword into the deck. "I still remember how to kick your arse, Irish."

I brought my blade up to strike. His fingers closed around my wrist like a steel trap, stopping my blow inches from his face. I clenched my teeth, arm shaking.

Black covered the sclera of his eyes like oil spilled in the ocean.

I knew what was coming.

It was as though he tapped an unknown reservoir, something none of us had but him. That extra power he took from my fallen kin, perhaps, or he was simply Anord's favorite. It was the reason why no one could defeat him.

And I had to infuriate him, bring out that tenebrous side of him, the one all bradaís feared.

"You can beat me, Edward." I leaned toward him, whispering, "But you'll never have what makes me different. That I can assure you."

His face contorted, and he twisted my wrist while darkness erupted from him.

It felt like being entombed, naked, within incandescent lava. His power penetrated my skin through his contact. Black spots danced in my vision and spread like octopus's ink.

My sword fell to the deck.

"You angered me, Irish," he said, his voice distorted to my ears. "And this was supposed to be fun."

"What's the matter, Ed?" I grunted with effort. "Lost your touch?"

I tried to breathe, but even thinking was hard. Every movement felt sluggish, clumsy. Edward threw me to the planks, then pressed a foot over my chest so I wouldn't move.

Something between a grunt and a guffaw came out of my mouth. I couldn't move even if I tried.

"Are you upset I wounded your dainty face?" Edward said, increasing the pressure. "What a pity. You'll have to be disabled for a while. Your *lover* will be so sad."

Bloody hell. I roared in anguish.

He *knew*.

SEVEN

Ryanne

Two distinct voices carried from the deck above, one of them Titus's. Other than their voices, only the swoosh of the waves and the flap of the sails reached my ears. I carefully climbed the steps up, my hand pressed on the wall.

A man dressed in a blue navy uniform stood at the top of the stairs, with his back facing me. A black ponytail came out beneath his cap.

Was he the bradaí Titus feared? Edward?

My heart thumped while I leaned my body forward, but I couldn't make out what was discussed on deck except for the clash of swords and a conversation that was not meant for my ears.

Then, Titus appeared in my line of sight, fighting another man with brown hair sweeping his shoulder. And then they were gone.

The navy outfit man spun, and our eyes met.

"Well, a little bee got out of her hive," he said as he grabbed my arm and took me back to the cabin before I knew what was going on.

He was medium height and had a golden earring adorning his left ear, like Titus. His white pants and navy-blue jacket looked custom made, elegant lines marking his shoulders and lean body.

He nudged the door closed behind him. Could he be Edward? No, Titus was facing that bradaí as much as I could tell. And wasn't all their crew human? Titus was the only one with a supernatural being as his first mate, wasn't he?

I straightened and held my chin up. "Are you a bradaí?"

"The Irish told you." His eyes narrowed dangerously. "What do you know about us?"

"That you, ah, like to sail in wooden ships around the world and dress in eighteenth-century clothes." I gave a small laugh. Now that was a good save! "I guess only Titus does that since your clothes are modern. They're nice. So you're not Edward."

"No," he all but snarled.

His expression returned to flat, and I held onto the Ryanne Special Fake Smile. He was a bradaí too! Titus mentioned they were loners, so why was there another with Edward? Who was this man?

I smiled sweetly and laced my hands behind my back in a smooth move while commanding Aine to stand still—it was like pressing a foot over the power and making it small, like a mushroom. The mushroom popped into my mind, a fluorescent blue one.

"Your skin's flawless." Minho slid a finger over my cheek.

The power-turned-shiny-mushroom pulsated, and again I had to push it down. I took a step back to avoid using my hands to swat him. Last thing I need was for him to discover what I was. "Don't," I warned.

The odd twitch in his lips grew into a distorted grin. It was then that I noticed his misshapen ears as if someone had cut the top of them with a knife. His dark opaque eyes looked me up and down.

My gaze darted to the bed, short nails digging into my palms.

The chuckle coming out of his lips sounded wrong, like a wild animal snorting. "Oh, no, little bee. I'm not into that sport. Not with little girls like you." He retrieved a wicked-looking knife from inside his jacket and held it at my eye level.

"No," he continued. "I'm an artist. I paint." He rotated the knife slowly, its long, serrated blade shining.

"Oh, ah, that's—that's awesome! Is your work in a gallery? Maybe I've seen it before."

That odd chuckle burst again. "You're funny, yah. No, little bee."

He pressed the tip of the knife against my collarbone. "Not that kind of work."

The stairs creaked with the weight of someone heavy. The bradaí swung behind me, the tip of the knife against my ribs. By the gnome's beard, not again. My teeth clattered but in fear or anger, I wasn't sure.

Homkar burst into the cabin, nostrils flaring. "Leave her, Minho." His baritone voice dropped to chilliness.

"Nay, Homkar. Come close and she'll feel the bite."

Homkar clenched his fists, jaw locked. "You do that, and I'll throw you overboard myself."

"Let's call it a truce." There was a hesitation in the bradaí's voice. "Let's see what my captain says, yah?"

Homkar stepped away from the door and waved a hand toward it.

Minho seized my neck and pushed me above deck. Geez, why does every villain have to manipulate us like rag dolls?

Because rag dolls can't fight back.

I'd screwed it up, but maybe I could touch them without them realizing who I was. Feel them. But how?

The strong salty breeze swirled around us. The crew was gathered at the other side of the ship and . . . I sucked in a breath and took a step toward Titus, lying face-first on the planks, but Minho held me back. A tanned, brawny man, dressed in navy clothes like Minho, pressed Titus's back with his foot.

"Now, that's an Edward," Minho whispered in my ear, his breath tickling me.

I winced.

Edward lifted his gaze and set it on me. I slapped a hand to my mouth and stifled a cry. There was something evil in this man's gaze, even colder than the bradaí holding me. He was dressed in a similar manner to Minho, but the clothes didn't fit as well—this was a man who didn't care much about clothing, but the power he radiated was enough to make you dismiss fashion.

Then again, it was enough to dismiss everything else.

Aine vanished with a *pop*. It was like I had a void in me, a void that made me feel too human.

Too vulnerable.

Edward hauled Titus up. All the *Scáil Dragún* crew was being herded below deck, all but Homkar. No one of the other ship's crew seemed brave enough to face him, and yet the huge man wasn't moving a finger, his glower set on Edward.

Cruelty lurked behind Edward's brown eyes, reminding me of the Erlking statue back at the taigh. Fear covered me like thick tar, and I swallowed painfully. These bradaís looked capable of anything.

Capable of killing fae without having second thoughts.

Edward took me in from head to toe, and my pulse raced. My shaking legs couldn't obey a simple command, and my dry throat held the bumbling words prisoner. I stared at him without being able to discern any details.

There was something in him, something I couldn't put into words, that made my skin crawl, and wished I was nothing more than a simple human who didn't deserve being noticed by him.

A cockroach not worthy of this attention.

"Is that your lover, Irish? I thought you had better taste. With so many gorgeous women out there, you had to pick the girl next door?" Edward clicked his tongue, affecting a sad expression. "Just some nights ago Minho and I went to this exclusive nightclub, where two ravishing females usurped all our time."

He was talking to Titus as he would a friend, not seeming to mind Titus's injured state.

Titus leaned his shoulder on the mainmast. Blood covered his face where a gash ran from his forehead down to his chin, his expression grim. He clutched his arm, covered in slashes as well as his chest and legs. I felt glad he was immortal.

"I could give you an invite. Drop my name, Irish, and you'll see what I'm talking about."

Edward patted Titus's back. When Titus flinched, I had to resist the instinct to do the same.

Instead I swallowed, fearful my legs would buckle under me if I moved. What had been my plan? Use my touch of fae with *them*? *What a joke*, I thought shakily. I couldn't even call Aine, couldn't even find it; surely it was cowed. As cowed as I was.

My mind conjured a colorless blob. I'd been able to transform my power into an ogre when Haru threatened my life. But this time was different.

This time, it wasn't a human, but two full-fledged bradaís.

Minho swiped a clammy finger over my cheek. "She ain't so bad. Her skin is flawless; it'll make a perfect canvas for my art."

Oh dear Cuidi, what's wrong with this guy?

A sound behind me made me jump. Was that the wind? Hopefully not Bricius. *Please, Bricius, keep hidden!*

Beads of sweat covered my upper lip, and my hands turned clammy. Edward's words weren't reassuring. There was a cold tone in them, and Titus wasn't in a position to fight either of them. He wasn't even attempting to. His feet slid, and he struggled to stand.

Danger floated around them. What was I doing here? Why hadn't Cuidi trained me properly to fight them?

But then, I was no fighter. And the fae sent me here despite my shortcoming, despite the fact I couldn't physically fight back.

Dammit.

For the first time in my life, I wished I knew self-defense. I wished I could defend myself and not be at the mercy of supernatural beings.

Edward placed himself in front of me. "Not even fun, Irish. You've dressed her like old times, and nowadays women like to show skin."

In a swift movement, he ripped the gown's neckline. I gasped, raising both hands to cover my chest. He scrunched his nose and turned to Titus, still silent, still leaning on the mainmast.

"You puzzle me." Edward looked back at me, stroking his bearded cheek with a finger.

He then grabbed a silk handkerchief from his jacket pocket and handed it to Minho. I'd been discarded—the rag doll no longer held interest to him.

"Make her walk the plank."

EIGHT

Titus

Bloody hell. Curse all these bradaís and their non-existent spawn.

Throw Ryanne into the ocean? The ocean she hates when she's by herself? I stiffened but forced myself to relax, despite the fact I wanted to gouge out their eyes.

Yes, attack.

All my body, my mind, pulled me to fight. A few weeks ago and I would have. But this wasn't about me now. She would fare worse if I reacted, so I showed just a mild annoyance, nothing like the turmoil inside me.

Worse, my head was about to explode. Nausea pumped my dry throat with bile. My arms and shoulders ached as if they were dislocated. My eyelids felt tar-smeared and heavy. The stickiness in my lips and tongue made me yearn for water.

Water. What Ryanne still feared. Where Minho was going to throw Ryanne into. Let Morrigan's crows guard over her.

Edward patted my shoulder. "I'm doing you a favor. You can do better. And I'm sorry about this unpleasant situation, Irish," he said with a half-smile, white teeth peeking under his lips. "But you must understand your reputation precedes you. It's truly fascinating."

He was playing a game. He was watching me, intently, like the Erlking when he releases his *Wild Jagd*. Cold loomed behind his gaze, as thick as paste, as dark as the beast when it growled within me.

And I had to play nice. Bow to his Highness and avoid moving an inch to help Ryanne.

"Come," he said as he walked toward the other railing, forcing me to turn my back on what was happening behind me.

She was asking Minho something. Of course she was, the woman couldn't keep quiet even if her life was on the line. Homkar loitered nearby, but there was nothing he could do.

"Have you ever wondered what it is to be human, Irish?"

I followed his gaze. Near the *Thunder's* railing, two sailors laughed, thumping each other's backs, surely celebrating the victory of his captain over my crew. Which was absurd, given he'd never been defeated. Stupid humans.

"Not really," I said.

Ryanne yelled. Minho laughed. A splash. And here I was, leaning sideways on the railing, stifling signs of interest on what was happening. Anord's balls.

Edward folded his arms over his chest, tilting his head and looking at the sailors as I had seen humans do with caged animals. A mixture of fascination, curiosity and, in some cases, disgust.

"Their lives are short, full of suffering, pain, and disease. When we do them the favor of depriving them of that pathetic existence, instead of thanking us, they dread and cling with their nails as if all this suffering was good. As if in the midst of the rubbish they find meaning."

"The Supreme Being," I said. I'd found monks in my travels and their sermons of a better life, but I never stopped to hear them in full.

Edward snorted derisively. "Pitfalls. Priests are sent to fill their heads with lies so they'll put up with whatever you give them." He stroked his short beard thoughtfully. "And yet they are happy. Their eyes sparkle when they see their stinking kids rolling in the filth, when two lovers meet. Why is that, Irish?"

I shrugged. "Love. They feel that."

"Do you know what that is?"

"No. Why would I? We bradaís can't feel."

Feel.

Like when I held Ryanne in my arms.

How would she fare by herself, alone in the ocean? She wouldn't drown. By the Morrigan, she'd better not.

Edward eyed me. Uncomfortable with his scrutiny, I watched the waves, away from where she must be, terrified and alone. Rain-leaden clouds covered the sky, and gulls cried above us. Panama's ink blue coastline loomed starboard.

"I wonder what they feel," Edward said, so quietly his words trailed with the wind.

I raised an eyebrow. He, the most powerful of all, wanting to feel? To know what humans felt?

"Surprised? Come." Without waiting for an answer, he headed aft to my quarters. "I need something to wet my throat."

Bloody hell. I kept my gaze away from where she'd submerged. Minho certainly was watching my every move.

Cursed lapdog.

She'd be scared, terrified, without me protecting her in the ocean. No, I couldn't think like that. She'd survive. She was stubborn enough to do it.

I expected Edward would leave soon; it wasn't like him to remain after he'd made his point, so he must have an agenda and it had nothing to do with Ryanne.

Edward waved a hand toward my cabin's door, and I staggered inside.

He opened a cabinet and pulled out a bottle of red wine. After uncorking the bottle with deliberate calm, he poured it into two glasses, offering me one.

"The nectar of the gods," he said as he raised his glass and sipped.

I emptied mine in one gulp. "Why are you here?" I asked.

"I want you to be my first mate again. It hasn't been the same since you ran away with that white-haired fae. Remember her?" he asked nonchalantly.

Aghna. Aye, I remembered her. "What about Minho?"

"He'll have your ship."

"That's a crappy offer, Ed, even from you. What do you really want?"

"That." He took a sip from his wine and closed his eyes in enjoyment.

"Did Anord send you to kill me?" That was the only thing that made sense.

"If that were true, Minho wouldn't be calm, would he?"

Images of those times when Anord called us to hunt a bradaí hit me with force. The blood call, our minds taken with his will until we found the bradaí whose power he wanted taken.

What was it with this bastard? Was the killing of two bradaís what made Edward superior to us?

And how in Anord's hell did he manage to kill those bradaís?

"You killed Luc. I was there."

"Oh, please, Irish. We're not back to this, are we? I killed Luc, I killed Thomas; you even blamed me for Sergei's lover's death."

"First mate."

"Whatever. And I'm the Alpha, your leader. It doesn't matter how hard you try, nothing will change that."

"You took Luc's power. I saw it clearly."

"That was all I did."

"Do you take me for a fool?"

"Believe me, it was an Eadrom who did the actual killing. Though I wasn't going to let Luc's power be wasted, would I?" He grinned and leaned forward as though sharing a secret. "Helps to kill fae quicker, yes?"

Bloody liar. He'd blamed the deaths on Eadroms, the Guardians of the Hawthorn and the most powerful of the fae. Luckily for us, Eadroms were scarce. "How convenient you arrive first both times. How?"

"Oh, but I'm not telling you all my secrets, Irish. You also managed to avoid the second call."

"Like you, I have a trick or two up my sleeve." I'd had to use all my control but even that wasn't enough, so I commanded Homkar to throw me into the sea. There, the call was subdued.

"But of course you do. Anord created you in the same manner as me." His gaze pierced me.

A shiver ran down my spine. I'd been in the dark regarding my creation, unlike all bradaís. All knew, all remembered how they were created, their first glimpse at Anord. All but me.

But I had to tread carefully. "Not different from the others, I would assume."

"You'd be surprised."

My thoughts raced. Did Edward have the same peculiarities I had? Hadn't Anord told me once that I was defective?

Edward walked to the large window and looked out. "You and I are different from the rest. The first and the last. Alpha and Omega." He laced his hands behind his back. "Oh, yes. I am perfect. His first creation. He tried to replicate what he achieved with me to no avail. You are the second best. *Almost* as perfect." He turned around. "You have . . . imperfections."

"Sure I do."

I needed this to end so I could get to Ryanne. She wouldn't fare well alone in the ocean, riddled with her fears.

Anord's balls.

"He talks to me from time to time." He tilted his head. "Doesn't he talk to you?"

"Sometimes."

"Every bradaí feels something when created. Once our beloved Creator Named us. What did you feel when Anord gave you your Name, Irish?"

"My memories are fuzzy."

"But you know your Name." He didn't look surprised.

My true Name, Aodhán. I could only recall darkness surrounding me, flashes of a cave. I'd dreamed of the sea and something else, but my memories were blurred and confusing.

I clenched my fists. Why couldn't I remember? I'd heard Anord a couple of times, when I discovered my bradaí pocket and when he commanded us to hunt those two bradaís whom Edward ultimately killed.

Edward threw me against the wall, my head bouncing against the wood. The glass I'd held crashed against the floor.

Bloody hell.

I seized Edward's wrist as his fingers dug into my throat.

"You felt something. What was it?" His nose was centimeters from mine.

"I. Don't. Know."

"What is your Name, Irish? Tell me!"

Do not give him your Name. It is yours. Your own.

"No! It's mine, my own!"

"Give me your Name!" Edward hesitated, then turned his head to the side. "I need it; it should be mine!"

I had the suspicion he wasn't talking to me.

That was unexpected.

I condensed *dorcha*, all that I had, all that I was, on my hands, and latched them over Edward's throat.

I'd never attacked him with *dorcha*, never felt my darkness was up to par. But I wouldn't give in, Anord be damned. Black thorns sprouted from my fingers, tiny lances of *dorcha* engulfed his throat.

Edward yelled in pain, and he released me. All my power spent, I fell to my knees, though I quickly regained my feet, pain notwithstanding. He couldn't know the vulnerable condition I was in now.

His eyes glazed over. "Yes, my lord," he said so quietly I almost didn't hear him. Anord. He was talking to our creator.

"Get off my ship," I commanded, pointing at the door. "Now!"

Edward rubbed his throat, where the black thorns were already fading. "This is not over," he said, coughing. "Someday, Irish. Someday you will fail. Anord will give me a signal. I'll be waiting with a smile."

He jabbed something into my stomach. Something pointy, painful like a blade forged in fire. With a flick of his wrist, he twisted the blade, and I grunted.

"Enjoy your recovery, Irish." He retrieved the weapon, a dagger shining a sickly green hue.

I sucked in a breath. A goblin's blade.

He stormed outside.

Staggering, I held myself against the wall, only to fall again. Blood tainted my shirt. Shooting pain erupted from every muscle but another ache stormed my guts.

Ryanne.

Darkness covered my vision like squid ink, my head lolling to the side. A small pinpoint of light suspended in front of me.

Am I going to die? I thought stupidly while I clenched my bloodied stomach.

"Hang on, pirate," the point of light said. "There is too much blood, yes, yes, yes."

"Ryanne," I managed to stutter.

The point of light grew bigger, and I sighed in peace. Then, I knew nothing else.

NINE

Ryanne

I let out a desperate scream and flapped my legs, the steely waves rushing at me, hands tightly bound by Edward's handkerchief. Wind hit my face. Too fast, too . . .

I sank, confused, my body turning around. Darkness and freezing water enveloped me. My torn dress, my *heavy* torn dress pulled me down.

The surface, where was the surface? Which way was *up*? I kicked wildly. Couldn't breathe.

Silence.

Then shrill sounds.

Whales? *Nymphs?*

Muddy, dark green and darker shapes beyond. *Oh, dear Cuidi, am I going to die eaten by sharks?*

My lungs burned, demanding oxygen. My eyes stung, but I had to keep them open. Which way was *up*? I kicked my legs desperately, only to move in circles, the soggy dress too heavy.

God, I need air. Can't keep eyes . . . open. Hurts.

Where was Titus? Why wasn't he already in the water? I couldn't breathe. It was too cold.

Bubbles slipped from my mouth.

Titus wouldn't be able to come. It was up to me.

My limbs were numb, the heavy dress slowed my movements.

I focused and called Aine. In a moment, it was there, swirling inside my chest like an eel high on caffeine. I didn't have Titus's strange powers, but I had Aine.

My lungs were about to explode with a blazing fire, the pressure in my ears growing. But once Aine took over, strength came to my limbs, the heaviness of the dress a simple leaf on my legs.

I released the last oxygen reserve, following the bubbles going down. Aine nudged me. No, they were going *up* toward a bright patch. The surface!

With the last of my strength, I kicked toward the patch of clearer water and broke the surface, sucking the coveted air in gulps.

A wave crashed on my face, salty water flushing into my mouth. I spat some out and blinked, trying to clear my vision. First, I needed to remove my binding. Taking a long gulp of air, I sank back and wriggled my body to pass my hands beneath me.

Thank Cuidi for all their training with the trolls and ogres that helped me be nimble and flexible.

With my teeth, I tried to remove the silk handkerchief, but it wouldn't give in.

No one was in sight. No Minho looking down or any of the crew.

"Help!" I croaked. Were they going to let me drown? The dress felt bothersome and heavy. Uncontrollable shivers made my teeth clatter, and not just because of the ocean's temperature.

I was alone here, without any way to climb back onboard. Even if I could, would Minho throw me overboard again?

"Oh, for the Erlking's horns," I sputtered. Where was my pixie guardian?

"Bricius," I hissed. "Help!"

I looked up the hull, frantic. An orange mollusk was glued above the water line. I squinted—not a mollusk but Bricius. The butterfly wings of my little friend sprang. He glanced down and put a finger to his lips.

Relieved that I wasn't alone, I nodded and swam as close as I dared to the hull, my hands tied in front. My beautiful friend slid down but there was no way anyone could see him from the railing.

He stopped when he was at my eye level and again, put his finger to his lips. He barely moved and his wings were now glued to his body like a resting fly. I lifted my bound hands and his wings perked up.

Without a word, he worked on the binding and removed the handkerchief.

"Edward?" I whispered from a corner of my mouth, as I did back in the human world so no one to notice I was talking to an invisible pixie. The heavy dress kept pulling me down so I squirmed out of it—Edward having ripped it open made that process a lot easier than it should have been.

Bricius nodded and climbed up using his hands. I swam backward to be able to see where he was going. He slipped back into the porthole.

The waiting felt unbearable, and I kept glancing down to the depths of the ocean, certain my life would be cut short in the jaws of a shark. Shouts came from faraway; they didn't originate with our ship, but from the other one.

Then I realized the boats weren't on this side. Were they leaving? I hoped so.

The *Scáil Dragún* rocked, and small waves disturbed where I was. Oh damn! My teeth clattered, and I did my best to stay near the hull but not so near it could hit me if it moved. My frozen limbs felt heavy. Aine was like that little fluorescent mushroom, always present in my mind. There was a connection between the fae power and my brain, where I "saw" Aine, waiting for my next command.

What a wuss, being afraid of sharks, so I hummed a song, the vibration in the water of both Titus's and Edward's ships a caress.

After what felt like an eternity, Bricius returned, as silently as a ninja. A pixie ninja. The little guy was resourceful, that he was. I approached the hull again.

"The bradaí stormed out," Bricius whispered, so low I had to strain my hearing to catch the words.

"Titus? How's he?"

Bricius shook his head, a worried expression etched on his face. Oh, no. I needed to get back up and . . . do whatever to help.

My shoulders tightened and my teeth clattered. Now what? I couldn't keep floating here forever.

A big man dove into the ocean, and I yelped. Homkar surfaced next to me and tried to grab me.

"I'm fine," I said.

"No." Homkar reached out again and pulled me against him.

"What will—" Bricius started.

"Be quiet." He glowered at Bricius, as he usually did, but my little friend grinned, and Homkar's glower vanished.

Bricius flew to the back of my head and grabbed wet locks of hair to hang on.

Homkar's body released the warmth that I needed, and I opted to forget how inappropriate it felt. Survival first.

Titus next. All my body itched to go up and see for myself.

Some minutes passed and Mouse appeared above, waving a hand against the hull. Mouse was the hacker on board—a dark-haired woman, the only female in Titus's crew, the kind of person you can never guess their age—she could be twenty-five, or she could be forty.

A rope shot over the side and into the water.

"He's gone," Homkar said.

He released me and offered me the rope. "Take it," he said. To Bricius, he said, "Keep hiding, insect. They're still close by."

Images of huge, white sharks swimming below me boosted my panic, and I grabbed the rope. There was a knot at the end of it. The rope tightened under my weight, and they started to pull me. My hands slipped a couple of inches, the rope burning them. Wind caressed my shaken, goosebump-covered body.

Bricius stuck to the hull once again and climbed up in the same manner as before toward the bathroom's porthole.

I grabbed the rope as tightly as I could with my trembling hands, knuckles turning white. A salty taste lingered in my mouth. I held for dear life until my body was completely out of the water. When I placed my feet on the hull, a tingling appeared at the touch. The image of a dragon flashed in my mind, and Aine traveled down to my feet.

Feihnum, the dragonwood sang.

My feet connected to the wood as if they were glued to it, making the climb easier like I was horizontally pushing myself forward. The tingling spread through my limbs.

Several hands grabbed me, hauling me over the railing. I coughed, teeth chattering.

"You're a natural climber, that you are, Miss."

I squinted at Mouse and coughed some more. Someone thumped my back. Another one placed a blanket over my shivering body. I clenched and unclenched my hands, trying to get the blood circulating.

Images blurred and danced. I blinked several times until they focused. Mouse and the redhead Stephen stood near me. Titus was nowhere to be seen.

Where the heck is he?

Stephen grabbed my arm to help me stand. The *Thunder* was sailing away. Dark spots danced in my vision, and my knees buckled. That coldness, that power of his blinding me, cowing me into a shivering wuss.

Dear Cuidi, let him be gone and never come back.

Edward had barely taken notice of the rag doll. What would he do if he knew who I really was?

Taking a deep breath, I brushed the wet hair from my forehead and looked around as casually as I could. Homkar was back on deck, dripping water. I closed the blanket tightly around me. The *Thunder* was moving away but still close by.

My legs buckled again.

"Whoa, Miss." Mouse steadied me. "Take it easy."

I willed my legs to steady. I coughed up more water. Lungs tight and breath wheezy, I felt like I'd swallowed pure salt, and my eyes still stung. Someone offered me a bottle of clear liquid, and I took a healthy swig. The burning liquid scorched my parched throat. That was not water. I coughed up the vodka and handed the bottle back.

"You dumb ass, she needs water," Mouse whispered. "Someone get her water."

Another sailor handed me a bottle of water. I poured it into my mouth and onto my face, trying to get the sting out of my eyes.

I glanced at the sea where Minho had thrown me, where sharks might be lurking beneath.

Great. Let's add a new nightmare to my water-related ones. Besides the nymph-drowning, now sharks. It was one thing to dive with Titus, another entirely by myself.

I let out a shaky breath. The *Thunder* was now a distant shape—Edward and Minho were added to that increasing list of Supernatural Things to Fear, though Edward was at the number one spot right next to the Erlking.

"Titus?" I asked Homkar.

He pointed below at the cabin.

I headed there with Homkar following me. I slipped, and he steadied me. The planks had red stains. Blood. I'd slipped on blood.

Images from my nightmare sprung: Titus gushing blood.

I dashed inside the cabin, heart pounding wildly. Could Edward hurt Titus and bleed him to death?

Titus lay on the bed, eyes closed. He looked like a dead man except for the twitch in his eyelids or the slight tremble in his legs. Blood was splattered on the sheets, and I sucked in a breath. It was then I noticed Bricius hovering anxiously over Titus as if he was worried about Titus's fate.

"Quick, Ryanne! He's not waking up!"

I rushed to the bed and pulled aside the ripped and bloody shirt, where crossed slashes bled on his chest, besides a nasty yellowed-green wound in his stomach.

Bricius paled and retched.

"It doesn't seem anything of consequence—no mortal peril in sight," I said while I pressed two fingers to his neck, near his windpipe. It was a reflex, but it was always perplexing to find no heartbeat.

Bradaís had no heart.

"Are you sure?" Bricius landed on my shoulder.

Dark tendrils wove in and out of the wound like slithering worms, and I placed a tentative hand over it. His dark energy was at work. It prickled my hand and made Aine expand and contract as if preparing to attack.

"Is the brute pirate gone, then?" Bricius asked.

"Yes, Bug."

The cuts to Titus's thighs had torn his pants. One eye was swollen shut. Bricius flew to Titus and poked gently his cheek, which made Titus stir awake.

Both Bricius and I exhaled in relief.

"You're soaking wet," Titus mumbled, his words slurring.

"Don't speak," I said. "Homkar, bring me some towels."

The giant scowled. "I'm taking care of him."

"No, you're not. Just bring me the damn towels."

He started to argue but decided against it. Shaking his head again, he did as told. I felt in control. Not to mention this task helped me feel useful.

"If you get sick, use this." Homkar placed a bucket near me.

"Blood doesn't make me sick. I'm a nurse, remember?" I pointed to the cabin's door. "Go outside. I can help here."

With a gentle pat, I cleaned the blood from Titus's face, uncovering the deep slash from his forehead to his chin. He had a cut on his left ear.

Nightmares aren't visions, I reminded myself. *Just pesky dreams that bother you awake.*

"I didn't like it. Being in hiding, no, no, no."

"You did well." I reassured Bricius.

Titus pushed himself with his elbows and glared. "You are fine, aren't you?"

I tilted my head, a bit surprised at his cold tone. "Yeah."

"Then why the hell didn't you heed me when I said to hide? Was that so hard to understand, woman?"

I pressed my lips tight. "I was busy drowning."

"Because you didn't stay put!"

"I needed to go out—"

"Do you have a death wish? Why the hell can't you obey a simple command?"

I stood up, livid. He was certainly *not* bleeding, and if he could shout like that, he must be fine. "You wouldn't understand."

"Leave me." He let himself fall.

"Oh, you stubborn goat!"

With Bricius on my tail, I stormed out of the cabin, only to remember I was still in my skivvies with just a blanket atop my shoulders. So with my chin up, I returned and slipped a dress over my wet underwear.

Without a glance in his direction, I stormed out again.

TEN

Titus

"Captain." Homkar strode inside. He gave me a once over. "You made him mad. No doubt about it."

I tried to smile but grimaced instead. I hadn't been hurt so badly since Edward and Minho thwarted my first and only attempt to bring the bradaís together against the Alpha. Bradaís were all cursed, bloody traitors who weren't worth my time. And Ryanne wondered why I never wanted to talk about my kin. Whatever for?

Ryanne. Bloody reckless woman. To survive in the sea, a mortal needed to follow orders. There was no questioning. "Have Ryanne sleep below."

"Sir?"

"I need my space while I heal. Have you notified the network?" I said, struggling to prop up on an elbow.

"Yes, sir. Kara sends her sympathy."

"So nice of her. She was hit too, then."

"Right before us. She sent a message, but it arrived when Edward did."

"A bit late, wasn't it?" I let myself fall on the pillow.

Homkar stood near the bed, hands behind his back and legs spread apart, thoughtful. "It was a test."

I grunted.

"He wanted to know about the girl." His lips quivered as though attempting a smile. "She's reckless. Stepping out to Minho without a clue."

"I should have tied her up and gagged her inside the head." I tried to wave a hand, but it fell flat on my stomach. "Stupid woman."

He jerked his chin to me. "She's taking care of you."

I could see the approval in his eyes. Taking care of me had given her top marks.

Blindness and ignorance ruled her, aye, yet for some unbeknownst reason, I fancied her. Perhaps too much. Aye, it was better we slept in different cabins, for the time being.

"But there was something else," Homkar said, thoughtfully. "With Edward."

"What gave it away?"

"The blood."

"He used a goblin's blade."

"Forged in blue fire," Homkar said, thoughtfully.

We both shared a look. When I first met him, goblins were torturing him with those bloody daggers. As my kin, dannan-dhubbs were highly resistant and hard to kill, but those daggers cut deeply, and he'd been on the verge of death.

My beast hadn't wanted me to rescue him, and out of spite, I did. A life debt that Homkar had taken seriously all these years, thank the Morrigan.

I patted the wound, sensing *dorcha* hard at work. Aye, nasty wounds and harder to recover, but I would in a few days. Curse Edward.

"I want you to focus on the Japan failed coup."

"Those amateurs?"

Aye, amateurs, but Haru had almost succeeded. He would have maimed her. I clenched my fists. It'd been my fault. I myself left her there in the lab for those humans to analyze her touch of fae and try to extract it. The fools didn't know it could not happen—the touch of fae was a power given by the fae themselves, not a chemical concoction easy to reproduce.

That wouldn't stop those humans, though. And I'd handed Ryanne to them on a silver platter. No wonder she had a hard time trusting me.

Even as I'd given in and killed in front of her, ruled by the beast, it had been easy to pull out. Easier than other times.

There was another pressing matter.

"It's imperative to know who hired Haru."

"You should talk to Kara," Homkar said. "Perhaps she knows about it."

"Kara better not be involved."

"Whoever did it knows the plan failed. If it was a bradaí behind the coup, you left your signature over their bodies. If it's not her, you can tell her the girl is your lover and nothing else."

"Too many *ifs*."

"Aye, sir, but worth considering."

Just the idea that one of my kin knew Ryanne had a touch of fae churned my insides. If Kara was the one responsible for Ryanne's kidnapping attempt, she could have tapped into my network or had a spy with my clients. It wouldn't have been hard to put two and two together and found out Ryanne had a touch of fae.

What a gobshite had I been.

"It wasn't Edward, that I can say."

"Edward would have killed her on the spot, yes. What if it's someone we contacted? We did send the notice on the board about the seer."

"Sanders? The man didn't take my refusal to sell Ryanne to him well and kept insisting . . ." I met Homkar's stormy eyes. Of all the people we contacted about Ryanne, Sanders had been the less viable option since he enjoyed torturing those who fell in his hands.

"That's a possibility, sir. But he couldn't have known you'd accepted Wataru's offer. The transaction was held under our regular tight security. I'll tell Mouse to check if there was a leak just to make sure."

"Can any of our customers spread the word?"

"Mouse has made sure all of them are under scrutiny."

I could discard Kara's involvement right away if I met with her . . . or increase the risk. If my sister knew, it was better to let it out in the open. Keep your enemies close and all that shite.

Sister. The word felt odd yet right at the same time.

"Contact her," I said. "She should be nearby."

"You need anything else?" Homkar asked.

"Sleep. Get out."

Without a word, he left.

I grimaced, my hands clutching the sheets. I should have heeded the fae's warning immediately and locked Ryanne inside with someone guarding her. Too reckless.

What a gobshite. I'd acted carelessly.

I fingered my sore throat and asked myself the same question that had been prowling my mind. Edward needed my Name to retrieve my powers—that might be why Anord never wanted us to give it away. It made sense.

And Anord hadn't wanted Edward to kill me. That was why he stopped, the bastard. It wasn't like Edward to disobey Anord.

That time in Corsica, when the first blood call arrived and Anord told us a bradaí had fallen, I'd pushed that question aside, not having an answer then.

It'd been odd Anord had called us all when Edward had accomplished the deed, but after the second call, I came to the realization that Anord wanted the best of us to reach the fallen first.

Edward had managed to arrive first both times. How? I'd never known. That was why he was the best of us, power wise.

Why fallen? What had Luc and Thomas done to anger Anord and make him send his pitbull to them?

Only Edward knew the answers. He'd blamed the killings on the Eadroms and, all the while, taken the fallen bradaís' powers for himself. No wonder he alone had eradicated half of the fae.

But he'd failed with me. So unusual how he'd argued with Anord. Or was it the beast inside him? Did he know the difference between them?

Was Edward getting loose?

Too many unanswered questions. My hands grasped the sheets in tight fists.

Cursed, bloody Edward.

ELEVEN

Titus

Nanjing, 1860

After an uneventful voyage up the Yangtze River, the *Scaíl Dragún* arrived at Nanjing at dusk. Single-masted, flat-bottom boats filled the waterfront, with some European ships here and there. For the sake of the trade, I'd made the ship visible before arriving. It took little effort from my side—touch the wood and concentrate on the other vessels.

The *Scaíl Dragún* responded to her rightful owner.

The Qing officials believed our facade of textile merchants. We'd already sold our real shipment some hours ago.

China had been the market for opium in recent decades, yet it fell into Shen's territory. I'd struggled with him since he didn't want to share—the human Opium War might have ended, but not the bradaí version. Minho had claimed he deserved part of the deal since he'd been in the area for many years.

I'd been better at negotiating. And more charming. By showing Shen maps and numbers, I convinced him the market was big enough for both, and he granted me one-third of his area. Minho gracefully abided by Shen's decision and retired, yet I needed to be careful and have my eyes open.

The stench of dead fish, sweaty humans, rotten vegetables, and raw sewage wafted in the warm breeze, making bile rise in my throat. Shouts rose in Mandarin from the dock by merchants, officers, workers, and good-for-nothing passersby. Seagulls cried as if wanting to join in.

The crew shoved each other in their haste to disembark, most likely to spend their share of the loot in spirits and wenches. *Humans.*

Only Homkar and I remained on board. I smiled to myself, proud of being a bradaí, not subject to the animal impulse seizing humans, rolling in the filth just because their hormones—

My vision turned black, my legs buckling beneath. With a trembling hand, I grabbed the rail.

"Are you all right, Captain?" Homkar's voice sounded distant.

Images of blood and death overwhelmed all thoughts. Mutilated bodies, swords cutting limbs, sticky blood inking my hands. Human faces distorted with fear, with hunger, pain smeared on their blank eyes. Beautiful.

Destroy. Kill. No mercy.

I unsheathed my sword and jumped over the rail to the dock, ready to thrust it through the first human daring to cross my path. Two Chinese bilge rats shouted at me in Mandarin, lifting pistols.

The flame lit within me burned unquenchable, indestructible. I raised my sword to slay the men, but a powerful hand stopped my movement. The gray eyes of my first mate met mine.

"Avast, Captain. I don't know what's happening, but this isn't the time." He glanced briefly at the humans, who looked undecidedly at Homkar.

I shoved him aside, and he staggered back. "You don't understand. I must go."

"Where, sir?"

I hesitated. What was happening? Death pounded inside my head, the claim of blood bursting out.

"*Go, Aodhán,*" boomed Anord's. authoritative voice inside my head. No one else knew my true Name. "*Return to your ship.*"

Aye. I had to return to the ship. "Move, Homkar."

The two officers shouted again, and when I didn't oblige to their unreasonable commands, shot at my chest. I didn't even feel the bullets and inhaled the gunpowder greedily. The razor edge of my sword greeted their fragile necks, and their heads rolled to the ground. The crimson liquid poured like an artist's hand painting the canvas of his masterpiece.

Blood. More.

My sword rattled as though calling for more blood too. From the end of the dock, more Chinese rats, wanting to try my steel. I obliged them, right through their tonsils. They fell face first over spilled guts and blood.

I yelled in defiance, lifting my bloodied sword.

A child ran out from behind barrels, stopping short at the sight of me. I raised my sword, clenching my teeth. A feeling flickered over my chest—that alien energy, *préachta*. Staggering, I looked at the frozen child.

Something lurked behind his eyes: a silver light shining, dissipating the fog in my mind. The child smiled—too wise for someone so young —then skittered away.

What was I doing? What had overcome me? I lowered my sword and pivoted, eyeing the pool of blood beneath my feet and the dismembered bodies. Air came and went into my body like a bellow, my lips dry. Was I no better than my crew, letting my beast take over my actions?

"*The others will arrive before you. Return to your ship,*" Anord commanded, his voice resonating inside my brain. "*You're wasting time. Focus.*"

I nodded and headed back to the ship. The fire within gave wings to my feet, and soon I was back on board where Homkar waited for me.

"That was stupid, Captain," he said. "They will track the crew and—"

"Loose the moorings and unfurl the mainsail. I need to go. You can stay." I cared not. I needed to get out of here, go . . . where?

Images of a Mediterranean island flashed through my mind. I sucked in a breath. "I have to go to Corsica."

"We need the crew. How are we going to . . .?" Homkar's nostrils dilated. "You're going to call the Dragon."

"Aye."

I walked over to the scuttlebutt to wash. Shouts came from the end of the dock; soon Qing officers would arrive, but I would be long gone by then. The tepid water splashed against my skin, cooling the hot rage inside me.

A tad cleaner, I held the helm tightly. My mind conjured a gale taking away the stench.

"Ready, Captain!" Homkar shouted a few moments later.

Grand. Having him with me made things easier. Homkar unfurled the main sail for the Dragon to use—that was all it needed.

I filled my lungs to their maximum and let the air out through my mouth, slowly, concentrating to isolate the screams of my beast, the images of destruction. My mind focused on the Valley of the Dragons. Wood vibrated beneath my feet, feeling the call. Its essence entered me, taking over my body.

The vast face of a dragon appeared, suspended above the mainsail, its muzzle wide about to devour. I watched its mesmerizing eyes and allowed its strength to pour out of the dragonwood.

With a roar, its head exploded in millions of colored lights that seized the ship and the sails, then pushed us down river. The dock erupted into chaos, men, and women shouting and pointing at the sail. This was a sight they would always remember.

I allowed myself a smile. I alone from the bradaís had discovered the power of the Dragon within the wood. Though I had to concentrate, allowing the Dragon to be part of me. For a moment I furrowed my brow, worried that Shen's men could have seen what I did and reported back to him. I shook the feeling away—it was necessary, and I would deal with it if needed.

Air shimmered in front of the ship. The Dragon had called a portal to Tír D'aois.

The ship passed through, a cold feeling washing over me as we did. Despite the portal, this would be a challenging trip that demanded my full attention and energy.

For hours, I kept focus, my legs and arms numb, my eyes strained. The endless ocean was identical to that of the human world, except sometimes the wind carried a lullaby from sea nymphs and the sails flapped in response like two lovers who had been apart and desired nothing else but to reunite.

The air shimmered again, and the ship went through the portal, back to the human world.

Corsica appeared before us. My body ached from the strain. The violent images, which had been isolated during the journey, pounded again inside my brain. I let myself fall to the planks, exhausted after using the Dragon portal for so long.

"You should rest, Captain," Homkar said, brow creased.

"Nay. I cannot."

The fire swept over me, giving me new strength. I removed my jacket, boots, and shirt, leaving only my breeches on.

"Lower the anchor and wait here," I said to Homkar, who nodded.

Rocky cliffs loomed proudly, and a small beach was nearby.

I felt extremely exhausted after the long trip. My body would pay the price later, but I cared not. The fire within gave me the energy I needed.

"Go to the island," Anord said in my head.

Aye. I dove into the sea. As my body hit the water, the fire withdrew. I let myself sink, confused.

Why had I come? What did I have to do?

A dainty woman smiled through the water, crimson curls like quivering fire. She felt familiar, somehow. The anxiety that had nestled in my chest since I saw the first image of destruction back in Nanjing disappeared altogether. She beckoned me. My body refused to obey her command, my beast roaring inside of me. I recoiled.

The woman dissolved into the water. A hallucination.

I spread my arms and felt the pulse of marine life, throbbing into me as if I were a part of it. I let that peace take over, all traces of my beast gone. I sank further, cool water balancing the heat inside.

I spent a long time underwater, grateful that whatever controlled me, what had made me kill before, was no longer. My energy slowly came back to me—water infused me with added vitality. I could not understand why I'd reacted the way I did, stronger and blinder than when I obeyed my beast. Perhaps Anord's call reinforced the beast.

The answer was on the island. I had to go and henceforth avoid my killing impulse.

With this resolution, I swam to the shore and reached the small beach. A stony path snaked up between the cliffs.

I climbed, the call diminished after the water submersion. At midway, I looked back. I could only sense the *Scáil Dragún* gracing the bay, but I knew deep within me others would arrive soon. Anord hadn't called just me, but all bradaís. The Mediterranean sun's intensity burned my skin. A warm sea breeze swirled around my sweaty chest. Black-throated loons made their peculiar *kwow* call while waves crashed against the cliffs.

Do not stop. Keep going.

Not Anord's voice anymore, just the beast. Anord had been cut from me since the submersion.

Did I want to follow Anord's call? I paused and reflected upon it. The beast wanted this, so what the hell was I going to do? Anord's balls, I would rather keep submerged in the water than blindly obey.

And yet, I had to see for myself why he wanted me there. Why he wanted all of us.

The path continued upward; I used hands and feet to grasp rocks and disregarded the pain in the soles of my feet, the scorching rocks blistering them.

When I reached the top of the cliff, I looked back at the horseshoe-shaped bay. Blurred images appeared at the corner of my eyes—a couple of bradaí warships. They must have been in the northern Atlantic; the rest would rely upon goblins to open portals for them.

With renewed strength, I darted between trees and bushes, disregarding the snap of the branches on my naked torso, my feet trampling wild, rough grass.

I must arrive first. The others would react as I did before the water submersion, and having my head clear would be an advantage.

The call now intensified like approaching a bonfire. Controlling the flame within me, I slowed down, trying not to make noise.

Whatever called me was ahead, in a clearing amongst gnarled trees with tall branches that formed a green canopy above. I wiped the sweat from my forehead with the back of my hand and recovered my breath. Extending my senses, I felt bradaís nearby—a fire within like walking barefoot over burning coals. I slid my hand vertically in the hair, a silver line following my fingers to open my bradaí pocket, then retrieved my sword, and hid behind a wide trunk. I glanced at the clearing.

Two bradaís. One dead, one alive.

Luc, the Frenchman, lay on the ground in a pool of his own blood. The coppery smell mixed with urine hit me. His guts spilled to one side as I'd done with the Chinese officers. By the Morrigan! The sight of one of my kin dead struck me to the core. We were supposed to be immortal. Unkillable.

What had changed?

Edward stood before him, wearing a blood-splattered white shirt under a black vest edged with golden buttons. The killing had happened recently by the bright color of the blood. I furrowed my brow.

He squatted and thrust his fist *inside* Luc's corpse. Morrigan's crow. A cruel grin spread across Edward's face as he stood. The bloody fist began to shine, and his body was wrapped in a coppery halo. He inhaled, closing his eyes. A shockwave of power hit me.

Hell and damnation. He had killed Luc like Anord had commanded. It all made sense now. Our creator had wanted us to destroy one of our own and take the fallen's power, the bastard god.

Edward panted, and his expression changed, something I could not fathom, then shoved the shiny fist into his pocket. His body trembled but not with exhaustion, no. Something powerful had hit him. I watched the scene before me, making sure no other dangers lurked. A dead woman lay not far from Luc, her hand outstretched as though wanting to touch him with her last breath. His human lover, caught up in the crossfire. Grabbing my sword tightly with both hands, I stepped into the clearing.

Edward turned, surprised. Which was odd since he should have been able to sense me as I did him. Mayhap he'd been too enthralled with the power lust.

"Irish." His bulldog cheeks were covered by a well-trimmed beard. His stocky frame reminded me of a carronade.

The glow disappeared from his body but lingered in his eyes. Eyes I could bet had been completely black a moment before. The light dimmed, leaving him with a cold shark-like bearing.

"Did you feel the call?" he asked, his expression changing to perplexed. Fake.

I nodded, putting one foot before the other, wary of both pirates—dead and alive—and any suspicious movement around.

"Who would think an Eadrom could kill one of us?" He shook his head in mock sadness.

Eadrom my arse. There were not many of them among the fae, thank the Morrigan, yet Edward was lying. How had he managed to kill one of our own?

"Anord called us here," I said casually, gauging his reaction.

"He did, so we could stop the Eadrom and kill her." He stroked his chin, thoughtfully.

Bloody liar! I made sure enough space stretched between us. "You saw the Eadrom?"

He let out a sigh. A good actor, seeming genuinely remorseful. "I tried to fight her, but you know it's almost impossible to beat a fae, much less one of those."

His clothes had blood splatters, but it was not his blood. He didn't have one scratch.

"Curious you came through unscathed," I said. "Eadrom are extremely powerful."

His smile didn't reach his cold eyes. "Fighting me is not an easy matter, Irish. I managed to wound her. Though it was too late for Luc."

Bastard. The knuckles of my hands whitened around the sword's hilt. I forced myself to relax.

He took a step toward me. Darkness covered his sclera. My body tensed again. He wanted more power. My own.

I held my ground. He would not have it easy.

He took another step, and wavered, hesitating—an invisible wall between us. His lips tightened and his brow furrowed as his eyes returned to normal. He'd changed his mind, then. I suppressed a grin. Edward wouldn't risk going against me face to face, the coward.

"Bradaís are coming," I said, nodding at the way behind me. "They'll arrive any minute."

He cocked his head. "Where were you when you felt the call?"

"Nanjing," I answered before thinking it through.

His eyes narrowed dangerously. "China."

Hell. I smiled at him. "Chez Nanjing. France. You should try it. Best dumplings on the continent."

Pounding footsteps nearby saved me from his scrutiny. A few bradaís stormed into the clearing, eyes wider than normal. A pack of rabid, disoriented hyenas finding their prey gone.

Edward eyed me, stroking his beard as if comparing my calm and controlled attitude with theirs, my lack of proper clothes and bare feet. I refrained from cursing. Goblins would have been a better answer if it weren't for my ship waiting in the bay.

"You look too calm," I said to him. Nothing better for throwing suspicion away than to turn the tables.

"I was in Rome dealing with goblins, it wasn't hard for me to come here."

And yet, both him and I were the only ones with a clear mind.

The bradaís stopped short, stupidly watching the dead pirate—they were returning to their old selves. Kara was with them, but Sergei was yet to come. She locked gazes with me, her chest heaving.

Edward leaned toward me. "Shall we wait for the rest, Irish? I wager they would all use a goblin's portal."

There was more in his words. He was testing me.

I shrugged. "I don't think they'll wait. These might try to rip our heads off before they know what's happening."

Edward nodded and raised his hands. "My beloved companions. A fae managed to do what no one thought possible. One of us has fallen." He removed the tricorn he wore, placing it on his chest. "Let's have a moment of silence for him."

The gorgeous Parvaati stepped forward. "Who did this?" She spat the words, a spasm of anger contorting her beautiful brown face. "Who killed one of us?"

Screams and shouts of all but the Alpha and me.

"The culprit was an Eadrom," Edward cried in a clear, firm voice. "We shall return this affront to the fae! Anord wants us to."

"Impossible!" Shen shouted, shaking a fist in the air. His bald head shone, the long braid quivering with his brusque head movements. "Eadrom are too powerful. If they can kill us, we stand no chance."

Edward twisted his mouth, his eyes flashing dangerously again. For a second, I thought they had once again become black, but they were as brown as ever. "We will do what we do best. What Anord created us for."

The complaining stopped, and the bradaís' anger subsided. I whipped my head up. The beast was silent within me, although it could be giving the same advice it gave me when I used to be Edward's first mate: *Obey the Alpha.*

They all nodded, all with the same, cruel grin. Aye. The beast's doing. Morrigan's crow, why did Anord want us to obey Edward?

I glanced at Luc. Edward had taken his power. Whatever for?

"They are more powerful, but we are stealthy and devious," Edward said, raising his voice while the bradaís kept nodding stupidly. "Tackle the distracted, those who are alone. Let us return their blow!"

The enraged bradaís raised their fists and shouted. Kara took a step forward, her focus on Luc and his lover. Her lips pressed together, and I nodded at her. She was finally gathering her wits and shaking the beast away. Aye, it had to be that.

I glanced at the fallen pirate, trying to understand what had happened. It was then I noticed that the human's hand wasn't the only one reaching for her lover. Luc's arm also stretched toward the dead woman as though attempting to touch her. That was odd. Why would a bradaí care for his lover?

Though more importantly, if Edward achieved what we thought impossible, then Anord had helped him. And that bothered me more than anything else.

TWELVE

Titus

My body hurt like it was being pierced by rusty nails. And yet, I'd be up and about in a day and fully recovered in five days. I'd been playing Nanjing in my mind over and over and comparing it with what happened the day before.

Edward had wanted to kill me after Luc, but Anord had stopped him then too. Although what had happened with Luc was still muddled. Nothing made sense.

Ryanne entered the cabin, alone, her expression set. "Look, Titus, I know it's important to obey orders, you being the captain and all—"

"It's not about that." I pushed myself up with my elbows. "If you can't heed a warning, then you'll end up dead."

She sighed. "I wanted to see Edward up close."

"Why?"

"It's just . . . fae and bradaís hate each other so much, but you said you didn't like to kill fae, and I wanted to see if Edward was like you."

"You'll be the death of me, woman. Next time, heed my command or I'll throw you overboard myself." I let myself fall on the bed.

Ryanne sat next to me and laced her fingers with mine. Bloody hell, it felt good. But her gaze was far away, her jaw clenched.

"Something troubling you, *ashtore*?"

"I'm tired of being bullied around. You"—her lips twitched—"Haru, now Minho. And the nymphs, who love to bully me. I'm tired."

"You're way over your head with all those creatures." My turn to twitch my lips. "Even me."

"Ha ha. I know. I'm just a human." She sighed and retrieved her hand. I didn't like that. "But the fae trained me to face them, somehow. I just don't know how."

"To fight?"

"Well, no."

"I'll teach you."

"You will?"

"Aye. You need to know the basics. I can teach you swordsmanship."

"That'll take me years to master! Can we start with something easier?"

"Mouse practices kickboxing when the crew is on deck. I'll ask her to teach you if you'd rather."

"I have a question," she said in that sweet tone of hers.

"Hell woman—"

"—you ask too many questions," she said with a straight face.

I gave a dry chuckle. "And I promised I'd answer, aye. What do you want to know?"

"First, why, if Minho is a bradaí, is he with Edward? Is that common? You said you were loners."

Not a full-fledged bradaí, I wanted to say, but I kept quiet on that account.

My mind brought up Minho's blank eyes pleading, his weak grasp raking at my arm.

"*Please,*" he'd said.

I clenched my fist and shook those thoughts away. "All bradaís use only human crews, all but me and Edward. I have Homkar, albeit that's quite uncommon. Edward used to have me as his first mate for six years."

"Why would you do that?"

"I wanted to learn from the best."

"And now Minho is with him."

"Aye. I once led a rebellion against Edward, and Minho betrayed me then." Right after Corsica. "Since then, Edward took him under his wing. Is that all you want to know?"

"I need all that you can tell me. If I'm taking this path with you, I need to be more informed."

"As in?"

"As in who the bradaís really are. I know everything from the fae's point of view, I think, but it takes two to tango."

"That's a hell of a question. But fine."

I reached out for the whiskey tumbler resting on the night table and told her about our kin as I savored the drink. She nodded at times, indicating she already knew Anord was involved with destruction and chaos and created us to be his tools.

"We might not be immortal, but it's extremely difficult to kill us. Your pointy-eared friend has tried for centuries, though only Edward has been successful."

"Wait." She leaned back. "You can be killed?"

"Fae don't know that? Interesting." I took another swig and closed my eyes for a moment. This was a hell of a whiskey—thirteen-year single malt. "But it shouldn't surprise me. Fae *can't* kill us. But our Alpha can."

Edward and his bloody lies, blaming the deaths on Eadroms when it'd been him. Always him.

"So Ed's more dangerous than I thought." She squeezed her hands, and her moss-green eyes grew bigger.

Grand. She was finally realizing her folly. "Every time he kills one of us, he gets stronger, since he takes away the power of each dead bradaí."

She looked confused. "Why does he need the extra power?"

"To kill fae quicker. He alone has disposed of half the fae our kin have managed to kill."

She hugged herself and rubbed her arms. "I thought he was going to kill your crew."

"No. After the 1907 Council, we decided humans weren't disposable anymore due to the difficulty finding hands that could accept the strangeness around us."

"A council? Really?" She gave a small smile.

"Aye. Edward orders us to come together once every few decades." I scowled, remembering that last stupid council I went to, the last where I still counted Kara and Sergei as friends, right before Edward accused me of being Ivan's killer.

Corfu, 1921

The impossible blue of the Mediterranean Sea glittered in the distance through the open windows in Edward's spacious and sunny villa. Bradaís sat on fluffy sofas, feet propped on ottomans. Greek women in white robes, with twisted and braided hair gathered at the top of their heads and gold bands on their arms, offered every kind of spirit and wine. Olives, feta cheese, and small fish lay on silver plates. In one of the corners, a woman played the clarinet while another played the lute.

Edward laughed with curvy, gorgeous Parvaati, who acted as if the Alpha hadn't attacked her ship recently. His good mood echoed through the rest of the bradaís. The only one in a sour-mood, besides me, was Sergei.

Sergei lounged about on a comfy chair, his big frame barely fitting, his long whitish-blond hair tied behind his neck. He didn't bother to look at me or even acknowledge my presence—it'd been like this since Ivan's death.

As a matter of fact, Sergei had never been the same with me since Ivan appeared, his attention always on that human and paying less and less attention to me. We raided less together. Hell, we weren't at all like we used to be.

Curse Ivan. I brooded and wished Ivan had never appeared. Even his death was a ghost over our friendship. Lucky me, attempting to deal with humans regarding a profitable business in Haiti, and Ivan had been there in that hut, alone with several stacks of gold ingots. We'd both been surprised at the coincidence. The lights went out, then someone attacked me. When I recovered, Ivan laid dead, my sword stuck in his back, the gold gone. Sergei and his crew had been monitoring the lonely hut, and no one had seen anyone but me enter. I'd been careful to sense for any bradaís before entering the hut, but only Ivan had been there.

I'd promised Sergei I hadn't touched Ivan and that I'd been framed by Edward. After some weeks, too many gold coins, and a ton of rum, I'd finally found the proof I needed. It was a matter of timing correctly when to shove it in Edward's face. It hadn't been complicated, since the murder happened on the day of the treaty of Berlin, and one of his crew had confessed about Edward's whereabouts that day.

Like Parvaati, Shen looked comfortable. He sauntered over, taking his time to chitchat here and there until he finally reached my side. His red and golden *changpao* didn't do much to hide his protruding belly. My kin was getting lazy.

He spoke in Mandarin, a language I mastered when involved in the opium trade. "Can you believe them? They have fallen under his spell."

I kept silent for a moment, taking rum from one of the servants' trays. Shen grabbed a shot glass of ouzo.

I emptied mine in one long gulp. "I take it you're not."

"By the way, I didn't know you love dragons." He kept his expression serious, but I stiffened.

"Who doesn't?" I answered in the same careless tone.

He knew about the Dragon portal, there was no doubt about it. Would he use that information against me? Of course he would. When it was convenient for him.

Edward stood and clapped his hands twice. The servants closed the windows and hastily retired.

"Nothing here is what it seems, Doyle. Be careful." Shen nodded at me and withdrew.

"Thank you all for responding to my request for this council."

Edward took his time to look each one of us in the eye. "I would not have expected otherwise, yes?"

Those sitting shifted uncomfortably. All but Minho, who seemed to enjoy their distress.

"A matter has been brought to my attention, a matter that must be dealt with swiftly." Edward caressed his clean-shaven chin and paced around the room.

The bradaís strained their necks to follow his movement. There was an advantage to standing in the opposite corner. No one was at my back.

"I have been informed of a vicious attack."

I scoffed. The only vicious attack had been his. Eyes shifted toward me, and murmurs in the room grew. I arched an eyebrow.

Edward stopped and looked me in the eye. "Yes, we are bradaís. Yes, we've killed each other's crews when there were . . . misunderstandings. It's our nature. But"—his features darkened, as his voice lowered into a steady growl—"it's one thing to openly fight while we are on deck, sword to sword. Quite another to lure a bradaí crew member with the promise of gold, cowardly kill him, and then blame it on me!"

His arm shot forward, index finger pointed at me.

Either Edward was genuinely angered by my accusation a few months ago regarding Ivan's death, or he had been taking acting classes, the bastard.

Though I had to pull my strength here. Besides, this was my golden opportunity. Corner him.

"You hit me and then killed Ivan. Who's the coward?" I advanced a step, chin lifted.

"Irish, stop it," Edward said. "I'm unfurling the Jolly Roger, not the blood flag. Admit it."

I dropped the anchor on his head. "Your ship was there in Haiti. You were there. One of your crew confessed." A slow smile spread on my face. "You did it; I know."

"Did I? I wasn't in Haiti that day but in Prague."

"No. You were not. Your ship anchored in Port-au-Prince that same day. Coincidence? Not anymore, Edward."

Take that, you bastard.

"Oh, Irish"—Edward put on his sad face—"tell me you didn't offer gold to my crew. They're unreliable, and I had to fire them all."

"Of course you did." I arched an eyebrow. "How convenient."

"I'll prove it to you." He turned toward Kara. "Kara can testify."

Kara paled. Sergei rose, jumping from his seat, angst etching on his clenched fists and locked jaw.

"You're lying," I said, knowing Kara wouldn't be swayed like Parvaati or Shen. Not her. Not ever.

"Tell him, dearie," Edward said. "Tell him what day it was when we had that lovely chat, hm?"

"August 25th." Her eyes pleaded. "The day of—"

"The treaty of Berlin!" Sergei roared.

My confidence wavered. Kara on Edward's side?

Edward smirked and addressed the group. "See? The Irish killed Sergei's first mate. He's the one lying. How could I have been in Prague in the day and Haiti at night? Impossible."

"C'mon, Ed," I said, "you used a goblin and reached the hut where Ivan was. Be the bradaí I know you are. Admit it."

"Lies!" The bloody finger was aimed at me again. "You want to turn everyone against me."

Sergei said through clenched teeth, "There was no goblin portal, Doyle. No one approached the hut but you."

Edward closed his eyes and took a deep breath. Then, he adopted that sad, disappointed expression he often used. "Why are you so against me, Irish? I've always been concerned about our kin. Taking care of you all."

Bloody bastard. I glanced around the room. Kara's gaze wavered, going back and forth from me to Sergei, his breathing ragged and neck muscles bulging.

"You attacked Shen," I said to Edward. "And Parvaati before him. What do you have to say about that?"

Parvaati stood and said, "It was my punishment because I interfered in Shen's business."

Shen waved his hand dismissively. "I stepped on Minho's. That's why I was punished. No need to blame the Alpha. *Méi shí.*"

I clenched my jaw.

Edward opened his arms. "You're acting like a desperate, cornered man. The charade is over, Irish."

Minho stood next to Edward. "He should be punished as well."

"Nay, Minho." Edward waved a hand. "He murdered a human, and who cares about them?"

"He stole Sergei's gold."

Bastard. Sergei didn't care about the ingots. Charade, indeed.

"Ah." Edward's eyes brightened. "Yes, a punishment is in order. You are to pay Sergei ten times the ingots you stole by the end of the month."

Minho thumped his fist on his open palm. "By Anord, someone must lead, to keep us in line. Edward did what he had to do. Otherwise, we'd run wild. Just like him." He pointed at me. "Do we want the likes of him stabbing a knife in our backs, pretending to be our friend the whole time?"

The rest of the bradaís nodded, except Sergei, whose fists shook, and me, who glared and tried to come up with something fast.

Nothing came to mind. Edward must have opened a goblin portal after killing Ivan. But why didn't Sergei's crew spot anyone besides me? I was missing something. What?

Minho continued, "We can't let someone like Doyle try to take away the Alpha's lead. Doyle said Edward killed Luc and Thomas, and took their powers, but . . ." He paused for an evident dramatic effect. "Who's the one who can do things no one else can?"

Eyes shifted to me, suspicion painted on them like tar on wood. Morrigan's crow.

"What are you trying to say, Minho?" Parvaati asked. "What things?"

Edward eyed me, a shadow of a grin tempting to break his mask. "He can stay underwater for an unreasonable time."

All bradaís murmured among themselves.

"And you disappear mysteriously," Minho said, then turned to Edward. "Didn't he vanish from your ship once?"

"Yes," Edward answered. "We were marooned, having a nice time with a fae, and then he was gone with her. Vanished. What is it about you, Irish, that you can do things not one of us can? Did you make a deal with someone? A fae, perhaps?"

Sergei blanched.

"Fae," Minho spat. "The Irish didn't respond to Anord's calling when Thomas was murdered. Yah, he has good friends among the pointy-eared. He's a fae lover."

"That's a lie, and you know it," I said through clenched teeth. "I'm good at escaping though Anord can send the call right here, right now, before I tell you what I've learned. I'm only surviving."

Shen glanced at me, and I waited for him to give the last strike—how I could call the Dragon from my ship. That information would brand me as a fae-lover forever.

Instead, he reached out for his ouzo and sipped it.

"I'm like any bradaí." I folded my arms across my chest and scowled. "I'm not any different."

"A bradaí hungry for power," Edward said. "*My* power. You've been against me and telling lies since Luc's death. Didn't I spare you all when the Irish led you against me?"

Mumbles of agreement echoed.

"Me, wanting your power? You have balls, Edward. Balls the size of a dragon. It's the other way around." I glowered at the rest of the bradaís. Not one of them would dare to oppose him, the cowards.

"I must stop you before you jump into your own grave. Everyone knows about you now," Edward said, still with that fake concerned expression. "You killed Sergei's first mate because you were jealous, and the gold lust had you by the balls. But come clean, Irish. We all understand that allure, yes?"

Sergei seized my jacket and dragged me outside. I didn't stop him, hoping he'd come to his senses.

Once outside, he threw me against the wall. "You lied to me."

"By the Morrígan, how can you believe him? Edward has been after me. He might be after all of us, trying to take our powers."

"You always blame him for everything."

"Because he is to blame!"

"You know Ivan was like a son to me." He let me go, disappointment and something else flashed in his eyes. Hurt. "You *knew*. And you killed him. My son. You murdered my *son*."

"I did not. And why would I have killed him in that hut? I could have killed him dozens of times—"

"Because you let your beast dominate you. You let the gold dictate your actions. And you *promised*. I'd expected at least you'd come clean with me. Face me with the truth. But no. You blamed it on someone else. You hide behind Edward's back."

"You don't trust me," I said, not believing my ears. "I'm telling the truth and yet—"

Sergei's nostrils flared, eyes bloodshot. "From now on, you and Ivan are the same to me. Dead." Without looking back, he walked away.

My body shook, and my legs trembled. I placed a hand on the wall for support.

Kara stepped out of the room, her lean, tall body covered in leathers, as was her wont, her dirty, wavy blonde hair loose. "What a bloody mess you're in, by Odín."

"Why are you siding with Edward?" I scowled. "You, of all people."

"I'm not," she said through clenched teeth. "Edward was with me that day, persuading me to abandon a job where Parvaati was involved." She rubbed her chin. "He succeeded."

I ran my hands through my hair. Could I trust her? The bloody bastard set me up somehow. How? What was I missing? The beast had blinded them all back in Corsica when Edward fooled them so easily. It was the same here; it was like the beast whispered to them to follow his orders. Puppets. All bradaís were bloody puppets.

"You broke our family code by murdering Ivan." She spat. "Where does your act leave us? How can I trust you now if you kill anyone for gold?"

"Kara—"

"We're supposed to be *family*, Doyle."

I flinched at the use of my name. She'd never said it before. Never with that bitterness.

Her jaw locked, and I knew she was beyond reason.

She continued, "You *knew* what I felt when Minho murdered Philippe. I told you. And you do the same to Sergei? To our *brother*? By Odin, Doyle. You disappoint me." Her voice broke. "Perhaps you also told Minho about Philippe. Were you jealous then too?"

She trotted after Sergei without bothering to glance back at me.

I watched her go. Tightening my lips, I turned away. If no one would believe me, fine. Perhaps the beast had been right all these years, and I should trust no one since no one seemed to trust me.

Yes. Trust no one. You are better alone.

Present Day

I shook my head to dispel those painful memories. "We bradaís are cruel. Heartless."

Ryanne took one of my hands between her slender ones. "I can't see you like that. Not anymore."

My thumb slid over her skin, relishing the contact. "The absence of evil doesn't make me good, Ryanne."

"When we are underwater, what you showed me . . . It has nothing to do with the destruction and chaos you described."

"I know. I've always wondered about that." I placed the tumbler back on the nightstand and leaned back on the pillow.

"What I saw, what I *felt*, was love for life, for creation."

"Aye, there's that." I shook my head. "But there's something inside me, something that continually whispers. My beast."

"Beast?"

"So I call it. It's a bloodthirsty monster, demanding I destroy. What I showed you underwater helps me to balance. But I can't always, Ryanne. In fact, for most of my life I've succumbed to it because it's hard to ignore its calling. You asked me about the killings back in Japan. I let it take over. I could pull back, thanks to you. Yet . . ." I shut my eyes, grimacing.

She brushed a damp lock of hair away from my forehead.

"That's why I need you," I said. "You helped me to drown the beast back in Japan. And I don't want to succumb to it anymore. I want to be free of it."

"You can't do it by yourself?" she whispered.

I squeezed her hands and shook my head once.

"Is this related to why you couldn't kill Aghna?"

"No, that's . . . That's not an easy confession. I'm not used to feeling—"

"Vulnerable?"

"Aye. We can't show vulnerability; it's not in us. I believe it has to do with Edward killing those bradaís. We're not supposed to feel." Was that what it was? Something about those murders bothered me, but I couldn't put my finger to it.

"Did you have feelings for Aghna?" she asked softly.

"Hell no!"

She seemed to ponder about that. Feel about a fae. Not in Anord's hell.

I was no fae lover.

"It's so odd to see you so—"

"Weak?"

"I didn't want to say it like that, but yeah."

I grunted, and was about to keep quiet, but she deserved my trust. Partly. "Edward infused *dorcha* in me."

She glanced at her hand. "Like you did with me?"

"When bradaís mark our prey, it's a small amount. He raised the blood flag."

"The what now?"

"Blood flag. Pirates of yore would use that to mean they wouldn't give no quarter. No prisoners."

"So he meant to kill you?"

"He wanted my powers. His greediness blinds him. Unfortunately, his *dorcha* is the darkest of all, so I'll take longer to heal. And he gave the killing blow with a goblin's blade." I grimaced. "I'd never been hurt like this before."

"We're not going to Paris, are we?" she asked softly.

"Not for now. Too dangerous."

"Then?"

"Kara's coming. Since you're so curious about bradaís, you'll meet another."

"This Kara," she said, "she's nothing like Edward?"

"No. Not quite."

Ryanne glanced at her hands, trying to hide her disappointment. No wonder, I promised her Paris and now, the only thing for certain was that I needed more information from Kara, and then, figure out our next step. Edward at sea, and fae at land.

Which of them would blow the man down?

THIRTEEN

Ryanne

N o, no, no, you're doing it wrong," Bricius said, bobbing up and down like one of the waves hitting the hull.

"She ain't so bad," Homkar said.

"She's learning fast," Mouse said in response to Homkar since she couldn't hear or see Bricius, sweat beading her forehead. "Now, jab." She put herself into defense position and, movements slow and precise, she jabbed again.

And here we were on deck, side by side, for the best part of the morning, with Mouse teaching me the basics. Clear skies and a bright sun shone down on me while a steady breeze played with us.

Bricius flew around me, inspecting my position while stroking his pointy chin. "Your arm is not quite correct, no, no, no. It should be aligned like Mouse's." Then he flew beneath my arm and pushed it upward an inch.

I grunted, and Homkar's lips twitched.

But Mouse had been right. This was fun and not as complicated as I thought, and it turned out I hadn't had any problem following Mouse's instructions. Thank Cuidi for all that training with the trolls and ogres! One learned to be nimble in that land, or else.

And fae never told, always showed.

Titus stood behind me and grasped my wrists. "You look good," he murmured in my ear, "maybe too good."

"I'm sweaty," I said.

"You need strength in your arms. That's why you need to practice more."

"You sound like Bricius."

"Practice is important, yes, yes, yes!"

Homkar placed himself before me and, without any warning, threw a light punch to my face.

"Hey!" I sidestepped at the last second, my reflexes not rusty at all.

"Don't your visions predict when he's going to hit, little seer?" Titus smirked. *Little seer* was the moniker he gave me when we first met.

"By Cuidi, it doesn't work like that." I groaned.

"Once you improve with kickboxing, I'll teach you karate."

I squinted at him. "Aren't pirates supposed to like weapons? Dunno, swords, guns, lasers?" Though weapons and me—ugh, not a good combination. "Why karate? Do you have infatuation with Japan and that's why you took me there?" I gave a playful smile to let him know he was forgiven—partially.

He shrugged in that lovely way of his, with a small tilt of his head, a corner of his lips curving up. "I spent several years there. I've always loved to learn, and Kara told me about these monk warriors in Ryukyu who trained with their bodies in a way that none of us did. And it mesmerized me. We bradaís are fast, but those monks had moves, as you say."

"Kara, huh?" I said nonchalantly. "You went there with her?"

"No. With Sergei."

"What happened with him? He was your best friend, right?"

Titus straightened; the relaxed posture gone. "Kara's about to arrive. Pixie, hide."

"Again?" Bricius grunted, not unlike Homkar.

"You know the drill," Titus said. "Bradaís can't know who she is."

"Why not hide her?" Bricius asked.

"Because that never works. Your human charge is a wee too curious."

I had the decency to blush. Curiosity killed little seers who got too close to bradaís.

Titus stood beside me, hands clasped behind his back and his gaze on the horizon, an unreadable expression on his face.

Bricius had grumbled—quite loudly if you ask me. Instead of the bathroom, he hid in the sails. By now, it was impossible to find him up there even if one knew where he was.

Emotions swirled within me at this encounter; excitement to see a new bradaí and dread that the Edward experience would be repeated. The darkness he'd projected crept into my memories—that was one bradaí who could never be redeemed. He might not even have the spark I needed to find. Would this new bradaí be more like Titus?

The *Panther* arrived. It maneuvered alongside the *Scáil Dragún*. Her ship looked like Titus's but smaller and slender, with two masts and large sails. A black flag fluttered in the wind, a panther's face with its maw open.

He turned to me, the serious expression lingering on his tight lips. "Don't let her take your hand. Understand? It's the only way for us to sense what you have."

I nodded. "Wait, wait . . . Why can we see that ship? Or Edward's? Doesn't the dragonwood make the ships invisible?"

"From ship to ship it's possible. While we're in contact with the wood, we can see each other."

Homkar approached and said, "Edward messed up her ship."

While Titus answered, I squinted at the ship. One of the masts was half-way broken, and several of the crew had bandages. A section of the rail was destroyed.

A lean, blonde woman waved. "Ahoy! Permission to board, Captain!"

"Aye. But only you, Kara, and no tricks!" Titus yelled.

I leaned over the rail to watch an inflatable boat descend from the *Panther*. A man took the oars while the bradaí called Kara proudly stood with a foot on the bow, her balance impeccable. When they arrived amidship, Homkar threw her a rope. She hauled herself up gracefully, landing like a cat on deck.

Leather pants hugged her hips, matching her wide-heeled boots. She wore a loose, long-sleeved white blouse with lacy, ample wrists, and a neckline low enough to show the swell of her breasts. Dark blonde curls brushed her shoulders, swaying to the rhythm of her hips. Like Titus, she looked in her earlier thirties.

"She's still got it," Homkar said when Kara was a few feet away.

Titus grunted, his stance stiff.

As with Minho, I pushed Aine down in my mind, and it morphed into the fluorescent mushroom. It was like when you're listening to someone but at the same time you're thinking about something else, so that picture is clear in your mind even as you're seeing the real world through your eyes.

Aine-slash-mushroom pulsated with a happy bright blue as if I had a VR headset and the mushroom was ever present in the screen.

"Are you still wearing that old red jacket?" Kara's tone was clear, firm, and musical. "Tsk, tsk, you should see my designer, love."

"I'd rather kiss the gunnar's daughter."

Kara gave a crystalline laugh. "Always so charming. And who is this?" She gave me a glance over.

"My lover in turn," Titus said, emotionless.

Titus had explained he'd say that for her to avoid any suspicion.

She tilted her head, her lips suppressing a grin. "A new lover." Her accent reminded me of Peter's—someone who learned British English but wasn't a native. Kara looked Nordic, perhaps Swede; she was tall enough with her six-foot-frame. A true Valkyrie.

"Now that you're here, what do you want?" Titus asked in what seemed a flat tone, but it felt forced. Strained. Like those people who tried to act cool and uninterested yet oozed yearning.

Kara dismissed him and grabbed my chin. "Watcha, look at those eyes! And you must tell me what shampoo brand you use. I adore your hair."

Her smile was so warm I smiled back, making sure to lace my hands behind my back in a casual gesture. Titus had changed from charming to predatory when he touched my hand the first time, and I didn't care to see how she'd react. Like Titus, she could be one to hang with until her darkness peeked.

What was it like to be a female bradaí and a captain of her own ship? Did she enjoy killing? Was she good at it? Did she kick ass? Did she ever meet someone like me? Questions swirled my mind like Bricius near coffee.

"Whatever you want to say," Titus said, growling, "I'm sure it wasn't beauty advice."

"Don't be daft, love. I'm getting to know your woman. You never give us a bell, and you've stopped coming to our cozy family gatherings, little brother." She whispered to me loud enough for Titus to hear. "He hates it when I call him that."

Little brother? Huh. There was something attractive about her, something so different from the flat, dense energy I felt with Minho and Edward. I itched to touch Kara, see if she also had cold energy within her. Would it react as Titus's? Cuidi had said Anord imbued something to control them. It had to be that beast, whatever it was.

But then, why did Kara and Titus's energy feel different from Minho and Edward?

"Kara," Titus warned, "state your business."

She winked at me. "And I'm his favorite person in all the world, besides my boy Homkar. Hey"—she smiled at the big man while jerking her chin up—"what's up?"

Homkar grunted, but he somewhat chuckled. It was that, or he just burped.

I tried to understand their link by observing Titus. There was a yearning in his posture. For just a moment, his lips parted, and he leaned his body forward as if to take a step toward her.

Then the moment passed, and his eyes returned to the hard expression he had during the exchange.

Titus had said she was something like family but also a friend. Could she be a former lover? Maybe that "little brother" thing irked him because he saw her as something else? The pit of my stomach clenched. The feeling that Peter had it wrong about them increased.

They could feel more than my fae mentor thought.

FOURTEEN

Titus

My muscles tensed, my body ready to intervene. I relaxed enough not to appear concerned and resisted the urge to pull Ryanne to my side. Kara had to believe Ryanne was only a lover, someone unimportant.

Lover. Something that might come true once Ryanne trusted me more. Though she would never be a typical one, not when the fae-power she had within helped to balance my darkness, my bradaí soul. My beast.

Homkar was at ease, even attempting a brief smile. My first mate and only friend thought he was protecting me by letting Kara talk to me. The Morrigan knows I'd stall any advance from her part. As the eldest of what used to be my family, Kara had set our code of conduct —a family, where we trusted each other, something unheard of between bradaís. The code had grappled Sergei, and he didn't hesitate to adopt the puny, gaunt ten-year-old Ivan as his son, back in London where the one who used to be my brother and I were raiding. The why still eluded me. Ivan had been a wedge between us since that time.

Kara smiled at her, a warm smile Ryanne returned. My jaw clenched—Ryanne was too trusting, despite everything. She should have learned her lesson when Edward came and kicked my arse. My body felt stiff, and my wounds had yet to heal completely. By the Morrigan, I was in a vulnerable position. Too vulnerable.

Although there was no sign Kara knew who Ryanne was, the real reason I'd allowed her aboard. Kara hadn't tried to take her hand, though I had to be alert.

Kara finally stopped ignoring me.

"We need to talk. Alone," she said.

"Like hell."

"Then let's talk here." She winked at Ryanne.

"Not a chance. This way." I waved at the stern.

Kara beamed and led the way, the crew parting to let us pass. This had been my intention all along, but one couldn't be straight up with bradaís. It was better they thought they had the upper hand.

There had been a time I didn't need any subterfuges around Kara, but that time was gone.

Once we reached the captain's mess, I closed the door and turned to face her.

Kara raised a hand and strode to the wooden table in the center of the cabin. She unsheathed a knife from her belt.

I retrieved a dagger from my belt, point down. I was as quick as her if it came to a fight.

She scoffed and nailed the knife to the surface, right next to the globe I kept there. The knife was completely black, both in handle and blade, with a serrated edge on one side.

I tightened the hold on my dagger's handle, not taking my eyes from her—distracting your opponent by surrendering a weapon while having others concealed was her favorite stunt. "I didn't know you had a thing for knives. Looks wicked."

"It's not mine," she hissed, a fierce scowl on her face replacing her previous light mood. "It's Minho's."

"Minho? He let you keep one of his knives?"

"As if. I stole it from him in payment. Edward smashed my ship." Kara's nostrils flared, and her pupils contracted. "He made up something about me messing with Parvaati's casinos. Lies! I don't even like gambling."

"I'm sure your customers do."

She scowled. One of the few rules we abided by was not to mess with another bradaí's territory. Kara traded weapons, and her customers were high profile and usually on the most-wanted list of any government on the globe—a good portion of her clientele enjoyed their times at casinos.

"I don't know why Anord made Edward so powerful," she grunted, then pounded both palms on the table, her jaw locked. "I'm tired of Edward's attacks. I'm sick of him always getting away with it. It's time to take away his impunity, Doyle. Finish him once and for all."

"So now you believe me?" I said in a flat tone. "After all these years, when everyone isolated me?"

And there it was. The invisible wall between us. She evaded my gaze and shifted uncomfortably.

"Why have you been contacting me?" I said, eyes narrowed. "You scolded me for ditching you and Sergei back when we got our ships. And that's exactly what you did to me when Edward put all the bradaís against me. You gave up on me. Was it payback?"

"No," she said, sadly. "Look, we can't continue like this. We need to stand together again. Edward's putting his nose into *my* business. He's closing the noose around our necks, and if we don't kill him—"

"We *can't*."

"That you know. We can try at least."

"You believe I murdered Ivan."

Kara caressed the knife's handle. "I've always believed in you." Her whisper carried to me, yet it bounced against that invisible wall.

"Anord's balls." I spat.

"You've always blamed Edward for everything, but let's focus. We must neutralize him. You, Sergei, and I ought to join. Like old times." Her tone was anxious, a hint of nostalgia laced in it.

I slid my hand across the globe. "Sergei turned his back on me when he saw Ivan dead." His *adopted* son. Why would a bradaí want a son?

"You two are a pair of dumbasses." Kara sighed. "We're getting off-topic."

The globe kept swirling, its blue and green colors hypnotizing me. My fingers slid over its surface, feeling the movement. Stop Edward? Madness.

"Shen might join," she said.

"The hell he will."

"He's been on your side, believe it or not. Parvaati was upset after Thomas's death. She might jump in."

"One of us will betray the rest. History doesn't change." I pressed a finger, and the globe stopped. "It only repeats itself." Shen was saving that Dragon portal knowledge for a time where it'd suited him; that was all.

"Then let's not call everyone. Forget the rest, just us three together again."

"Sergei would plunge a knife into my back the moment I'm distracted."

"So what? Do we stay with our arms crossed while Edward gets stronger each time?"

I sighed. "I don't see how we can beat him."

"We have to try!" Her lips tightened. "I need you, Doyle."

Minho's knife caught my eye. My fingers closed tightly around the knife's hilt, the same way I wanted them to close around Minho's throat. If only I could have the bastard alone, I'd make sure he'd suffer long enough for him not to recover so easily.

"I'm leaving it there as a peace offering," she said, "so you know who's really between us."

"We'll get burned. Forget it. Learn to live in his shadow," I said.

She looked away. She didn't understand why it took me so long to know playing defense was the best way to pass unnoticed under his radar. I'd learned my lesson the hard way. Confronting Edward was like confronting Anord, and I wasn't stupid enough.

Not anymore.

Is fearr lúbadh ná briseadh, as an Irish saying goes. It's better to bend than to break.

We stayed in silence for some time, each lost in our thoughts.

"All right," she said at last, pushing herself up on the table, then crossing her legs. "Let's talk about a more pleasant subject. Your lover's cute. Different from what I'd imagined. Yet, I like her."

I grunted.

Kara smiled too innocently. "Bring her to me. I want to talk to her."

She might only be curious. If I refused, she might think it odd. Not only that, but I still had to make sure she didn't have a part in Ryanne's kidnapping attempt.

"Sure, why not?"

Ryanne walked inside, curiosity and excitement shining in her beautiful, moss-green eyes, as though the Edward experience was only a blurred memory.

Kara grinned, a twinkle in her eye as if Ryanne were a lost friend to whom she couldn't wait to share the latest gossip. She sashayed toward Ryanne.

Ryanne smiled sweetly and clasped her hands behind her back. Good.

I leaned on the table and dipped my chin, pretending to be deep in thought, yet my senses were on the edge, and I strained my hearing, something not needed since the mess's walls blocked the sounds from outside. Our senses might help us to know if fae were around, but the touch of fae in humans was too slight to notice.

Kara stood in front of Ryanne, one hand on her hip. "Tell me, is he good?"

Ryanne blinked, confused, and I arched an eyebrow.

"Don't worry, love, I don't get off with mercenaries, not my cup of tea." Kara glanced behind her shoulder, her grin widening at her knowledge that every uttered word fell on my ears. "But tell me, I'm dying to know if he's naughty."

For once at a loss for words, Ryanne looked past her into my eyes. I managed a blank expression.

"Come on, is he smashing?"

Kara's insistence grated on my nerves. She was seeing through Ryanne's confusion and would notice something was amiss.

Ryanne's ears blushed into a deep crimson. "That's, er, none of your business."

Kara gave a clear laugh. "You're definitely cute." She looked over her shoulder. "I *am* surprised."

I pushed myself from the table. "Enough. Your silly talk is boring me."

"Not silly talk," Kara said, grinning. "Girl's talk. Why don't you leave us for a moment? I'm sure your girl would open to me without a man in the room."

Ryanne tucked a loose strand of her shiny chestnut hair behind her ear, her nervous tell. I tensed. Quick as a cobra, Kara seized Ryanne's hand.

Kara sucked in a breath, her eyes wide. In an instant, I was right beside them, prying Kara's fingers away.

Too late.

Kara *knew*.

FIFTEEN

Titus

Morrigan's crow. Why had I trusted Kara to go near her?

"I knew it! She-she's like Philippe! Blimey, Doyle!" Kara rubbed her face.

Ryanne cringed, mouthing, *I'm sorry*.

I grunted. It'd been my mistake, not hers.

A zoom, and the pixie flew inside through the slightly ajar door. "Avast, ye scurvy pirate! Remove your filthy hands from her!" His little sword flashed in his hand.

"Anord piss on all of you! Can't you heed one bloody command?" I scowled at the pixie.

"And she has a fly," Kara hissed.

"I'm *not* a fly!" The pixie pointed his sword to Kara, ready for the kill. "And I sensed Ryanne was in danger, pirate. She needs me, yes, yes, yes!"

Ryanne stepped between Kara and the furious pixie, a hand lifted. "It's okay, Bug."

"It better be." Still with his sword in his hand, he landed on Ryanne's head, gaze not leaving Kara. "And we're *not* flies," he grumbled.

"You two," I growled, "are addled."

I thought of taking Ryanne away from Kara, but the rum was already spilled. Time to confront Kara.

"Were you behind it? Don't lie to me, Kara."

"Behind what?" She pointed at Ryanne. "You have one of *them*. Are you *stupid?*"

No lying tells. She sounded genuinely surprised. "Look me in the eye and tell me what you know about her."

"Besides having bloody, tainted energy within her?" She jabbed a finger at my chest. "You're clueless, aren't you?"

The pixie hovered in front of Ryanne. "*Tainted* energy? You—"

"Hush," Ryanne hissed. She grabbed my arm and, on reflex, I covered her hand with mine.

Kara glanced at our joined hands, then looked at Ryanne. Comprehension lighted her eyes. "Bugger. You *feel* something."

"No." I let go of Ryanne's hand.

"Feel?" the pixie echoed, stroking his pointy chin.

Ryanne hissed something else, and the pixie sat atop her head again, folding his wings and scowling fiercely. I liked that.

Kara sighed. "By Odin, when are you going to trust me? Yes, I screwed up in Corfu. I should have sided with you. But I've never betrayed you. And more to the point, I've been where you are now."

"We can't feel," I said, straightening to my full height and looking as menacing as I could be. "It's impossible."

"We *shouldn't*, that's different," Kara continued, unimpressed by my stunt. "Sergei had his son fetish, protecting Ivan as a momma bear. He always wanted to have a son, did you know?"

"No."

"Of course you didn't." She wrinkled her nose. "Sergei wanted a kid, cursing Anord because of our sterility. Then Ivan appeared, and he took him into his care. Ivan called him Papa." She arched her brows, daring me.

I folded my arms over my chest and deepened my frown. "I knew that."

"It's obvious something similar is happening to you, too; I can sense it. We feel something. Not love," she added quickly, looking at

Ryanne intently as if to give her a warning. "That's something we don't understand. I know from experience."

Ryanne sidestepped me, the pixie taking flight but hovering near her. "And do you know why? Why it is like this with you three?"

There was no disappointment in her regarding the lack of love. Grand.

Kara shook her head. "I have no clue. But I'm ready to bet my right arm some of the others are like us. Shen, perhaps Parvaati. They both have been involved with humans, just like us."

"Except Edward," I grunted.

"Except Edward and Minho. Remember Luc's death? His lover was killed with him. He had a warning he didn't heed."

"I remember. But she was killed in the crossfire." I tried to block the image of them reaching for each other in death.

"No." Kara's jaw was set. "I was with Philippe back then, and something bugged me. I should have paid heed before it was too late."

I brooded over the subject, but something wasn't adding up. There was something else.

"Was Philippe like me?" Ryanne asked, softly.

Kara turned her head to the windows, hugging herself. Ryanne and I traded a look, and I put a finger on my lips. She nodded. After some moments of silence, Kara sighed.

"I was with him for two years. It's the most emotional part of my life. The only one. I knew who he was and didn't care. I felt . . . happy." She looked me in the eye. "I watched Philippe die under Minho's knife. Edward said I couldn't be distracted by humans. To have fun, yes, but Anord," she lowered her voice to barely a whisper, "didn't want that. Feelings were for the defective, and obviously I was. He gave me a warning, that next time it would be me."

Miyuki's face came into view, the only woman with whom I had some relationship more than a passing night—a woman with a touch of fae. When I'd thought of going back to her and taking her away, Edward appeared, the son of a gun. Coincidence, my arse. Perhaps Anord sent him to keep an eye on me. Good thing I pulled back then.

Could I pull back again? Could I keep Ryanne safe?

The pixie and Ryanne talked in whispers. Most likely he thought they should leave, back to safety. Back to the fae. I scowled.

"Did Anord warn Sergei to dispose of Ivan? Perhaps Sergei didn't heed Anord, so Anord sent Edward."

"I don't know. I told Sergei what I'm telling you, but he wouldn't get rid of his so-called son. Said Ivan was more important than us."

"It's more than that," I said, mostly to myself. "There's another reason for Anord to send us his bully. You're alive, and so is Sergei." And so was I.

Kara scowled but didn't say a thing. Perhaps she sensed that too.

"If Anord didn't send a warning, then no wonder Sergei thought Ivan was off the hook. That's why Sergei was so troubled."

"That's right, Sherlock. And then he was murdered." She lifted a hand when I opened my mouth. "I know it wasn't you. I was scared back then by Edward. Though I think Edward wanted to get rid of your developing leadership and Ivan in the same coup."

"I didn't have a developing leadership."

She clicked her tongue. "Edward follows Anord's commands blindly. You don't. I'm sure some of the bradaís looked up to you. You could have that leadership, if you try."

I waved my hand in disinterest.

"Right. About her." Kara nodded at Ryanne. "Perhaps you lovebirds can be together for some time, but make sure to part ways before you get too attached."

Just like with Miyuki. Albeit it had hurt, it hadn't been difficult to put her aside. The idea of separating from Ryanne churned my insides. "You spent two full years with Philippe. And Ivan lived until he was sixty or something."

"I was lucky." She shrugged. "Though it took me a long time to be where you are now." Kara looked at Ryanne. "Sorry, love. It's obvious you have affection for him, and for that alone I like you. But this is for the best. I know what I'm talking about." She addressed me. "You don't want to see your girl in Minho's hands. You don't want to see what he'll do, and believe me, once Anord knows of your feelings, he'll send his hound after her. You might keep your hide intact, but she won't. So keep your head under the radar."

I nodded. "Thanks for the heads up. About Edward . . . let it go."

"Let me put it this way. If you kill Edward, you might be able to keep her longer than any of us has been able to."

"It isn't worth the attempt. If by some miracle Edward dies, some other bradaí would take his place."

"That someone is you. Think about it." She turned to the door.

I grabbed her arm and gave her a menacing look. "I like her; that's all. If they get the wrong idea because of you—"

She pinched my cheek. "Nice one. But you should start trusting me for a change. You knew about Philippe and never said a word. Even if you weren't my little brother, just for that I'll keep quiet. Cheerio, love."

An idea formed in my head. A crazy idea.

Ryanne blurted, "Would you stay for dinner?"

Hell.

She gave Ryanne a predatory grin. "Sure, why not? Maybe I can convince Doyle. Word of advice: shag him while you're here since it's obvious you haven't done so. Word on the street is that bradaís are good to have. I wouldn't know. I prefer to be on top, and they *hate* that." She rolled her eyes.

The sound that erupted from Ryanne's throat was something between a chuckle and an indignant gasp.

"Oh, bloody hell." I seized Kara's arm and pushed her out of the cabin. "Anord piss on you and your senseless blabbering. Wait outside. I need a moment with Ryanne."

She laughed while I shut the door.

"What is it?" Ryanne asked.

"Quintus."

"Who?"

"Who?" echoed the pixie.

"Remember when you asked me about how I learned to walk in the Shadows? You need to hear the full story. I believe he can help us."

SIXTEEN

Titus

Rome. 1800

Umbra Gente. Shadow People. The nádhúrthas—beings akin to the fae, hidden to humans' perceptions—made their home in the sprawling Roman catacombs. They venerated the shadow as if it were a living, throbbing being. I'd struggled to trace them, leaving the dragonwood search, the quest that would make me a full bradaí, as soon as I found their whereabouts.

Beneath the paths that make Rome, dark labyrinths of underground tunnels harbor millions of buried people. Pillaged shrines for martyrs abounded. Skulls and femurs adorned arches among statues of robed monks. My kind of place, albeit a strange abode for nádhúrthas.

Quintus—the leader of the Umbra Gente—stood next to a semi-demolished column under a triangular facade inside the catacombs. Roman frescoes decorated the walls, the air of a bygone era trapped within them.

I knelt before him. I could see no more than the outline of his chin, his features hiding beneath a dark gray cowl. Fifteen hooded Umbrae

100

surrounded Quintus and I with torches. Flickering shadows slid across the walls as though alive.

He spoke, his loud voice echoing off the walls. "What is your name?"

"Titus," I answered. Having a Roman name was essential to join their sect. I had researched many names, but the story of Emperor Titus caught my attention because of his dogged determination to overcome obstacles. Now I added a new name to my previous two.

"Follow me," Quintus said, signaling to one of his people, who gave him a torch.

I knew he liked my choice of name. They would not have allowed me to join them otherwise.

We entered a dark, narrow tunnel. The torches the Umbrae carried cast a dim light. Walls gouged out with musty burial niches. The musty, enclosed odor disturbed me, but I pushed it aside. If Quintus could endure the smell then, by Anord's balls, so could I.

Quintus stopped beside an empty spot on the wall. He raised his hand, and an opaque, yellow light illuminated a frame. A door appeared, opening at his touch. He entered, and I followed him into an obscure cave.

Humid air replaced the putrid smell of the tunnel. Water drip-dripped on the dank cave walls, the only sound besides our footsteps. We passed a dark opening, and a light breeze flickered the flames, forming capricious shadows on the walls around us.

Quintus stopped, while the Umbrae made a circle with us in the middle, torches held high. I raised my eyes to the ceiling where a thick, swirling shadow hovered. By the Morrigan, it looked like a living being indeed, spreading its long, gloomy fingers toward us.

"Walking in Shadows is no easy feat." Quintus steepled his hands and took slow steps around. "None of your race has achieved it because something unbeknownst to you is required. But I know you are different, Titus. You have proven it." He paused, tilting his head slightly to me. "Let go. Allow the Shadow to invade you. Lose control."

This is not for you. Stay away. We do not belong here.

My body shook, my feet attempting to back away. With a long, deep breath, I remained in my place. I had to beat the bloody beast.

Everyone kept saying I was different, no matter what I did to prove otherwise. So be it. I would be as different from my kin as I could.

Under the sea, my consciousness drifted, connecting me to life within the water. None of my kin felt that, I knew. I could stay in that peaceful state as if I were part of the current. It was what had eluded me since the day I woke up. I had tried to find it on firm ground but couldn't as the voice of my beast kept nagging me.

Quintus resumed his circular walk. "The Shadow is a subtle art that requires all your concentration. Accept the Shadow. Regulate your breathing until you are like her. Be like her." He paused, looking at me. "You have successfully passed all our tests, and I'm proud to teach you, Titus."

No. Retreat.

My hands shook, and I struggled to accept. Bloody beast.

Quintus touched my shoulder, a cold, dreary feeling like a corpse. But it helped me, and the beast retreated. For the time being.

"Thank you, Master." I bowed my head before him. I would do anything to learn.

To be more different.

Quintus lowered his cowl for the first time before my eyes. I sucked in a breath. A shadow covered him, blurring his contours. "Take my hand, Titus. Lose yourself in the Shadow."

And so I did.

Present Day

"This Quintus," Ryanne said, "he's a nádhúrtha, right?"

"Nádhúrthas are not evil, no, no, no." The pixie flew in that way he did when he was upset.

"Who said anything about evil?" The pixie couldn't understand anything else than the light he was born to. "Just because there is darkness doesn't mean it's evil. Besides, nádhúrthas mirror humans; or rather, humans mirror them. They are light and darkness."

The pixie traded a look with Ryanne. Both had an uncanny ability to understand each other without words. That made my chest ache with a longing—that longing that had erupted since I'd been a prisoner back at the taigh.

A need to belong.

I looked through the door of the cabin where Kara had left, but I shook my head. We might have talked, but the barrier between us was real. I could never have with her what Ryanne had with her guardian.

"Let me get this straight," Ryanne said softly. "Your kind thinks they're above humans—"

"We *are* above humans, little seer." I smirked, only to push that annoying feeling away. Being superior was, real or not, a familiar notion. Tangible.

She rolled her eyes and, funny enough, so did the pixie in the same fashion.

"Be serious, Titus," she warned. "I want to have this clear. No bradaí has ever felt the need to ask for help, or train with humans or any other beings."

"Correct."

"But you did. With Quintus."

"Not only with him, but I even learned from humans how to escape. Some are quite resourceful, and that's why I always keep items that help me escape in my bradaí pocket." I waved a hand toward the air, if only to emphasize the point. "But aye, I took Quintus as my mentor, and I let him teach me, despite the beast wanting to interfere."

What an odd notion, being so open. So vulnerable. And yet, I felt it was the right thing to do. Not to mention the beast was subdued with Ryanne next to me. The more we felt at ease with each other, the more it was silent. Grand.

"That's how you control the Shadow," she said, pensive. I liked it when she had that look, of someone older than her twenty-two years, assimilating information. "Because you learned."

"Aye. And since we're both in danger at sea and at land, I believe Quintus might be able to help us."

"How?" the pixie asked, stroking his pointy chin.

"To hide for a while from both dangers—fae and bradaís—and plan our next step."

"What about Edward? Would you heed Kara and fight him?"

For the first time, I didn't fight the notion. "That's the other thing. I can't fight him head on; you saw that. But perhaps Quintus can teach me something else, and then, maybe . . ." I dared not say out loud, so I tilted my head backward and exhaled hard. "Maybe if I learn a new trick, a way to defeat him or at least rend him temporarily disabled, then I will."

"So you're willing to ask for help," she murmured, more as a rhetoric question.

A plan began to take shape in my head. Find Quintus. Defeat the Alpha. Stay with Ryanne without danger.

A voice nagged me from the depths of my brain. A voice that sounded much like my beast.

No bradai can escape Anord. He sees everything.

SEVENTEEN

Ryanne

Having dinner with Kara had been an adventure. She was loud while Titus was quiet, laughed while Titus brooded. She would prod me about the fae, and Titus would hush her. But despite her good humor, her eyes were sad when Titus wasn't looking.

An invisible wall, Titus had said.

We ended late, and she was so drunk that Titus left her snoring in the captain's mess.

Aine kept sending me images of the taigh, and my body responded to that invisible command, filling with longing. Bricius said not to linger on those images, but it wasn't easy.

It was still dark, and Homkar carried a lantern so we wouldn't trip. The *Scáil Dragún* had anchored near the coast, Kara's ship not far behind. Titus, Homkar, Bricius, and I were on the luscious Costa Rica shore, out of sight of the ships, in case Kara had awakened or someone from her ship followed us.

"Are you sure I cannot go?" Bricius asked, zigzagging nervously.

"Bug, we talked about this," I said. "Besides, we won't be long."

"And it's clear you can't follow commands, like your charge," Titus said with a hard edge in his voice.

He'd adamantly prohibited Bricius to come with us because of the dangers involved. Me? He needed his beast subdued, so he couldn't part ways with me. Such a romantic. But I knew bradaís couldn't feel love. It was what it was.

Even though I didn't like it.

"What if that nádhúrtha doesn't let you go?" Bricius insisted. "How would I know?"

"You feel me when I'm in danger. You can always open a portal if you need to."

"I would have used the Dragon Portal," Titus grumbled, "if it weren't that Kara's too drunk to return to her ship. Another promise with a taste of the cat."

"With a what now?" I asked, frowning.

"Full flogged." He sighed in exasperation. "It's she and me, pixie; if my kin see you, they'll know who she is. I cannot put her in such danger. We'll return before dusk." He turned to Homkar. "Make sure to dispatch Kara as soon as she wakes and dump her at her ship. Tie her up if you need to."

"Yes, Captain."

"Come, *ashtore,*" Titus said. He slid his hand through the air, and a seam trailed after his fingers, suspended in the air.

Titus and I stepped through his portal and onto what looked like ruins. To avoid startling passersby, Titus had chosen to arrive before the crack of dawn. Still, a drunken man swore loudly when we appeared out of nowhere.

"Where are we?" I whispered.

"Forum Romanum."

I glanced around the ruins shrouded in darkness. Only the drunken man was in sight, who swore loudly in Italian while leaving.

Titus swaggered across the place with me on his heels. Soon the light broke over our heads, and I gasped in awe.

Ancient stones sucked the morning light greedily and turned the gray shapes into pinks. The soft blue above seemed jealous of the beauty of the temples, monuments, and triumphal arches.

We walked in the wake of time. I could almost hear a toga-wrapped

Roman haranguing passersby with a stentorian voice or elegant Roman matrons walking with entwined arms and whispering about the new gladiators with a twinkle in their eyes.

"This is amazing," I whispered.

"Aye, that's why I love being here. The past whispers through the stones and the grass," he said with reverence.

"Is this where we'll find Quintus?"

"Sometimes he's here. I've always found him in the remains of Rome's past." He cracked a smile. "Though you'll see that everywhere in this city. Everywhere you look, you're reminded that you are standing in what was one of the most powerful cities in the Old World."

We trudged through the Roman Forum, but after an hour of looking, Titus conceded that Quintus wasn't there. We took a cab to the Colosseum, the Trevi fountain, the Pantheon, and other magnificent places, but no sign of Quintus.

It was midday by the time we sat in a trattoria. I hadn't realized how hungry I was after so much walking.

"It's unusual to find Quintus once the sun is high," Titus said after swallowing a mouthful of pasta. "We could return to the ship and wait for dusk to set. He's a night creature."

"No wonder, if he's a master of the Shadow," I said, then took a bite of my calzone. "But can we walk some more? I'd love to look around."

He closed his eyes while extending his arms.

"What are you doing?" I whispered, casting a glance at the few patrons at the nearby tables. They weren't paying attention to us.

"Hush, woman."

He remained that way for a few seconds, then opened his eyes and rested his arms. "I was sensing for fae. Remember, we're on land, and we must be careful."

A flash of my nightmare interposed with reality. Titus bleeding, his face contorted in a grimace, while he shouted my name. I rubbed my temples—nightmares didn't come true. It was a fear deep inside me. Nothing more.

"Something wrong, *ashtore*?"

"I had a nightmare about you." I wasn't used to discuss anything of the sort with anyone other than Bricius. But Titus had been open with me, so it was only fair.

He frowned. "Tell me."

I did, and his frown creased.

"You saw the worse that's happened to me: beaten by fae, then beaten by Edward." He played with his wine glass. "Unless Anord decides to erase me, I'm good."

"How does he decide that?"

"I'm not sure. That's why we should go to Quintus. He's a more powerful being than I thought at first."

Could Quintus help with the spark? No, that was my job, a human's job. I reached out and held Titus's hand. With all the excitement it'd been hard to attempt a reading. But then, if I were to come clean with him, it'd be easier. How?

"Are we safe here?" I didn't want to be reckless by touring Rome, but what I'd seen had awed me, and despite knowing we were on a quest, my feet itched to stop this frantic pace and enjoy for once.

He covered my hand with one of his. "I promised you Paris, and we ended up here."

"I'm sure we'll go there eventually, and Rome is . . . mind-blowing."

"Let's fly low then. I'll be sensing for fae or bradaís, and any sign of danger, we'll escape through my portal right away."

Danger, excitement, and Rome. What more could I ask for?

The last portion of the quick Roman tour ended in the Vatican. I gaped in awe at the enormous structure and pulled Titus to the pillars around it.

Titus stopped me in my tracks. "Oh, no, I don't think so."

"Why? Are you going to scorch or something if you put one foot on holy ground?"

"My kin never go inside churches. I don't think the warriors from this dimension would gladly let us in."

"Warriors? What are you talking about?"

"Nádhúrthas. Humans call them angels. I prefer warriors."

Angels. "You mean the winged variety? Because I thought nádhúrthas were like fae."

"Not quite. They're more varied, for one, and they have different levels, some connecting to higher planes of existence. Those are the most skilled warriors, the angels."

Light and dark. Bricius and I had discussed this earlier on, that maybe I'd been able to call ogres because of that duality in humans. But then angels!

I'd met a nádhúrtha. The dark-skinned man I'd seen outside Starbucks and who'd appeared to me again in Japan. Amriel, that was his name. What was his level, I wondered?

"I'm no expert on this topic," I said, "but isn't it the other way around? Don't angels look for repentant souls?"

"First," Titus said, entwining his fingers with mine, "I'm not repentant for anything except for what I did to you. Second, a soul is required."

Oh, yeah. There was that tiny little detail. Bradaís were heartless and soulless, and not figuratively. And that was why I was here. To find out about a way to cut his connection to Anord through the spark, and gain him, what, a soul? Did it work like that? Cuidi had left that detail out as well. I rubbed my arms while gawking at the awe-inspiring Vatican. Was that why Amriel had appeared to me?

An angel. A freaking angel.

Maybe my task was more complicated than I thought at first.

"And third," Titus continued, "it's getting dark, and it's time to go to the catacombs." He glanced at his watch. "Midnight if possible. If you're too tired, we can rest for a couple of hours, then head there."

"Oh hell no. I want to see all I can before meeting with Quintus. Are you sure he's in Rome?"

"He's usually here. He loves this city so much, he never strays far away. We'd be unfortunate if we can't find him at the catacombs."

We walked for an hour more until Titus stopped at a jewelry shop window. His jaw locked and his nostrils flared.

"Why such fascination with gold?" I asked, worried at his stare. He certainly acted like a gold-aholic.

He shivered and took something out of his pocket. He held up a small, golden rock with soft, rounded edges.

"Imagine that all you care about in life is to have this in your hands. No values, no friendship, nothing else but this. What would happen?"

"Is that gold?"

"Aye." He made a forward movement, hesitated, then locked his jaw and put it in my open palm.

It felt heavy yet malleable at my touch. "Is that what happens? You do whatever it takes?" I said in a shrill tone.

"We leave a path of destruction behind us, without looking back. That's our purpose. Destruction."

"That's terrible."

Titus seized my chin tenderly. "Do you know that your lips are sweet? That their softness doesn't compare to anything else?"

He caressed my lower lip with his thumb as if to print the sensation on his fingertip, making my heart flutter.

"Gold won't kiss me back," he said with a smile that soon died. He closed my fingers around the nugget. "Whatever's happening between us is stronger than that. I can't be the same. Not anymore. Not after I held you in my arms."

"What about your beast?" I asked softly.

"It's in the back of my mind. I feel it, and sometimes it protests. But our proximity has helped to tame it."

"It's not gone."

"Alas, no. Imagine a tiger waiting to pounce the moment I'm distracted. That's exactly how it feels."

I pondered about that and how this could help him in the long run. Finding and activating the spark might help to nullify his beast; all the more reason why I should try to find it.

And what better with that task than come clean with Titus.

"Titus," I started tentatively. "There is this thing—"

Cold swirled within me like a miniature maelstrom, and my chest felt like a troll punched it. Sounds faded, and sepia splashed in my vision like in an old movie. The images showed men in black fatigues with guns. Something flashed at the bottom of the image—a red circle.

Dainséar, it said with a sense of urgency.

I scanned the narrow street nearby. "What does *dainséar* mean?"

"Danger." He furrowed his brow and glanced at the dark street, tensing his body. "No bradaí, no fae—" Footsteps erupted down the street. He spat. "The Morrigan take me!"

At the drop of a hat, several men surrounded us. Men who had come out of the shadows like cockroaches from the sewer. Titus cursed and pulled me toward him.

Muscular like professional wrestlers, dressed in dark fatigues and military boots, they pointed assault rifles directly at us. Titus inhaled sharply.

I slapped a hand to my mouth.

"Well," one of them said, a woman. "The informant was accurate, Mr. Doyle." She lowered her gun with the confidence of knowing she had backup. "You should not appear like that in Rome."

"Who are you?" Titus demanded.

"I advise you to stay put." She pointed with her head at those around us. "Unless you want to test how many bullets a bradaí can take."

EIGHTEEN

Titus

Morrigan's crow. The mercenaries circled us. These were professionals who wouldn't hesitate to pull the trigger. I could take bullets, but not Ryanne.

More to the point, this woman knew who I was.

"You should know then that you're making a mistake," I said, *dorcha* gathering in my hands.

"I made a mistake by suggesting my boss bribe Haru," she said, voice hard. She stared right into my eyes. "But these men aren't Wataru's nephew. They know their job."

"Haru?" Ryanne glared at her, her fists clenched. "You were the one who wanted me out of the lab! You sent Haru to get me!"

She took a step forward, fists clenched, but I shoved her behind me. The moment I did that, I sensed her power gathering inside her, like that time back in Japan. An angry power.

"Don't," I said quietly to her while I let *préachta* take over *dorcha*, for now. I didn't like the odds, not with so many guns. We should wait for the right opportunity.

My own *préachta* reached out to her through my hand and found her cold energy expanding and then collapsing on itself as if preparing to attack.

"Why?" she seethed.

"Listen to him, sweetie," the woman said.

"You're working with Sanders." Sanders was the one who'd requested Ryanne back when I was selling her for gold. I'd denied the request since he was a sadist, and I didn't want Ryanne to be hurt.

Her slight grin told me I was right. Darkness swirled within me. Sanders's days were numbered, and so were this woman's.

Kill them all.

Aye. I would. *Dorcha* again condensed in my fists. They would all die tonight.

I gritted my teeth. No, I couldn't put Ryanne in danger. If I fought them, one might injure her.

Cold prickled between our palms. Her power swirled inside her, looking for an excuse, but what could it do except . . .

Call Bricius. Homkar. If I gave her a window, she could escape; she was fast enough. Mentally, I pushed my *préachta* toward her, not as a warning like before, but to get ready. "Bricius," I whispered to her, then released her hand.

She inhaled, her energy whirling faster. Grand.

I positioned myself in front of the woman, hands at my sides. "How'd you find me?" I asked. My old self would not have asked and hit instead, but I needed a diversion.

"You're not as good as you think. My boss received a notice about a couple appearing out of nowhere this morning. Our informer kept close to you and sent us a description."

The drunk man from the Forum Romanum. I all but forgot about him, Anord be damned!

Two vans screeched their tires and pulled near us. Hell! They were going to separate us. I cursed under my breath.

Bradaís were a force to be reckoned with. One of us could dispatch these mercenaries with hardly a scratch, especially if we attacked from behind.

This time was different.

This time I wasn't alone.

But then, she wasn't helpless.

Before the mercenary woman could blink, I lurched toward her and seized her gun. A shot fired and lodged in my thigh, but I dismissed the pain. Chaos, that I could do. And I counted on Ryanne's quickness to seize the opportunity.

"Get the girl, quick!" the woman shouted as I broke her arm. She let out a howl that quickly died. A professional.

"Run!" I shouted while I retrieved my sword from my portal and buried it into the chest of the nearest mercenary. The man gurgled blood and dropped to the ground.

The gunmen shot at me, and while I moved quicker than a human, some bullets lodged in my abdomen and my arm.

"Stop!" a man shouted.

Ready to behead him, I angled my sword . . . and froze.

He had a gun to Ryanne's waist. It was clear to me she'd tried to run, since they weren't on the same spot she was a moment ago and her breathing hitched.

"Drop your weapon."

Anord's balls, not again. Ryanne's arms were captured at her sides, so she couldn't do a thing either. Her chest heaved, and her gaze promised hell, a hell that couldn't be unleashed.

Aye, I wasn't alone this time. She was valuable to them and yet, Haru's words came from that time in Japan: *"Maybe I won't kill her, but I can maim her."*

She was more valuable to me. I couldn't risk her.

I slid my sword back into the portal and raised my hands, all the while my gaze focused on the lead mercenary. What an irony. The pixie had to be left behind in case fae or bradaís spotted us, but now that humans captured both, he could have been invaluable.

"Titus," Ryanne hissed. Something shone in her eyes, something I'd never seen before.

One of the mercenaries yanked my hands behind my back and cuffed them. Another did the same with Ryanne. Grand. Getting rid of handcuffs was as easy as stealing a doubloon from a sailor.

"We need to move, Oz," said one of the mercenaries to the leader.

The woman who'd spoke first, the one called Oz, was glaring at me with a mix of hatred and awe, but nodded, clutching at her broken arm.

Break her neck.

Aye, beast.

I hurled at her, thumping her shoulder with mine. Several mercenaries threw themselves at me like pirates after pieces of eight.

Run, Ryanne, escape, I thought.

From the corner of my eye, I saw her punching the man holding her, like we practiced, then slipped away as fast as was her wont.

Having hands tied was no handicap for a bradaí. With Ryanne escaping, I was free to kick as many as I liked.

More shots. Morrigan's crow, I hoped all were directed at me. Annoying discomfort lodged in my body—it would eventually dissolve the bullets.

"Restrain him!" the woman, Oz, yelled.

Alas, with so many professionals, they could do so. These mercenaries were no daighs—the fae warriors—but they were trained. They dragged me to one of the vans, and from the corner of my eye, noticed another doing the same to Ryanne, who squirmed and threw punches wildly.

Damn them all!

She might be safe until reaching wherever they were taking us. The fear of Sanders hurting her tightened my chest.

I had to get away fast.

Two mercenaries restrained me at each side.

"Let's go, Oklahoma." Oz said to the driver. Then she turned and pointed her handgun at my head, her fear masked by arrogance. "Don't try any more tricks or I'll blow your brains out."

I stared at her.

"Hold your tongue, Oz," said Oklahoma. "The boss warned us about him, and he was damn right. He was shot—a lot—and look at him." The dark-skinned driver glanced at me through the rearview mirror. "Buckle up, this might get rough."

Oz pointed at the man to my right. "Check to see if he has a bullet-proof vest, Portland."

Portland patted my chest. "Negative."

Oz pointed at my head, her chest heaving and struggling to keep the gun steady. "What the fuck is this man? How many bullets did he take?"

"Lower that weapon, Oz!" Oklahoma exclaimed.

"No. I'm taking no chances. How many, Portland?"

"I'd say more than ten," Portland answered.

"No wounds?"

"None that I can see."

I grinned at her, making her shift in place, and picked a bobby pin from my back pocket—never leave your ship without it. Without taking my eyes off Oz, I began to work on the handcuffs. It was a matter of knowing when to attack. I had to wait for the right opportunity, but knowing Sanders, whose pockets ran deep, he might have more mercenaries waiting for us. I couldn't risk fighting with more.

The less, the merrier.

Oz snuck a look out the front. "Hey, I can't see the other van. Did we lose it?"

"Negative," Oklahoma said. "We're to take different routes in case someone is following us."

"Roger that."

"And buckle up, goddammit!"

"I can't," she hissed. "Damn arm is no good."

"Lower your weapon then."

"Not a chance," she said, gun aimed at me.

The handcuffs opened in a matter of seconds. The van zigzagged between streets for a while until we left Rome. Calmly, my mind blank, I continue to stare—as long as the driver lived to take me where Ryanne was, I could kill the rest. Oz shifted uncomfortably.

"Three minutes 'til rendezvous," the driver Oklahoma announced.

This was it.

"Stop looking at me," Oz said, restless. She raised the gun with her good arm and pointed it at my chest.

I winked while I shook off the cuffs.

"Fuck! I *said*—"

I unbuckled and seized her gun hand, twisting it. Oz fired. Portland cursed. I slid my hand down my bradaí portal to retrieve a dagger. Wasting no time, I plunged it into the silent man's chest at my left. Oz pointed at my chest and fired twice. I recoiled. Oklahoma yelled words in the background. Locking my jaw, I discarded the pain when another shot boomed on my thigh.

Kill them. Do not hesitate.

I jabbed the dagger into Oz's throat, then bumped my shoulder with the van's walls at a sharp turn. Blood spurted while she gurgled, eyes wide. More shots. Metal burned in my left thigh and my shoulder. I whipped to Portland, who'd emptied the gun's chamber and was refilling it.

Steadily, I plunged the dagger into his chest. The man convulsed, waving his arms and legs.

More screams. The van jerked from side to side. Oklahoma shot his handgun blindly, but I ducked behind his seat, avoiding most of the bullets. Pain dizzied me.

Half-crouched, I pressed the tip of the dagger to Oklahoma's neck. "If you want to live, keep driving where you were headed."

The van skidded off the road, but Oklahoma regained control.

"Don't try any tricks or you won't fare any better than your companions."

My vision blurred for a moment. How many bullets had I received? My body burned as though I had a fever, and my hands trembled, sweat dripping from my forehead. I must stay conscious.

The road was dark ahead. Oklahoma took a turn off the highway onto a rural road. Suddenly, the vehicle skidded and whirled. By the Morrigan!

I was thrown back. We kept turning like a loosened barrel during a storm. The van rolled over. My head hit something hard, and my vision went black.

No, I must stay conscious. She's in danger. I can't fail her.

We turned twice more and stopped. I tried to catch my breath.

Images danced before my eyes. I touched the side of my head. Blood covered my fingers.

"And that's why one buckles up," Oklahoma said, pointing a gun at me. He fired between my eyebrows.

Red. Dark.

NINETEEN

Ryanne

Sweat clung to my skin, to my hair. Cold air blew through the broken multi-panel windows in the dingy room. My hands hadn't stopped trembling since those men shoved me into the van.

The metal chair I sat on was cold and hard, and there was a wooden table before me, small enough to resemble a school desk. Shackles restrained my hands to the armrest. Another chair had been thrown into a corner.

How long had it been? My head kept sagging, my eyelids demanded their rest. But I dared not. I shot a quick glance at the couple of armed men standing guard at the door. Fear squeezed my heart with a skeletal hand, remembering how they yelled at me when I dozed before, their putrid breath so close to me.

Titus had been shot. But he hadn't been bleeding, not like that nightmare that kept plaguing me. He was okay. He *must* be okay. Knowing him, he'd free himself.

Was he looking for me? Where was he?

They had stripped me down to my underwear. That dream about being naked in the middle of a crowded room? This was worse. I was left vulnerable. Terrified. I grabbed the armrests of the metal chair to counter my uncontrollable spasms, my bare feet brushing the dirty floor.

After the frantic van trip, I'd been dragged to an old building and left with the guards in this room. I didn't know if the pale lighting was from morning or evening. Sobs escaped my chest, despite my poor attempts to restrain them. Foul odors came from the corner, where a small toilet sat, one I'd used once, with guards watching me.

Aine was coiled inside me, my power useless. Or maybe it was me who was useless and weak, not able to call it.

"Cuidigtheach, Cuidigtheach, Cuidigtheach," I mumbled as I'd been doing in the past hours. Her name gave me peace, even if temporary. And fae believed in the power of three. Maybe if I repeated her name long enough, she would hear. Bricius had a way of calling them, perhaps I could too.

Bug. Had he felt something off with me? He should be worried by now. Was he in Rome with Homkar, wondering what happened? I shouldn't have left him behind.

"Bricius, Bricius, Bricius," I whispered. Could he hear me? Aine expanded and contracted at each mention of his name, so I kept repeating it.

The door creaked open, and I lifted my head, weary, shoulders tight. A portly man with hooded eyes slinked inside.

He grabbed the fallen metal chair and dragged it opposite me, the scraping sounding like nails on a chalkboard. "I hope you're comfy, my dear. Let me introduce myself. I'm Sanders," he said in a light, happy tone.

Fear rippled through every inch of my tired body, but I forced myself to look him in the eye as expressionless as I could. He sat with a groan, the table between us flimsy protection.

He opened a little velvet bag, pouring its contents onto the table: rusted two-inch nails. Then he pulled a small hammer from his belt and pushed the nails to the side with it, leaving it there as if it was unimportant.

"I want you to feel yourself at home, my dear. Imagine I'm your favorite uncle." Sanders gave me a smile clearly meant to make me feel at ease, but instead my lower lip trembled.

"Oh, but don't look so panicked, child." Sanders feigned concern and lifted his head a notch, eyeing me through his short lashes. "I'm sure you'll answer all my questions, unlike your partner."

Had Titus failed to escape? *No, not Titus!*

The ghost of a rage that had faded in the past hours wanted to stick those nails into his toad-like eyeballs and gouge them out. "You're lying," I said through gritted teeth. "He escaped."

He had to have.

Sanders laughed merrily and slapped a meaty hand over his thigh, then sobered up so quickly it threw me back, his hooded eyes drilling into mine. "I want to know everything you know about the bradaís. Especially Mr. Doyle."

I jerked my head back, a heavy feeling settling in my stomach.

"Were you expecting me to ask you about the land of the fae?" he asked in mock surprise. "All in due time, my dear. We'll have plenty of it." He pumped a fist in the air. "But having a bradaí in my power . . ." He closed his eyes and a ripple of pleasure shot across his face.

My clammy hands felt even clammier.

"I want to see how many bullets they can take." Sanders leaned his meaty forearms on the table as if wanting to share a secret with me. "He received more than twenty when captured, and he passed out. We've shot him about ten times more, and he's still breathing. Isn't that exciting?" He leaned back and gave a sick smile.

"S-shot?" I croaked.

"Oh, yes! And guess what? He woke up not so long ago, and we tried this beauty on him." He lifted one of the rusty nails and observed it. "It seems their pain threshold is very high. Can you imagine what I could do with that? And their blood could be useful."

"B-blood?"

"Certainly! We've pumped just a few drops so far, sadly. Hellish to extract. Bradaís don't have a heartbeat. How can they function without a heart?"

"Where is he?" I managed to ask, my throat scorching.

He waved a hand. "Upstairs. Now—"

"Water. Please," I panted.

"How did you meet Mr. Doyle?"

"I-I, ah," I stuttered.

"I'm not a very patient man," he said, stroking the hammer's head with a chubby finger. His toady eyes zeroed in on me. "Talk."

I began to tell him about the Starbucks encounter when Sanders stood up and paced around.

"Tell me about your family," he interrupted.

I shut my eyes tight but had nothing left in me. I talked about my parents, and he interrupted me again to ask about how I'd met Titus. Sanders paced behind me now.

Not being able to see him was worse than having him glaring at me. So I repeated the encounter, just for him to ask about my father's occupation. His voice sounded far away as if he retreated to the opposite wall behind me.

"H-he's a scientist and I-loves chess," I mumbled.

"Louder!" he shouted in my ear, and I started. "How many bradaís exist?"

"I don't know," I managed to grumble.

"What's their power?" he whispered in my ear, his horrid meaty hands rubbing my shoulders.

"Immortality." *You ass.*

Aine felt like a blob, like it was before I took this path. Powerless.

Sanders kept questioning me about the bradaís, about my family, about how I met Titus. He repeated the questions once, twice, thrice, all in different ways. I could hardly speak. He gave me no quarter, sometimes standing and placing his meaty hands over my shoulders, caressing my skin while demanding answers. Sometimes he'd walk away and kept behind me for a long time, then yelled like a maniac, startling me. He'd walk away again, and then come back at different intervals. Sometimes he cooed and stroked my hair, his lips so close to my face, his stinky garlic breath nauseating me.

It went on forever.

I could barely speak. Instead of water, he gave me a sour, bitter drink so I could stay awake. My legs trembled without control, yet he kept pushing with his questions, repeatedly.

Where was Aine? It pulsated as if sensing I needed it. But my hands were tied. What could it do?

"Please," I begged after the last question, sobbing though no tears came to my dry eyes.

He grabbed my hair and yanked it back. "You'll rest when I want you to, my dear. Do you understand?"

I nodded with jerky movements.

"Good." He picked up one of the rusty nails and rotated it between his thumb and his middle finger. "Do fae feel pain?" he asked absently.

"Please, don't." I hated myself for begging, hated his toady eyes, hated how my voice came out weak and panicked.

He pressed the nail to my collarbone, and I shut my eyes. "How much fae power do you have, I wonder?"

The nail pierced my skin, and I bit my lips to avoid screaming.

"Please . . ."

Fear quashed Aine, like it was a drained water skin. It was struggling, I knew, but I could hardly breathe.

I heard Sanders moving away, and I let out a shaky breath. My eyes flew open, wanting to know what he was up to.

Sanders was hefting the hammer.

Oh Gods, no.

A knock sounded at the door. Sanders glanced at his watch. "Ah! The guard change. Arizona, open."

One of the men nodded and opened it.

A blonde woman in leathers stood there. It was Kara, and her grin was the most beautiful thing I'd ever seen. "My, my. What a fantastic array of testosterone." With her hands on hips, she thrusted to one side. "Whom to pick?"

TWENTY

Ryanne

ara! Oh, thank you!

"Get her," Sanders growled.

The guard moved his hand toward his gun.

A sword flashed in Kara's hands. "You, love, you're first." And before anyone reacted, she thrust it into the guard's chest. "Now, who's next?"

Sanders sprang to his feet, the chair falling with a loud bang. "What the—!"

Crimson spread, soaking the man's fatigues. A huge, black man came into sight behind Kara. Homkar! And flying above a pixie, my lovely, darling Bricius!

A second guard drew a gun.

Kara was already sprinting toward him and hacked his hand. The gun fell with a dry *thump*. Blood sprayed on his face. The man gawked at his own bloody stump then went for another gun behind his back. Kara kicked him.

"Ryanne, are you okay?" Bricius asked next to my ear.

"Bug! Thank Cuidi, you're here!"

"I should have never left you, no, no, no." He landed on one of the handcuffs. "How does this open?"

Homkar had already taken care of the third guard.

"It's too strong!" Bricius was hacking the handcuff with his little sword's pommel.

Quick footsteps receded, and I glanced around. Sanders wasn't in my line of vision. A door shut close behind. The coward!

"He's gone!" I screamed, hoarse.

"Quiet," Kara said with a sense of urgency. "There're still mercenaries alive in the building." She wiped her sword on one of the men's fatigues, then sheathed it into the scabbard upon her back. Homkar loitered under the lintel, keeping guard.

Still? Alive? I wanted to shout. Instead I panted, "Sanders escaped."

Kara looked at me blankly while Bricius kept hacking at the handcuffs.

"Fat guy." Blood covered the floor, and an acrid smell wafted through the air. Bile rose in my throat, and nausea blurred my vision. *Can you hate someone so much?*

"Then let us hurry." She slid her hand through the air like I'd seen Titus do, then retrieved something from her bradaí pocket. "Step aside, pixie." She worked on the handcuffs, and before I blinked, they fell to the floor with a *clink.*

"Homkar, help her." Kara gave me a once over and grinned. "You're in prime condition, love, no wonder Doyle is enchanted with you."

"I hope it's not just because of my looks," I managed to say. Kara's grin grew wider.

So tired I could barely walk, I let Homkar grab my waist to steady me. I slipped on the blood at the entrance and hung on tight. Bricius landed on my shoulder, his familiar weight assuaging my fear.

"Where's the captain?" Homkar all but growled.

"T-testing h-him. Upstairs."

Homkar's chest rumbled with a low growl.

"They'll pay, Homkar," Kara said, lips tight. "Let's get him first."

The image of Titus bleeding came with force. Had Sanders bled him?

Oh dear Cuidi, no. Let him be all right.

"We need to take you to safety, yes, yes, yes," Bricius said, worry tinging his voice.

We walked out to the poorly lit hall, the bulbs flickering above. I'd been blindfolded when they brought me here, so I didn't remember anything of the gloomy building, seemingly abandoned—ripped wallpaper, graffiti covering every available space, cobwebby corners, and an invisible *drip-drip*.

Stealthily, we turned one corner. Two dead bodies blocked our path, sword wounds on both chests. My shoulders tightened. The garden, back in Japan, when Haru showed his true colors and Titus killed them all in cold blood. More death, more blood, all because humans wanted to test me. No, because *Sanders* had wanted to test *me* to get to the bradaís. And he'd escaped.

I felt Bricius shivering, hanging tight to my hair.

We stepped over them, and I tripped, falling to the bloodied floor before Kara could catch me. I retched bile. Bricius whispered words of encouragement, and I nodded, trembling.

We took wide stairs to the upper level, garbage littering the steps. My bare feet hurt, so I stepped carefully. Kara stopped, raising a hand. The stairs had directed us to a wide double-height room with what could have been an elegant staircase.

We reached the second level and entered a long hall. Around a corner, we heard a muffled conversation.

"The guy here's a piece of work, Oklahoma," a man said. "Gave us a hell of trouble to restrain him."

"I know, I saw what he did," another said. "I'll be careful."

Homkar grumbled, "I'll get them both."

I restrained him. "Please, no more blood. No killing."

"Let me," Kara said, and sashayed toward them. "Hey, boys, Sanders sent me here to have a bit of fun. Y'all in?"

Bricius zoomed after her.

I pressed my back to the wall, Homkar scowling, maybe because he wanted to break their skulls. They'd hurt his captain.

Damn, *I* wanted them hurt too, but the blood . . .

After some whacks, thumps, and swearing. Kara returned in no time. "Come."

Both men lay unconscious on the floor, crumpled next to a door in a long hall. They were no match for one bradaí.

"She is something," Bricius whispered. "She is strong, yes, yes, yes."

Strong. Yes. I stood taller, though right away I grew conscious of the fact that I was down to my skivvies.

My hands shook, the nightmare vision playing again and again in my mind. Titus, bleeding to death, calling my name.

She opened the door. I heaved a sigh of relief. Titus was tied to a chair just like I had been. His head hung, but no blood pooled at his feet—no blood at all except for a few dried patches on his clothes. Two people with white coats were inside. The woman was sticking needles into his forearm, and the man checking his vitals. The place was a makeshift lab with trays, syringes, a microscope, and operation instruments, among glass containers.

Bricius went to Titus, but instead of jabbing him as he would before, he placed a hand on Titus's cheek and closed his eyes.

The woman started and squinted at Kara. "Who are you? Didn't the boss—"

Homkar strode toward them and punched both before they could speak further.

"I thought you were going to kill them," I squeaked.

"You said no more blood." He paid me no further heed while inspecting Titus's restrains.

Kara slammed the door behind me. "Filthy humans who do research on things they cannot understand are not worthy of living." Kara's lips were livid, and her voice barely restrained her fury. "But for you, love, we'll spare this crap. Here, big guy." She glided toward the wall where a key hung, then threw it to Homkar.

Bricius flew back to me. "Your pirate is drugged. But he isn't injured, no, no, no."

Titus's mouth was slightly open, saliva drooling, and eyes glazed.

"Odin's balls, how are we going to get him out?" Kara slapped his cheeks and Titus jerked awake. "For a bradaí to be this drugged, they must have used an inordinate number of concoctions."

"What?" he slurred.

"I'll carry him," Homkar said.

"Wait." I searched for water and held a glass up to Titus's lips, my hands unsteady so a few drops of water slid over his throat. "You're okay," I whispered. "You'll be okay."

He drank eagerly while Kara removed the coat from the unconscious woman. I refilled the glass, drank some, refilled it again, and poured the rest over his head to shake him awake.

"Here, love," Kara said, offering me the lab coat. "Put it on. I don't mind watching you as you are, but Doyle would object."

I quickly donned the coat, feeling a little better. Aine swirled in my chest, now present. Images of the taigh flashed in my mind and a longing stirred.

Homkar glanced at the door and then exchanged a look with Kara.

"Time's running out," she said. "We don't know how many more are in the building and, it's only me and Homkar."

"I'll crush some skulls," he said, thumping his big fists together, then glared at me. "No blood."

Kara retrieved her sword from her scabbard and placed herself at one side of the door. Remembering some distant memory from my childhood, I muttered a quick prayer for all the dead and those soon to be.

"Get ready."

She opened the door, and I stood like a dazzled fawn. No one was outside.

"Clear. Come on." Sword gripped, she stepped out.

Homkar lifted Titus in a fireman's carry.

We sidestepped the crumpled guards and into the hall. My knees were so weak I prayed I could carry on for the next minutes, sure to pass out any second. How many mercenaries remained?

The corner was a few feet away when footsteps echoed around it.

"Steady," Kara hissed.

Gulping, I tried to still my breathing. The footsteps receded down the stairs. Kara jerked her head toward the corner and stealthily we carried on.

Shouts came from the basement below. They'd found the bodies!

Titus's breath was laborious, and I feared for him. But he'd heal. It'd been a nightmare that felt like a vision, but a nightmare nonetheless.

Finally finding the way out, we stepped outside the building. Yellow, dry grass grew all around us, but there was no street, only trees and the unkempt garden. Weary, I looked up. This was a mansion. Or had been.

More shouts from inside the mansion. Homkar grunted, and Kara nodded. She pressed a finger to her lips and placed herself at the entrance.

"Come," Homkar said, jerking his head toward the side of the mansion.

Shakily, I obeyed, Bricius on my heels. The cement of the sidewalk hurt my bare feet, the morning chill making my teeth clatter, so I closed the lab coat tightly around me.

"She's not so bad for a bradaí, no, no, no," Bricius said as he turned his head toward Kara.

"Do you have a crush?" I managed to smile.

"What?"

"You like her," I croaked. It was wise not to speak any more.

He scratched his orange head. "What does a crush have anything to do with that?"

Some shouts but they were brief.

Kara returned to us while we walked—well, Homkar strode, Kara trotted, and I stumbled. Kara seized my arm and pulled me up.

"Come, love, we're almost there."

"Open the portal," Homkar said to Bricius, then to me, "You'll take care of him again."

His tone didn't leave room for discussion and despite all, I cracked a smile.

Aine, the one I liked, burst within me and covered me whole. My chest vibrated like a tuning fork, and unexpected joy grew in my chest.

Levity took my limbs, and for a moment, my exhaustion vanished. At the same time, Bricius's wings perked.

"I called Peter," he whispered so low only I caught his words.

"Oh." I stopped in my tracks, straightening as much as I could. "Oh," I repeated dumbly.

The air shimmered before us.

Homkar grunted and, with a delicacy at odds with his size, placed Titus on the ground. Titus stumbled like a drunk, and incomprehensible words came from his drooly mouth.

Kara swore loudly and unsheathed her sword with a metallic sound. She pointed at the shimmering. Bricius zoomed around the portal, his gossamer wings catching the sunlight.

A tall, reddish-brown-haired man in dark tights and a loose robe secured by a leather belt stepped out from the shimmering, his fist raised. Energy crackled around him.

Peter! The sight of my fae mentor was a relief in my heart. I rushed toward him, as much as my tired legs let me, and hugged him tight.

"Peter, thank Cuidi, you're here!" I sobbed against his stiff body.

His arm secured around my waist.

"*Mo thiarna!*" Bricius exclaimed. "Do not charge against them. They helped Ryanne, yes, yes, yes."

"What's happening here?" I heard Kara say.

Something nagged at the back of my mind, but it felt so good to see Peter after the ordeal, that I couldn't let go, not to mention Aine felt overjoyed and—very important detail—my rubber-legs weren't going to be able to support my weight much longer.

"*Dannan-dubh,*" Peter said. "What is one like you doing with the likes of them?" he spat.

"That is none of your business, fae," Homkar answered in his baritone voice.

"He is not bad, no, no, no," Bricius said fondly.

It finally clicked. The temperature around was icy, and not because of the fae cold power or the weather. Still shaking, I turned around, hands seized to Peter's robes to avoid greeting the asphalt with a thump.

Peter had a sword pointing at Kara. Kara returned the gesture with her own sword.

Homkar glared at me, with Titus now on his feet but staggering, eyes half-closed. Everyone's lips were tight, and they shared the same sour expressions.

"They helped, yes, yes, yes," Bricius insisted, suspended in the air just inches away from Peter. "Do not hurt them, *mo thiarna.*"

"Pretty fae," Kara said, thrusting her hip to one side. "I'd fight you, but it seems this human girl likes you. Let's call it a truce, shall we?"

"I don't trust you, pirate," Peter said, his sword steadily pointed at her.

She winked at him. "You're cute, and I'd love to shag you, but I don't trust you either."

"Don't get any wrong ideas, *pirate brocach.*"

"Oh, but I want to get all the wrong ideas with you, pretty fae," she purred.

Peter blushed. "My business is done here."

My numb brain finally put two and two together. Weakly, I released myself from Peter's hold and took a trembling step like a toddler toward Titus.

"Don't," I croaked. *Don't take me away, please.*

Titus lifted a trembling hand to me. "Ryanne."

I extended a shivering hand to him. Gravity failed, and I stumbled, my knees giving way. Peter caught me before I hit the ground and swept me into his arms.

"Get away from her, pirate," he said without turning back. "You were lucky this time. Next time we meet, it won't be as civilized."

"Titus," I said weakly, tugging at Peter's robe as if my hand was boneless.

Titus tried to take a step but fell again. What had those bastards done to him? Vaguely, I noticed Peter opening a portal and stepping into it. I craned my neck at Titus, who was yelling.

But I couldn't hear his words.

TWENTY-ONE

Titus

The Morrigan take all the fae.

My mouth, throat, and stomach felt gritty and painful as if I'd chewed and swallowed broken glass mixed with acid. I tried to walk but fell to my knees, the furnace within me suffocating. The bloody dryshite and Ryanne disappeared into Tír D'aois. A portal. Anord's balls, I needed to open one. I stood up, my legs shaking. I raised a hand and tried to focus on Tír D'aois. Nothing.

No. I had to. She couldn't up and leave me now!

"Ryanne!"

I tried again and again, but focusing on that land was like trying to grab a pixie.

Closing my eyes, I focused on my ship. This time, the silver line appeared from my trembling fingers. Someone grabbed my arm, someone who smelled like blood and Coco Channel. Kara. Aye, that was who.

I crossed the portal right into my cabin, Kara next to me. With trembling steps, I reached my bed and fell upon it, face down.

"Rest, little brother," came Kara's voice from far away. "I'll talk to Homkar. Later you'll explain to me how the hell you can open a portal."

Gain strength. And come back to kill those humans.

Aye, but, what about Ryanne?

Forget her. She has forgotten you. Left you.

No, she didn't. The bloody dryshite took her away.

The image of her in his arms churned my stomach, and the cabin swirled around me. I'd get her back. Whatever the cost. Even if I had to take the taigh by assault, I would.

That dryshite would never have her.

Never.

Part Two

TWENTY-TWO

Ryanne

Multicolored bright spots danced on my closed eyelids. Where was I? I was lying, limp, on a soft bed, that much I could tell. Something was wrong, but I couldn't remember what.

Images of bloody, mutilated, and headless bodies drilled my head; someone was in danger. Water touched my dry, scorched lips, and I drank without stopping, the cold liquid rushing down my scratchy throat. A bittersweet taste clung to the back of my tongue.

Nonsensical words echoed far away and then, blessed darkness and unconsciousness. I fell into an obscure dream, where an arrogant blue-skinned being stood in a cave—he exuded so much power, he could be a godlike being from Tír na Vraoichta, the dark dimension. The sound of crashing waves and the strong smell of the ocean made me think this was real.

A vision.

Titus, young and naked, stood in front of the god. Clean-shaven with wavy raven black hair brushing his shoulders, Titus was expressionless, like a wooden doll the artist forgot to paint. A cowl, shimmering orange-red like a river of lava, hid the god's features. He muttered words in a foreign language—an enchantment. The god lifted a gold coin while his chant rose in intensity, and the power in the cave turned tangible, electrifying. My skin crawled. Tendrils of darkness rose, as thick as ivy growing right from the soil, wrapping both him and Titus. The god shouted like a fanatic while Titus remained still, eyes still blank. Despair and corrupt energy tore my heart open.

Warm water enveloped me like a womb, and fear vanished like footsteps on sand swept away by a swift wave. The temperature dropped until my teeth chattered. I turned around as dozens of bull sharks swam around, sharks with strange eyes, brown wicked eyes like Edward's.

I yelled, bubbles erupting from my mouth, heart pounding too fast, too intense.

With a kick, I pushed myself to the surface, gulping air into my lungs. There was no moon on the chilly night, yet I could see clearly. I floated in the middle of the ocean, teeth chattering, the sharks waiting for something.

Titus appeared, leaping over the fins. He yelled, "The sea crashes and sweeps, but there's peace within!" What he'd told me it felt like so long ago back at sea. But there was no peace here.

A hooded figure jumped behind him, sword raised, ready to strike.

"Titus!" I cried. "Watch out!"

He swiveled to deflect the thrust. The sharks circled me while they kept jumping nimbly on their fins, exchanging strokes.

The hooded figure thrust their sword into Titus's chest and blood gushed. Titus widened his eyes, gasped, and fell back to the sea. A bright-crimson stain spread on the surface.

Blood. Blood around him, on my hands, in the water. Sharks mobbed him, mauling him as he screamed.

Screaming too, I awoke, beads of sweat dampening my forehead. The only light came from a hearth. The fire spread warmth and the fragrance of burning wood. Sparks crackled. A shadowed figure sat before it in a solid, wooden chair. He rose to his feet, his tall, lean body highlighted by the fire behind.

Titus?

"You had a nightmare." Not Titus. Peter.

Peter crouched next to me, a worried look cracking his marble face. "You're finally awake."

The memories of what had happened rushed through me. Rome, the search for Quintus, Sanders, and the abandoned mansion. I pushed myself up and tried to talk, but my throat was too dry.

"Here, you need to drink this."

Peter placed a rustic wooden bowl to my lips. The same bittersweet taste drifted in the water, but still I eagerly drank. Tiredness took a back seat, and energy returned to my shaken limbs.

"Thanks," I croaked.

"We will wait here a while longer until your strength fully returns. Rest."

"Titus. We need to go back."

"You're delirious. Drink some more."

I glanced around. "Bricius! Where is he?"

"I sent him back to the taigh."

I nodded. The only times Bricius left me alone was at the taigh and when Peter was with me. Peter was the only one Bricius trusted to keep me safe. Cuidi would too, but then she hardly left the taigh.

We were in a hut with a dirt floor and a wood-beamed ceiling. The window was dark, so it was night. A different hut from the one we arrived in several weeks ago after Titus's failed kidnap attempt back when we first met. Peter used the same point of entry to Tír D'aois every time, a hut similar to this yet different in little details, like the position of the fireplace, the flagstones, and the window's size.

"I don't recognize this hut. Are we far from the taigh?" I asked.

"Because of where we were and what happened there, I couldn't arrive at a nearer point. But worry not, we have different means of transport other than the capalls. She's agreed to help me. Now, drink a little bit more. This will help you."

"She?"

"You'll see."

Fae couldn't just appear directly in Cuidi's taigh or even in her valley. Her power was too strong, not to mention the balance of energies on either side of the portal should match, so usually we had to ride to the taigh in capalls—wild creatures that were a mix of wolves and horses. I didn't have a clue about this new creature, whoever she was.

Peter offered the bowl again, and I drank more, energy rushing to me, mixing with the cold inside. I felt rested and full of vitality as if I'd taken a long, restoring, dreamless nap. Aine quivered and filled me whole.

It was always stronger in Tír D'aois.

"Titus! Where is he?" I jumped to my feet, fully awake now. My legs failed and, staggering, my butt landed on the cot again. Was he far away? I shook my numb thoughts; of course he was.

"You're safe. That pirate cannot hurt you." Peter's emerald eyes glowered.

"No, Peter, he wasn't hurting me. He—"

"He kidnapped you, can't you remember?" He furrowed his brow and placed a hand on my forehead. "You're still feverish."

I grabbed his hand and held it between mine. "Oh, Peter, I need to know if he's all right."

Peter grunted. "Unfortunately he shall be. He's survived for hundreds of years. I'm sorry to say he'll be up and about in no time."

"It's not like that now. He's different. He's sorry and even offered me an apology."

"Apology? It was certainly a trick," he said, dismissing my comment with a wave of his hand. "But apology or not, you mustn't be afraid anymore."

It was time to set him straight.

"That's what I mean, Peter. There's *nothing* to fear from Titus. I spent enough time with him and—"

"And he tricked you. Pirates are untrustworthy. He must have taken advantage of your innocence. You're just *cailín*, after all."

"No, Peter," I said, strangely calm despite the child moniker. "Fé Erie sent me on a quest. Didn't Cuidigtheach tell you about it?"

"I know our Lady is worried about the fate of the fae." He thumped a fist on his open palm. "Those *brocach* pirates have only one thing on their corrupt minds—exterminate us until there is no one left." His breathing came ragged.

Brocach. Filthy.

"A quest, Peter, to understand them."

"Ah." His eyes brightened. "To know how to kill them, is that so?"

"No. *Understand* them. I am to find a spark in them."

But Peter's thoughts were faraway, his eyes still shiny.

"Titus isn't like the others."

His pointy ears twitched. "But of course. He's different, is he not?"

I furrowed my brow at his mocking tone.

"And don't say he made you believe he was *good.*" He snorted. "They are masters of deception, don't forget." He dropped into the chair in front of the fire as if to terminate the discussion.

"I know he's not *good*—what you would call good. But he isn't evil, and he's changing for the better. There is something in him, an energy within." I steeled myself, determined to get this out. "That energy reminded me of you. Of the fae."

"How absurd. Have you developed feelings for him, perhaps?" He stared at me. "Do please tell me it's not so."

I sighed. "It's not like that."

He rose, clasping his hands behind his back. "You let him deceive you. You wanted to see something in him that doesn't exist."

"It *does* exist, Peter." Oh, this strong-headed mule! Why did he have to be so one-track-minded?

"Then enlighten me. Why did he kidnap you? Was he scared of asking permission to take you on a date?" He lifted his chin in that fae-arrogant expression of his.

I stood up and lifted my hands, torn between strangling him or calming myself. "Okay, he messed up. But he repented."

"He took advantage of you, Ryanne, and your feelings."

"No, you're mistaken. Please, listen to me."

Peter looked at me with a mixture of pity and exasperation but listened in silence.

I told him about Edward, Kara, and the experience with Sanders. Peter cocked his head, an expression on his face as if I were just a little kid trying to excuse a bully on the playground . . . or a kidnapper from a Stockholm Syndrome perspective. I tightened my lips before I reached the part about the strange power in Titus.

"I cannot believe you're so naive, Ryanne. This bradaí woman is certainly his lover and wanted to get rid of you. Why else did she come for him? A sense of loyalty or companionship is unbeknownst to them."

"No! She's like his sister."

He blinked. "Are you *serious*?"

"You're misinterpreting *everything*, Peter."

"No, Ryanne. You see only what you want to see. You forget I've fought them for hundreds of years, and I know them quite well, especially the one you call Titus. You've forgotten about the fae he tortured," he said with a grimace of anger. "Aghna was her name." He shut his eyes for a moment, pain flickering on his face.

"He told me about her. He didn't—"

Peter ground his teeth, the muscles of his neck tensing. He got closer, his handsome face disfigured by hatred. "And he told you how he killed her at the end?" He swiveled to watch the fire, the flames' reflection flickering on his face. "I shan't stop until every pirate *brocach* has been wiped off the face of the earth."

"It wasn't like that," I whispered.

"You weren't there," he said in a chilly way. "I was."

I cringed. There's always two sides to a story, and I only knew Titus's. As a bradaí, Titus hated fae as fae hated them. He was changing, but that change was gradual.

Titus and I hadn't discussed Aghna in full, and I doubted Peter would believe Titus's assertion of not wanting to kill fae because of her. Which we didn't talk about either.

"Peter," I said as softly as I could, "not all bradaís are that evil. Edward is worse than the others and—"

"I saw it with my own eyes. I rescued her from him." Peter's face darkened, and I took a step back at the ferocity of his features. "He destroyed her, Ryanne. He killed her spirit, her joy, her kind being. Her face was beaten, swollen when I took her from him . . ." His pained words shattered, and he sobbed. "She was my everything. My world."

A lump formed in my throat. Peter's words were like acid burning me and creating a little hole inside me, a small hole that threatened to turn into a dark cave.

"I'm sorry." I attempted to place a hand on his arm.

Peter stepped back, inhaling deeply. "They're a disease that must be eradicated." He slammed a fist into his palm. "And that pirate who caught you is no better than the others."

"But I saw another part of him," I insisted.

Did Titus tell the truth about not killing Lhotto when he escaped from the taigh? His turnaround happened afterwards. Could I ever forget the blood tainting Titus's hands? He'd said he only repented for what he did to me. What about every evil thing he'd done before? If he didn't repent, he would murder again and again. Could my feelings survive that?

I didn't dare ask Peter about Lhotto and Otto, the daighs who guarded Titus back at the taigh. What if . . .?

Peter placed a hand on my shoulder, his expression softening. "You were a victim of his deception, Ryanne. You mustn't blame yourself. And you should not worry. We'll find a way for you to be safe from them. For good."

"Fé Erie gave me this quest, Peter. *I* need to be there."

"We fae have trouble understanding her since she sees beyond our own paths. Do not assume you do."

I opened my mouth again but, after a moment of hesitation, shut it. Peter had chosen to heed the fae side who thought bradaís were beyond redemption.

The nightmare. Anord and Titus . . . Titus bleeding. Edward and Minho's cruel smiles flashed before my eyes. Sanders and his men. Kara rescuing me, even getting Titus out.

And what had I done? Nothing.

Nothing.

Not a thing.

I was way over my head.

"Peter, would you help me train?"

"I've trained you."

"Yes, to talk to ogres, but I need to learn how to fight. To defend myself."

"You'll be safe from the bradaís in the taigh."

"Apparently I'm not safe anywhere, and I need to be able to defend myself."

He lifted a hand. "May I?"

Without any idea about what he had in mind, I nodded. He placed his palm on my forehead and closed his eyes.

Aine responded immediately, like a little kid who sees their favorite uncle. Or Grandpa. Peter might look in his thirties, but he was several centuries old. A favorite great-great-great-grandpa.

Memories from my failures flashed like hitting fast-forward on a movie. Me before Minho. With Haru. Edward. Sanders.

He lifted his hand and stared into my eyes without a word. I told him about how despite the fact my power had been growing, it had coiled before Edward and dispersed before Sanders due to my terror.

Peter listened to me without interrupting once, his eyes never leaving mine. I had the feeling he wasn't looking at me but seeing—or feeling—Aine.

"When I was *cailín*," Peter said the moment I finished, "I played with what you would call clay, but it's a slightly different texture. I felt it in my hands, felt the grains dispersing on my skin. I did this in different scenarios, never paying attention to the surroundings but only the clay. I finally shaped it into what I wanted."

And then, Peter walked to a rustic chest, pushed against the wall.

That's it? Clay?

"What did you shape it into?"

"You need some clothes." He stared at the chest. "Aghna used to keep human clothing here, male and female." With a slight shake of his head, as if to dispel unwanted recollections, he grabbed some clothes. "They will not fit you properly, I am afraid."

Trousers that reached just below the knee and a long-sleeved undershirt.

"I shaped it into an ogre," I said. "My energy. Bricius didn't like it."

"You're human; it's not unexpected," he said in a lighter tone. "I have a surprise outside. It'll make you forget this ordeal. Come out when you have changed." He closed the door behind him.

I swallowed. My stupid hopes to return to Titus vanished like smoke rising from the fire. My throat ached, and I shut my eyes for a moment, then threw the lab coat to the floor and slipped on the garments, which were a bit loose. Aghna had been a tall fae, for sure.

The moonlight hit my face as I crossed the threshold. My jaw slackened. But it wasn't the beauty of the moon that dazzled me and dissolved my doubts, nor its unusual size, or how its brilliance stood against the velvet cloak of night.

What made me gape was the giant fire-breathing lizard taking all the space in the clearing. *She* was our transport? "A dragon," I whispered in awe.

She had a long, sinuous body like a thick snake with legs, her big head had an elongated snout ending with two big fangs. Her color was burning red, yellow scales adorning her back. She was what Americans would call a Chinese dragon. I wondered what her real name was.

"Close your eyes now, you don't want to see into the depths of her gaze."

"Wait, aren't dragons on the Erlking side?" I said as I closed them.

"Not her."

I was going to ride a frigging dragon! I would have done a silly dance if Peter hadn't drag me along, his hand firmly on my elbow.

"How can you control a dragon?" I whispered in wonder.

"I don't. I asked."

At one point, I felt his hands on my waist, lifting me onto what I assumed was the dragon's body.

"You can open them now," he said behind me.

His arm closed around my waist, bringing me closer to him so I wouldn't fall, which I was grateful for when the dragon took flight into the starry night, slithering like a snake in water. The warm breeze soothed me.

Tír D'aois lay at our feet. Forests, lakes, and deserts were illuminated by the soft light of the moon as far as my eye could see. Strange rock formations stood on my right. Groups of giant pines surrounded a monstrous mushroom village, divided by a strip of sand where trolls walked, all dragging maces, even the little ones.

Farther up to my right, lava swirled in blackness, puffs of smoke emanating from caves even darker than the night. Danger surged from there. The Erlking's lands, a place that made my skin crawl. I turned my head left, and the pressure in my chest lifted at the sight of a river shining like molten silver. A herd of bison-like creatures rested nearby.

"This is unbelievable, Peter," I whispered in wonder. My worries took a back seat. There was no space for them when upon the back of a dragon in flight. "I never thought Tír D'aois would look like this from above. It's . . ." The words stuck in my throat, emotions swirling inside me.

The wind whipped my face and played with my hair, making me feel free. The dragon flew higher and gained more altitude.

Joy bubbled in me. I laughed as I hadn't for a while, feeling brave for the first time, believing I could reach the stars with my hands if I tried. I placed my hands on the dragon's scales, feeling their hard yet smooth texture. I smiled from within—I'd been in the ocean and now high up in the sky.

Below on a plain, a redheaded fae ran as fast as we flew, her laughter rising to our height. It was like the sound of a thousand singing fountains joining to create the force of a waterfall.

Looking down, I could clearly see the fae, despite the distance. Her long, fire-red tresses floated like a cape behind her, her starry dress as a trail marking her passage. She opened her arms, and wispy fog shot out of her fingers, covering the plain.

"Fé Erie," I whispered.

"Can you see her?" Peter asked with a hint of surprise.

"Perfectly," I shouted merrily into the night.

"You surprise me, Ryanne."

Yeah, now you believe me!

After some time, a valley appeared. Green mountains surrounded the taigh. The lake outside reflected the silvery moonlight.

Two emotions mixed within me. Sadness because the dragon flight didn't last as long as I'd have liked. Relief because I'd finally returned and could talk to Cuidi.

I frowned. Where would the dragon land? There was no space for a creature this big. Its sinuous body curved like a ribbon in a gymnast's hands.

The dragon flew low, right over the small lake within the walls.

A song flashed through my memory.

Dream, dream, little girl.
Come with us, mouth wide,
Eyes glazed, you shall see
How wonderful it is death to thee.

The inside lake.

"Do you know how fae become adults? How the *cailín* moniker is lifted? We must face our biggest fears. And we don't give advice to our children. We show them."

"That's not so different from humans," I wheezed.

"Have you faced your fears before? Your deepest one?"

I glanced at the lake and their song boomed in my head. "No, no, nooo."

Peter tossed me off the dragon. I plunged toward the water before I realized what was happening.

Nymphs.

Drowning frigging nymphs.

TWENTY-THREE

Titus

The burning debris surrounded me, and by Anord, it felt good. Charred bodies and blackened, smoking furniture littered the old mansion. I kicked a desk. Bloody humans. There weren't many when I returned, but the few remaining satisfied my beast's cries of revenge.

Yes. You did well.

One of the mercenaries lay at my feet, twitching. I crouched and watched him dispassionately. Black thorns covered his face but were fading.

More.

I fastened a hand on this throat and poured *dorcha* in him. From my fingertips, those black thorns spread, and he convulsed, foam sputtering out of his mouth until death claimed him.

Homkar exited the room where they had drawn blood from me, his brow as dark as mine. What had they done to Ryanne? In how many ways had Sanders hurt her, while I sat here, impotent to stop them? I found my thoughts again hauled to the manner of her dress—or lack thereof. To how Gallchobhair had swept her into his arms, as though he had the right. The muscle in my jaw twitched, and my fists clenched, demanding to be launched against Pretty Boy's smug face.

He'd stolen her from me, whisked her from my reach. My beast stirred, claiming his blood. For once, I agreed with it.

Kara stepped inside and stood next to my loyal first mate. "The police have arrived. You want me to get rid of them?" She flashed a grin.

"No. Our job here is done. There's no longer any trace I was here. Or Ryanne." My nostrils flared, and I flexed my fingers. "Let's head out that way"—I pointed at a window—"to avoid arriving somewhere we don't want to end. We need parks," I said as way of explanation as I headed to the window and opened it wide.

Kara went through first, then Homkar. I took one last look at the demolished place. At the blank faces of the dead. An odd feeling of being unsatisfied with what I did, grabbed me by surprise.

Did I really have to kill them?

Yes. You are a bradai. You kill.

I shook my head and followed suit, landing with a thump. Two stories was not a challenge for any of us.

"Over there, then?" Kara asked, pointing with her head toward an open area with trees.

"Aye, that would do."

"Hard still to believe you manage to open a portal like the goblins. Mind-blowing, little brother." She tilted her head and stared right into my eyes. "I'm beginning to think Anord might have made you different, after all."

Yells behind us, up in the building, but trees now hid us from the guards. My fingers cracked with *dorcha*.

"It's time," I said to Homkar. "Are you sure your brother will help us?"

"Count on it, Captain."

I addressed Kara next. "Are you in?"

"Bloody right I am." She thumped a hand on my shoulder. "I deserted you once. Told ya, little brother, tell me to follow you to the depths of hell and I'll go right beside you. With a smile."

"Not Hell, but close enough."

The fae's realm.

TWENTY-FOUR

Ryanne

I fell with a tremendous splash. I kicked to the surface, frantically. Silvery moonlight bathed the surroundings, giving a phantas-magoric, ethereal brilliance to the lake surface. The nearest shore was too far away for my liking—the crazy nymphs might be lurking beneath the water surface.

"Where are you?" I yelled while wiping the water dripping from my brow. No need to talk in hushed tones. Those maniacs knew when someone was in their domain.

There was no dragon above. No Peter.

I cursed loudly. Spending time with sailors tended to change one's own vocabulary. "Nymphs, Peter, they like to drown humans! Where the heck are you?"

But they wouldn't dare, would they? Peter isn't far, shouldn't be far.

Thankfully, Aghna's clothes didn't hinder me in the water or weigh me down like the fancy dress had.

Ripples formed around me, and the hairs at my nape bristled.

No. A soft breeze rippled the lake, not the nymphs. This was worse than being thrown overboard. Images of a silver-haired nymph throwing a net and pulling me into the depths of the lake to *dance* with her flashed in my mind. If it weren't for Bricius's warning Cuidi back then, my seer career would have ended at the tender age of ten.

Oh, no, not again! I started to swim to shore.

Here and there the surface broke as if tiny fishes gulped air. A chill traveled down my spine, and my heart beat painfully against my ribcage.

Crapcrapcrap!

Something brushed against my leg, and I yelped, shoulders tense like sails in a gale. Laughter erupted—maniac, crystal noises surrounded me. Darker shapes moved below me.

"They're here!" I turned around this way and that like a broken musical figurine at double speed. "Peter! Stop playing games!"

Several heads broke the surface in a circle around me. The nymphs smiled like sorority sisters about to bully a freshmen. I quickly counted ten maniacs.

Down, down, little girl.

"But look who it is," sang a nymph with braided blue hair. "A toy for us!" She clapped enthusiastically.

They broke into titters, and goosebumps erupted on my skin.

Gritting my teeth, I started to swim again—better to take some action than wait for those crazy nymphs to toy with me.

"What's the rush, beautiful Ryanne?" another nymph said, red braids atop her head. I knew this one: Layla. In the faint moonlight, it was hard to see the details of their crocodile-like skin. "Play with us for a while. It's been a long time since you came to see us, and we've missed you." Her beautiful full lips pouted.

"Yes, Rynny Tinny, play for a while as you did before," said a third one. Her silver, slick hair matched her shining eyes.

Not Zadora. Dammit.

Then, I saw Peter, standing on shore, a black figure contrasting with luminescent flowers. "Peter!" I called.

"Gallchobhair?" some of the nymphs asked, turning their colorful heads toward my fae mentor.

Seizing their distraction, I turned to escape and swam towards shore, far from where Peter stood. The lake's coldness didn't bother me at all. It caressed and embraced me instead. At least I learned to enjoy this part of the water from Titus. If only he was here to chase the predators away.

A slimy hand grabbed my ankle.

One of the nymphs pulled me down. An arctic gale covered my limbs and my reasoning. I glanced back. A flash of silver hair. Fear gripped me, the memory of my near-drowning robbing strength from my body.

Down, down, little girl.

The surface rushed away from me quickly and, holding back a scream, I flapped my arms and legs in a vain attempt to escape.

And then, she released me.

I kicked and swam back to the surface. Gods, it felt so good to breathe.

Before I got too comfortable, I was pulled back into the depths.

And she released me again.

With a wild kick, I swam desperately toward—

Zadora pulled me back before I reached the coveted surface.

I threw another wild kick, this time aimed at her face. She laughed, and her maniac giggles boomed in my head.

And she released me.

Wasting no time, lungs burning, I paddled toward the surface again and took a frantic breath.

Zadora grinned at me just an arm's distance away.

Nononononooo.

She grabbed my arm and pulled me toward her, showing her sharp teeth in her creepy signature smile. Her slimy, cold webbed hand cupped my cheek. The scent of lilies and raw fish mixed in the lake's breeze. I cringed.

A game of killer whale and seal—or nymph and seer in this case.

"Rynni Tynni, so glad to see you again. Look at you, so pretty. But your face looks so pale." She pouted, then flashed a fake big smile. "I know the perfect remedy!"

"Zadora," I said in the same tone I used with ogres, a tone I'd always struggle to have but after spending time with Titus, it came naturally. "You can't come near me. You know Cuidigtheach will be angry."

"Oh, what are you talking about, Rynny Tynny? That was long ago, and you and I are sisters."

The nymph—still clutching my arm—laughed like fingernails on a chalkboard. I had to suppress the fear in me. She'd sense it.

"You smell so good, Rynny Tynny."

"You smell like rotten fish," I snapped.

She purred and caressed my cheek again with that slimy, nasty hand, then kissed me on the mouth, her lips full and soft.

"Swim with us!" a nymph shouted, surely at Peter.

Zadora released me, her attention on them. Peter was still on shore, but the nymphs were clamoring like groupies to a rock-star. Zadora turned to them and clapped her hands.

Keep Calm and Swim to Shore.

I quickened my strokes, gulping air between them.

Strong arms pulled me back. Water entered my nose and pain drilled in the back of my head, burning me. The stink of raw fish lingered in the air.

Zadora wrapped her arms around my waist and neck, squeezing like an anaconda.

Time to remove the never in this never-ending game.

"Rynny Tynny," Zadora sang in that tone nuts use when they get what they want. "Why do you want to go? We're getting along so well."

"I'm not your toy, crazy nymph."

I'm always their toy, their rag doll.

Zadora's bright laughter rang loudly while I fought for oxygen. She squeezed her arm tighter around my neck, and I struggled in vain to remove it, digging my nails into her scaly forearm. Desperate, I grabbed her arm and pushed it away harder with Aine's help.

Zadora didn't react.

"Peter . . ." My voice came out as a strangled, weak whisper.

"Our beloved prince is too busy with my sisters to come with you, Rynny Tynny. If it weren't because I missed you so much, I would join them. He hasn't visited us in forever," she said in a pouting tone.

My insides churned, and a weight settled on my chest. Why did I have to be rescued all the time? Granted, I was out of my league with a nymph, but I couldn't keep going like this.

"Zadora," I said, struggling to inhale air, "let's play if you want, but let me breathe."

Giggling, she pressed harder. "But that's the fun part. I love the face humans make when they go with me and turn purple, purple, and then they leave their eyes open wide. It's so cute! You are so pale. Purple will suit you."

"Release me," I wheezed. Black spots danced in my vision.

I need . . . to fight . . . back.

"Aw, but we are doing just fine, look." Placing both arms under my armpits, she lifted the corners of my mouth. "See how happy you are?"

I gulped air and coughed.

"Zadora. Let me loose," I breathed.

"But I don't want to," Zadora said in her pouty voice. "You're so cute." She hugged me tightly, resting her head on my shoulder. "I want to see your face purple, purple."

"Zadora. Let me loose."

She giggled in my ear and squeezed my neck.

I kicked and thrashed wildly. But she was so strong.

Aine whirled like a wild beast waiting for my command. I stopped thrashing and focused.

"Thrice I ask. Zadora. Let me loose." My voice sounded empowered with intent.

In Tír D'aois, saying something three times has power. It was in their nature. Yet, I could sense Zadora resisting, her arms loosening then tightening again, her breathing ragged—I wasn't powerful enough to make her stop.

Zadora whispered in my ear, "Nonono, Rynny Tynny. You play with me." And with that, the craziest of the lot dragged me to the bottom of the lake.

The surface vanished. There would be no more chances.

No one to rescue me.

My body stiffened and my chest crushed, my fingers in a rictus.

I was going to die.

Powerless.

The surface was so far away. Darkness engulfed me.

An imaginary Bricius whispered in my ear, "*You can do this. You're not* cailín *anymore.*"

I wasn't.

And I had Aine.

Edward's threats. Minho throwing me overboard. Sander's interrogation.

Enough!

I wouldn't go like a frightened child, like the *cailín* I used to be.

"*I played with what you would call clay. I felt it in my hands, felt the grains dispersing on my skin.*"

Right! I did the same with Haru. It hadn't worked with Edward or Sanders, but I didn't have time to ponder why.

I could do this.

Aine reacted at my call, expectant.

"*Never paying attention to the surroundings.*"

Forget I was drowning.

"*I finally shaped it into what I wanted.*"

Someone strong. Capable.

Aine transformed into a creature rippling with muscle—a dryad on steroids with the green tinge skin of an ogre. It filled me completely as I extended my arms and closed my eyes.

I had those muscles, that strength.

We were underwater though.

"*. . . shaped it into what I wanted.*"

Into what was needed.

Only a nymph thrived here, not an ogre.

Aine morphed into a dark nymph with canines poking out from its lips. My legs straightened, and I could feel them like a tail. Powerful. I willed the energy to my hands, a mini supernova traveling to my fingertips.

Zadora had stopped as if sensing something was off, and we floated underwater. She had her arms tight around my chest and bubbles exploded in my ear.

"What are you doing, Rynny Tynny?"

"This."

When in Rome. I let myself be guided by my touch of fae, a power I used to dismiss, since it had appeared randomly and of no use to me.

A power used to show me snippets of a romantic pairing in the future because that was what I'd wanted.

Now I wanted to be stronger, capable to face supernatural creatures. I didn't have the physical strength, that much was clear. But I had my fae connection, one that had been a stranger inside me but not anymore.

I could feel the water sliding down my torso, the change of vibrations as Zadora rocked me back and forth.

"You can hear me," she said in awe.

The water was not a tomb, but a delicious sensation firing me up.

I lifted my arms above my head and twirled. It was as if her arms were made of butter and couldn't hold me any longer. My legs-slash-metaphoric-tail propped me up and kicked her face while at it.

"That is amazing, Rynny!" She laughed. *"You* are *really my sister."*

I swam back to the surface, faster and stronger than before, Zadora right next to me, giggling. I turned as I broke the surface, her head breaking the surface right beside me, her silver hair reflecting the moonlight.

She grinned, her canines shining white.

I punched Zadora in the face, all the energy focused on that spot. Her head recoiled and her nose bled a viscous thick dark blood.

I was free.

Free!

Damn, it felt so good!

I swam to shore as fast as I could, Aine's nymph tail helping. Hazy figures stood by the shore. Friendly, I hoped.

Two strong arms lifted me and helped me out. I coughed water, kneeling on all fours, all strength vanishing and Aine coiling back, exhausted—I was human again. Air rushed into my lungs in gulps. I pressed a hand on my throat, feeling the too quick beat of my heart. Someone helped me to stand. Someone sturdy, with a mass of unruly orange hair that stood on end, and a scar crossing his right cheek.

Lhotto.

"Whoa, missy!" Lhotto said, steadying me. "Watch your step. Big scare, huh?"

Otto appeared at Lhotto's side, identical to my friend but without the scar. My heart eased. Titus had said the truth. He hadn't killed him!

"We are glad you are safe," Otto said in a formal voice, but strangely omitting the *cailín* moniker he always gave me. That all fae gave me.

"Yeah," Lhotto said, "that was quite a punch."

"Lhotto!" I stood and hugged the surprised daigh until I felt the breastplate on his chest. "And, Otto, you survived! You-you fell down the stairs." Yeah, I believed that all along, but it was still nice to hug the confirmation.

Otto puffed his chest while pointing at his hairline. "It was nothing, just a tiny scar now."

I was dripping wet, so I removed the wet clothing, thankful of the summer-like weather of the taigh.

"Hand me your cape, Lhotto."

"May the Force be with you," Lhotto said. "I got that right, didn't I, Ryanne?" he whispered while he unclasped his short cap and draped it around my shoulders. He was an uncommon fae who loved watching movies with me and Bricius back in Seattle.

Cuidi stood a few feet away from us, her long, dark hair stirring around her, her striking figure clad in white robes.

She strode to the lake's edge and said in a booming voice, "Zadora, you shall be punished for attempting to hurt my guest."

"Aw, Lady," Zadora said, a slimy hand covering her bloodied nose. "I only wanted to see her purple. We're sisters, Rynny Tynny and me."

Cuidi lifted a hand, silver power emanating from it.

The silver energy hit Zadora. With a shrill screech, Zadora jumped over the surface and transformed into a great silverfish. She dove back into the water with a big splash. I let out a sigh, releasing all the fear and stress of the last moments. If it weren't for Aine, I'd be like Zadora wanted, with my face purple, purple.

"Thanks," I wheezed, tightening the soft material of the cape around me. The temperature might be nice enough, but I was tired of being half-dressed.

Cuidi winked at me, so fast I thought my imagination was tricking me, but she definitely winked, a playful smile hovering on her lips, then bowed her head gracefully like the queen she was. "I welcome you, Ryanne. You are, as always, pleasing to our eyes."

I knelt on the soft grass, and despite my shaking voice, I repeated the greeting Cuidi expected and encouraged. "Lady Cuidigtheach, I appreciate and accept your invitation. I am honored, and while I am here, you will find me to be a respectful and obedient guest."

Cuidi nodded, pleased. Manners were important to the fae, and showing respect to the Lady of the taigh was the number one item when arriving. Even if it was via the lake and half-drowned by a crazy nymph.

"Come." She walked back to the taigh.

Before I followed her, I glanced back at the lake. Peter was in the lake! Did the nymphs get a hold of him? The rest of the nymphs were laughing, apparently without concern for Zadora's fate. Or maybe they hadn't noticed and were way too busy fighting over my fae mentor.

"My Lady, wait!" I said, pointing at him. "Peter's in trouble!"

Cuidi looked over her shoulder. "Peter has been focused on fighting pirates for too long. It's time for him to relax."

"To relax? With that bunch of lunatics?" I couldn't believe Cuidi would leave Peter in the nymphs' hands. I picked up Aghna's clothing and hurried to catch up to her, my legs still wobbly and my bare feet pounding on the soft grass.

"Nymphs love him."

"Like Zadora loves me?" I insisted, still worried about him. I glanced back but they were just a dark misshapen blotch contrasting with the lake's brightness.

"Peter is fae. Although you have tried to humanize him by that name, he belongs to us."

"He doesn't know about the bradaís—"

"There has been no change from our last conversation."

Where she explained how most fae, like Peter, didn't believe bradaís could be redeemed.

She signaled to the path leading to the southern entrance of the main building, at the moment a looming black figure, and we followed it, Lhotto and Otto behind us. Their strange, eerie eyes shone bluish-white against the darkness, their orange hair like wild flames atop their heads. Lhotto gave me a thumbs up, winking, and we both grinned.

Oh, Gods, I was so happy to see my dear daighs.

I gazed back at the lake, a small reflection in the darkness. I tightened the cape once again around my still shaken body.

"Cuidigtheach." I hesitated a moment. "I've never thanked you for everything you've done for me."

Feihnum, my fae power sang.

Cuidi's smile grew, and somehow, I knew she heard it. "It's not easy for a human to understand us or open their minds as you have. It has been an honor to accompany you in your growth."

"Still, I want you to know how grateful I am. All this time you've cared for me and . . . Thank you."

"Many humans who used to see us when young, as adults decide to forget about us, convincing themselves we were only a figment of their imagination." She shook her head, sadly. "Few manage to arrive where you are and continue to accept us." Cuidi briefly touched my cheek and my fae power lit, a pet wanting to be caressed. "Rest now, you have been under a lot of stress from what happened to you with the bradaí. Later we shall talk."

"There's much to talk about, yes." I sighed.

The adrenaline dissolved from my system, an empty void replacing it when my thoughts drifted to Titus. Where was he? Would I see him again?

Most importantly, how the heck was I going to get back to him and how was I going to convince Cuidi to let me go?

TWENTY-FIVE

Ryanne

The second-floor hallway on the western side of the taigh showed glimpses of the silvery lake in the distance. I leaned my shoulder against one of the stone arches, inhaling the scent of damp soil. It'd rained earlier that morning, and everything in the forest looked mysterious, with fog swirling among the vegetation. Clouds heavy with unshed rain covered the sky in different hues of gray.

Satisfaction blossomed into a smile on my face. I'd been able to fight a nymph away. Clumsily, but a start was a start. My first defeat of a supernatural creature.

I pumped a fist and scrunched my face while at it.

Aine swirled as if agreeing with me. Then it pulled me forward, and I almost fell but managed to grip the stone railing. I frowned and decided to follow its beckoning, so I descended the stairs and to the garden. The warm morning breeze played with my silk dress that rustled against my legs. Eucalyptus, mint, and juniper tickled my nose, and I inhaled the taigh's scent greedily. A helpful pixie had braided forget-me-nots in my hair, which brushed the middle of my back. Silky slippers covered my feet that barely felt the stone beneath them.

Aine pushed me toward one of the winding paths in the southern area. I caught a faraway song. Invisible beings sang here, sometimes somberly, sometimes in a vibrant staccato. Their notes touched my heart and made it leap; they infused my feet with a grace almost akin to the dryads.

And off I went, skidding along, skirts dancing around my legs, until the Hawthorn came into view. Aine coiled and purred as if satisfied it achieved its goal.

I stood before the humble tree, the one the fae revered. A tree I could never approach due to my human energy, power throbbed from it and pulsated in tune with the song. Its roots sank deep into rocks, its many branches spread like a funny hat, leaves green and stirring to the invisible tune like an old woman enjoying herself at a concert, her eyes closed.

The Hawthorn was known as the faery tree in Ireland and England. The reverence they paid the species here gave merit to the tradition. Some farmers wouldn't cut down the tree, considering it back luck. If the faery tree was killed, the faery might seek revenge. I wouldn't blink if some of that was true.

My vision narrowed to a tunnel where only the tree mattered.

The power of the land.

I'd never felt its energy, not like I was feeling it now. Never had I understood how the tree connected to the taigh, but now, I could picture its roots deep into the heart of the land, feeding it, an energy that pulsated like an underground river.

A river with three branches. Three Hawthorns.

My fae power expanded and covered me whole, light seeping from my pores. No, it came from the *tree*. I felt it through the soles of my feet, a cold, tingling energy that my body greedily sucked in.

A vision flashed before my eyes. The Hawthorn dried, and fae laying asleep . . . no, dead, at its base. Other fae walked like zombies, black thorns spread over their skin, their eyes empty.

"*Heal*," a voice said in my mind.

The vision vanished, and I gasped, a hole gnawing at my chest. This land, this gorgeous land would be destroyed along with the fae if bradaís kept on their destructive path.

The Hawthorn energy left my body, and I was once again just Ryanne.

I needed Bricius. He wouldn't be inside any of the three looming buildings, buildings that had risen from the ground by Cuidi's will, but in one of the many gardens. The Lady was the proverbial dame with an iron fist, so peace shrouded this place: jets of water shooting from the many fountains coordinated with the delightful chants of invisible beings, pixies flew in unison and dryads danced. The black stone wall that surrounded the taigh vibrated with energy and trapped beings who had claimed the wall as their domain.

Yeah, we had to find a way to stop the bradaís. Titus had stopped, perhaps Kara would too, but Minho and Edward and who knew who else wouldn't. I was certain. Not until we found a way to disconnect them from Anord.

Two daighs strolled nearby and greeted me, *cailín* absent from their words. They were tough fighters and never shied away from a foe, not even a bradaí. Lhotto and Otto had looked over Titus when he'd been imprisoned here, and even as he'd been bound, he managed to escape, with me as his prisoner—well, alleged prisoner.

I had a strong suspicion Fé Erie had a hand in letting Titus escape from here when I chose to take the fae path and find about the bradaís' sparks. It couldn't have been otherwise—here, I'd been safe, but Titus guarded his true self. On his ship, he'd been his own man, and I'd been able to see through him, partially accomplishing my goal.

But then, I hadn't been able to find that orb of light and remove Anord's tight hold on Titus. That could be the clue, though I wasn't sure yet how to find that orb. Titus wanted to eliminate Edward, but what if Edward also had that spark, deep beneath layers of darkness? Could Edward or Minho turn into softer bradaís, without Anord's command to destroy fae?

Would they even care?

Thoughtful, I arrived at a small, high-walled garden filled only with white flowers, like soft snow surrounding me. A red stone trail wound through the plants and stone benches, carved with faerie designs. I had always avoided those with an engraved depiction of the Erlking, and still did, even now.

A familiar hum buzzed, and my spirits lifted. Bricius flew to me, his tousled hair matching his orange pants. A yellow jacket and bright green shoes complemented the fashion garden look, his seven-inch figure elegant despite the strident colors.

"Hey, Bricius."

"You look sad, yes, yes, yes."

"Well, yeah," I lowered my voice, "I was taken here against my will. I need to go back to Titus."

"Hush! No one here wants you to go back," he said in the same hushed tones. "What did I hear about a nymph?" he asked, now in his normal shrill tone.

"Oh, you wouldn't believe it!"

I told him everything about the fight, his gossamer wings catching the sunlight and making him bright. He kept silent during my telling, which was odd for him.

"I'm not *cailín* anymore, Bug."

"You are not, no, no, no." He grinned mysteriously. "Now here's something new for you: you were destined for this. That is why Fé Erie chose you when you were a baby."

"Wait a minute. What the heck do you mean?"

"Have you ever wondered why you encountered us when you were young? When you found the light?"

I poked his belly with my pinky. "Bricius, I asked you that when I was about nine. And then at twelve. And you always said"—I placed my hands on my hips and imitated his shrill little voice quite well—"'Ryanne, that's the way of things,' and I said, 'That doesn't make sense,' and you said, 'You're too human to understand.'"

"I do not talk like that!" he yelled in the same shrill little voice.

I leaned toward the annoying bug. "Yes, you do. Now, talk."

"You're getting bossy, yes, yes, yes."

"Come on, spill it."

He landed on the bench's armrest, stomping his little foot. "That is what I am doing. As I said, you're no longer *cailín*, and that is why I'm telling you this now. You came through a portal."

"No, I remember it well. I ran after the light and came to the brook. There was no portal."

"Did not you say you felt as if you went through millions of bubbles?"

I pinched my brows. I'd forgotten that, and not once whenever I told his story to Muriel or any of the elders back at the nursing home, had Bricius reminded me of those bubbles.

Millions of bubbles. My memory took me back to that spot, and I saw it clearly, how my eight-year-old self laughed, delighted at the sensation.

And I'd felt cold. But I dismissed it to dash after the pixie.

"I went through a portal? Why? How?" I sat again on the bench. I knew they'd chosen me, but all this time I thought they gave me the touch of fae because I'd been able to see the pixies.

"When you were in your crib, you looked at me and giggled, and I knew you were special. You could accept our gift. So when you turned eight, we made sure your family could go near the portal Tuiren had prepared."

"Tuiren?" I asked surprised. Tuiren seldom visited Cuidi's taigh and certainly never deigned to even look at me.

"She's an Eadrom."

"A Guardian."

"Yes, yes, yes, a Guardian of the Hawthorn. There are three: my Lady Cuidigtheach, my Lord Gallchobhair, and my Lady Tuiren."

Three Hawthorns. Three Guardians.

"I didn't know that, except Peter had a taigh, which Titus told me about some time ago back in his ship." The thought of Titus made me sigh.

"I'm sure I told you in your first lessons, yes, yes, yes."

"When I was eight. Gee, Bug, one wonders why I don't remember a thing."

But then, I'd never paid attention to his long sermons, daydreaming about adventures instead.

"And all have taighs, right?"

"Tuiren and my Lady, yes. The Hawthorn in Lord Gallchobhair's is dead." His wings lowered.

"So it wasn't by chance that I met you guys?"

"No, no, no. The Eadrom never do things by chance." He puffed his little chest. "A pixie always helps to find the next human, and it was I who was chosen. And I chose you."

Fé Erie had wanted me to help with the bradaís, with Titus. Had she chosen me for that task since I was a child?

I scoffed. Free will my ass.

There was nothing better to clear my thoughts than to walk the narrow path winding among the bright flowers. My steps took me to a small fountain in the center of the garden. I sat on the border, dipping my hand in the water while orange minnows pecked my fingers between floating lilies.

Sweet energy came from them, caressing my skin in greeting. "Hi," I said, and one of them did a flip.

Bricius landed on the edge of the stone fountain.

"I miss him, Bricius."

"You like the pirate too much."

He took off his shoes and dipped his long feet into the water. A tiny red fish jumped up to his hand. The small fish cartwheeled in the air, entering the pond in a perfect dive.

I drew circles in the water. One of the orange fish followed my finger, like a small carousel. These weren't like those fish that fed on bread. Here they ate from my own energy and were overjoyed to do it.

"It's more than that, Bricius," I said, my voice choking.

Bricius flew near me and caught a tear in his hands. His gaze fixed on the trapped bead. "Oh," he said, furrowing his little brow. "Interesting."

"What's interesting?"

"Your pirate *is* different. Hmm!" Gently, he deposited my tear on a lily, like a precious package. "He misses you, and he is suffering."

"How do you know that?" I pressed a hand to my chest, trying to calm my beating heart. A beating heart that didn't have an echo in Titus's empty chest.

"It's reflected in your tears."

That night in Rome rushed to my memories, all those confusing images.

Visions.

"Bug, my vision warned me of danger. Then it happened immediately." Ache pierced my chest at that memory. How stupid!

"Can you remember that vision?"

I drummed a finger over my lips, trying to remember. Aine rushed to my mind and the vision showed itself for a couple of seconds, the images clear.

"Bug, I just saw the vision again! I just had to use Aine." I rose, a tingling in my legs and arms as I walked from side to side as Bricius had done.

Bricius flew toward me smiling proudly. "About time, Ryanne."

"Give me five, Bug."

Bricius hit my open palm with a tiny fist.

The peek into the future that my visions showed had changed, as Cuidi had predicted. My last vision had showed Wataru back in Japan with his newborn and . . .

I sucked in a breath. I hadn't talked about my discovery with Bricius!

"What is it, Ryanne?" Bricius asked. "Your eyes are brightened, yes, yes, yes."

I inhaled deeply. "Bricius, I had a vision back in Japan, and I saw something at the bottom of the vision, what you've been asking all these years."

"At last! What did you see? A gnome? A dancing troll?" His eyes glowed. "Or a red pixie? I like the red pixie, yes, yes, yes!"

I blinked. "No, Bug. No dancing trolls, gnomes, or pixies. I saw some symbols at the bottom of the image."

"Symbols? Who sees symbols? No, no, no."

"That's what I saw, Bug. I had a vision of a man with his child, and the Roman numeral for nine blinked at the bottom."

"What?"

"Hold on." I searched for a stick and then drew on the ground what I saw with Wataru: *IX*.

"Who are the Romans and why do they have numerals?" Bricius scratched his head.

"Aw, Bug, one would think after attending school with me you'd know that."

"And why would I pay attention to your teachers? They said pure nonsense like gravity only pulling you down."

I chuckled and drew the next symbol. A circle with a tilted slash. "This also appeared right next to the nine."

"That one is the symbol of the moon."

"Nine moons. Nine months." I straightened. "But why does my vision combine human and Tír D'aois symbols?"

"You are starting to accept your visions. Perhaps you're mixing realities, like when you shaped your touch of fae into an ogre." He scowled.

"But thanks to that Haru released me, and Titus was able to defeat him."

"There's that," the bug conceded.

"When those mercenaries appeared, only a red circle was at the bottom. I'd seen it before, but I hadn't paid much attention. Does the red circle mean immediate danger?"

"Red circle? That must be one of your symbols, yes, yes, yes."

I nodded in thought. Now it was only a matter to return to Titus and finish my quest.

As soon as possible.

TWENTY-SIX

Titus

Zorkar watched the valley with a slight frown. Taller than Homkar by an inch, he dwarfed his brother by sheer musculature. I pinched the bridge of my nose, attempting to calm myself or, by the Morrigan, I'd punch either of the brothers.

Kara stood with hands on hips, assessing the stretch of land below us. Fae power rippled across the valley. I'd tried to Shadow-walk, but the Shadow slipped away the moment I placed a foot inside the protected valley. I'd been pondering why was I able to use the Shadow when I escaped from the taigh, when I took Ryanne with me. The answer was simple: I'd already been inside.

"Is it possible?" I asked Zorkar.

Zorkar let out a sigh. "Nay, Captain. Lady Cuidigtheach would sense us the moment we stepped into her domain. A great lady, she is," he said, admiration coloring his voice.

Kara patted around as if touching a wall. "It might be impossible to get inside without the bloody fae noticing. But we might be able to take it by assault."

Homkar grunted. "Impossible. She would crush us before we could even reach those walls. Not even with more of us."

Cursing loudly, I punched a tree. I couldn't lose Ryanne, not now. I'd lost the battle with the beast in that building, following every instruction it gave me. I shook the trunk. I missed her, missed her flowery perfume and her arms around me. Missed every inch of her. Her lush chestnut hair and moss-green eyes that reminded me of the high seas. Anord's balls.

I pressed my forehead against the tree, my hands latched to it. Something had changed within me.

Feeling, Kara called it. Annoyance, I described it.

Whatever it was, it kept growing every bloody hour I was away from her. I pulled at my jacket, trying to make this *feeling* disappear so I could get back to who I was before. Yet, I didn't want to.

This was so bloody confusing.

Homkar thumped a heavy hand on my shoulder. "Don't despair, Captain." He smiled, flashing his white teeth against his cedar-brown skin. "Not possible for *us* to get in, but we'll stand watch. You will know."

Hope swelled within me. Nothing like dannan-dhubs to know their away around Tír D'aois.

Kara winked. "There you go, little brother. You'll get her back."

I clasped my sword from my bradaí pocket and plunged it into the black damp soil, if only to have my hands busy, then looked over to where the taigh was and memories of that time I spent as prisoner flooded my mind. Ryanne taking care of me, wanting to know more about me, and that spirit-fae appearing to me right before I was about to escape. How she reached out to me.

A thought began to form in my head. An odd thought. A dangerous one. What if that spirit-fae wasn't trying to obliterate me, but help me instead? Strangely enough, I felt peace around her.

My fingers tightened around the pommel.

"You came for me," I said to Kara. "Although I don't trust you."

"You wouldn't be a bradaí if you did." Her playful expression turned serious. Honest, as true as a bradaí could be.

I reached out for her hand and squeezed it. "You still came. Thanks."

She squeezed back. "You dimwit. You have no idea how many years I banged my head for not being there for you."

"That's why you tried to reach out to me back then."

"Yes, but by Odin, I didn't do a great job. I should have tried harder. Same goes with Sergei. That other dimwit has kept me at bay too. We're pathetic. Our differences should make us more united."

"Why, Kara? Why have you been so determined to win us back?"

She looked away. My distrust gained force at her hesitation. Aye, I didn't trust her in full. Time would tell if my sister was what she said she was. But by Anord, I needed friends.

I needed people by me, and I had to start trusting. Even if that trust was still weak.

Ryanne showed me that.

"Immortality can be lonely," she finally said. "I've seen people die around me, my crew, lovers . . . and it's not fun anymore. I miss you both. At least you have Homkar."

I glanced at my loyal first mate, who was talking to his brother some meters away. Warmth spread through my chest—he'd been the only friend who'd stuck with me for more than two hundred years.

"Why, Kara?" I retrieved my sword and leaned my back to the tree. "Why are we different? Why do we feel?"

"Beats me." She shrugged. "But even as I lost Philippe, I would do whatever it takes to feel the same again. I hadn't realized that until I saw you with your woman." Her eyes softened, even as pain lurked behind them.

"I want to have an opportunity with Ryanne," I said. "Get off Edward's radar. Even take a long vacation from being a bradaí."

"Ah, little brother! That you never can. It's within us." She smiled sadly.

"The beast."

"Can't get rid of the pesky creature. Philippe inhibited it while we were together. It was nice. I thought I could be just me." She paused and glanced at her hands. "Suddenly, I'm in a killing frenzy, and I don't realize it until after I'd killed. And I despise myself for it, remembering Philippe's disappointment."

I slashed the air with my sword, picturing the beast as an ugly troll. "Perhaps we can get rid of it."

"We're Anord's creatures." She looked up at the sky, grimacing. "Wherever that bastard is trapped, he must enjoy knowing we abide by him. No, Doyle. We can't. It's our nature. As much as we want to fight against it, it's a lost battle. We can't win against a god. Against our creator."

"And yet, it seems I'm defying him by taking Ryanne."

"It seems you will still do that even knowing the odds."

"It seems I will."

She winked. "You will stir the nest, are you aware of that?

"I care not. I only care about getting rid of the beast. Edward doesn't know he has it. Or blatantly lied, the bastard."

She furrowed her brow. "Did Anord want us to realize we have it? Perhaps Edward really doesn't realize he has it."

"He's different from us."

"From *all* of us. No other bradaí has that degree of darkness." She nodded her head in thought. "There's something off about Minho as well. Why did Anord create a lesser bradaí?"

"Anord didn't create Minho. He used to be fae."

She gaped. "That's impossible. How?"

"Edward converted him with Anord's help. He's no fae anymore. Did you ever wonder about his ears? Edward cut them when he captured Minho."

"When was that?"

"It was during my initiation."

"Ah." She clicked her tongue. "He wanted to see if you could kill one of them."

"Aye. But something happened. I'm not sure what." Minho was the only fae that Edward—with my help—had been able to convert. There was nothing left of his fae essence, though. He couldn't open portals, even though Edward had counted on that particular characteristic of the fae remaining.

"What do you mean, you're not sure?" Kara said, approaching me with that fire in her eyes. "All fae die. No one has—"

"I know. All others do. He's the only one." I sighed. "Minho begged me to kill him before we corrupted his energy. I thought I'd did that but, as you can see, he lives. Edward did something after my initiation, but he's been tight-lipped about it since then."

"Tell me all about it."

"It was the first time I met Edward, back in 1756. Right when you and Sergei went to find the dragonwood for your ships. I had yet to acquire one for me, and Edward and Shen captured me. Minho was a prisoner."

TWENTY-SEVEN

Titus

High Seas 1756

Burnt wood and charred flesh wafted in the wind. Flames engulfed my ship, giving an eerie light to the darkness while dense columns of volute smoke drifted upward. The cries of my crew faded away along with their miserable lives.

The mainmast cracked and fell to the sea, and I ground my teeth, watching the destruction from the quarterdeck of Edward's ship, hands tied behind my back and muscles screaming in pain. Edward and Shen stood by my side. My own kin had been hunting me down to teach me a "lesson." They used a fire-ship, loaded with powder and tar, and set my ship ablaze. Edward had prevented the crew from escaping the doomed vessel.

Flames reflected in Edward's brown eyes as if they too were burning. Walnut brown hair peeked from the back of his neck. A thick beard covered his cheeks, giving him a menacing look. Not undeserved after the way he single-handedly killed several of my crew.

A fading scar crossed his face, a gift from my knife when he'd boarded my ship earlier. He paid me back in kind with several gashes on my arms and chest. Those fleeting moments where we could hurt the other were a bright light in our dark lives. Grand.

"I'm overjoyed that we finally met, Ed." I attempted a crooked smile that hurt as though my face was coated with smoldering tar.

A cruel grin deformed Edward's face. The leader of the bradaís, the first of us, had acted like a brute so far. I had the dubious pleasure of becoming well acquainted with the force of his fists.

It'd been a lovely chat.

Anord had created one of our kin every few decades and in different places. Though in the last fifty years, he'd remained silent, therefore I continued to be the youngest. Created two hundred years ago in England, Edward nonetheless looked around twenty-five years of age, barely older than me. I had thought we did not age, but we did, albeit rather slowly.

A whiskey bottle dangled from his hand. I licked my bloodied lips; the metallic tang clung to the back of my throat. Hell, just a tiny sip would do wonders right now.

"You need to learn to be a true bradaí," Edward said, "instead of playing pirates in a pond with your friends." He spat the last word as if it was poisonous.

My expression remained neutral. Edward disliked that Kara, Sergei, and I had joined together. Yet, he did not have a problem joining forces to hunt me down, the bastard. Joining was acceptable when destruction was the aim. To be friends, not so much, as alliances were formed with a common purpose rather than a desire for camaraderie. My kin were warm and amiable, indeed.

"You know where friends are, nuh?" Shen asked. He looked like an ordinary Chinese pirate, up to his red tunic embroidered with yellow designs. His brown eyes sparkled dangerously. Brown like all bradaís. Except for mine. He nodded to my burning ship. "They went to get wood for ships. Real ships, not toys. Left you behind."

You are better off.

A nagging sensation tugged from the pit of my stomach. They wouldn't . . . My family would never leave me.

Bradaís have no friends, no attachments. Learn that.

Bloody beast. All it kept saying was, work alone, be alone. Perhaps that was why my family was different; we acted differently than the others. Because of what I had learned from my wondrous kin, we three killed and destroyed less. We took less pleasure in the killing. I was sure Kara and Sergei had fought to dismiss the beast as well, though we'd never talked about it.

Had they left me behind?

"Shen, lad," I said in a light tone, dismissing any odd feeling harbored within me, swirling and threatening to rage and slash like a storm. "I'm overjoyed to see your brute face." I glanced behind my back to see a young man standing a couple of meters away, eyes glazed —a prisoner. A nearby lamp lit his features.

With fae, I felt a cold tingling in my body, like an alarm heightening my senses. With my kind, it felt like walking barefoot over heated coals. Quite charming.

Something was amiss with the prisoner—a mix of that cold tingling and the heat.

"What a horrible excuse for a beard." I jerked my head to where the man was, in the hope that Shen would shed some light. "Nothing like a good pair of sideburns, aye?"

Shen had none. His skull was clean-shaven, except at the top where a long braid swung back and forth. It was I who had impressive sideburns.

I showed him my teeth in a broad smile. "Ed looks like a bulldog chewing a wasp, so don't feel bad, Shen. You're a handsome lad."

Edward folded his arms across his hideous ornamented jacket. "Having fun, Irish?"

I grinned. "A whale of a time. Nothing better to celebrate my first half-century than with you ugly brutes." I jerked my chin at Edward's bottle. "Would you share some whiskey, Ed? Have some compassion for a poor fella."

Edward smirked and took a long gulp. Hell.

He yanked back my hair. I gritted my teeth—they would not hear a complaint from me. Whatever was building in the fathoms of my being at the thought of my family leaving me dissipated like black smoke after a spent cannon.

"You're just playing bradaí, Irish. You're not even a full grown-up."

"I'm a captain. I have a ship." The flames shot higher into the night. Laughter rang.

"You had," Shen said with disdain, pulling a knife from his belt and placing its tip on my sweaty chest. "Until you have one like ours, you're no captain but an ordinary pirate. Can't you smell the reek of defeat?"

Anord's balls. I needed that dragonwood. This was the second ship these cursed bradaís had burned. Shen captured me the first time, and I thought I could give them the shoulder this time. No such luck.

Kara, Sergei, and I had spent years trying to get to Tír D'aois. Blasted goblins were a tough lot, always asking for more gold—the bastards knew our desperation. Once there, we'd lost our way countless times. Kara said she'd found how to get the dragonwood and was waiting for me on shore, just before Edward and Shen caught me.

These bilge rats were lying. Kara would never leave me. Neither would Sergei.

"*We stand together. You, Sergei, and me. You two are my family.*" She'd repeated those words to me countless times. She would abide by them. She would.

I glanced back at the prisoner. He looked from the far East, brown-skinned and dark hair gathered in a ponytail at his nape.

"Have you met fae?" Edward asked amiably.

So a fae, then. I shrugged. "Aye. Seen them from afar."

Edward crooked a finger. Shen grabbed the fae's arm and pushed him toward us. The way the fae held himself reminded me of men in the gallows who couldn't fight their fate.

The hairs at the back of my neck bristled, yet warmth sizzled at my guts.

What in Anord's beard?

The fae swayed, chest heaving. His eyes blinked rapidly as if he was trying to wake up from a nightmare. The black thorns that sprout from my fingertips from time to time when I killed humans faintly covered his face, pulsating beneath the skin.

Edward brushed away the fae's hair, revealing rounded ears. I squinted. No, not rounded. Bloodied at the top. "They—"

"Have been cut, yes," Edward said. "I hate those bloody pointy ears, don't you? I found him in Vietnam, helping humans. Why would they do that?" Edward cupped the fae's jaw, almost in a caress. "Do they feel something?"

Feel. "I have no idea," I said.

Edward squeezed, and the fae trembled, eyes darting everywhere, pleading. The fae gasped, and his hands clawed at Edward's grasp. The Alpha parted his lips in ecstasy—the same way he had when killing my men—clean nails digging into the fae's flesh.

I'd never seen a fae in a weakened state. Always strong and tough, the bastards. Seeing one like this made me feel . . . good. Like a cat giving the final strike to a dying rat.

Foam slipped from the fae's lips, and thick beads of sweat rolled down his cheeks. Black thorns spread from the touch of Edward's fingernails over the fae's skin, and the previous ones throbbed, feeding on the Alpha's energy.

"Do you know they're immortal?" Edward said. "They can't be killed by natural means." He gave a cruel grin. "Good thing we're not natural."

Yes.

"Yes," Edward echoed my beast, gaze focused on his prey. "He's strong and tries to fight it. But he can't." He cupped the fae's face with his other hand, curiosity brightening his eyes as I'd seen in men while inflecting pain to their own kind. "He's not begging for his life to end because he doesn't understand his life is mine now. I might call him Minho."

Naming him like a pet.

Préachta within pinched my chest. I clenched my jaw and stepped forward. This should not be.

"Enough," I commanded.

"Enough?" Edward didn't take his gaze off the fae, clearly enjoying what I did not. "You aren't a fae lover perchance, are you?"

"No," I said deadpan. What was the matter with me? Fae were our enemy, and I should hate them as Anord advised. Aye, I despised their sight.

"Good. Finish the job." Edward removed his hands.

The black thorns vanished gradually from the prisoner's skin. The fae staggered, hair plastered to his skull.

Shen removed my bindings, and I clenched and unclenched my fists to get my blood moving. "Is this some sort of bradaí initiation?" I asked.

Edward waved a hand. "Sort of. Prove yourself one. If you can, that is."

I glanced at Shen. He stood a few feet stoically behind. No sniggers. Nothing.

Once, my family and I had captured a fae. Kara had tried to hurt her, yet nothing at all like Edward had done here and, in the end, we only annoyed her. She'd escaped shortly after, mostly unscathed.

Energy condensed in the pit of my stomach, like a shark in a blood frenzy, then spurted to my chest, arms, and toward my fingers. *Préachta* quivered and cooled the frenzy, exactly how it'd happened with that captured fae. I hadn't touched the fae then, but none of my family noticed in their lust to hurt the creature.

I'd failed then. A mere half-bradaí yet to show his worth to our creator.

My jaw clenched. I could sense Edward watching me. Sizing me up.

My fingers twitched and, drowning the cold sensation, 1 latched them around the fae's neck. His eyes widened with fear as the energy burst into him. A jolt of ecstasy coursed through my cold veins, and the power increased and hissed.

"Yes, Irish," Edward whispered, "keep going."

Better than bedding a woman, the empowering sensation took over. Darkness swirled within me like a pit of hissing snakes. My vision dimmed. Everything blurred except the fae in front of me. The power inside me found his—silvery energy that was fading. Like a bright, pure river meeting a torrent of putrid waters. I knew with certainty Edward had been trying to kill him for some time because of the foul energy already present. It was as though the fae's inner system had been fighting Edward and still retained some strength.

Destroy it.

The fae's energy twinkled. Something else lurked behind it. A bright globe that blinded me. My energy seeped into it, tendrils of black bradaí essence crushing his core. So easy to kill a human, and so hard to crush a fae.

And then . . . A gasp. An awareness, as though Anord himself watched.

Pride swelled in my chest. I would prove to my god I was worthy.

The fae was losing the fight, and he knew it. "*Kill me,*" he whispered in my head. "*Please, I beg thee.*"

By the Morrígan, I would.

The awareness increased. Curiosity. Greed.

Préachta seized my chest, and the river surged, hiding the energy orb.

My darkness recoiled, angry like wasps trying to find an outlet but trapped in the dark.

Something was wrong. I could feel it.

Forgetting about the orb, I focused on pouring in more dark energy. My power rammed the fae's core like a Spanish galley. The fae's face turned into a rictus of agony, his weak hands trying to swat mine away.

The fae collapsed, clearly unable to resist. I couldn't sense his silvery energy anymore. He was dead.

A dead immortal creature.

"Well done, Irish," Edward exclaimed and clapped my back. The smile on his lips was absent in his glare. "And here I thought you didn't have it in you. Perhaps you could even be my first mate, yes?"

Shen stared at me, surprise reflected in his eyes. The night didn't let me gauge his expression, but something in his rigid posture, in his eyes not leaving mine, made me wonder if it was unusual for a bradaí to kill a fae so fast.

The awareness retreated and left a void.

Anord wasn't happy, I knew. Why? I'd successfully killed a fae. I was no longer a wee bradaí.

Yet, I had failed in something. And I had to find out what.

Present Day

"Why didn't you ever tell me that?" Kara asked.

"I was in the dark, believing Minho had died, until I became Ed's first mate and found him on his ship. He demanded I not tell anyone, so the rumors of the malfunctioned bradaí remained. We tried to replicate it later." The white-haired fae, Aghna, came to my memories. "But that fae died like the rest."

"Is that why Minho hates you so much?"

"That and because of the opium trade."

"Let me understand this. You used our *dorcha* to kill him like we all do, but you went deeper and crushed that orb of light."

"Aye."

"That's it? Fae turned to bradaí?" She snapped her fingers, distrust reflecting on her eyes.

"I thought about this a great deal back in the day, but it's now that I'm telling you that it's becoming clear to me. Edward must have done something else."

"Still, we bradaís were created by Anord. He was born fae."

"That's why he's just a half-fledge bradaí. *Dorcha* is what reigns in him, not light. A bradaí is ruled by *dorcha* . . ." I left the sentence unfinished and waved my hand for her to connect the dots.

"Thus, he's now an honorary bradaí. Why aren't there more of them?"

I shrugged. "No idea. Whatever Edward did, he never said."

"How many did you kill after that? Fae, I mean."

I glanced at my hands. "Not many."

"Did you do the same with those?"

"No."

She stared at me, hard. "How many fae have you killed, Doyle? Give me a number."

Trust. Hell, it was hard. My first natural impulse was to lie, but we knew each other too well. "Two. Minho, which I didn't really kill, and I helped Edward with another one."

"What happened to that fae?"

The white-haired fae with the caramel skin—Aghna. "She died."

She pondered about that, then said, "I'd never seen an orb. Heck, I'd never seen anything like you described. And evidently Anord is fine with Minho, so why hasn't Edward done more like him? He should have a small army of Minho's at his beck and call."

I opened my mouth, then promptly shut it.

"I'll tell you why, little brother. It was *you* who converted Minho. That's why Edward's obsessed with you."

Again, I opened my mouth, but there was nothing I could say.

Her eyes were ablaze, and I knew more questions I was not prepared to answer would come.

"Enough sharing, Kara."

I plunged the sword back into the soil with more force than I intended. How could I have converted Minho without knowing?

Edward wanted me back as his first mate. Anord didn't destroy me despite my nascent feelings for Ryanne.

I scowled and glowered at the valley where the fae had Ryanne. Anord telling me I was defective.

What else was afoot?

TWENTY-EIGHT

Ryanne

The taigh barely showed behind me as I jogged, lost among the leafy foliage and the dark gray clouds whirling above, promising more rain. The fountains shot water jets at the rhythm of the sweet, melodious singing of unseen beings. Patches of bright red entwined with happy yellow and dull green. It was always amazing how Cuidi could change the season at her whim.

Bricius flew right beside me. "Faster, faster, faster," he mumbled. "We're almost there, yes, yes, yes."

I sped up, sprinting for the last stretch, the exhilaration of exercise pumping through my veins. I shouted in defiance, fist raised as I crossed the finish line—two giant bushes with fuchsia colors.

"Well done, Ryanne!" Bricius's chest puffed with pride.

"Yeah," I panted, hands on my knees. "Don't know how this will help us find Titus."

"It helps to clear your mind of worry, yes, yes, yes."

I straightened and stretched to the side. "There's that." Sweat coated me despite the colder temperature. "But we need to come up with a plan."

We strolled toward the taigh, me taking deep breaths to return my heart's beat to its usual rhythm, Bricius bobbing and zigzagging. I *was* getting stronger. This past week, Bricius and I had been running around the gardens, and I'd tried to do some kickboxing, even tried to replicate Peter's movements when he trained.

"The Lady is about to call for you." He looked up to the tower.

"How do you know?"

"I can sense her focus on you, yes, yes, yes."

"About time." I hadn't seen Cuidi or Peter since the lake incident. That wasn't odd; for them a few days were like an hour to me. That's why time was different in this realm, due to their time conception.

Still, I usually didn't stay more than a week because my body couldn't take the energy of this place. I usually felt a bit heavier at the end of my stay. Curiously now I felt lighter. Most likely due to the increment of my fae power.

"*Ryanne,*" a lyrical voice sang in my head. "*Welcome home.*"

I turned my head to see a dryad peeking behind one of the oaks—Aine, the real one that I'd named my power after.

Her long, fine greenish hair moved like thin branches stirred by the wind, her terracotta skin and big, oak-brown eyes blended with the leaves covering her body, patched together like a quilt. Dryads were thought to be spirits of trees, but in reality, they favored oaks—oaks were to dryads what water was to nymphs.

The ethereal being smiled, then disappeared in a flurry of leaves—one of the things I loved about this place.

A place that could be no longer if bradaís kept killing fae.

"Aine just greeted me," I said, pensive.

"Your power?" Bricius furrowed his little brow.

"No, no, the real dryad."

"I didn't hear her," he said, looking this way and that.

"In my head."

"Oh!" His orange eyes grew big. "You could hear her!"

"And Zadora too. Interesting." It was. I'd never heard Aine talk before. The dryad, that is. Hm, maybe I should give my fae power a different name.

At the end of the path, Lhotto strolled toward us. "Heya, Ryanne," he said when he was at earshot. "My Lady Cuidigtheach is expecting you in her quarters."

Bricius's chest puffed again. "See? I told you!"

"Thanks, Lhotto."

"Sure thing." He shifted his weight from foot to foot and cleared his throat.

"What is it?"

"Been meaning to ask you, if you don't mind. What happened with the dude pirate? I was worried sick, but everyone here was freezing."

"What?"

"You know, not worried."

"*Chillin*'s the word you want." I smiled.

He scratched his head. "What's the difference? They're both cold."

"You're right, say freezing if you prefer."

"So what about him? Did he get his due? Because next time I see him, I'll punch him right in that mocking face of his." He mimicked a punch in the air while his eerie whitish-blue eyes darkened.

"Lhotto, he's my friend now," I said softly. "Maybe next time you're in town you come with us and watch a movie, all right?"

"Ah, Ryanne! Have you forgotten how he escaped?" He grabbed the pommel of his sword and squeezed as if imagining Titus's head. "Won't forgive the dude easily." He pivoted on his heels and marched away.

I stood there, watching his back. How was I going to reconcile both fae and bradaí? I was the darned bridge.

It was clear to me what my path was—not just to find the spark in Titus or any bradaí for that matter—to smooth the road ahead. This was the perfect time to talk to Cuidi and see what she had in store for me.

Peter waited at the tower's entrance.

"I owe you an apology," he said as if the nymphs' incident happened recently. Which to him, surely it was.

"Nah, don't worry. I was able to defeat Zadora on my own."

"I knew you would. No, I'm referring to our talk in the hut."

My jaw slackened. Had he pondered about what I said about Titus?

"You are no *cailin*."

Oh. *That.*

"I shall escort you to my Lady's quarters."

He waved a hand forward, and we strolled under the trees. A fresh breeze swirled leaves around while sweet song surrounded us like in a concert—a song coming from invisible beings.

We walked down a hallway between towers, with broad arches that opened onto a garden on one side and the lake on the other.

"A suggestion," he said, gaze focused forward. "You ought to learn not to show your emotions because you give your enemy the advantage. Let them guess."

"You mean when I was at the lake?"

"It applies in any case. When you showed me your memories back at the hut, I saw your expression as well. Your fear."

The hairs on the back of my neck rose. I twisted around to glimpse two pairs of odd yellow eyes lost between the leafed trees.

"What are those beings?" I asked.

Peter turned, but there was nothing to see anymore. My gaze met his questioning one for a second.

"Could have been anything," he said nonchalantly.

He took me to an adjacent hall on the first floor, where Cuidi's private garden was. A draft of warm air blew through small arched openings into the area. Candleholders adorned the austere stone walls.

Peter waved a hand to a small opening at the end of the hall, one that would take me to the garden.

Once I stepped outside, Peter retreated into the shadowy hall.

The garden was full of light, with the scent of pine mixed with roses, a contrast with the stark hall outside. It was supposed to be an inner garden, but size was deceiving—a willow tree stood nearby, its branches reaching wide. Creatures chirped and twitted in sweet, melancholy notes, and the sound of a brook mingled harmonically, as if they were in a concert hall. The temperature felt perfect, neither cold nor warm.

I wiped my clammy hands over my skirts. This was it. My opportunity to convince Cuidi that I should return to Titus, wherever he was.

Cuidi sat at a circular marble table beneath the willow tree, her long jet-black hair partially pinned at the top with the same forget-me-nots that were braided in my hair, and the rest of it cascading over her shoulders. Her dark, wide-set eyes looked at me unblinking.

"You must be hungry. Eat." She waved a slender olive hand at a cut-glass bowl, full of fruits from this land. Fruits I'd never been allowed to eat.

"Are you going to let me eat your fruit now?" I asked, surprised.

She nodded.

I picked a black, hard-shelled fruit from the bowl and sat down.

Cuidi cocked her head. "Not that one," she said. "There are beings here who don't show themselves, and this fruit would open your consciousness."

I let go of the fruit. I didn't want to see what bumped in the dark.

"Try this one instead." Her fine fingers seized what, at first glance, was a bunch of purple grapes, though their bright color proclaimed their fae origin.

I accepted her offering and bit one. "Mmmm!" It exploded like a concert of flavors in my mouth, one of them strongly like cherry pie. I greedily ate one after another, as I felt light, weightless.

"Wait." Cuidi laughed. "Your body is not used to this fruit and must be done little by little. Remember how you felt when Bricius gave you our gift."

"It does the same? Open doors that we keep closed?" I squinted at the last little fruit.

"Our fruit helps us to stay in this realm. But you humans are like a horse with blinders. You cannot see or understand more than what is placed in front of you."

I sighed. Sometimes it was hard to understand fae, but it was harder for them to understand *us*. I observed the tiny grape-like fruit as if it was something magical.

"So this helps to open my perception?"

"Something of the sort. But too much of it could make you insane, with no ability whatsoever to judge what reality is and what fantasy is. It's better you eat little of it."

Ah. No wonder they'd never let me taste their fruit.

The bright fruit throbbed like it had a little heart. Titus's face reflected on the skin, his aqua eyes staring at me anxiously. I threw the fruit away, wiping my trembling hands on my dress.

Cuidi waved her hand in a dismissive gesture. "What you have seen, may or may not be real. Don't give importance to it."

Easier said than done.

"It's time for you to tell me what happened with the bradaí."

"You were right; they can be redeemed."

She steepled her hands, her eyes shiny black pearls.

I talked about the time on the ship, what happened in Japan, Edward, and Sanders. Unlike Peter, her expression was peaceful, and her head tilted to one side like an eager student before their favorite teacher.

I withheld the most important part, wanting to hear her thoughts first and what was her impression of Titus.

"Your fae power helped to control his darkness, then," she said.

"His beast, what Anord imbued in them to have thoughts of destruction."

"Thus, he is aware of the energy within him." She cocked her head like a swan would. "Such a riveting revelation; I'd believed they were mindless of such influence."

"Titus knows. What I saw inside the sea is what balances him. And what I have inside me helps him even more, to quell the beast."

"Tell me about the spark."

And it was then when I talked about the underwater experience and how I felt his raw energy reacting to mine. How Titus apologized and began to change.

"I sensed something while inside the water, and I thought that was it."

Her eyes shone with excitement. "Tell me exactly what you felt."

"When I saw him enjoying the submersion, my touch of fae reacted to his energy within. And a flickering light shone. You said I'd feel it deep in my being, deep in my own soul."

"Yes. A bright orb of the purest energy, filling you with joy."

"It filled me with joy, yes, but I didn't see that bright orb, just that elusive light. I thought it was the spark at first, but now I'm not so sure."

She lowered her head, dark lashes shadowing her defined cheeks. "Come with me," she said, her expression not hinting at any emotions or thoughts.

I followed her in silence. Lances of light shot though the hulking dark green-leafed trees.

Cuidi glided through the grass, her dress trailing behind her. She stopped under the shade of a cedar-like tree. The black fruit hung from its branches.

"Between bradaís and fae there's a long feud, as you know," Cuidi said. "It's not the first time a human who has a touch of fae within them has fallen in the middle of it."

"Fallen? Or have you pushed us to them?" I furrowed my brow. "Titus told me that my predecessors died before their time."

"The question is, can this pirate change if you are not by his side? Is he redeemable on his own?"

"I believe he is. He began to change with me. But it's not done."

"Hm." She gazed into the distance, thoughtful. "You have been compromised, though. Those humans you spoke of, the people who want to analyze you, to understand our kingdom." She sneered. "As if they could. If we were to give a gift to them, their heads would explode before they even knew what happened to them."

Cuidi reached out, taking one of the large fruits hanging from the nearby branches. With a small flick of her wrist, she tore the fruit. Her nails dug into it, peeling the rough opening. She carefully extracted a piece of white pulp and placed it in her mouth.

A little gnome ran behind a tree, and with a jump worthy of an Olympic gymnast, snatched the fruit from her hands, grabbing his hat without stopping until he disappeared behind a bush.

"These gnomes are crazy about the fruit," Cuidi said with a smile that made me realize she'd expected it. Perhaps she'd taken it down for the little gnome.

"Titus still needs my help," I said as I twisted a branch of a bush.

"He needs to prove he can change without you."

"Yet it's my path. One I took with my eyes open." I didn't wish to talk about my feelings, certain she wouldn't understand them. But I had to put my foot down. "I *can* help him."

"Our error has been that we left humans too long with bradaís, and they all died before their time. There was only one who remained alive for longer than we hoped, somehow escaping Anord's notice. In the end, he was murdered too. I do not seek that for you."

"And did he find the spark?"

"He forgot his purpose. He was too young, merely ten summers when that bradaí found him, and took him in."

"Which one?" I asked.

"One who was created in that land you humans call Russia."

Sergei, then. Was that Ivan, the one whose murder caused the rift between Titus and Sergei? "What happened?" I asked. Cuidi was more talkative than usual, and I had to seize the moment.

She stared at me for a few seconds, as if considering whether to indulge my curiosity or not. Then she nodded and said, "The boy was an orphan, and this bradaí took him in like a parent would. The boy's need for a parent was stronger than his love for us, and he relished in the small amount of fae power inside him for a longer life. You are the only one who has continued with your purpose."

With that, she looked away, her tell that it was all I would get from her. Something nagged me. I'd been following their rules and instructions to a T, and yet I felt they kept me on the sideline.

"You have passed the test," Cuidi said.

"What test?" I asked, confused.

"Your touch of fae is not a touch anymore. It has evolved." She stretched her hand, palm toward me as if sensing the energy. "Your body accepted our food without repercussions."

Let them guess, Peter had said. He wasn't referring to the fae, but I had to practice, right?

So Keep Calm and Fool the Lady.

"I'm quite delighted," I said. I resisted the urge to pat myself.

"You shall stay here in Tír D'aois, for another turn of the sun—"

"*What?* A year here!" She wanted me to stay inside the walls for a full year? "Why? I thought I'd return home in a week or so."

"This is your home."

"Uh, yeah, but you said I could visit my human friends and family, and I want to."

"Not yet. Your fae power needs to anchor to the land for it to grow."

"I can return later."

Cuidi stared at me, and I cursed inwardly. So much for trying to fool her.

"You want to return to find the bradaí."

Time to remove the gloves.

"Yes," I said, chin up. "You know I haven't finished my task. I have yet to find what you asked me to. Let me finish."

"Your power isn't strong enough for you to recognize the spark, let alone ignite it."

"I almost did."

"You shouldn't have doubts then, thus you need to practice more."

My lips pinched. Her voice had that final tone I'd heard so many times before. It'd be utterly useless to try to change her mind.

"Your fae power grew too fast in such a short time, and you need to slow down, let it take root here. Let it breathe. You don't want to rush it, otherwise it shall grow unstable. Once you've balanced it, then you might return to Tír na Donna to establish your humanity, to avoid losing it altogether."

I looked away. Yeah, that was important, but returning to Titus was more important. Why couldn't she see that?

She stepped closer and reached out. Her fingertips skimmed over the line of my jaw. "You are indeed reckless."

"That isn't such a bad thing. That's why Fé Erie choose me for this."

Cuidi dropped her hand, then turned her back. I was being dismissed.

I sank to one knee, teeth gnashing, and bowed my head. "Thank you, my Lady. Until the light of the Hawthorn brings us together again." I might not like the outcome of this visit, but manners were manners.

"And so it shall," she said without turning.

I stormed out of the garden just to find myself face to face with Peter, waiting by the opening.

"Since you'll be staying, I could help you train instead of Bricius."

About to protest, I clamped my mouth shut. That wasn't such a terrible idea. In fact, it was perfect while I conjured a plan to return to Titus.

"Would you? I'm no warrior, but there must be a way I can defend myself."

Peter grinned. "If you're so determined."

He framed my face with his hands and pressed his lips to my forehead. An icy cold took possession of my body, starting at his lips, down my throat, and freezing my chest. I couldn't breathe. My vision blurred and dizziness took hold of me.

Feihnum, my fae power sang, mixing with the new one.

And the cold feeling vanished. It was now a delicious sensation that made my limbs like gossamer.

I opened my eyes, not remembering having closed them. Luminous energy covered Peter, making him look ethereal.

"Gallchobhair," I murmured, blinking. Naming him Peter had been irreverent. He was no ordinary fae.

"Peter." He beamed. "I'll always be Peter for you."

"I can't call you Peter," I stammered, ashamed of the familiarity I'd used with this powerful being.

"I gave you permission, and that's how I'll be called. Peter."

The light faded, and he appeared as before. Gallch . . . Gallzo . . . I scrunched my nose. Now that the light vanished, I couldn't pronounce his name adequately.

"What did you do to me?"

"I enhanced the fae energy within you. Yet you need to keep working on it. I shall help you."

"That new power . . . Will it help me against the bradaís?"

Will it help me against Edward?

Even though I was in a sanctuary against bradaís, the temperature dropped and my vision blackened for a moment.

"*I* will help you against them," Peter said, chest puffed. "Your gift might help to thwart them for a moment in such a case. That is why you need to keep on working with our gift. But make no mistake: it isn't a new power. I only strengthened what was already there. A new layer, if you will."

I pressed a tanned hand to my chest, nothing like the pale hue I had before, thanks to the time spent on the ship. It contrasted with the coral hue of my dress.

I felt like a pawn, but whether I was still on the board or pushed aside, I couldn't tell.

Peter walked down the hall, and I stood alone, whispers from an unknown language reaching me, a song without words.

Be clear of heart, be clear of mind.

Fé Erie's warning as she pressed a hand on my chest, my power responding to her touch. Cuidi's warning that it'd grown too fast. Did I misunderstood Fé Erie's warning the first time?

My humanity. When Cuidi told me the truth about why they needed a human, she said that my fae power would grow, making it difficult to interact with humans for a while.

Humans, not bradaís.

Titus was out of reach. He'd been able to escape from here because the Lady let him. There was no way in hell he could get back in. And there was no way I could get out of here.

Not without the Lady's permission, and she didn't trust me to carry on the task. A year here, trapped?

My fists shook. A fire blazed inside me as it never had before, consuming me.

I sprinted toward the oak forest, wanting nothing more than to dampen the anger eating my insides. Thick roots and small rocks littered my path, slowing my pace until I reached a small clearing. The drizzle returned, and thunder rumbled in the distance.

"Arghhh!"

I threw my fists in the air and paced around like a caged troll. The nightmare where Titus bled to death played again and again in my head. I plopped next to an oak and leaned my head on my raised knees, raindrops falling steadily on my head.

"*Do not despair.*"

The soft, lilting voice made me lift my head. Aine, the dryad, was sitting next to me, her expression peaceful and friendly.

"*Do not despair,*" she repeated without opening her lips, placing a slim hand on my shoulder. Her long, green hair fluttered around her thin face.

I blinked. "What?"

She rose in a graceful movement, her sheer clothes billowing over her slender body. Then, she spun like a ballerina in a music box and embedded within the oak behind me.

Great. More confusion.

The stress and worry slowly abated, leaving me space to breathe. I closed my eyes and rested my head on the oak's trunk. As the dryad said, I wasn't going to despair. Titus'd said that only Edward had been able to kill another bradaí, and he'd survived Edward's attack. Survived Sander's torture and even Peter's mistreating of him back when he was a prisoner here.

He was fine now, I knew.

His intense kisses barged into my memory, the way his lips took mine, claiming them for himself.

His pained expression when Peter took me away from him.

Nothingness consumed me. I hid my face in my hands, sobs lost in the sound of the wind whirling around the oak's branches. The rain intensified, but it was like a caress, easing my pain inside.

I let the water soak me until my limbs numbed. The rain stopped and birds chirped sweetly above. A bright rainbow appeared on the gray sky, and I smiled—a beautiful reminder that light always conquered darkness.

Heck. It was up to *me* to decide *my* fate, not the fae's obscure rules.

Not Cuidi's mistrust of what I could do now.

I returned toward the outside passageway. Giant anemone-like plants bordered the path. The strange plants expelled greenish, innocuous vapors.

I thought about what Cuidi said about the spark, how it should be ignited. She didn't say that at first, but perhaps she didn't think I could. That could be the missing puzzle.

Odd yellow eyes glanced back at me from behind the plants, and a rustle of leaves showed a pair of hairy arms. I stopped, trying to remember if I'd seen a creature like that before. It reminded me of a humanoid chimpanzee, jaw protruding below tiny beady eyes.

It pointed a finger at me, and garbled noise echoed in my head, like a foreign language I was far from grasping.

Laughter rang not far away. Several fae with linked arms approached the path. I glanced back at the foliage. The creature had vanished. I shrugged. Surely one of many that visit the taigh.

To avoid the fae, I retraced my steps and took another path, flanked by statues. The Erlking grinned malevolently; his huge antlers, long beard, and snow boots gave him a menacing look. The two growling dire wolves flanking the statue didn't improve his PR.

It was just a statue. Stone made, just like my heart if Cuidi and Peter managed to keep Titus at bay.

TWENTY-NINE

Titus

The forest was quiet after the rain. Only birds chirped above our heads. Clouds parted, and a bright rainbow appeared. My nostrils flared, and my breathing increased its rhythm at the sight. Leprechauns! They must be up and about, hiding some of their gold. I exhaled loudly and leaned back upon the tree, forcing myself to relax. The bark was smooth like polished wood, cold to the touch. Just like gold. Anord's beard, I missed gold as much as I missed Ryanne.

Kara plopped next to me and pointed to the rainbow. "Want to find some little rascals?" She grinned. "You loved to chase them."

"Aye. Blasted little green devils hate the sight of me."

We shared a laugh. The memories of those times when the three of us worked together suspended like the mist around us. Other memories flashed in my mind, of that time when Sergei and I went to the Far East.

"You sent me to Japan," I said.

"I did? When?"

"1910."

"Ah." She clicked her tongue. "Ryukyu. The monks."

"Aye. That's where Edward went after me."

"Did he?"

"I had a lover. A woman with a touch of fae."

Kara nodded. "Seems that lot keep appearing to us."

"It's no coincidence, aye, and Edward suddenly appearing wasn't either."

"Why does he do that?"

"Corsica. Do you remember the dead woman, reaching out to Luc?"

We traded a look, and a nasty feeling clenched my gut. Ryanne might be safer behind fae walls than with me. No. We'd be vigilant for not only fae and bradaís, but for anyone.

I had many safe houses. We could be together.

But Kara had been right. Edward should be confronted and defeated before that happened.

"I've been thinking about how to take Edward down."

"You're in?" she said, eyes brightened.

"Aye. If us three—"

"Three?" She tilted her head, trying hard not to smile.

I grunted. "I'm not sure if that hardheaded Russian would ever listen to me, albeit it'd be harder if it's just the two of us. No bradaí has sided against another except when I tried to take Edward down, and that rebellion dissipated with a betrayal. We've been too cowardly to face him since."

"What's your plan?"

I clenched my hand in a fist and willed *dorcha* to it. "His *dorcha* is too powerful. If we attack him with our *dorcha* combined, we might have an opportunity. We could use a goblin's dagger to finish the deed."

"I'd never used *dorcha* against any bradaí."

"It wasn't meant to attack us. But it can injure."

I told her about Edward's last attack and how I thwarted him, if even a little.

"There you go, little brother. Now we have a plan. Get Sergei on board and blast that bastard Alpha out from this world."

"We must have him alone, without Minho."

"Then once you regain Ryanne, we find Sergei."

"Aye." I sighed. "That part will be as difficult as trying to kill Edward with our *dorcha.*"

"We should ask Shen. The more *dorcha*, the merrier."

"I'd rather have only us three." Shen had always sided with me on the surface, but he was a bradaí. He might have been pretending, for all I knew.

She clenched her fist. "Killing a bradaí with our *dorcha*," she whispered. "It can work. It kills fae, after all." Her eyes brightened. "We can do this."

I was regaining Kara's trust. Being with her sparked memories of our time together when she and Sergei were my only family.

The only ones I could trust, besides Ryanne. Perhaps I could regain that again and be whole.

Whole.

I wished I could rip the beast away and find out who I was. Would I take glee in killing if I didn't have it? Would I stop fighting against the gold allure? I'd never know.

Anord doomed us from our first breath of life.

THIRTY

Ryanne

I threw a glance around the spacious and elegant place that was my room. What was my position here? Just a darned pawn they could move whenever they pleased? The subsided anger returned with a vengeance and my lips tightened.

"Dammit!"

Bricius zoomed inside the window. "Are we leaving?"

"No, Bug, Cuidi says I have to stay here because . . ." I jerked my head at him. "Bug! You can open portals!" I paced around like a maddened ogre. "You can open portals, and we need to return."

He shook his head. "I cannot without my Lady's permission."

"Oh," I said, dejected. Nothing happened without the Lady's permission. "But . . ." I lifted a hand.

"I don't like that look on your face, no, no, no."

"You can open portals *outside* the taigh."

He widened his big orange eyes. "I can, but—"

"We can find ourselves a capall. I think I might be able to call one now." I hoped.

"It's dangerous."

"Danger is my middle name now," I said, thumping a hand on my hip and throwing it to the side as I'd seen Kara do.

Bricius rolled his eyes.

"C'mon. I need to return. You know why."

He sighed. "Fine. But I have no idea what I'm doing, no, no, no."

"We leave at first light. No, wait, before. We need to slip by."

"And how do you plan to trick the daighs?"

I slumped my shoulders. Right, how the heck could we bypass them?

"Wait. I have a plan."

A flimsy one, but it was all I had.

Gray light shrouded the central courtyard. One daigh stood guard, his orange-flame hair flowing free in the soft breeze. His armor shone like mercury over white robes and red leather boots. Not Lhotto or Otto, but some other. Morka, a daigh I hadn't interacted with much.

Which suited my plan better.

"Ryanne," Morka said formally. No *cailin,* not anymore.

"Hi!"

"What do you require?" He didn't look suspicious that I was strolling before dawn.

I bit my lip as if unsure. "Do you know about Zadora? The nymph the Lady turned into a silver fish?"

He grinned. "Yes. That was quite a feat!"

I had the suspicion he wasn't talking about the fish, but how I fought the nymph. Warmth spread in my chest.

"Do you think I can see her?" I craned my neck toward the direction of the lake outside.

"Why?"

And here was where my human nature, the incomprehensible one for any fae, played a role. "I want to make sure she's fine. She's a nymph. She can't help it, can she?"

Morka shrugged. "Sure," he said, opening the gate. "But don't take long. I'll be watching from outside."

That hadn't been unexpected, though my human side was hoping he wouldn't. This wasn't the first time I'd done this, always wanting to explore beyond the walls, and it was safe if I didn't get too far.

It wasn't as if the Erlking was waiting outside to snatch any stranded fae. Safe as a taigh.

I peeped outside, my steps unsure. "What if she thinks it's a trap and doesn't come out?"

"No problem, I'll leave the gate ajar, and you call me if you have any trouble."

Not yell like a human, but "call" as a fae would do—Cuidi used otherworldly means to call them. Perhaps it was how Aine, the dryad, had been communicating with me.

Huh.

Muted-green grass spread outside the walls. The lake at my left was a gray shape in a gray world.

And here I was going, walking toward the nymphs.

This time of morning they should be tired, about to sleep away in the bottom of the lake. Hopefully, a few were still up and about, especially when sensing a human on the shore.

Sure enough, a silver head broke the surface.

"Rynny! So glad you came to see me!"

"I see you're back to nymph," I said, making sure my feet were away from the water line.

"Oh yes," she purred, "and you're here. Come, come, and let's play together." She was already half out of the water, her movements slow and sensual, her skin no longer crocodile-like but smooth and luscious. White algae covered her curves leaving nothing to the imagination.

Her full lips puckered in a kiss, and she threw a lazy hand toward me. Lilies surrounded me with their sweet smell.

The feeling of those soft lips on mine made me step forward. Yes, it'd be nice to play with her in the water, feel her caresses. My eyes should grow wide as she dragged me below.

It made sense.

Cold energy covered me completely and rooted me before my feet touched the water. And I saw her as she was—a deceiver, a succubus with crocodile-skin and fish-rotten smell.

The lake held no mystery. Nymphs were gathered below the water-line, watching in anticipation and giggling.

"Look at the silly human!" I heard inside my head.

"Oh, this is going to be so much fun! How long 'til she stops breathing?"

"I can't wait!"

"Wait. Something's wrong."

I grinned and cocked my head, my hips to the side. "Oh no," I purred back. "That is not how games go, Zadora."

She pouted and crossed her arms across her algae-dress. "That's not fair. You're no longer only human."

Whispers of discontent came from the lake as Zadora turned and splashed back, her long tail iridescent silver.

My smile grew wider until her words reached my brain.

You're no longer only human.

I staggered back, Aine coiling inside and purring like a well-fed Bandersnatch. It was happy, happier than I'd ever felt it. Without turning back, I sprinted to the forest line.

"Hey!" came Morka's voice from far away.

In my *head*. He was talking *inside* my freaking head.

"Where are you going? Come back!"

Oh, Gods.

"Ryanne," Bricius hissed by my ear. "What are you doing?"

"Don't, Bug," I said through gritted teeth.

Tears welled in my eyes as branches snapped against my arms. It wasn't supposed to go like this. I still had my Return-to-Human card, didn't I? I didn't want to go all fae.

Wasn't this what you've always wanted? a little voice asked inside my head. My own voice.

No! Yes?

My fae power helping me when Minho threw me overboard; feeling like a nymph while defeating Zadora, me purring at Zadora, aware she didn't have a hold on me anymore.

Because I was turning fae.

I stopped, panting, my hands on my knees, my eyes shut.

"What is wrong, Ryanne?" Bricius asked near me. "You did well, yes, yes, yes, but now the Lady has been notified and they'll come after us!"

"I don't care," I breathed.

"I cannot open a portal here." He lifted my chin with both hands, and I opened my eyes. He was so close he was blurred.

Or maybe it was the tears.

"Your pirate, remember? He's waiting in Seattle."

"I don't want to turn fae, Bug."

"What?"

"I don't want to lose myself. I don't want to be anyone else. I want to be me."

"Can we talk about this later? This will be your only chance, yes, yes, yes."

That took me out of my stupor. Right. Keep Calm, and worry about being fae later.

Voices from the taigh carried over. I straightened and looked back.

"Run!" Bricius said.

And I did. I dashed through the underbrush, sensing when I had to jump and when I had to duck, knowing when to contort my body to pass between trees without breaking stride.

I'd known this forest for years, and I was an accomplished jogger and agile enough, but I'd never been *this* good.

Eyes followed me. I glanced around but saw nothing.

Capall, I had to call one. I pictured the wild horse-wolf animal and said its name in my head three times, hoping it would work.

We kept running to the eastern side of the valley until we reached a dirt road weaving through a sea of trees growing together, their tall and leafy branches creating an autumn-colored dome above our heads.

I couldn't shake the sensation someone was watching us. Up in the trees, dark shapes with odd-yellow eyes watched us.

"What are those beings up on the trees?" I asked without stopping, squinting to try to get a good look at them, but they were like a blur out of the corner of my eye.

"Apelings. But nothing to worry about, no, no, no. We're still in milady's territory. They're harmless."

I nodded, yet my goosebumps remained. Images of daighs behind me and someone else. Someone stronger and powerful.

Peter.

My apprehension grew with each tree we passed; every rock seemed to hide a danger. I seldom came through this part of the valley, so I didn't know when the protection ended.

The image of one capall burst forward in my mind. Was one responding to my call?

The trees at our right vanished as we climbed a winding path. The sound of water gurgled from the ravine below. A warm drizzle fell, blurring the colors around us.

We reached a clearing at the top. A light mist covered the ground to our left. The forest was so dense I couldn't see beyond the first row of trees. Without being told, I felt the protection of the Lady fading at my back. We had reached our spot!

A wild capall trotted before us, the one I pictured. I stiffened.

Perhaps it was because of its jet-black fur, unusual for a capall.

Or maybe its fiery golden eyes. The eyes of a pooka.

Pookas didn't belong to either side, fae or Erlking—they were mischievous spirits who loved playing tricks on humans. They were amazing shapeshifters, usually rabbits or horses.

I met one recently, when Titus had tried to kidnap me and Peter thwarted his attempt, taking Titus as a prisoner to the taigh. Pookas were gifted prophesiers too. So it was no coincidence one stood before me now.

"Quick, Bricius," I panted. "Your portal."

The bug spread his hands in the fae way and moved them like painting an oval.

The pooka stopped before us and grinned.

"You're not using that, are you?" It gestured toward the newly formed portal with its head.

I dashed to the portal. The pooka vanished from where it was and teleported itself into my path in less than a second where I bumped right into it.

"Bricius!"

"It isn't holding up, no, no, no!"

The portal vanished with a *pop*. Shouts came beneath me.

A young man with pointed ears and jet-black hair rolled on the ground, laughing. The changeling was pulling a prank, the bastard.

"Open another, quick!"

"Oh, he can't," the pooka said, sobering up and rising to his feet, his fiery golden eyes brighter. "We don't want to miss the fun."

Capalls broke behind us, daighs mounted and, yes, Peter. Dammit!

The pooka grinned mischievously then vanished. But unlike before, where he'd been one moment and away the next, I saw him gradually transforming into some sort of ghost or spirit.

It was as if his body traveled through planes of existence in the blink of an eye.

The shouts brought me back to my predicament, and I prepared to dash into the trees.

Before I could do anything, Peter intercepted me, his capall puffing through its nose, ears pinned back. Lhotto and Otto were right behind him and, before I could take a step back, both were at my sides, grasping my arms.

Dammit!

"Ryanne, what were you thinking?" Peter shouted.

Cries bellowed from the trees before us.

Small humanoids burst from the branches. They had longish arms and apelike features. Measuring about five feet, robust and swift, they wore rags over their hairy skin, yellow eyes shining.

The same yellow eyes I saw back at the taigh. These must be apelings.

From one of the trees at our left, Titus landed with a smirk.

THIRTY-ONE

Titus

The Morrigan take all fae to hell and leave them to rot there for eternity.

But it wasn't unexpected. The apelings warned us on time the fae were about to catch Ryanne.

I cast a quick glance to Ryanne, being held by two daighs. Fire blossomed in her eyes, a determination to reach me. I liked that.

Except Gallchobhair had already dismounted and was headed toward me, naked sword in hand, shoulders squared, and chin lifted. The grip on my sword was strong, my determination fierce.

I was not to be deterred. Every cursed being wanted us to part: Edward, Sanders, now the dryshite.

Not anymore.

We bradaís never fared well face to face on level ground against fae. Pretty Boy had already bested me in a similar circumstance, though back then I'd only cared to kidnap Ryanne. This time, certainty that I could best this fae rammed me like a Spanish Galleon.

I am the sea. Inside me lives the storm and the calm altogether.

"Get out of my way, Pretty Boy," I growled, sword pointed at him.

"I warned you, pirate, next time we see each other as enemies."

He'd barely finished those words when he thrust forward.

Bronze clanked on bronze.

The fae struck again, and his blow glanced off my blade. I slashed downward at his waist. In a blur of movement, he slid away and struck at my side.

In another time, he might have hit home. I grunted, whirled, and sliced my sword against his arm.

He jumped back but not fast enough. Now his robe sported a cut.

In another time, I would have smirked and smart-mouthed.

This was not that time.

I went for his throat, my feet nimble over roots and rocks. He counterattacked and slashed my chest without making a dent.

"You've improved, pirate," he said, awe tinting his voice. "But no matter, you shall fall."

Aye, he was fast and undoubtedly superior, but the fire stoked me —a purpose, something I didn't have before.

And he was losing ground.

I am a tsunami. Inside me destruction arises.

A gale seized my arms and an undercurrent my legs. My foot work impeccable. The force of my strikes pushed him toward the ledge of the ravine. His eyes showed uncertainty for the first time.

He parried a blow and lifted his sword. Like it was encased in thick tar, his arm froze.

"What's the matter, Pretty Boy?" I said. "Troll got your—"

My muscles stopped working, the word stuck in my throat.

I couldn't move. My surroundings blurred as if I was seeing everything under water. A figure with fire-red tresses solidified beside Pretty Boy. The mysterious fae. My beast roared, trying to keep me away from her. But only my eyes could move.

She reached out and cupped my cheek. Her touch made my skin numb with cold. Then she slid a hand over my chest and down my left side, just above my hip. She squeezed. Unbearable heat sprouted like boiling tar over bare skin.

She seemed to convey a message with her eyes.

Stay put.

Like I could go anywhere.

Then she leaned toward Pretty Boy and whispered something in his ear, her eyes still not leaving me, then vanished.

What in Anord's hell?

Noise returned and so did the control over my body. I stumbled then regained my footing. "Who's she?"

The dryshite looked at me dumbly. "Did you see her? How could you, pirate *brocach*?" His eyes narrowed. "I'm not going to fall for your lies as Ryanne did."

Bright light streamed from his pores like white lava sprouting from a volcano, his eyes glowing intense green.

By the Morrigan!

I lunged at his neck. He blocked my attempt smoothly.

"No more games, *Aodhán*."

Anord be damned. How could he know?

"This is when you face your creator, *Aodhán*."

"You cannot—"

"I can, *Aodhán*."

At the third mention of my Name, he plunged the sword into my side where the red-haired fae had burned me.

His sword cut my skin effortlessly. Hot pain blinded me.

I staggered and glanced down stupidly. The sword bypassed my usual defense system. No, he couldn't. This wasn't real. Wasn't happening.

A goblin blade, I thought. Albeit it didn't feel like Edward's dagger, not at all. There was no *dorcha* this time. I couldn't feel it inside me.

"This isn't possible." I gasped, seizing his arm with numb fingers.

He drew his sword out before my eyes. I stumbled backward. Then crashed into a tree. I pressed my wound while blood spurted, my fingers soaked.

My sword slipped to the ground. How could he cut me? Why was there was so much blood?

"She-she told you my Name," I breathed.

His marble face came in and out of focus. Pain throbbed in my wound, taking over. A rooted, haunting pain as I had never known, threatened to drown me.

Threatened to kill me.

"My revenge is complete," the dryshite said. "Fé Erie, as I, wanted you dead."

"No, she-she did not."

Could not.

I had felt peace with her. Was it all a hoax? A cruel hoax? The Morrigan piss on all fae!

That bloody bastard Edward had told the truth. An Eadrom Caomhnoir had killed the other bradaís, not him. With effort, I leaned my head on the trunk of a nearby tree and gave a faint laugh. How ironic.

I slid down the bark, my legs unable to hold me up. Cries boomed from somewhere. Ryanne and Homkar came running toward me. Everything blurred but her, her chestnut hair flowing around her. She looked like an angel. I smiled.

The dryshite yelled and lunged at Homkar.

My life slipped through my blood-covered fingers. I struggled to open my eyes. Ryanne, she-she . . . I coughed a thick liquid. A metallic taste lingered on my tongue.

I couldn't tell her how I felt for her.

Feel.

Never more.

THIRTY-TWO

Ryanne

Something inside me broke. Darkness covered me from the tip of my mind to the shaking of my soul.

Blood. Just like in that frigging nightmare. So much blood.

Time slowed.

Fight sounds muffled, slipping away to unconsciousness. Colors disappeared, except red. Bright red gushed from Titus's wound.

He slipped on the trunk, his hands on his bleeding abdomen, a glazed look in his eyes.

Tears blurred my vision as if thousands of tiny water pixies clogged it. With the back of my hand, I wiped them, wishing I could do the same with the fog numbing my heart.

An enraged Homkar fought with Peter, not giving quarter. But Peter, he was a Guardian. He would defeat Homkar too, maybe even kill him.

"Ryanne! Your pirate!"

Bricius's shrill voice brought me back, and I dashed toward Titus.

I tripped on a root and regained my balance, then knelt beside him. Blood bubbled on his left side, his chest rising and falling in an unnatural way as if a heavy burden rested on him. He coughed, his eyes unfocused.

"He doesn't look good, no, no, no." Bricius sounded sick. He didn't like the sight of blood, I recalled numbly.

Shouts resonated dimly in my ears, far away.

"Right, Ryanne," I said in a shaky voice, "stop acting like a wimp."

I shook off my sweater and pressed it against the wound.

Yells boomed in anger. Kara knelt beside us.

"What in Odin's hell! A bloody Eadrom Caomhnoir." Her voice broke. "No, little brother, you can't die. Not you." Her haunted eyes locked on me. "I have to kill him. Odin help me, I'll kill that fae. You got this?"

"Don't kill him, Kara. Only stop him. Please."

She pressed her lips together and thumped a hand on my shoulder. "Just help my brother."

I nodded dazedly, and she jumped to her feet with a deafening cry toward Peter.

I felt Bricius landing on my shoulder. "Bug, make sure Peter doesn't kill everyone. But stay safe, you hear?"

A zoom, and he was gone.

Titus's lips had a bluish tinge. A small pool of blood coalesced next to him. I took a deep breath, controlling my trembling. I kept squeezing the wound. It was stupid; he was going to heal; I shouldn't worry. But then, why was he so pale? Why was there so much blood?

Where were those dark tendrils that heal him? I couldn't feel a thing.

"Look at me." I seized his chin and forced him to fix his gaze on me. "Look at me," I repeated in a softer tone.

"Ryanne," he whispered, eyes glazed.

"Don't try to speak. You'll get better, you hear? You always heal." I tried not to think about the stickiness in my hand, how the cloth was completely soaked.

"Not this time, not . . ." His voice was so weak, I barely heard it. He raised his hand, his lower lip trembling. "I-I can feel it. Death."

I took his bloody hand in mine. "Don't talk. Concentrate on healing. I'll take you to safety." Nothing else mattered. No one would take him away from me.

Could Aine help? I closed my eyes and focused. It sprang forward in my chest, then stood by, expectant.

In my mind, I pushed it toward Titus. But it swirled inside me, confused.

"Dammit, Aine, go to him," I mumbled. "Help him!"

It pulsated once, then vanished.

Gone.

I cursed. It wasn't like with Edward or Sanders. It was just *gone*.

Damn! I tried again. And again.

But no power responded to my call.

"It's too late." His gaze lost focus. His lip stopped trembling. His hand felt heavy, lifeless. His head tilted to one side.

The sounds of the battle raged around me, but everything went quiet.

"No, Titus. No, you-you'll be okay." I cradled him and held his limp head. "You'll be okay, you'll be okay," I repeated again and again, pressing him against me. By reflex, I pressed two fingers to one side of his neck. No pulse.

His chest stopped moving. Titus was still.

The world darkened.

"Don't leave," I whispered, sobbing, knowing he couldn't hear me.

He never would again.

THIRTY-THREE

Ryanne

A bright light blinded me, then gradually faded. Sounds of the fight vanished, even those belonging to the forest. Colors dimmed under the mist that promptly covered the area. Time seemed to stop.

Fé Erie materialized beside the tree. Her long, fire-red tresses stirred around her glittering dress, though there was no breeze. Fog enveloped her ageless frame. No, that wasn't right. The mist came *from* her.

"He isn't dead, is he? He'll be able to recover as he always does," I said, my lower lip quivering.

"Time draws nigh for him to die. A sorry sight, for his wound is mortal."

"But h-he's immortal." I broke into sobs.

My own body felt cold and detached from reality, my lungs constricted, making it hard to breathe. His blood no longer flowed as if it'd stopped along with time.

Something nagged at the back of my mind. Cuidi keeping me at the taigh. My nightmare—or was it a vision?

I should feel anger. Hatred. I should lash out at Fé Erie. But I felt nothing.

I was empty.

"Please," I begged. "Can you save him?"

"He shalt not die while we are in this space; you shan't worry for now. A thin thread keeps him alive between this world and the void of nothingness, where his kin belong."

"So, that's it?" The emptiness began to fill with nascent anger, anger that wiped away any sob.

"Wait." She crouched next to Titus and her hand hovered over his wound. "It should be here," she mumbled, eyes half-closed.

She reminded me of one of the gnomes searching for a special mushroom and not the all-powerful Queen-Knight of Tír D'aois. Even the majesty of her voice had changed to a more youthful and sassy tone, just like Bricius and I. The shock of the change made my anger dissipate.

"Aha!" Her eyes flew open, and her face lit, *exactly* like a gnome. "I knew it."

In that moment she embodied all Tir D'aois's creatures: the majesty of the fae right down to the innocence and playfulness of pixies and gnomes. I wondered if she had a darker side, like that of the Erlking.

"Here is where you prove your worth," she said, now in a serious tone. "Come, child, crouch next to me."

I obeyed, feeling the weight of everything that had happened. Yet, above it all resonated a feeling that everything had led me here, to this moment.

Her hand still hovered over Titus's wound.

"What is it?" I asked.

"Patience, child. Listen first. This bradaí is the only one I've been able to appear to. None of his kind has seen me, so blinded with hatred and prejudice. But I could not know if what I was looking for was here. Two things were required: a deathly magical stroke and a human, one with a clear heart."

I didn't like the sound of "deathly," but I kept quiet. Titus's life was on the line.

"You are to thrust your fist inside his wound and grasp a coin."

"A coin?" I looked alternately between the bloody wound and her.

But there was no time to wonder how something like a coin ended up inside Titus and how the heck was I going to retrieve it. If Fé Erie said it could be done, then it could be done.

"Put this on first." She handed me a glove, one that seemed made from the finest, soft leather, bigger than my hand.

I complied, the leather as soft as I imagined, and then the glove shifted and fitted my hand as if custom made. "What is this?" I said in awe.

"Dragonskin. It will protect you and him. Now do it, but clear your mind. Don't let any thought linger in it for too long. If something comes, acknowledge it and let it pass. That is essential to the task. A clear mind and heart."

I clenched my hand into a fist. "Just like that?"

"Just like that." She smiled, like we were besties chatting over a slice of cake.

"Wait. How do you know this will work if this has never been done?"

"It must. Otherwise, he shall die."

My heart beat faster. Titus's life was in my hands. But this wasn't the time to be shy or fearful.

I steadied myself and thrust my fist, which went through as easily as if the wound was exactly fist size and the innards were just void fillers.

"Clear your mind. Steady your heart," she said.

Many thoughts passed through my mind, but I did as told and didn't linger on them as I focused on my breathing.

"Grasp the coin. Then swiftly, retrieve your hand."

I snatched something heavy, and once I secured whatever it was, I pulled my hand out.

My fist wasn't bloodied but swathed in a golden halo. Fé Erie rose gracefully to her feet, and her face darkened as her eyes fastened on my fist. "Wise, wise," she mumbled as if she'd forgotten I was here. "You trickster Anord, you believed thy magic would hide this from me."

"What is it?" I asked reverently and even a little fearful as I stood up myself. She wasn't the eager girl anymore, but she'd grown in stature and those eyes that hid eons of wisdom darkened like blood-red pearls.

"Open thy fist."

I did, palm up. A bright gold coin—encapsulated in an orb of light and surrounded by tendrils of dark smoke—hovered over my palm. It featured a detailed pattern comprising two concentric circles, with a prominently positioned skull at the center.

"His kin shalt know soon one of them has fallen. Like greedy goblins, they shalt be looking for this."

I reached my other hand tentatively toward the gold coin.

"If you touch it, you shalt take his power and vanish him into nothingness. There shalt be nothing remaining of him whatsoever, not in this world or the other."

My hand recoiled. The nightmare with the arrogant god flashed in my mind, and I saw Anord again clearly, lifting the gold coin while chanting a spell. "I had a dream. A seer dream. Anord inserted something bright in him. Is this it?"

She gave a curt nod. "Helpless is *Aodhán* now. Henceforth, the first bradaí who finds the coin shall claim it and absorb his power, obliterating him to end the cycle. It is inevitable."

With a graceful movement of her wrist, sparks flew out of her fingers and a bright flower made of sparks hovered in the air.

"Drop the coin there."

Once I did, the coin disappeared like a magician's trick—and so did the flower.

"Naught they shalt have now, bereft of what they seek."

I gasped. "Are you going to take his powers?"

Her now orange eyes twinkled with amusement. Right, she didn't need them.

She opened her palm to me, her eyes drifting to my gloved hand. I removed the dragonskin glove, which expanded to its original size, and handed it over.

"Is this why you needed me? A human."

She nodded. "That and other things. No fae would have ever been able to do what you performed, their thoughts focused only on destruction of these creatures."

"Lady Cuidightheach doesn't want them destroyed," I said.

"She is an Eadrom Caomhnoir. Her fae energy is so powerful it would destroy him even if her thoughts are focused on healing."

"What about the task you gave me? Finding the spark."

"You felt something."

"I did, but it was faint."

"You shant have no doubt whatsoever." She shook her head. "Hence why you are of the utmost importance to me. To feel something so powerful and yet so fragile as the spark of creation is no easy matter. There should be a deep connection, otherwise it would fail."

A deep connection. Something we'd started to achieve.

Fé Erie's eyes brightened. "Indeed."

"Will he survive?" I asked, hope swelling within me.

Fé Erie placed a hand on Titus's forehead. "He is feeble. A wound such as this makes him vulnerable for the kill."

"And yet, it was a fae who did it." The reproach in my tone slipped by my ever-present fae etiquette. But Peter, *my* Peter, had wounded him mortally.

"It was necessary."

And it was when I knew. Fé Erie had played a hand in this fight to retrieve the coin. Had it been her only purpose? Had the pooka stalled me by her orders?

"No," she said, her gaze drilling me. "I did not send the pooka, and my true and only purpose is to save the fae."

"You used him." My fists clenched.

"I did what I must for my kin."

"Would you do the same for me?"

Her lips quivered in a smile.

"You said the wound makes him vulnerable," I said. "Then his death is not inevitable."

"He shant, if the proper ritual takes place."

She'd bet on Titus's life and could have killed him. Could still.

"But I was right," she said. "It was a necessary gamble."

Oh, geez.

"Why do you want to save him?" Fé Erie asked.

"I love him." The words came unbidden. I hadn't even thought about love, but it was undeniable.

"Ah. Love. A great virtue, thy feeling is. You are blessed by the most wondrous of gifts! Yet, if he is saved, he cannot love you as you do. He has not the capacity."

"He has feelings for me," I said.

"You moved something in him which he does not understand. Alas, it can never evolve into true love. If you save him, your pain shalt be immense because your love shalt deepen, and his feeling would not. Despair shalt hold you prisoner."

"So? It makes no difference. Will you help me?"

"Even if it is for naught? Even if the price you pay is too high?"

I brushed the hair from his forehead, a gentle caress that left no doubt. "Yes. That is what I want." My voice cracked, and I looked up, expecting to see the reproach in her eyes.

They shone like two stars. A small smile lingered on her lips, a smile that proclaimed she knew I would accept this.

"And so it shalt."

Part Three

THIRTY-FOUR

Ryanne

Light blinded me again, and I shut my eyes. When the brilliance disappeared, I cracked them open. Titus lay at my feet. Otherwise, we were alone in a small cave.

Hope made a way through my despair. With my heart pounding and my hands shaking, I crouched to inspect Titus's wounds. Warm liquid wet my hand. The blood in his wound was flowing again.

"Oh damn it," I mumbled, pressing my hands to stop the flow and willing Aine into his body.

This time, the power complied and slithered like an eel but came back right away, swirling too fast, too anxious—it couldn't help.

Keep Calm and Assess the Situation.

Titus's inner system mended his wounds. His *dorcha*, what he said was dark energy from Anord. Black magic. But he had a mortal wound, something his *dorcha* couldn't heal.

Unless it needed help.

Not from the fae. Fé Erie would have healed him if she could, wouldn't she? But she'd depended on me to retrieve that coin, so maybe she wasn't able to alter physical states.

And she sent me here to help him.

Be clear of heart, clear of mind.

No thoughts. Or rather, no focusing on errant thoughts. Okay. I placed my palms over his wound and relaxed my body, my mind, like when I'd retrieved the coin.

I tried to visualize what was inside him. There was blood so there was something human in him, and yet, there was also his *dorcha* making him powerful.

Fae power and bradaí energy should combine to help.

That was it!

Okay, Aine, I commanded my power, *time to get cozy with his* dorcha.

I mentally conjured a white flag and had Aine flow like gentle water inside him. Nothing dangerous, nothing combative. The cold energy infused itself into Titus's body, covering him. There was also his *préachta*, which had already accepted Aine. They worked together to win over *dorcha*.

Images from the battle and worries invaded my mind, but I didn't fight them. I let them be, acknowledged they were there, then showed them the exit door. That same mentality commanded Aine.

Oily energy, stagnant, reacted to my fae power, but perhaps because of its gentle state, it didn't react proactively. But after some encouragement from Aine, it did flow toward Titus's wound as dark tendrils.

My hands prickled, and my first reaction at his *dorcha* was to remove them. But I let them be. Confused, Aine hovered between *dorcha* and me.

"It was like clay, and I had to focus."

Energy stirred and flooded toward my hands. Titus gasped, and his eyelids fluttered. Dark, thick energy flurried, blocking his *préachta*. Furrowing my brow, I willed Aine to back up *préachta*. His *dorcha* twitched, but it seemed distracted by the gentle blue-silvery snake that was Aine and stopped blocking his *préachta*, which traveled throughout his body to sense other damaged areas.

It was like his dark energy was the surgeon, and *préachta* with Aine's assistance were the nurses aiding it.

For I while, I focused on feeling the mix of powers. I had no idea whether this helped, but Titus's face looked relaxed when I removed my numb hands. Aine returned to my chest and coiled, purring.

"Get well, please," I whispered, stroking his hair. My throat closed, not letting more words pass through.

I took the down time to check out our lodgings. There was a water-fall to my left, some furs at my right, and something warm—a fire—in the middle. A wicker basket rested near the furs. Inside, it had food, clean cloths, and a bowl.

Clean the wound. Right, I should do that next.

The waterfall gave me the creeps, but luckily there was a small stream in the far side of the small cave.

With a cloth and the bowl now full of water, I crouched near Titus. Carefully, I removed his blood-soaked shirt and cleaned the blood off his skin. It was so eerie seeing the dark tendrils traveling through his body like creepy needles from hell.

His eyelids fluttered, and his face scrunched, like those having a nightmare. Sweat beaded his forehead and his body convulsed at times.

To check if he had other injuries, I removed his pants, leaving him only in his black boxers though I made certain all was well there too with a medical eye. No wounds beside the near-fatal one, only some scratches. With one of the furs, I covered his legs and part of his torso to control his temperature, though the air was warm enough.

Sitting on my haunches, I observed him to make certain I hadn't forgotten anything, but I'd done a good job.

"The sea crashes and sweeps, but there's peace within," I whispered in his ear.

That line he'd said back in our second submersion had come unbidden and the words slipped from my lips, as if my brain knew I must say those words.

His chest heaved, and his expression softened a little, though he still looked anguished.

The sea! Of course, this pirate missed his element. So I whispered those fragments about the sea I remembered, and then made up some. I told him he should imagine being on deck and laughing at a storm, while waves rocked his ship.

The more I talked about the sea, the more his expression relaxed until he fell to a peaceful dream. I'd seen so many older people battling with restless sleep to know his anxiety had faded away.

I placed a kiss on his cold forehead. I had to believe Fé Erie brought us here to help him, otherwise, I'd go insane. My emotions should be kept at bay until he opened his eyes.

Time to see if there was a way out. The cave ceiling was high enough to walk and still have some clearance. The walls were smooth polished rock with black obsidian veins. The thick and dense water curtain, wide enough for three people to walk side by side, prevented me from seeing what lay beyond. The furs lay in a sort of bed, and the trickle of water I'd wet the cloths with ran through a corner, disappearing behind a nook.

The floor was of fine sand, cold to the touch. Behind the corner where the creek turned, the nook acted as a bathroom spacious enough for privacy. Fé Erie had thought of everything, even giving me new clothes, neatly piled: white crop pants and blouse. Absentmindedly, I changed my dirty clothes.

The roaring water gave me chills. Bright, almost impossible white foam swirled on it. Capricious figures formed as if water spirits roamed in the water, not unlike that time in Niagara, but back then I *thought* I saw spirits. Here, I had no doubts creatures lingered in the water.

I shook from exhaustion, but I leaned back and watched him. Aine traveled through my body like inspecting a new house.

Huh.

Weird, my fae energy had been with me for more than fifteen years, yet it was like it'd been a tenant. Weirder, it didn't feel unnatural. It was like another arm or another head.

A creature with one arm, one eye, and a big head intruded in my mind.

"Oh, come on," I said, voice weak.

It felt like Aine chuckled.

I wiped the drool from my mouth and rubbed my eyes. It took me a while to remember where I was. The fire burned as if someone had thrown in more logs. Bright blue sparks crackled.

Titus moaned.

Titus!

I scrambled, relieved to hear him alive. His forehead burned, beaded with sweat, so I removed the fur and patted his forehead dry.

His bloodied clothes were gone. The sand floor was pristine as if blood had never touched it. My body tensed. I took several deep breaths.

He was pale and still. I swallowed, trying to keep the desperation at bay. I needed to be strong and not question whether he'd come out in one piece.

Despite my misgivings about anything fae now, I trusted Fé Erie.

To my surprise, there was only a dark purple line where Peter's sword struck him. The healing was even faster than when Ed wounded him. I looked around in awe and fear.

From the food basket, I took a loaf of bread and a chunk of cheese, then sat down to eat. How many hours had we been here? I had no idea. It was as if we were tucked in a hole in the space time continuum, a place that didn't exist. It was strange, but it felt that way. Impossible to know what time was; the waterfall didn't let enough light inside. The odd fire kept burning brightly. It was then when I noticed a thin column of smoke, trailing to the roof and then disappearing behind the rainfall curtain. I inhaled deeply—instead of the smoky smell, I found only the scent of pine and roses.

The same scent as in Cuidi's quarters.

I chewed the pungent-smelling cheese and plopped in some bread to join the cheese. This wasn't unlike when she let Titus kidnap me back at the taigh and shut down the guardians in the wall.

A head's up about Titus's mortal wound and search of his coin would have been nice but nooo. It was so like the fae, sending you on quests without instructions attached to them. Nope, you had to figure it out on your own.

Aine lazily traveled inside me, an owner happy with its home.

That Return-to-Human card . . .

"*Be clear of heart, clear of mind.*" Fé Erie hadn't blinked when I confessed my love of Titus.

"*I played with it and forgot about my surroundings,*" Peter had said.

Perhaps it just meant the same.

I sighed and finished the rest of the bread and cheese. I'd tackle that ogre once Titus was healed. That was my priority right now. So, for the next few hours, I continued to check our energies and have Aine help him in his mending. The cave provided constant fire, drinking water, and food. Fé Erie had abided by her promise.

"Ryanne."

Titus's broken and hoarse voice startled me. He lay on the sand in the same position I'd left him, but now his head was tilted toward me. The corners of my lips lifted as fast as my heartbeats.

I'd laid next to him, so I only had to prop myself up.

"How do you feel?" I asked.

"As if I died." He grimaced in pain.

"You're healing quite fast."

"Here, come to me, I need to feel you."

Before I knew it, I was encircled in his arms, his nose touching mine. Careful not to rattle him, I caressed his back, his breath warming me.

His lips searched for mine and placed a chaste kiss, a kiss that smelled of the sea.

"My pirate," I mumbled.

"My little seer," he croaked.

"Hmm." I tasted his lips again, softly, just enough to calm my hunger. "You better heal fast, Captain. This isn't enough."

He made a sound between a chuckle and a groan.

"Dead men tell no tales," I said jokingly in reference to the first time I set foot on his ship, "so don't die on me, you hear?"

"Nay, I won't."

"How does it feel being brought back from the dead?"

"I felt the same long time ago, when I first opened my eyes." He scrunched his face in concentration. "No, that was a dream," he said, hoarse.

"Are you thirsty?"

"Aye."

I filled the bowl with water from the creek. The water curtain was as intense as when we arrived. I propped up his head and helped him while he gulped it down.

"More."

I repeated the process twice. "This reminds me of when you were captive at the taigh. And when Ed beat you." I smiled at him even as he didn't seem to understand what I was saying. "I think you kidnapped me because I'm a nurse, not because I'm a seer."

He chuckled weakly. Oh he heard me alright.

A nurse. Did I choose that profession by myself? What if I was pushed into this? Fae needed not just a human, but a human nurse, it seemed.

"Do you want to eat?"

"No. This."

He reached out and latched his hand on my neck, pulling me to him. Like clay, I molded my body to his and sighed against his lips. The kiss was soft and tender, like a lazy wave slapping over the sand on a hot summer day.

He grunted, let me go, and closed his eyes. His face relaxed back to sleep, though with a shade of anxiety the dream couldn't get rid of. I gently brushed the hair from his forehead.

Titus moved slightly, murmuring. "Ryanne."

His call vibrated in me. "Thank you," I said to no one, grateful he had been given another chance.

To make certain his *dorcha* was working on him, I placed both hands on his chest and sent Aine. Nothing responded—neither his *dorcha* nor his *préachta*. Huh. But he seemed okay, so maybe his energies were dormant. Repairing themselves.

Was he different after the experience? I pressed two fingers to his wrist, where a beat should be felt, but as in prior occasions, there was none.

It wasn't long before I got bored waiting for Titus to wake back up. Wondering if the thunderous water was a magical entrance, I approached it. Perhaps we were behind a waterfall high up on a ridge. I could peek outside to make sure, carefully. The foam condensed, thinned, and swirled; my feet glued to the sandy floor.

Come on! It's just water!

Inch by inch, I approached, my trembling hand stretched before me. When the spray sprinkled my fingers, I held my breath. I plunged my hand into the water. A painful tingling ran from my fingers up to my elbow, turning into an electric current that threw me backward so hard I fell on my backside.

The noise the water curtain made sounded like a soft laugh. The foam figures grinned like happy ghosts.

"I guess that's a no," I mumbled, massaging my butt.

Titus

Shadows shifted in my mind. Red splashed against my conscience, yet a sweet voice lulled me into a restful sleep.

Waves crashed against my ship, and a salty breeze splayed on my face. Glorious.

Then pain. So much pain I dropped into the ocean, where sharks tore me apart.

I gasped awake and found myself on dry land.

In a cave.

What happened hit me like a ram. The ambush, Ryanne running away. Bloody spirit fae jabbing me in the back.

I blinked, attempting to understand the strange situation I was in. Wasn't I dead? Didn't I bleed to death?

I propped myself up, blinking at the light coming through a water curtain, still drowsy.

The first thing I noticed was Ryanne sleeping by my side, her gorgeous chestnut hair a beautiful mess.

What in Anord's hell?

"The sea crashes and sweeps, but there's peace within," she'd said to me in my dreams.

Or was it a dream? Perhaps I'd been in the nether world, a barren land without hope, and she'd brought me back.

Sweet Ryanne.

I caressed her cheek softly, not wanting to wake her up. She needed her rest, for the rings under her eyes. She'd been taking care of me, then.

A strange feeling harbored in my usual empty chest. Something warm that made me smile. My little seer, always attentive of me. What would I have done without her?

But I'd been dead, hadn't I? I inspected my body, though I felt no pain. The wound where the sword pierced me was no more. I frowned —how many days had I been here to have been brought back from the nether world?

Come to think of it, where was I now?

That was when I noticed something amiss I couldn't pinpoint, a feeling that upset me without understanding why. I rose to my feet, wary, and observed the closed space, taking in every nook, every crevice.

The place was sealed, and the only way out was the waterfall. Stranger though, my body wasn't sore. At all.

A pile of clothes lay beside me, and I donned a white shirt and beige pants. The water curtain had been whispering to me since I woke up to the land of the living, but it was just now I acknowledged its siren song.

Part of the nether world experience had been swept by water, waves that placed me on the only place on Earth I could be happy—my ship. I glanced at Ryanne and knew it was her doing as well. Ryanne and my ship, the only two things I cared about. No, not the only ones.

Homkar's image came to me, then Kara, and that warmth spread further.

I furrowed my brow, and coldness overtook the warmth, like a sudden gale in an otherwise cloudy day. Did that fae kill them too?

My fist clenched, but due to my weariness, the anger didn't hold, slippery like fresh tar on deck. A food basket lay nearby, and I picked it up.

Not wanting to disturb her well-earned rest, even though all I desired was to hold her in my arms, I limped to the water entrance and plopped down with a huff, the basket tipping to the side.

Everything was confusing, blurred. I'd been fighting that bloody fae and winning, then he'd skewered me to death. He hadn't been able to do it before until that fae-spirit told him my Name.

Go figure.

I patted my healed side and flinched. Anord's balls, this hadn't been my year. What happened after I'd been killed?

What happened to Kara and Homkar? The Morrigan take all the fae and the crows peck at their eyes for eternity if they'd hurt my friends, my loyal friends.

Ryanne stirred and mumbled, then yawned, her arms stretched over her head. I exhaled hard through my mouth—time to leave those ramblings that were getting me nowhere. Problem was, I didn't feel endangered here. This was the first time in my life I didn't feel the need to look behind my shoulder. What an oddity. Perhaps because Ryanne had been sleeping relaxed and peacefully.

"You're awake," I said. "Come to me."

Startled, she blinked and looked around.

I opened my arms wide, and she rushed to me to settle on my chest. Warmth returned to me again, a feeling of being whole. As I should be. She inspected me with a clinical eye.

"Are you hurt?" she asked.

"No." I hugged her tighter, not wanting to let go.

"Your recovery is incredible."

"Nay, something else is happening here. I've never recovered this fast." I paused while glancing at the water curtain. "Especially since I was brought back from the dead."

She closed her eyes and buried her face in my neck. Her familiar scent of eucalyptus and roses impregnated her skin. We stayed that way for a while, the warmth of her hands seeping through the thin material of my clothes.

Better than *dorcha*, her contact healed me in a different way than the dark energy. For that, I'd gladly be mortal and turn my back on the bradaí way.

"Why did you have to fight?" she asked.

"I had to get you."

"I was escaping. Bricius was going to open a portal back to Seattle. I thought you were there."

"It wasn't how I saw it. Pretty Boy had caught up to you."

She furrowed her brow, then rapped her knuckles lightly on my head. "What were you *thinking*?"

"I couldn't bear to see you with him."

"Peter? Oh, not that again. I told you, he's a friend. My fae mentor, that's all."

I took a bunch of grapes from the basket and placed one against her lips. "Open."

She raised an inquisitive eyebrow, surely recalling that time in the taigh when she hand-fed me.

"Please," I said, smiling.

With a grin, she did, and I pushed the grape gently, my fingers tingling at the contact of her lips. One by one, the grapes disappeared into her mouth. A tingling went straight to the center of my chest.

I locked her in my arms again and caressed her back. She all but purred.

"How did you bring us here?" I asked.

"Fé Erie did," she sighed.

"Who?"

"The spirit fae, the one with red-fire tresses."

"What?" I pushed her gently to look her in the eye. "*She* brought us here?"

"Yes."

Anord be damned!

I pulled out of our embrace and jumped to my feet, then sliced my hand in the air, but my portal refused to answer my call. I shut my eyes and extended my arms, attempting to sense this otherworldly space. A wave of white, cold fae power hit me right on the chest. The same one I felt before I met Ryanne for the first time, that day outside the Star-bucks in Seattle while I was pursuing the fae-spirit.

"Anord piss on her and all the cursed fae! I'm as good as dead again!" I brooded. This was not good, not good at all. "That spirit brought me here to finish me."

"No, Titus"—she rose too—"think about it. If she'd wanted you dead, she would have left you there after Peter landed the killing blow. You would be dead by now."

"I don't understand."

"It was necessary. She brought us here so I could heal you with Aine, my power. Just listen, Titus."

She puckered up her face then told me all about the conversation with the fae-spirit. She told me about the coin and how she'd extracted it, her arms waving in the air while she paced around. It was like watching an actress on stage recalling a scene.

My eyes widened in bewilderment. "By the Morrigan! I had a coin that Anord placed in me, and she took it?"

"Well, I handed it to her."

"Why does she want my coin? She doesn't need my powers."

"You don't have them anymore?"

"This place reeks of fae power on a level I can't even comprehend. Not even with my powers at full could I do a thing here."

I patted my healed side. My *dorcha* felt dormant, as the *préachta*. What in Anord's Hell?

"One thing I don't get. How could Peter mortally wound you? He couldn't before, and not for lack of trying."

"She told him my Name." I scowled. "That bypassed my defenses, and he was able to kill me as if I were a wee human."

"It's odd," she said. "I saw in a dream how you were wounded by a hooded man. Peter, I guess."

My scowl turned darker.

"That means I had a vision when dreaming," she said while scrunching her nose. "I saw your creation, Titus! But how? How could I?"

She began to pace around, her hands wriggling.

"This is a chessboard," she said. "A pawn. The fae played me as a pawn. Are you one, too? Or do you have a bigger role, and that is why Fé Erie did what she did? Fé Erie is playing the white pieces but against whom? Anord? Edward?"

A coin. Ryanne's bright fist. The golden object flashed in my mind, and I shifted in place. Something else was happening, although the final piece was missing.

"You said you dreamed you were dying when you were created." She walked around, unable to stand still. "Did you feel the cold power then? The one we both have and you call *préachta*?"

"Aye."

She sucked in a breath. "I felt icy cold when Bricius gave me the gift. A blue light came to me, and I choked, like dying."

"I felt something like that, but it's unclear, I—"

"Fé Erie has a plan for you. For me too, I think."

"And what's that plan?" I folded my arms across my chest.

She raised her hands in frustration. "I don't know. I don't understand the board. The chess pieces. But all this has a reason. She wanted this to happen. Your death."

"Do you trust her?"

She took a moment to think about it, which was odd by itself. Old Ryanne would have said "yes" in an instant.

Finally, she said, "I've been having trust issues with my fae mentors. We don't see eye to eye now that I've spent time with you. About Fé Erie, I believe she'd do whatever it takes to protect her land and the fae."

"That could mean she could push us aside if we're against her."

"Maybe," she said, pensive. "But I'm sure she wanted me to heal you."

"Because I might be useful. Otherwise, she would have left me to die."

She shrugged. "And yet, she didn't."

I patted my side again. "Why would I have a coin?"

"Do you feel different?"

"No. And aye, I do. My powers feel dormant. And yet I feel the same. This is so bloody confusing."

She flickered fingertips over my side and whispered, "Peter gave you the killing blow where Anord placed the coin."

"That's why she told him my Name. To get the coin out."

"Yes, yes, those two dreams were in sequence. I should have put the pieces together."

She bit her nails, pacing at the speed of her thoughts. I stopped her crazy walk and pulled her toward me. She rested her head on my chest.

"That's how fae killed the other two bradaís," I said.

"The fae? I thought Edward—"

"Aye, I thought so too until that dryshite killed me. It takes a fae, a powerful one, an Eadrom. Bloody Edward told the truth." I pushed her softly away to look into her eyes. "The cold power, why did it affect me so much when Edward tortured Aghna. You described the same sensation I felt." I shook my head. "It makes sense, though I don't understand why."

"What happened there, Titus? With Aghna?"

I seized her hands and pressed them to my chest. "I saved her from Edward's hands. Feel the truth in me."

I recalled that time back in 1792 and told her everything, not withholding any detail. Edward and I looming over a caramel-skinned woman, her white hair spilled like milk foam, her face in a rictus of pain. I picking her up, expression tightened, and fear hidden behind my steely resolution. Then running with her in my arms, Ed shouting far away. Then stepping into Tír D'aois, searching for a safe place.

"You wanted to save her from Edward," she said with a sigh of relief.

"Aye."

The rushing of the water returned me back to the cave.

"Was saving her the reason why you won't kill fae?"

I frowned and then all became clear. "She helped me to activate *préachta* and taught me to open a portal. But she was the first and only fae who looked at me. Really looked at me. That's why I won't kill them. *Préachta* activates and drowns the beast, and I felt connected to her back then. I wanted to save her, but it was all for naught."

Ryanne pushed away and her cheeks flushed. She let out a long exhale through her mouth. "Titus, I, ah, I need to confess something. I"—she glanced at her nails, then clenched her hands—"I haven't been totally honest with you."

"I know."

She whipped her hand up, her mouth opening and closing comically like a goldfish.

"*Ashtore*, you're a terrible liar. And you've been evading my gaze. When I told you I trusted you, I was hoping you'd come clean."

Her cheeks turned red right up to her ear tips. "You didn't kidnap me from the taigh," she blurted.

"Of course I did."

"Yes, but it was *my* choice. The fae . . . Cuidi and Fé Erie . . . They, ah, they wanted me to get close to you."

I pondered about that for a few seconds. "I see. It explains a lot, about how I could take you out so easily, why I could use the Shadow. You're a human protected by the fae, and after what I did to you back in Seattle, trying to kidnap you, you chose to take care of me. You asked me lots of things—hell, you keep asking questions." I jerked my chin at her. "What's this about?"

She reached out for my hands. "Oh, Titus, please don't be angry. I like you. I know I hid some things from you but—"

"From the bradaí who kidnapped you and sent you to that lab at Haru's mercy? From the bradaí who couldn't promise you he wouldn't sell you again for some gold coins?"

"There's that." She smiled. "It's just . . . the spark."

"What?"

"You have something within you."

"Aye, the beast."

"No, no." She waved a hand. "Something pure."

I gave a dry bark of laughter. "There's nothing pure in me, *ashtore*."

"You're wrong." She pressed her warm hands over my chest.

"There's something else within you: a connection with the Supreme Being. A way to obtain your soul."

"It's you who is wrong. I am what I am. A bradaí, a dark creature. There's only *dorcha* inside me." And *préachta.* "We don't have souls. Once we're killed, that's it for us."

This was so bloody confusing.

"That's what Anord *wants* you to believe." She scowled, her lips pressed tight. "I felt it, Titus."

And she told me. How the Lady gave her a path, and Ryanne chose to find whatever was within us. How she'd been trying to find that spark or whatever the hell it was, how she'd felt it after the sea submersion and now in this cave. I brooded over the subject once she fell silent.

It made sense. Everything did. Anord had limitations, after all, and unbeknownst to all bradaís, we had a possible connection. Something to get rid of the beast.

She reached out to cup my cheek, and something else became urgent. I bent toward her; her lips parted. I relished on the wondrous sensation of nibbling on her lower lip, my hands sliding over her back.

As if that slight touch wasn't enough for either, we melted into one another, hungrily seeking each other's mouths.

Her chest burst with raw energy. Something awakened inside me, aware of the energy she transmitted through the kiss.

I yearned for it and grabbed her shoulders, like a drowning man reaching for that coveted gulp of air.

The cold energy wrapped us—her own and my awakened *préachta,* one and the same.

We kept on kissing, kept on touching each other as if we were afraid to stop and break the connection between us.

She was my lifeline. I couldn't let go, or I'd drown. Hungrily, I kissed her with full force, hands roaming her skin. The more we touched, the connection got stronger.

It was so strong I couldn't cope with it. I needed air.

"No more." I pushed her gently and rested my head on the wall.

She rose and headed for the entrance, her legs wavering. Oh no. I followed her.

"I didn't mean for you to leave my side," I murmured in her ear behind her. I pushed her hair and kissed her neck while her breathing stirred.

She twisted to face me and stroke my jaw with her fingertips.

"You know?" she said, looking at me through her lashes in a sassy tone. "This is the first time we've really been alone."

"Aye?" I smiled.

She lifted my shirt above my head, then slid her hands over my bare torso and arms. By the Morrigan, that felt good.

"Keep going," I urged, yet remained still.

She kissed my hot skin. My hands tangled in her hair while the tip of her tongue tasted my skin.

"Come here," I said, barely a breath, and pulled her up to meet my own tongue. My hands ran down and up her back, wanting more. Wanting all.

She pulled away, and I felt disappointed yet didn't budge her.

"Should we remove this too?" she asked in a playful tone, lowering her hands to my waistband.

"Don't let me stop you."

Slowly, she lowered my pants and then my boxers. I sucked in a breath as she took a step back, taking her sweet time to roam her gaze over me.

"Your turn," I said, still not moving a finger. Letting her take the initiative.

"No. Wait." She stuck her clothed body to my bare one, pulling me toward her and kissing me thoroughly.

I trapped her in my arms while her hands slid over my back, then lower until she cupped my bare backside.

"Enjoying yourself?" I asked.

"Like you have no idea," she said.

I chuckled and pulled away, a question in my eyes.

Chewing on her lip, she slowly removed her clothes, moving to a rhythm that only existed in her head. Her eyes half-closed, hair sweeping shoulders and face.

"Woman, come here," I said, passion laced in my tone.

With a sexy smile, she offered me her hand.

I snatched it and crushed her against my chest. She laughed, delighted, until I caught her mouth in mine, and her merriment morphed to need.

The contact of her skin against mine felt like a small sun warming our bodies and getting into our skin, lighting a fire within.

She rubbed her leg against mine. The sensation of her soft breasts against my chest, glorious. Even better than anything else I'd felt before.

Feel.

"Take me," she whispered. "Take me now, Titus."

"Not yet, *ashtore*. I've waited for this for far too long."

I led her to the skins in the corner and laid us down, she against the furs and I hovering above her. I couldn't remove my gaze from her gorgeous moss-green eyes.

"What are you waiting for?" she asked, her voice reflecting her aching need.

"I'm getting drunk off you. You're my water of vitality."

She laughed. "Whiskey. Oh, Titus." She caressed my forearms and shoulders. "I'm already drunk. Now, come to me."

But I took my time. To kiss her mouth, her jawline, leaving a trace of my lips over her neck and shoulders.

I was grateful I'd died and was brought back here with her.

Heaven. The only one I could aspire to.

THIRTY-SIX

Titus

Bare back against the furs, I fixated my gaze on the rocky ceiling of the cave. Ryanne lay next to me, locked in my arms.

"I love you," she whispered, her face buried in my neck.

Love. The word passed by without making an impression.

Her breathing slowed, her arm around my waist relaxed. I stroked her hair, relishing its softness until she fell asleep. I played our previous conversion in my head.

Puppets. We were both puppets. Fae and bradaí, what the hell mattered. Grand.

The air near the waterfall vibrated, and the fae-spirit appeared. I rose to my feet, clenching my fists.

"You," I growled.

Fé Erie raised her fiery eyebrows.

I stepped toward her. "Did you come to finish what that dryshite couldn't?" Even as Ryanne explained, I couldn't trust the bloody fae.

The fae-spirit threw her head back and laughed, a musical sound like dozens of rumbling waterfalls.

"You'll wake her," I said, nodding at Ryanne.

"She shalt not. This is a space between you and me."

"You talk."

"Unquestionably. And no, Aodhán, I shant eliminate you."

"Ryanne told me what you did, but still, I don't understand why."

"Take my hand and you shalt, Aodhán. Time is nigh for you to know what happened when Anord created you."

"How do you know what happened during my creation?"

"I was there."

I was highly tempted to tell her to go to Anord's hell. I cast a glance at Ryanne's sleeping form. She believed this spirit had something in store for me. She believed in this fae.

Fine, I'd take the risk. This was my chance to understand what had happened to me.

Her hand was cold yet warm at the same time, then, her eyes brightened until nothingness covered me.

We reappeared in a familiar place. Too familiar. Ireland's coast, not yet dawn. But we were suspended on air near the face of a cliff.

"This is where you started," she said.

"Is this a memory of yours?" I asked.

"Yes. Look, Aodhán, look what happened."

And I saw.

Like the waves that slapped at the cliff in a continuous dance, Fé Erie—the one from the memory—vanished and reappeared, as though striving to take hold in this human dimension. Bare feet brushing the rocky, narrow ledge, she balanced above the ocean, high enough that the foam resembled a wisp of an old troll's beard, and so cautious she could be mistaken for one of the remaining shadows of twilight.

Atop the cliff, two different types of rock sat—rocks with green-gold eyes.

"Who are they?" I asked, sensing great power through the glamour of those creatures.

"The Guardian, the most powerful and oldest nádhúrtha. And Amriel, second to the Guardian. See that cave?" She pointed at one near her memory-self.

"Aye."

"Anord is hiding there. He was the last of the Dorchcréacht wreaking havoc in the human dimension, and he hid in my land, pretending to be someone he was not, all the while learning about the fae's weakness and preparing his black magic. He fooled everyone."

"Dorchcréacht? I asked.

"That is what I call the godlike beings from Tír na Vraoichta. In consequence, as you are aware, fae numbers have been dwindling at an alarming rate, and I could not have that. I could not let him continue and destroy my land. Balance had taken a strike."

"What are those nádhúrthas doing?" I asked.

"They're preparing the land around the cave with energy. You shall see." She gave a mysterious smile.

She'd captured Anord after my creation, I knew. I was the last of the bradaís, but none of my kin knew how he'd ended up trapped in Tír Na Vraoichta.

I watched as her memory-self claimed ubiquitous energy from within the cliff, from the power of the crashing waves, from the grass growing atop, from the cawing of the gannets, and the chanting of nearby men. Energy came rushing at her bidding like a grateful servant to its master.

The waves increased in intensity, their tune with the cliff increasing its tempo.

"I could feel Anord's energy increasing tenfold, putrid like an ogre's gnashing of teeth within an inch of my nose. Now, listen to the wind."

"You will be Named Aodhán," the wind whispered.

I sucked in a breath. That was how she knew my Name. A memory came to me, and a piece of the puzzle fell. It'd been the first words he'd said to me.

Memory-spirit rushed into the cave with a yell of defiance, a merciless gale ready to tear the god apart. Fé Erie took me inside, not like ghosts through walls—we were inside the cave before I could blink.

"You!" Anord boomed in a deep voice. Standing tall and powerful, he was clad in a black tunic, a cowl covering his dark blue tattooed face, except for his jaw and tight lips. The newborn yet fully grown man stood naked, head bowed, a curtain of black hair hiding his face —a puppet without cords. The god's *dorcha* pulsated within the bradaí.

Me. Memory-Titus. What I hadn't remembered, what every bradaí could, and yet the memory had fogged my brain. It was becoming clearer.

Anord spotted Memory Fé Erie and thrust energy toward her shaped like a javelin. She lifted her arms and deflected the attack. The javelin slid off the shield, the oily energy harmlessly sizzling on the cave's floor.

Memory Fé Erie breathed. It was just a misty trail that softly wafted out of her body. But as Anord's initial attack had been rash, swift, and dense, her breath was all-present and inescapable.

"I thought you couldn't do a thing in the human dimension," I said.

"An impossible feat in a different place, indeed. Here, my power solidified, aided by the beliefs of the people dwelling in this land."

The Irish folk. All the legends and beliefs helping her.

I approached my past-self, oblivious to what was happening, and placed a hand on his shoulder.

A memory hit me, and I staggered. I was him, there. Void filled me, and there was nothing. Then a light, a bright one, covered me like an underground river. Magnificent iridescent hues played on the surface, and I wanted to go there, swim in that river. A silvery light bound every element, and I felt light. Happy.

Feel.

A chant, and all vanished except for a prick of silvery light, trapped in the darkness. *No*, I wanted to shout. I needed that light.

Someone grabbed my arm, and I was back at the cave.

"It is dangerous to interfere in my memory. Do not attempt such a thing. Watch."

Anord seized my past self and threw him out of the cave before her energy touched him. He flew past me, arms flailing, and plunged into the raging sea.

Bloody Anord. He discarded me like a broken puppet, the bastard god. But I couldn't see what happened to my newly formed self—her memory anchored me to what she was doing.

Whatever putrid energy Anord sent her way, it met hers, a tidal wave advancing inevitably toward him. It deflected Anord's dark energy of the god and seeped into the cracks.

Anord paced around the cave while her misty breath reached out.

"If it touches him, it will paralyze him, if momentarily," Fé Erie explained.

He lowered the cowl and met the memory-spirit's eyes.

"A friend turned to foe, one who deceived while eating from the fae's table," she said with utmost sadness.

I hadn't known that; Anord strolling in the fae's lands like a friend. But it made sense, he'd been fooling them in the bradaí way for them to lower their defenses. Once he couldn't obtain what he desired, he turned to black magic, aided by his powerful parents—the Morrigan, goddess of battle, and Donn, the god of death. My grandparents, if there was such a thing.

Anord spread a hand toward the far end of the cave. A portal opened between wisps of fog and, with a smirk, he stepped through it.

"He escaped?" I asked. "I thought you'd trapped him here."

"Remember I told you the Guardian was preparing the land?" She pointed at the cave's wall.

It cracked and shifted for an old nádhúrtha to step through. He brushed the dirt from his shoulders and wriggled his toes. Behind him, another one pushed through, darker of hair and skin. That nádhúrtha looked at where we stood and grinned.

Memory Fé Erie bowed her head. "Thank you for your assistance, Guardian. My kin are indebted to you."

The Guardian pressed his hands together, the way some humans in the far East did for praying. "He won't cause any more mischief now, and that is good enough for me and mine." He grinned and his smile was so contagious, I found myself grinning too.

What an odd creature. "What did they do?"

"They modified the energy surrounding the cave and took Anord back to his dimension, now locked forever."

"And yet you didn't send us bradaís to that dimension." I couldn't complain, though.

"Alas, your kin do not belong in the same dimension as Anord, so neither me nor the Guardian can send you there." She smiled like an old wise woman to a child. "Anord created you all in human land, thus you belong here, even as your power comes from other places."

I was about to ask what other places when I noticed memory-spirit approaching the ledge. I'd finally understand what had been different with my creation besides being thrown to the sea.

The sea. My home, my power place. Fuzzy memories became clear —of me drowning.

Below, the waves crashed against the cliff's face, a rhythmic music that infused me. The energy of the land was changing; the sun had awakened and was ready to shine its light on the land.

"What about the newborn bradaí?" The Guardian craned his neck toward where my past self had submerged.

"Would I be able to destroy him in his fragile state?" Breeze swirled, and memory-spirit's fire-red curls danced around her lithe body.

The old man turned to his companion, shadows lurking in their expressions. "You know the answer as well as I."

"Anord completed his work."

Fé Erie said to me, "We stopped Anord, but he had already created you in full. You were about to be as dangerous as your Alpha."

"About to be?" Again I tried to see beyond but was not able to.

"Such a shame," the Guardian said while glancing at the steely waters. He clicked his tongue. "The bradaí isn't fully awake, but he'll start his path of destruction soon."

"Guardian, I thank you for that," Memory Fé Erie said.

"What? What did I say?" His expression projected innocence. He stared at the small cove beneath them. "He'll be in contact with humans soon. Fae will be displeased. Your power won't help the fae, though."

"Humans," she repeated. "I like it. It could work."

He grinned again, his eyes twinkling.

Memory-spirit laughed, joyfully. "Now, there is something I need to take care of." With her gaze steady on the sparkling ocean, where I'd submerged, she vanished into the wind.

Memories completed, and my old dream took shape. My own

creator had pushed me aside like a broken toy and left me to drown. Those dreams were real.

"Come," Fé Erie said. "You'll understand more."

A blink, and we were inside the sea. My past-self was drowning, and I could sense his confusion.

Death strove to claim me on the day of my creation.

The surface drifted away along with my life. Memory-spirit shimmered before my past-self. Long, vibrant red curls and a translucent gown hung, not bothered by the water. She smiled as she touched my chest. Cold burst from her hands, injecting vitality into me.

A touch of fae.

Fé Erie touched my chest and stirred my *préachta*. "I gave you a touch of my power. Only then could thee have a choice."

"A choice of what?"

"Of being you."

"I didn't understand the Guardian's words." I watched my past self, his brown eyes turning to blue, green, then brown again. He was struggling to return to the surface, yet something was changing in him.

"He would not explain in full, but it was then when I understood I could give you a touch of my power. You would have never let me approach you once fully awake. Although it wouldn't be enough. We needed a human to be the bridge between races."

Ryanne.

My past self opened his eyes and calm reflected on them; the peace I'd always looked for and only found in the sea. Memory-spirit had vanished. He kicked to the surface and took a deep breath. The Irish coastline was not far, and he swam toward it with ease.

"That's why I'm connected to the sea."

"You were drowning. I merged you with the ocean's energy."

We were now hovering above the surface, watching him reach the shore and lie down on the rocky sand. That was one of my first memories. I would start walking, confused with both *dorcha* and *préachta*. A battle of both forces attempting to claim me.

I would achieve my first kill not one hour after I'd awakened, my dark side winning then and *préachta* going to a slumber, exactly like that pinpoint of silvery light.

"Why? Why not let me drown and rot?" I would have returned to land eventually, but it could have taken years, and it would've been a tiresome endeavor.

She smiled like a mother to an inquiring child. "You have changed, Aodhán."

"Can you remove the beast?" Hope swelled within me.

"I do not wield that power."

She reached out and touched my forehead. Cold swept me and filled my lungs. Every fiber of my body tensed and froze.

I sucked in a breath like a newborn, gasping for precious oxygen. I found myself in the cave, lying on my back. She was gone. Just like that.

Annoyed, I latched my hands behind my back and stared at the cave ceiling. Anger boiled inside my chest. My fingers curled into fists, knowing she had been playing me since the beginning. And she had my coin. Was I vulnerable now? I clenched my teeth, my breathing agitated. Yet, if she hadn't interfered, if she hadn't given me the touch of fae, I would be like Edward, or perhaps even worse.

Mindless. Blood-lusting. Lost with the beast.

No wonder all the rest followed Edward blindly. It was all Anord. He only wanted the best of us for his dark deeds, and that was Edward.

He had to be terminated.

I scrambled to where Ryanne lay and held her in my arms. Her warmth eased the lonely feeling within me. She stirred, reaching for me. I responded with an urge born out of my desperation.

THIRTY-SEVEN

Titus

A stream of fresh air hit me in the back. The warmth of the cave disappeared. Muscles taut, I left Ryanne's side to observe, to feel around.

"What happened?" she asked, sleepy.

"I think the power of this place is going." Aye, something had changed, something subtle.

"Look, Titus, the fire." She pointed at the fire, down to coals, leaving only the darkness of the burned logs.

"It's time to go."

She sighed, her arms resting over her thighs.

"What's the matter, *ashtore*?"

"I want to take a break."

I arched an eyebrow. "Is that one of your modern words? I feel I've heard it before and, it's never good news."

She lifted her head up and smiled. "Not a break from *you*, but from the chase."

"Ah. I could take you somewhere safe. Hide for a while from bradaís and bloody fae."

"Can we go back to Seattle? Just for a couple of days? I need to be around humans." She glanced at her hands. "I can't believe I'm saying this, but I need to touch base."

"Aye, but only for a couple of days. Then we go into hiding."

"What about your ship?" She perked up. "Wait. Kara. Homkar!"

"What happened with them?" Anguish covered me whole. They had come with me, helping me out. The Morrigan take care of them. Let her crows guide them to safety.

"I don't know. After Peter gave you the killing blow, Kara and Homkar were determined to make him pay."

"Did they?" Warmth filled the hole in me. My sister and my loyal friend, fighting for me.

"Yes. I asked Bricius for help while I attended you, before Fé Erie took us here."

"Aye, it seems that spirit has great power." I furrowed my brow. "Do you think they're safe? Your fae protector was only able to give me that killing blow because of my Name." Did she know about all the Names?

"I hope they are."

"I hope so too." My fist clenched. I'd been about to best that dryshite while fighting clean. And what did I get? Tricked.

Killed.

And brought back from the dead.

I raked a hand through my hair. "I'll reach out to them once we're in a safe place. Let's get you to Seattle."

"I like that."

We put on our clothes and stood in front of the waterfall.

"Now what?" she asked, watching the water curtain with suspicion. It hadn't dimmed in intensity.

"Let me try to open my portal again."

Concentrating on my ship, I slid my hand, but couldn't create the portal. Although, the usual tingling in my fingers was there, a sign that perhaps I still retained my powers.

I despised the nature of Tír D'aois that prevented me from creating my portal anywhere but on neutral ground. But then, it now made sense why I from all my kin was able to open portals—I was the only one with a touch of fae inside. What an irony.

And then, the water curtain vanished. Morrigan's crow, hopefully, this wasn't another of their bloody tests.

Ryanne laced her fingers with mine, and together we walked toward the entrance. A lush forest appeared before our eyes. The cave was on high ground, tops of trees stretching as far as the eye could see. Leaden clouds covered the sky, not letting us know the time of day.

We wended our way down the slope; it felt like we were walking through sea foam.

I checked the vicinity, my body tense like an anchor thrown to sea. Anord could take me if I let my guard down. Fae energy surrounded us like a bell jar. As soon as we reached neutral ground, we'd get the hell out of here.

The trees at the foot of the hill covered our heads.

"A few more steps, *ashtore*, and we can get out."

Only some energy balls bounced off me. We were on the edge. Safe from everyone else, from fae knowing my Name and . . .

I stopped. "I need to tell you something."

"Can't it wait?"

"No. That redhead fae knows this, and we're still under her protection. I have a Name."

"Of course you do." She narrowed her eyes.

"My real Name. How Anord Named me. It has power and the reason why your fae friend could bypass my defenses." I'd never said it out loud, but the beast was still cowed. "It's . . . Aodhán."

"I like Titus better." She reached out and kissed my cheek.

I allowed myself a smile. My patience had been successful in the end. Ryanne was with me, and we would escape to some remote place where we couldn't be found.

The layer of fae-energy faded behind me, the keening of the wind music to my ears. As expected, *dorcha* reappeared, and with it the beast, though it was still cowed.

"Look, Titus," she said in a surprised tone. "This is the same place."

"Same place as?"

"Where you almost died."

She was right. A few apeling corpses lay on the ground. The ravine was in front of us, the sound of water gurgling at its bottom wafted through the fresh breeze.

I frowned; I didn't remember a hill.

We both turned at the same time. There was no hill. Just the forest. I approached one of the apelings and placed a hand on its skin.

"They feel like they died recently."

Ryanne crouched next to me and inspected the corpse with a keen eye. "Not an expert here but I say no more than twelve hours, unless apelings have a different biology."

"You turn me on when you talk like that."

She laughed merrily despite the corpses. "It does mean time worked differently in that cave. We had to have been there for a couple days, maybe three."

I focused on my bradaí pocket where I stored whatever I needed for emergencies and retrieved my sword. A weight lifted from my shoulders—I wasn't totally vulnerable, after all.

I patted my side where the coin had been. I didn't feel any different, although Anord had placed it there for a reason. The same reason why the fae-spirit took it away. I scowled.

"We have to leave this place," I said. "Not good opening a portal where blood was spilled. Too dangerous."

The hairs on my neck stood on end, my nerve endings prickled. We weren't alone. I extended my senses to feel what creature awaited us. Heat swirled inside me as though coals burned. Hell! A bradaí. Curse my kind!

"Get behind me," I hissed, tightening my fingers around the sword's hilt. Perhaps it was Kara, yet . . .

Ryanne complied without a word. Grand.

Minho stepped out from behind a tree. The bastard's forehead was sweaty, eyes widened, veins in his neck standing out as if he had run a bloody marathon. How did the bastard arrive so quickly?

I cursed under my breath. Anord had signaled my kin about my "death" so they could take my coin, even if they didn't know it yet. That was what Minho was after.

Morrigan's crow, we were in dire peril. I had to get rid of Minho quickly. That wouldn't be so hard given my success rate with him.

Minho steadied himself, seemingly taking control of the blood calling.

"Well," he slurred. "The little bee didn't drown. Who would say? You're fond of her. Is she your pet?"

"None of your business."

Minho grinned while caressing the hilt of his sword. "Interesting. You're protecting her. She's glued to you. Why is that, Irish? Ooh." His eyes widened. "She's a fae's pet! I'd been right all along. You're a fae lover, yah?"

"There's no one down. You're wasting your time."

"No, *freak*?" Minho's grin widened. "You fell from Anord's favor. Our Creator let me know."

"Get back," I whispered to Ryanne. Would he turn like Edward did back at my ship?

Minho smiled with triumph. "Now *I* will take your powers, Irish."

"That's going to be hard, *halfling*."

"I'm no halfling," he spat, face red. "I'm a full-fledge bradaí, *fae lover*." He lifted his sword in a mock salute. "And this is the end of the mighty Irish."

"You'll have to take me down first." I opened my stance and beckoned him over. I dared not look at Ryanne and hoped she'd heeded me.

Minho lunged, the golden chain around his neck glinting. I parried his strokes, ducking and stepping aside. His attack was relentless, yet each stroke well-thought.

Was I still immortal?

Could I be killed now?

Something odd and unfamiliar tightened my chest and quickened my breathing.

Fear.

"Finally." Minho rejoiced as if I was already defeated. "So many years under Edward's shadow, listening to how great you were and of those mysterious powers of yours. They shall be mine now!"

Aware of the uneven terrain and the roots and rocks littering the place, I tried to push forward to take him to the ravine. I'd send the bastard flying there.

In a fluid movement, he sliced the air, the blade directed to my left side. I twisted and took a step backward. A root entangled my foot, and I staggered. His sword swooshed just an inch above me, and I cringed.

I slammed to the ground. He lunged, and I rolled over. When did the bastard get so good? We were running out of time.

Jumping to my feet, I leaped over thick roots while Minho followed closely. My hands turned clammy. I readied my defense and for a second, we stopped and locked gazes.

Blackness covered his sclera, like Edward's back at my ship.

"Yah," he breathed, eyes momentarily glazed like Edward back at my ship. "I know how to kill you. Anord is whispering it to me now."

I risked a quick glance at Ryanne. She stood near a tree, eyes closed and hands together. *Préachta* reacted to her power.

If Anord guided Minho's hand, I wouldn't stand a chance. Neither would she.

The clock was ticking.

How long until the rest of my kin arrived?

How long until I died again?

"Your face turned ashen, Irish. Now why is that?" He clicked his tongue. "You're afraid, yah. The mighty Irish afraid!" He gave a bark of laughter.

Fear. I blinked my eyes from the sweat slithering down my forehead.

Minho attacked again. His strokes were fluid, slashing at my arms and chest, barely giving me time to deflect them, much less attack back. I was losing ground.

Was I bleeding? Perhaps it was just sweat.

"You will die by my hand!" he exclaimed.

I already died, you bastard, and here I am.

Aye. Fear was gripping me, although I pushed it aside. Keep him bragging.

He managed to slice my thigh, cutting through yet barely enough for me to feel it.

"If you're so mighty, why stay with Edward all these years?" I slashed at his arm and blood spurted.

"Because it was easier to have everyone blaming him." He stepped out of reach and cocked his head. "Like Sergei's first mate."

"What?"

"You thought it was Edward. See? I fooled everyone." His eyes narrowed to slits, still blackened to the sclera. "Sergei turned his back on you. It was as sweet as if Anord talked to me."

"You killed Ivan? How could you? I never felt you." I gritted my teeth. "You can't open portals. You lie."

He smirked. "Wouldn't you like to know. It was my payback for the opium trade, Irish."

"Only for that? I thought you hated me because Edward and I crushed your fae essence."

"I'm no fae!" His jaw muscle twitched and pointed his sword at me. "There is only *dorcha* inside me. And it wasn't Edward. It was you, Irish. You did it. But let's not waste time, Aodhán," he called, triumphant.

I gritted my teeth and attacked.

Minho deflected my stroke and slashed with a quickness I wasn't prepared for. My muscles tensed, getting ready for the impact. His face shone with glee.

He cast a glance toward Ryanne. "Don't worry, Irish. I won't give you the last killing blow until you see how I take care of her. I'm sure Kara told you what I did with her fae pet."

The blade reached my side, cutting through the first layers of skin. Exactly where the dryshite struck me dead.

Préachta burst in my chest. It felt . . . different. Happier. I traded a look at Ryanne, her face scrunched in concentration. It was then I noticed her energy *in* me, making my own *préachta* stronger.

My touch of fae.

Anord's balls.

I twisted and hit Minho with the hilt of my sword, my hand guided by the cold energy.

The hit impacted his skull with the force of two dannan's. Minho staggered, white taking the sclera again. *Préachta* took over, and I hit him again with a defying cry. And again. And again.

No mercy.

Minho's eyes rolled. Finally, he fell, unconscious.

And there lay the mighty Minho.

Ryanne rushed to my side. "Are you hurt? You're bleeding."

Blood seeped in the places where he cut me, but nothing of consequence. Pain throbbed, though it was manageable. Was it?

Am I mortal?

Grounding my teeth, I pushed the thought aside.

"Just superficial wounds. Let's go. This place will be swarming with bradaís the moment they figure out how to reach here."

How did Minho arrive, faster than the others? Faster than Edward. I crouched and placed a hand on his chest, my fingers brushing his golden chain. He groaned, but I couldn't sense anything inside him but *dorcha*. No fae energy responded. He was indeed a full-fledge bradaí.

Panting, I extended my senses for imminent danger. My skin tingled. Another one! Hell!

Homkar stomped from behind one of the trees, Zorkar at his side. Neither dannan looked badly injured. Kara burst right behind them. Wary, I assessed her. The wild look in her eyes worried me.

"You're alive! By Odin, I'm so glad you're alive!" She had blood covering her face and chest and looked exhausted.

"Bricius!" Ryanne shrieked.

And sure enough, the pixie hovered around Homkar, then flew directly toward her.

"Captain!" Homkar exclaimed. "We thought you dead until we heard you fighting with Minho."

Minho tried to stand up, but Homkar reached him and kicked him in his face. Minho fell down unconscious. Grand.

I stared at Kara, but blackness hadn't covered her sclera—she wasn't taken yet. "Stand back, Kara. I won't be taken down easily." I opened my stance and pointed my sword tightly at her.

She turned to Homkar. "Grab my arms and don't let me go. Do it!"

Homkar did as told and looked at me quizzically. Kara fought against him—her face showed her inner struggle. I nodded at her bravery—she was fighting it.

"I'm never going to try, little brother," she said in a strangled tone. "No matter if that bastard Anord is yelling for your blood. But you have to get out of here." Her haunted gaze locked with mine, her eyes still brown. "Anord has been playing the message again and again since that Eadrom killed—*injured* you a couple of hours ago. And I tried to kill him, Doyle, I did. But he beat me, and I had to run away. Odin help me, I couldn't."

"He helped." Homkar pointed at the pixie, who was talking to Ryanne in their usual hissing communication. "He led us here as well."

"Is Anord pinpointing me as he did with the other fallen?" If so, we were in deep trouble. We would never escape from him. For once, I was glad I couldn't hear his call. Perhaps the coin was what connected us to him.

"It's like you have a freaking Eat-at-Joe's sign over . . . Wait. The signal was strong at first but . . ." Confusion flashed across her face.

The call I couldn't hear.

"Something's off. Never mind. Go. I'll stay here to dissuade our kin. Perhaps we can confuse them, buy you some time so you can gather your bearings."

"No, I can't let you get hurt for me."

She jutted her head toward the nearest tree. "Don't be a dimwit. Go. Now!"

"Leave as soon as you can. We'll get Edward, I promise."

Fire lit her eyes.

"And . . . thank you. All of you."

Homkar nodded. Zorkar waved a hand.

Kara stared right into my eyes. "I heard him. Minho. He was the one who killed Ivan, didn't he?"

"Aye, he did."

We locked gazes for a couple of seconds. She turned her head, shutting her eyes. I grabbed Ryanne's hand and ran away from the clearing.

"Let's get away," Ryanne wheezed, her face paler than usual.

"Your pixie?"

Bricius had flown away.

"I told him about what happened and asked him to report back to Cuidi."

I furrowed my brow. "Fae are not to be trusted."

"Eh, I wouldn't say that. But I want Cuidi to be in the know. . . Wait!" She stopped in her tracks and pointed at a small creature, who hid behind a bush. "Was that a goblin?"

"I don't think so. It has a hat."

"But . . ." She pointed at it, confusion on her face.

"We'll talk about this later."

When we were far away enough, I opened a portal, and we both stumbled through it.

THIRTY-EIGHT

Ryanne

Still breathless from what had just happened with Minho and Titus, I thumped hands on knees, panting. The effort to push Aine toward Titus at such a distance had worn me out.

We'd arrived at a city street at dawn. Or was it dusk? A building loomed nearby, and a chill crossed my body. Energy swirled around me and then tightened, one I couldn't pinpoint.

"What in Anord's hell?" Titus spat.

"What? Where are we?"

"Somewhere we don't belong. Where *I* don't belong."

I straightened and looked up. The white building had the words *St. Joseph* on its whitewashed wall. A church.

He stared at his hands as if they'd tricked him. "I'd never appeared next to one before, but when I opened the portal, I felt something odd. A pull."

"Something *is* pulling us. I felt that too."

Titus wrapped me in a tight embrace. "You sharing Aine with me was amazing, *ashtore.*"

"I didn't know if it would work, but I had to try something."

"It worked, all right. Let's go, we need to hide from my kin."

"And from fae," I muttered.

He clasped my hand and pulled me toward the street.

"Wait." I looked up again.

Bradaís disliked churches, didn't they? And there was that pull toward it. A different kind of energy I'd never felt before. Maybe I was more sensible now.

"Come," I said, jerking my head toward the door.

Titus went rigid, refusing to move a step. "No. I won't go in there."

"Neither will your kin." I tugged him toward the entrance. "Just while we gather our breath." I wasn't feeling particularly tired, but Titus was, though he'd never own it.

Step by step, he followed, yet his body tensed as if ready to run until he froze in the doorway. As hard as I tried to pull, he wouldn't budge.

"I don't belong here, Ryanne."

I tried hard not to roll my eyes. *Very* hard. With a sigh, he stepped inside. Just barely.

"See? You weren't struck by lightning or anything." I let go of his hand and sat on a bench in the back. With a playful smile, I patted next to me.

Again he sighed and complied.

The church was empty except for an old man sitting in the first row.

"Now what?" Titus asked in a sharp tone, his hands grabbing the bench, his knuckles turning white.

"We wait until we both figure out a plan."

"We can't go anywhere," he said, shaking his head. "In any place here in Tír na Donna, bradaís will hunt us relentlessly until they finish me off. We can't go to Tír D'aois since the fae will be expecting us."

"Then we're doomed," I said joyfully.

Fae believed in Ard-Bheith, the Supreme Being. Or God or Yahweh or Allah or Vishnu or whatever name we humans gave Him. I guessed He didn't mind. Though He might be a She or They or whatever. I guessed He didn't mind that either.

So maybe I should pray for us to come up with a solution. I closed my eyes and took a deep breath.

"I don't feel your energy," Titus said. "Are you calling it?"

"No, I'm praying for a solution."

"That's a waste of time."

I looked up at him. "Got a better plan? We're in a church so why not? Try it."

"I don't know what that is."

"Just ask for what you want. With humility."

"What I want no one can give to me."

Something in his cold tone of voice made me decide not to ask what it was. But I took his hand, squeezing it gently.

"Where can we go, then?"

"Kara and I came with a plan to face Edward. I wanted to reach Sergei, but with the blood-calling, that won't be a good idea anymore. You saw Kara. Every bradaí is after my hide. Once Kara is over the blood-calling, we might put our heads together and figure out a solid plan to confront the Alpha once and for all."

"What is that blood-calling you mention?"

"Anord implants us a desire to kill the bradaí who've fallen. It's a force that doesn't let us think of anything else."

"That . . . sounds dangerous. Is your place safe?"

"For tonight only. We'll have to keep moving, though."

Cuidi had been right; danger swirled around Titus. Yet, as crazy as it was, I couldn't leave him. Maybe together we could activate that spark and remove the beast once and for all. I squeezed his hand, relishing in his warm touch.

The old man was now walking down the aisle with a slow, measured pace, head down and shoulders slouched as if he carried enormous weight. His clothes looked secondhand, worn and faded. His wispy white hair fell in disorder on his shoulders.

Titus stood up and retrieved his sword from his bradaí pocket, then pointed it at the old man. "Who are you?" he demanded.

With the same slowness the old man used for walking, he turned to us. Wrinkles covered his dark brown parched face.

"I know you," Titus said. "I've felt you before."

"Ah yes," the old man said with a raspy voice as if he hadn't used it for a long time. "We just saw each other in a cave."

"Amriel," Titus breathed.

Amriel? The nádhúrtha who liked coffee, but he didn't look like the one I saw back at the Starbucks, though that pull of energy from before felt the same as what I felt now: a bright, joyous energy, like that of a pixie but deeper. Stronger.

"What you desire," Amriel said to Titus, "is not within the reach of your kind."

"How do you know?" Titus asked haughtily.

"*Facta, non verba.*"

The old man bowed his head and stretched his hand to place it on Titus's forehead, eyes closed.

Titus fell on his knees, panting. I gasped. There was no old man now but a young one, with braided hair and colorful beads, and he had a bright sparkling robe. A dim light surrounded him, covering Titus's forehead.

It was Amriel, all right. Aine expanded and contracted . . . no, my *préachta*. That was the right name for my power.

"Where can we go?" I blurted. "We need a safe place."

"Safe. Interesting word. Can one be protected from danger anywhere? Danger looms in every corner, yet our choices make us meet them or skirt them. *De fumo in flammam.*" He stared at me with burning eyes as if wanting to brand his words in fire inside my brain. "Trust your heart."

He started to walk again, shrinking with every step, his light fading until he looked again like a tired, old man.

Trust my heart. Where could we go? My head felt about to explode until I noticed Titus sobbing. I knelt next to him and placed a hand on his shoulder.

"Titus . . ."

"Let's go." He rose, wiping tears with the back of his hand.

"What happened? Titus?"

He took my face in his hands. "You're so pure. I don't deserve you."

"Pure? Shit no, I'm full of flaws and I'm always making stupid mistakes."

"Compared to me, you shine bright."

"Don't say that," I whispered, cupping his cheek.

He kissed my lips softly. "Let's go to my place. I need a familiar place just for tonight."

"Just tonight," I agreed.

Titus

A black, endless hole sucked me in, leaving me breathless. I fell until I touched the ground. An endless plain stretched before me, and humans ran toward me, hatred distorting their expressions.

A sword appeared in my hand to decapitate the screaming enemies. Blood poured over my hands until I stood in a crimson pool with a crazy grin on my face.

Pretty boy appeared out of nowhere, jabbing me with his sword. Anguish tore me apart.

Above my hip, a wound opened—blood poured from it and joined the crimson pool at my feet. I staggered until I spotted a barrel of water, but the water was far away, and I couldn't reach it. My throat was dry, my thirst unquenchable.

I collapsed to the ground, sobbing without knowing why. Blood drenched my hands, blood I tried to remove with my tears, but the more I tried, the bloodier they became.

A guttural cry pierced the air.

Dozens of human creatures clamored for my head. Some I recognized—all I'd killed. I stood, stumbling backward until my hands found a wall.

My hands. Of course. I raised one to open the portal that would take me away from this nightmare. But no portal appeared. A plaintive cry rose, and I found myself surrounded, hands tearing at my clothes, demanding my death.

Humans knocked me down and kicked me mercilessly.

Sharp and unyielding pain skewered me like a new sword forged by fire. I ripped at bloodied clothes, trying to remove the torment assailing my skin.

The memories of my foul deeds pierced through my mind. One by one with unusual clarity, just like the old man showed me. Their scared and anguished faces as I'd killed them. Their screams pierced my ears, their unheard pleas nails through my skin. My sobs increased as I yanked my hair.

Would Ryanne forgive me if she knew what I'd done?

Ryanne's memory smoothed away the darkness like the coming of dawn, like a fresh balm over my sore wounds. I thought I heard her sweet voice, calling me.

I stood and found myself alone.

I took in the surroundings—an enormous room with walls so high I couldn't see where they ended. A bright light lit up the abandoned place. The hurt was gone, and peace shrouded me instead.

Blood no longer covered my hands, and my clothes were clean. I felt light, like a huge burden had lifted from my shoulders and I could finally breathe again.

"Aodhán."

I spun, searching for my sword to deflect the blow. But the dark-skinned man in dazzling white robes had no weapon. His hands clasped in front, his bright eyes piercing me as if knowing exactly what I had done.

I hung my head, ashamed.

"You are looking for something that none of your kind has attained. Or tried to find."

The words were familiar, belonging to the same wrinkled old man from the church. I ventured a glimpse. Not alike, yet there was no mistaking him for someone else. His gaze wasn't aggressive, but powerful and ancient, so old he made the most aged Tír D'aois being look like a baby.

"Who are you?" I asked.

"Dozens of names we have, depending upon who name us: Devas, First Movers, Messengers, Angels, Warriors, Nádhúrthas. You may call me as you desire. It matters not, though I like Amriel myself."

I squinted, finding it hard to discern his features under the brilliance. "Why are you here? I thought you never involve yourselves with us bradaís."

"Dire times call for dire measures."

"I want to find my soul," I said, slumping to my knees before him and trying to remove the haughtiness from my voice. How could I be proud in front of a being who could crush me like a bug? Perhaps he could show me how to remove my beast if the fae-spirit couldn't.

"You do not have one. *Certum est quia impossible est.*"

This is certain because it is impossible. Grand.

"Then I want to find a soul for me . . . please. I want to get rid of my beast." Somehow I felt that was the answer. Ryanne had wanted to find that connection within me. The spark.

"You have committed hundreds of atrocities, Aodhán."

I thought I'd escaped the throbbing pain. That I was indifferent to it. But I felt it inside, although it was hidden, waiting to pounce on me once I left this space.

"There is no real happiness if the suffering is unknown," he said as if reading my thoughts. "That is the path. Are you willing, Aodhán? *Qui audet adipiscitur.*"

He who dares, wins.

"My beast—"

"It is not present."

"Did you remove it?" I asked. "Is this why I feel light and in peace?"

Amriel nodded. "Unfortunately, that is because this is a special place. Only you I brought here. As you awake, you shall have it again."

"How can I get rid of it?"

"Do not let it control you."

"It hasn't."

He stared into my eyes, and the image of me in that burning building, the corpses at my feet blinked in my mind.

"When she's around . . ."

"She has helped you. But what happens when she's away? Control it without her, then, perhaps, we can talk again." He smiled.

A force pulled me down, and I plunged back into a whirlpool while the nádhúrtha's eyes shone above me.

"Do not let it control you when she's away."

I found myself laying on a bed, forehead beaded with sweat. Ryanne slept peacefully by my side. I sat beside her and stroked her hair. So pure, so good.

So unlike me.

I pushed aside the sheets and donned my trousers and shirt.

I left the bedroom and walked toward the French doors in my living room, leading to the balcony. I rested my elbows on the railing, watching Elliot Bay. The salty breeze reassured me, albeit I couldn't shake the feeling I was doing something wrong.

Would I get rid of the beast if I didn't let it control me? And how would I know if Ryanne inhibited the beast? I shook my head wearily. I would never find the peace I was looking for with the beast inside. Had I not killed all those humans in Sander's lab and let the beast dominate me yet again?

And if Amriel was right, I had to find my inner strength and not give in. By myself.

I was the first bradaí to survive their own death. Per Ryanne's explanation, as long as no one claimed the coin, I'd keep my powers, which made sense since I still had them. Who was to say the fae-spirit wouldn't offer my powers to another bradaí if I wasn't needed anymore?

Was that her way to control me?

De fumo in flammam. Perhaps that was what he meant. Out of the smoke and into the flame.

Could Anord feel there was no coin inside me now? What would he do, or instruct my kin to do, if all failed to kill me?

But most importantly, what had the coin meant? I had the beast. I had my powers. I replayed the scene where I found Luc dead and Edward crouched. Mentally I went through it all, taking all the details.

My head jerked up. Edward's fist had glowed coppery gold, something akin to what Ryanne experienced. Edward must have taken the coin after the Eadrom gave the killing blow. The fae-spirit might have whispered Luc's Name to the Eadrom, but his lover was not up to the task. Or Edward found both right away.

Perhaps that was why the fae-spirit took us to the cave, so I wouldn't suffer the same fate as Luc and Thomas. Both bradaís had been a bet the spirit lost.

The image of my rabid kin arriving at Corsica. Minho's eyes taken by darkness.

Any bloodlust-driven bradaí would seek to kill me. When they couldn't, *if* they couldn't, they might go after Ryanne.

To hell with them.

I patted my side where the coin had been.

I could be mortal now.

I *might* be mortal now.

The memory of Luc's woman, dead beside him—their hands outstretched to one another—burned my insides. What if that was me and Ryanne?

Too many *ifs*. Too many questions and no answers to satisfy me. For the first time, fear paralyzed me. Not fear for me, but for her.

I sensed the shift in the energies. Dawn was about to break.

Time to get moving. The question was . . . with Ryanne or without her? I was placing her in danger, anyway. I'd been lucky with Minho, but could I fight back more than one bradaí if I was hunted like a wild beast?

No way in Anord's hell.

And I didn't know how long I could stay ahead of my kin. Whether the fae-spirit had a plan for me, fae like the dryshite still hated me. Ryanne had tried to intercede for me, and yet Pretty Boy went for the kill. How many like him? Too many.

No, going to the fae was out of the question.

But she'd be safe behind their walls.

I headed to the kitchen, just to find it full of canned food. We'd been too tired to care for food last night, but she'd be starving when she woke up. I seized my jacket and stormed out of the apartment. Once I left her with them, I would make the bradaís go after me and leave her alone.

The sleepy security guard greeted me.

"Listen," I said. "There's a woman in my place. If she wakes up before I return, don't let her go out. Tell her I'll be back soon."

I didn't wait for his answer as I shoved my hands in the jacket's pockets and lengthened my strides. Find food, then return to Tír D'aois.

My chest hurt as though scorpions' tails stabbed into it. Would this pain accompany me every day for the rest of my life? This loneliness that tore me from the inside out? Was this what the nádhúrtha meant?

I walked without purpose for a couple of blocks, though I should be getting some food.

The hairs on my neck stood and burned like heated coals, and I spun, wary. Kara appeared from behind a corner. She didn't have the wild look she had yesterday and seemed more like herself.

"Kara! You're okay. They didn't come after me?"

She gave a crooked smile. "Oh, they did. But those guys . . . By Odin! Your first mate and his brother are good at dissuasion."

"Homkar? Is he okay?"

"Yes. He's with his brother. Needs a break, it seems. And some rest."

I felt relieved. "How did you find me? Anord?" My hands curled into fists.

"No, he's calling for your blood, but oddly enough he can't pinpoint your location as with the others. He sounds confused. We like that, don't we?" She winked.

I sucked in a breath. Anord didn't know where I was without the coin. I turned my head toward my apartment. Perhaps I could find a way to be with Ryanne, then. An oppressive shadow lifted.

"Do I have to worry about you?" I smiled yet watched her carefully.

"The call burns my blood, but I can control it if I focus." Her happy countenance darkened. "Not everything I have to say is good news, though. While we were distracted, Minho disappeared even though Zorkar had tied him tightly."

"How?"

"Beats me. That guy has tricks not so different from yours."

"He can't open portals," I said thoughtfully. I could because the touch of fae inside connected me with Tír D'aois. That was clear now.

"What if his fae essence never died?" Kara asked.

"Impossible. He tried several times to open a portal under Edward's surveillance."

"He could have faked it."

"Not a chance in hell. He's Edward's puppet." Or rather, he'd been until now. "And I felt for fae power right before you came into the clearing. It's gone."

"Never mind that. Where's your woman?" She looked around as if expecting Ryanne to materialize.

"She's at my place, sleeping."

She grabbed my jacket. "You left her alone, you dimwit? Sergei's heading for your apartment! That's why I came here, to warn you."

"The Morrigan curse him!"

Not waiting to see if Kara followed me, I broke into a sprint.

FORTY

Ryanne

I woke up with a start, my heart pounding. Something had nagged at me, preventing me from falling asleep, but what?

"Titus?" I called to an empty bedroom.

I checked around, but he wasn't there. I splashed water on my face, wondering where he'd gone or why he didn't leave me a message letting me know when he'd return.

What was I forgetting?

The sound of the main door closing signaled Titus was back. I walked with confident steps out of the bedroom.

"Titus, we have to . . ." I stopped short.

A huge, tall man stood in the center of the living room. Long, whitish-blond hair tied behind his thick neck. His faded jeans and T-shirt did a poor job at concealing his powerful muscles. Brown eyes peered beneath thick lashes, and a five o'clock shadow shaded his square, powerful jaw.

"What we have here?" His voice was deep and with a slight foreign accent. "Don't be afraid; you're comfortable with our kin, *da*?" Laughter rumbled in his chest, and I cringed, taking a step back.

A bradaí.

"You better leave. Titus will be here any second and—"

The man moved quickly and squeezed my jaw. *Préachta* swirled, angry like annoyed hornets. Following the energy, I twisted his hand and kicked his crotch with my knee.

With a gasp of surprise, he let me go. Letting *préachta* dictate the movement, I punched his ruddy face. He barely moved, then grinned.

"You're feisty. Good."

He hit back. *Préachta* warned me, and I ducked in time. I smacked his solar plexus, throwing my weight forward, directing the power that sprang from my chest at that point.

"*Bozhe moi!*" A look of surprise reflected on his face, and he stumbled, groaning.

More surprised than he was, I opted not to waste time and darted to the main door. My head jerked back, my scalp itching, and I let out a cry.

"You won't escape, as quarrelsome as you are."

He pulled my hair down while I tried to connect a punch. Wrapping my hands with one of his own, he forced them over my head then threw me against the wall.

I grunted.

The giant bent, sniffing me. "What's this?" He sounded perplexed. "You are one of *those*. How?"

He released me and took a step back, brooding.

"Pick on someone your own size, Sergei," Titus said, bursting in, Kara behind him.

I sighed in relief and took a few steps back. This was Sergei? Titus's friend. *Former* friend, I'd say.

"Ah. Here he is. Good." Sergei cracked his knuckles. The hatred oozing from him was a palpable shadow.

He launched at Titus, fists ready. Titus ducked in time, the massive fist ruffling his hair. Kara stepped between them, and both men froze. Sergei's nostrils flared.

"Stop! It's time to stop!" Kara yelled.

"Move, Kara. This doesn't concern you," Sergei said.

"Kiss my arse, Sergei," she spat, throwing a punch at his face. The big man stepped back.

Pushing Kara aside, Sergei seized Titus's shirt. "You treacherous Irish trash." He pressed his face close to Titus, snarling.

"I didn't kill Ivan, bloody stubborn Russian. Minho did."

"You're a lying bastard, Doyle. First Edward, now Minho? But you'll know how it feels to lose someone close. I'll do your woman, *da*?"

Oh, geez, really, this stupid macho stunt from last century. I clenched my stinging fist. If only I could hit like Kara. If only.

Kara jumped on his back and choked Sergei, making him loosen his hold on Titus.

"Listen, dimwit," she hissed. "Doyle's telling the truth. I heard it myself. Minho confessed before trying to kill him."

Emotions flickered on the huge man's otherwise impassive face. Confusion, hurt, doubt. Kara released him and rotated her shoulders while Sergei stumbled like a drunk.

"*Nyet!* Doyle was the culprit." He stared at Kara, his chest heaving. He slumped on the couch, hands pressing against his head. "Was there a witness? Who heard him?"

"I did. Loud and clear," Kara said. "Minho bragged about fooling everyone."

Titus sat in front of him. "Now do you believe me, good-for-nothing *friend*?" he spat.

"You said Edward did it." Sergei lifted his head; all trace of hate vanished from his eyes. He looked older, worn out.

"He *always* says Edward did it." Kara scoffed. "Everything."

Titus grunted.

Relieved that the feisty mood had cooled down, I sat next to Titus. He put his arm around me and pulled me close.

"I thought it was him," Titus admitted. "Seems the bastard hadn't been lying. At least not all the time."

Titus told him what Minho said in the clearing, word for word. Then, about how Peter was an Eadrom and how he nearly killed him. Kara kept interrupting him and adding information.

"Your woman." Sergei stared at me, weary. "She's like Ivan. I felt her."

"Ryanne," I hissed. "Name's Ryanne."

"Aye," Titus said as if I hadn't talked. "I'm sorry. For not under-standing you and Ivan."

"*Da*. I guess not easy to understand my desire to be a father."

"Why?" Titus asked, befuddled. "Why would you want that?"

He shrugged. "I just did."

"Enough with this chitchat," Kara said, thumping open palms over her thighs. "We're now together, and we need to plan our next step, by Odin."

"What's that?" Sergei asked, befuddled.

"Kill Edward," Titus answered, fist clenched.

"We tried that before, Doyle," Sergei said. "Half of the bradaís betrayed us."

"We're not doing it with the rest," Titus said. "Only us. You in?"

Sergei glanced at Kara.

"We are," she said with that fire in her eyes I was beginning to recognize as one of her traits. "With *dorcha*." Her fist clenched, and I could sense darkness in there.

I leaned forward. Could they defeat Edward with their *dorcha*? Three bradaís joining their darkness against their Alpha.

"Give me something to wet my throat, and I'll listen to that crazy plan," Sergei said, his lips breaking into a smile for the first time.

Kara smacked her thigh. "And some food, by Odin! I'm starving."

Titus's pantry had only canned food and bottles, so we prepared an improvised breakfast with tuna and crackers and grapefruit juice. And a bottle of whiskey. Sergei grimaced at the whiskey but drank it without further complaints.

Titus and Kara talked about using their combined *dorcha*, both excited and interrupting each other. With the set up carefully planned, Sergei kept quiet, obviously unconvinced.

"How did you find me, by the way?" Titus asked.

"Remember how you bragged a long time ago how you've learned from humans? I did the same. I hired a pri—"

"This flat isn't in my name, and I've only had two months with it."

Sergei exhaled hard, seemingly upset by the interruption. "I hired a private investigator years ago to follow you and record all your favorite haunts. Then I hired this expert on break-ins, who boobie-trapped your places. She found this place a few weeks ago. You were right; humans can be useful." He guffawed.

Titus stared at Sergei. "You aren't taken by the blood calling, then. Can't you hear Anord?"

"*Da.* I hear him. I'm not good at listening, it seems." He tapped his head. "Hard skull."

"You got that right," Titus said.

The hairs on my arms stood, *préachta* swirling like a blasting siren. A vision splashed in my conscience, a past one. What had been bothering me since last night.

The vision with the dead guard, the one I had the day I met Titus and entered his building. But now it had more elements: a bradaí pushing the body to the floor. A bradaí I knew too well, darkness emanating from him. A red circle, like that time when the mercenaries trapped us, flashed at the bottom of the vision.

Dainséar, it whispered. Danger.

"Edward," I whispered as I stood, knees trembling. "He's coming. Titus, open a portal! We have but seconds!"

Titus shot up, but he didn't make a move. His gaze fixed on the door, fingers tensed as if they were squeezing Edward's throat.

"Titus?"

FORTY-ONE

Titus

The door cracked open. In a second, the Alpha would enter, and we would be trapped here. There was no doubt in my mind why he was here.

Me.

My coin. My absent coin. Anord had sent the call, and here he was, ready to kick my arse with a smile and blast me to the void.

He's the Alpha. Obey him.

Ryanne's face was ashen. "We're not leaving?" she asked.

I turned to Kara. "Plan be damned. Ready?"

She cracked her knuckles. "Let's kick his sweet arse, little brother."

You cannot win this time.

"You're forgetting a little detail," Ryanne whispered.

The door swung open, and Edward stood in the frame in a grand entrance, a smirk on his face as he swept his gaze to all of us. *Dorcha* gathered in my fists.

"What?" I whispered back.

"Me."

My body tensed with worry. What a gobshite, so focused on Edward I forgot Ryanne shouldn't be here.

"Try to get away," I said quietly. "He won't even look at you." It was me whom he wanted.

Anord be damned. But then, one had to seize opportunities when we could. Sergei worried me. A couple of hours together after decades of estrangement didn't assure his participation.

"I'll be . . . A cozy family reunion." Edward sauntered inside, all the world at his feet, as he'd said when he beat my arse.

But we stood united. Kara at my right, Sergei at my left.

You have no friends. They will betray you.

I gritted my teeth. With Edward here, the beast had awoken despite Ryanne's proximity. And it was obvious Anord wanted me gone this time.

Minho entered after him. Aye, so much for plans. How did that Irish proverb go? There's rarely a perfect time to do something, so you may as well get started now.

I glanced at my friends. Friends.

Another proverb rang in my head. There is no strength without unity.

I smirked.

Edward arranged his silk shirt and tucked it into his gray pants.

"What a pleasant surprise. I came to pay a friendly visit to the Irish, and I found the three of you. Together. You aren't planning anything against me, are you?" He smiled benevolently.

"How the hell did you find me?" I asked, defiant. I needed to know if indeed Anord couldn't pinpoint me.

"Sergei led us here."

Sergei was silent.

I fought hard not to look at Sergei. He could betray me and make me pay, if not for Ivan's murder, then for not standing with him and understanding his relationship with Ivan. Or only because he was a bradaí.

I took a step forward. "Welcome to my home, then," I said with a bright smile, my arms opened wide. "Wine, Ed?"

He waved a hand. "Let's leave the pleasantries for later." His face darkened. "I'll drink wine over your cold body, Irish. It's time. Sergei, drop the pretense."

Sergei walked to Edward and placed himself next to the Alpha, then folded his arms across his broad chest. My scowl deepened, and Kara cursed. Aye, once a bradaí, always a bradaí.

You have no friends. You are alone.

Except for Ryanne. Although if I didn't win this, she'd die at Edward's hands. My head fogged with worry, but I gritted my teeth and forced the worry away.

Fear would not help Ryanne.

"You, Odin's bitch," Edward said, pointing at Kara. "Leave. This doesn't concern you. Sergei can watch as I finish the Irish, yes?"

This was the moment of truth. Sergei had betrayed me, and Kara could have a change of heart. Odds weren't in my favor.

Kara thrust her hip to the side. "Love, don't be daft," she purred to Edward. "This is not my ship, and I'm not alone. Mess with my brother, you mess with me."

I grinned.

Edward shrugged, then thrust his hand into his pockets and showed me two golden coins, larger than usual, each featuring a skull. "We need a third, yes? Yours."

Gold. Something nagged me, but I pushed it aside. Focus on Edward was the only thing that mattered.

"I'll take the Irish. Sergei, prove yourself to Anord. Break this bitch's bones and throw her into the ocean with a dead weight. Make sure she doesn't come up for decades. Minho, dispose of that fae's pet for me, will you?" He waved a hand toward Ryanne.

Sergei cracked his knuckles. Bloody cursed traitor.

Why did I trust that Russian again? Ryanne wouldn't be in danger if he hadn't switched gears.

I couldn't get distracted. Ryanne was stronger now. I called *dorcha*. It erupted in my gut, then pounded and buzzed like angry wasps. The darkness within me traveled to my arms, my hands, a fire spreading on dry twigs.

I'd never let myself be taken by *dorcha*, not entirely.
This was it.

FORTY-TWO

Ryanne

un, préachta seemed to say. But Minho stood in my way to freedom.

The same darkness Edward emanated in the ship shrouded him. I gazed down and retreated backward until I stuck my back to the wall.

A fly. A damned cowardly fly.

What could I do? If Titus had never been able to fight Edward back, what were my chances with Minho?

None. Zip. Nada. But I flexed my fists and ordered my *préachta* to stand by—a pebble could trigger a landslide, after all. I glared at Sergei. How could he?

He's a bradaí, my own voice whispered in my head. *Traitors,* Titus had said.

Minho sauntered toward me, unsheathing his wicked knife. I glanced toward Titus, engaged with Edward. Had something changed since his coin had been removed?

I couldn't see Sergei and Kara well. Before I craned my neck, Minho's knife flashed before my eyes. Black with a sickly green hue.

"Ah, little bee, so glad to see you again. You wanted to see my work, yah?"

"I changed my mind," I said, surprisingly steady. "I think your work sucks."

He chuckled.

I'd defeated a nymph, hadn't I? Granted, *préachta* worked best with Tír D'aois creatures, and I had no idea how it'd work against a bradaí.

But I called it to my fist, as I'd seen Titus do with his *dorcha*, and got ready to strike.

Sergei jumped on top of Minho and wrapped his hands around the knife-wielding bradaí's neck. I started. I hadn't expected someone that big to move so fast. Or be here.

Did he want to take me himself? I scowled and willed more *préachta* to both fists.

"You piece of crap," Sergei hissed to Minho.

Minho plunged his knife deep into Sergei's thigh and he roared in pain. The Russian pushed Minho away and removed the knife, throwing it to the floor.

"What trick is that?" Sergei exclaimed.

"Goblin's blade," Minho said, taking a quick look behind him. "Bites like a bitch, doesn't it?"

Kara and Titus were fighting against Edward, a dark gray mist floating around them. The couch and chairs had been thrown to the side, and Kara was standing on the coffee table.

Their fighting felt in slow motion while Minho and Sergei thrashed around.

"You killed Ivan!" Sergei spat.

I let *préachta* go and stuck to the wall to avoid being hit.

Unfortunately Minho seized that moment to slice his blade across the big man's chest. Sergei grunted.

"So? He was a fae's pet. I'm glad I did!" Minho retorted.

The path to the door cleared.

I could run. I could dash away. This wasn't a place for me. I was only the fly on the wall. Sidestepping Minho and Sergei was a feat in itself. One false step, and I'd get smacked.

I reached the door, heart thumping. How could I leave Titus to this fate? But what could I do here? I was scared to leave and terrified to stay.

Sergei and Minho were on equal footing, and there was no way to know who would win.

Kara lay on the floor, seizures taking her body as black thorns spread across her face. Her eyes rolled, white foam coming out of her mouth.

What the heck?

Titus and Edward were locked, hands on the other's throat, eyes intent on their foe.

Fear coiled my insides. The only ones who could stop Edward were the fae. The Eadroms. Cuidi and Peter. Not seers.

Oh shit. If I could shout to Cuidi, call Peter, this would be over. No, Peter would attack them all, including Titus and friends.

Préachta was cowed like me, an insignificant portion of my power. Insignificant. Cowed.

Then it hit me. My fae power was feeding from my fear. And I had to block that fear.

A green glint caught my eye—Minho's knife on the floor. Sticking to the wall as much as I could to avoid Sergei and Minho's fisticuffing, I reached the blade and crouched.

As I seized its handle, a tingling spread through my fingers. Darkness of a different nature than the bradaí, whispers of a foreign language invaded my mind.

And then, a vision splashed before me. Bradaís reaching the lobby and stepping over the dead guard. A red circle shone at the bottom.

"Titus! More bradaís!"

Minho panted and said to Sergei with glee, "You and your friends are done. They are all coming because of the calling. Anord sent them to finish the Irish!"

Sergei smacked his fist on Minho's face, who staggered and fell. "Done here." He crouched and seized Mino's ankles. "I'll take the garbage out."

Kara was standing now, weak but the fire in her eyes hadn't

dimmed. "Let's give Doyle some space, Sergei." She hiccuped but slogged toward me. "Stay out of the way, love."

"What happened?" I asked.

"Bloody beast tripped me; it didn't want me to fight the Alpha. I tried . . ." She glanced at her hands. "Odin knows I tried, but my *dorcha* attacked *me*. I have no idea what Doyle's doing now . . . he's certainly a different type of bradaí."

She glanced at the knife in my hands. "Be careful with that. Not a toy."

Yells came from outside.

"Come, Sergei, let's have a cozy reunion with these idiots."

Sergei closed the door after Kara left. I glanced at the dagger. What could I do? Bradaís couldn't be killed. At least not by me. My eyes met Edward and Titus.

Edward thrust his fist *inside* Titus's side. Titus howled in pain and staggered.

Something swirled in me.

I stood with my feet firmly on the floor, the blade in my hand. A bully was about to kill Titus again.

I wouldn't let him.

Préachta blossomed inside, no longer cowed.

I was no longer cowed.

No, it was up to me, and I wouldn't fail Titus.

FORTY-THREE

Titus

Fighting with *dorcha* was taking a toll.

You are done. Let the Alpha win.

Bloody beast had broken through Ryanne's cleansing and whispered to let the Alpha kill me.

His hands fastened on my throat while I clenched mine over his. Kara was out.

It was up to me.

"Didn't I tell you one day you'd fall, and I'd be there?" Edward grinned. "Today is the day, Irish."

"I couldn't care less, Ed."

"You wanted to know how I reached Luc and Thomas first. Because I'm not overpowered by the call as the rest. My head's clear, and I act faster. You would too, if you weren't taken by that odd power of yours. You from all the rest, have something that doesn't belong but allows you to be different."

Edward lifted me up a couple of centimeters. His eyes darkened like blackness from the pits of hell. His fingers closed as if pressing into dough, burning, scorching. I clawed at his hands. My inner self-defense counteracted, pushing his fingers outwards, but it was too much.

Dark tendrils of smoke surrounded his hand. My attempts to remove it were futile; my skin burned at his touch. I squeezed his throat harder. He didn't even flinch. With a half-smile, he raised his free hand and wriggled his fingers in front of me. Fingers which began to turn white as milk, purple veins highlighting, nails growing, blackening every second.

What the hell?

"Oh, yes, Irish. It is time for you to leave for good. You turned your back on Anord, on the bradaí way. You're no longer required, Aodhán."

That was the final piece. Why I'd been marked as a dead man. "Anord might whisper my Name. Much good will it do."

Would it? Would I die at Edward's hands?

The bastard raked my chest with the white milky fingers. "Doesn't this feel nice, Aodhán?"

"You're not . . ."

"Oh but I am, Aodhán. I *will* feel. Nothing like killing your kin to give you a kick, yes? Oh, yes . . . you felt something when created. When you're dead, I'll feel that too."

Pain exploded as though his hand was forged in fire. I gritted my teeth so hard I thought they were going to crack. Something salty and unfamiliar ran down my cheeks. Tears.

"I've been waiting for so long, Aodhán. Minho tried, yes? But you and I know who he really is."

My skin was torn, my chest about to explode as if several muskets shot at a single point.

"Where the hell is your coin! It should be here."

Préachta awakened.

"What is that?" he said with annoyance. "What the bloody—"

Préachta swelled in my chest, and coldness erupted from my fingers, closed tightly against his throat.

Edward gasped, but his hand remained inside me. "That's-that's fae power! Cursed Irish, that's why you're so different!" He glared at me. "Mighty fae had tried before and failed. They're all dead."

"Aye, but they didn't have what I have."

"And what is that?" He pushed more *dorcha* inside me, his jaw set.

I lifted my gaze and found Ryanne's intent eyes, eyes that reflected a mighty creature. And she had a knife in her hands. A goblin's blade. "Wouldn't you like to know."

FORTY-FOUR

Ryanne

Gripping the weapon with my shaking hands, I snuck toward Edward, a determination and ferocity born in my chest, giving strength to my arms and lightness to my feet. *Préachta* swirled inside me like a miniature hurricane gathering power.

"I played with it and shaped it in the way I wanted."

What I needed was a dragon. A mighty one. Red eyes floated before me, and I felt taller, even as it only happened in my head.

"I shaped it in the way I wanted."

It wasn't only in my head. I was powerful; I was mighty.

I was Ryanne.

Titus's eyes bore into me.

"Bollocks!" Edward withdrew his hand, the black nails still visible as well as the dark tendrils of smoke. "Whatever game you're playing, whatever bond you made with fae, ends now."

Although Titus's stomach convulsed, there was no apparent injury except for a dark purple blotch. Edward raised his hand, about to reinsert it.

Time slowed down. My vision blurred except for Edward.

All my focus was on him—my aim, my purpose.

I wasn't useless.

I wasn't weak.

Préachta didn't flow through me. I *was préachta*. It was me, and I was fae.

I jabbed the knife into Edward's trapezius. With a mental push, *préachta* launched itself like a catapult.

The dragon in me roared, and the blade glowed a sickly green.

Edward bellowed, clenching his unnatural hand into a fist. I couldn't sink the blade in more than a third.

I met Titus's eyes, eyes that mirrored my determination.

And then, I felt it. Titus's *préachta* had been fighting with Edward's darkness. Mine was the reinforcement, the infantry aiding the cavalry.

No. The general that would lead his army. The dragon about to scorch them all.

As if his energy lit mine, my whole body shook with power like when we were in the cave, and I focused all that energy into my hands, pressing as hard as I could. The knife cut through the hard skin up to the hilt.

Préachta battled inside Edward, and images flashed before me. An old man, crouched, slumped in a barren dark land. Red eyes floating in a mist. I was running, lost and confused.

A vision? No, not now!

A howl returned me to Titus's apartment.

Edward dropped Titus and turned to me, then raised his other hand as if wanting to dig his blackened nails into me.

I pushed him away, all my power focused on that push.

I was a dragon.

He staggered back.

Titus clutched his abdomen, breathing hard.

"We have to leave," I panted. Pain shot through me, and my knees buckled beneath me, not in fear, but in exhaustion.

"You!" Edward howled like a wounded dangerous animal.

His gaze froze me. My body dissociated from my mind as if floating in a sticky liquid. Ancient hatred oozed from him, like layers of rot accumulated for centuries by a being who only cried for vengeance, by someone who didn't know the light. The courage I'd gathered dissipated like drops of water on a hot rock, my chest aching as if his nails were already stuck inside me, tearing my heart open. I was no longer master of my will, and I waited for him to give me a punishment for my boldness.

Warmth like the fire in a rustic cabin, like two lovers kissing for the first time, shook me out of my daze, cleaning the hatred of the being in front of me.

Titus had taken my hand.

"Come," he said in a hoarse, raspy voice.

"Doyle!" Kara cried from the hall. "There's more coming from the stairs. Hurry! Sergei and I are holding them!"

"It's your doom, Irish!" Minho cried. "You won't get out of this building alive. Neither will that pretty thing of yours. But don't worry! I'll take her with me while you're busy fighting the others."

Edward took a shaky step toward us. "There's no place to run, Irish. I'll get you anywhere you go. Anord will guide me." He panted and attempted to grab the dagger, but no way in hell would he reach it.

Tír D'aois, my power whispered.

My heart beat faster.

Trust your heart, the nádhúrtha had said.

"Titus, let's go to Cuidi; she can help us." I urged him without raising my voice. "Please."

Titus's eyes flicked to the door, worry etched on them.

"Hurry!" Kara yelled from outside. "We can barely hold them!"

"I'll help you!" Titus yelled back. "I can't leave her alone," he said to me.

Kara yelled once more. "Are you an idiot? They can't kill me. They want you."

I cast a glance at Edward, who yelled in frustration, trying to reach the dagger. Frustrated, he staggered and panted.

I should be terrified, but instead, I felt dizzy. My fae power was now exhausted.

"Bloody hell!" Titus said. "All right."

"They're here!" Sergei bellowed.

Kara's battle cry boomed in my ears.

Edward fell sideways to the floor, yet his gaze didn't leave us. "I'll kill you!" But he sounded weak, his chest heaving.

Titus cursed loudly and opened a portal. We rushed through it.

And stumbled into darkness.

Hooded humanoid beings jumped from the treetops and surrounded us, making it impossible to retreat.

Oh, geez. Now what?

Part Four

Ryanne

orest green cloaks covered the humanoid beings, shadowing their features. Twilight made matters worse, altering the landscape into shades of muted greens and browns.

My vision—the normal one—blurred, and I blinked, resisting the urge to drop my hands to my knees until I could breathe normally again. The power spent was taking its toll.

Titus stepped in front of me and drew his sword.

"So it is true," said one of the beings in a familiar voice. "You're not dead."

Peter. *My* Peter. He removed his hood, revealing his reddish-brown hair and emerald eyes. Conflicted emotions swarmed in me. My fae mentor had always been stern and sometimes cold—okay, most of the times—but I knew he cared about me in his cold-fae way.

But he'd tried to kill Titus, even if it was part of Fé Erie's plan. He hadn't listened to me, hadn't taken into consideration my feelings for Titus.

For the first time since I met him, I glowered at him.

The other hooded beings uncovered their heads, showing hair in all lengths and hues—fae warriors, ten of them. Despite the fog and the dim light, their eyes shone brightly, their ethereal beauty contrasting with their rough cloaks.

"Your skin is thicker than I would have liked." Peter's voice was oddly calm, as if he had come to terms with Titus.

Wary, I narrowed my eyes. Why the change?

Titus lifted his sword, menacing. Peter also lifted his sword, yet his countenance was still calm. Geez, really, were they planning to resolve all their squabbles through sword fight?

I guess so. And yup, I'm the bridge. Hooray.

Unexpected anger boiled inside me, and I put myself between them, stretching my arms out while their swords hung over my head. "Stop," I said in a commanding voice.

"No," Titus muttered without removing his gaze from Peter. "If it weren't for you, this fae would have killed me for good."

I growled. Loudly.

That made Titus glance at me, brow slightly furrowed. I mimicked his frown.

"It truly surprises me that after what my Lady explained, you still want to go after my throat." Peter lowered his sword. "Your turn."

"Easy to say when you have backup," Titus snarled.

Peter waved a hand. The other fae retired to a distance. Still staring at Peter, Titus lowered his sword too, lips tight.

"This doesn't mean anything, pirate. Call this a necessary—but temporary—truce. There is still the fact that you killed my partner."

My arms fell at my sides, that anger still swirling like *préachta*, but different—thicker, for starters. "You're a bloody stubborn fae, did you know that?"

Peter's eyebrows shot up in surprise.

I positioned myself before him and jabbed him on the chest. "He. Did. Not. Kill. Her. Capisce?"

"You don't—"

"Oh, bloody hell!" The cursing flew unbidden from my lips. Perhaps I'd been spending too much time with Titus. "It wasn't him."

Peter's eye twitched.

If this brute fae kept with his stubborn mindset, he'd never hear the end of it. My forehead throbbed, and I rubbed it with both hands. That encounter with Edward still had me shaking.

"Fé Erie came to me." He scowled. "I understand I am not to harm him, unless he tries something." His fists clenched and unclenched as if waiting for Titus to make such a move.

Titus snarled, and I lifted a hand. *Préachta* expanded and contracted, too fast. It wanted to take a shape, it wanted to go out and strike something.

It seemed to be on a high after what we did with Edward.

"*Your fae power needs to anchor,*" Cuidi had said.

Or that.

"Titus, it's time you tell Peter what really happened. And stop that macho nonsense. Just tell him the freaking truth."

Titus shrugged. "Well, dryshite, I was actually returning Aghna to Tir D'aois. Edward, our Alpha, was the one tainting her energy, although I wasn't completely innocent."

Both men glared at each other. Dislike oozed from them, but at least it was restrained.

"I need to see it for myself. Although you'd have to open to me, pirate."

Titus arched an eyebrow.

"He wants to see into your mind," I explained.

"No way in Anord's hell."

"Only those memories, pirate. You need not show me anything else."

"In another time, I would say nay. But strange things are afoot. I'll grant you access only to that time back in 1792. And only that moment."

"It wouldn't work with any other pirate. But I understand you have something *special* within you."

If Titus could glower more, he certainly would.

Peter closed his eyes and pressed his hand to Titus's forehead. Titus tensed, and his fists clenched.

After a minute or so, Peter removed his hand. His expression was stony, yet his eyes watered. He'd seen her, his love, on the verge of dying. Of being tainted by Edward's energy 'til she couldn't take it anymore.

He turned on his heels, then signaled the others to follow. I guessed he must need time to digest the idea that Titus wasn't the culprit after all. The anger must be crusted upon his soul like burnt cheese stuck to an iron pan.

And speaking about anger, my own dissipated and left exhaustion in its wake.

Titus said to me, "I can't go to the taigh; I need to find Kara and make sure she came out unscathed."

"Oh damn." I slapped a hand to my mouth. I'd forgotten about them. "Sergei."

"That traitor," Titus hissed.

"No, Titus, you didn't see him. He went for Minho."

"He didn't touch Kara?"

"At all."

"Then how . . .?" He sucked in a breath. "Edward always knows how to find us, though that's usually at sea. Maybe Sergei spoke the truth. But more the reason I need to find them."

He wanted to believe his friend. I reached out and squeezed his arm. "Kara was better after she fell to the floor. She said her beast was telling her to obey the Alpha."

He nodded. "It did the same to me. Now, we're between two enemy ships, and until I find a way out, you must remain there." He placed a finger on my lips when they parted to speak. "Fae are not my friends, Ryanne, understand that."

"Indeed we're not," Peter said even as he was a good ways away.

"This doesn't concern you, Pretty Boy."

"Oh, but it does." Peter approached us, ears twitching. "I'm to bring both of you."

"I don't answer to fae," Titus growled.

Steel flashed beneath the other faes' cloaks. Peter hadn't moved a muscle, but then he didn't have to with so many of his kind around.

"You're not giving me a choice," Titus said through clenched teeth.

"Be satisfied you aren't bound this time. But play no tricks, pirate.

Any attempt to escape, and I'll be forced to bind your arms." Peter took the lead once again.

I couldn't blame Titus for not wanting to return to the taigh after the way the fae treated him back when we met. I truly hoped, though, that Cuidi wanted to help him. I scowled at Peter's back, my fists tightly clenched. This time, I wouldn't let them mistreat him.

By the Hawthorn, not this time.

My normal vision blurred again, and I felt sick, my legs barely supporting me. Titus passed an arm around my waist, and I leaned into him. Kara had looked so pale, yet she fought others to give us time. I wasn't sure how to feel about Sergei, but he'd removed Minho from the equation and fought too.

"Can Edward kill them?" I asked, anxious.

"He shouldn't. He came for me, and he looked like someone who kissed the gunnar's daughter, not to mention that goblin's blade in his back."

"I saw about five bradaís in your lobby."

"Kara and Sergei know their way around our kin. If Sergei attacked Minho, that bastard shouldn't be up to par. They can tell lies and say they were confused. But as soon as the fae release me, I'm checking on them."

The bare, whitish branches of the trees entwined above our heads like the long fingers of a skeleton. Patches of dried grass were scattered here and there until we arrived at a clearing where several capalls grazed on a greener pasture.

At Peter's whistle, the wild creatures trotted toward us. One of them, gray and white matted fur with oblong silvery eyes, snarled, its canine teeth showing. Familiar with them, I approached and placed a hand on its snout. Once the creature blinked its eyes once, I knew it was safe to mount. Peter did the same and nodded at Titus for him to mount.

"Are we close to the taigh?" I asked.

"We are right on the edge of the west valley," Peter answered.

We rode on a wide path where sparse trees lined the road, surrounded by the fae. Night had fallen, studded with stars. A waning moon peeked between wisps of white clouds, shining light painting every branch and every blade of grass with a thin layer of bright silver hue.

I dozed, my exhausted body clamoring for rest, glad the capall followed the others.

We reached the taigh's western side, right on the edge of the big lake outside the walls. Nymphs sat on rocks, greeting Peter with enthusiasm. Among them, crazy Zadora waved to me like I was her best friend. I snorted. I liked her more as a fish, but at least she was outside the walls.

Once we dismounted, the capalls broke into a gallop, disappearing into the forest on the eastern side. I clasped Titus's hand and walked toward the entrance. Exhausted and hungry, I wouldn't be able to stand on my feet for much longer.

"Where's Bricius?" I asked.

"Inside. You'll see him soon enough," Peter said.

At the entrance, Peter stood before Titus. "We have arrived at my Lady's taigh. By her own request, I give you the option to enter as my prisoner, or you can choose to enter as a guest."

"I choose guest."

"And you know what that entails?"

"Perfectly."

"Titus," I whispered. "You need to follow certain rules—"

"I know."

"You have to tell the Lady you'll be an honored guest—"

"I know what to do."

Titus crossed the stone-arched gate with firm footsteps, and I followed, silently praying he wouldn't smart-mouth the Lady. Inside the courtyard, several fae gathered around Cuidi, where lamppost light gave enough clarity to their features. Titus returned the fae's hostility with a stare, except for Cuidi, who remained neutral.

I whispered to him, "If you don't play nice, you'll suffer the consequences. Be smart, Titus."

He gave me an arrogant look.

My eyelids felt heavy, legs trembling, but at least I felt peace here. It was like a troll-weight lifted from my shoulders. I gave my oath as a guest as Cuidi required.

"Titus Doyle," Cuidi said, loud enough for everyone in the courtyard to hear. "You walk on your own feet inside my home. Hence, I require your word to conduct yourself as an honorable guest."

"Lady Cuidigtheach." Titus's voice was deep and resonant. "I will abide by the rules of your taigh as a respectful guest while remaining within the confines of it." He fixed his eyes on Cuidi. "As long as my host respects me."

A gasp echoed between the gathered fae, but Cuidi didn't flinch. A playful smile touched her lips.

She addressed the gathered fae. "Titus is the first bradaí to be my guest and will be treated as such." She then addressed us in a lower voice. "Lhotto will come for you before the sun awakens the land."

"We thank you, Lady Cuidigtheach," I said.

I led Titus to my room, too tired to demand food despite my stomach's rumblings. The candleholders upon the walls gave a cozy feeling while smells of the outdoors and scents of flowers wafted in the warm breeze. It felt like home, and I smiled.

"Ryanne!" a shrill voice exclaimed before we reached the first set of stairs.

Bricius, dressed in a yellow jacket and green pants, hovered near me.

"You look like a traffic light," I said, drowsy and wanting so much to hug him.

Bricius smiled widely. "I'm pleased you came out unscathed, yes, yes, yes. There is some food in your room. I took care of it as soon as I knew you were to arrive."

"Thank you, Bug."

"Let's go," Titus said. "I'm swaying on my feet, and I'm tired of all this."

I couldn't agree more.

FORTY-SIX

Titus

Ryanne and I talked for another hour despite our exhaustion, going into details about what had happened with Edward and the rest. She was certainly worried about Kara and couldn't stop talking about her. For my part, I was obsessed with every detail about Sergei and whether it had been another trick.

Ryanne glowered and told me I should trust him and shut up. Hell, she was right.

Shortly after we woke up, one of the daighs came to take us to the Lady of the taigh.

"Lhotto!" Ryanne shrieked, hugging the daigh. "So glad to see you."

"Me too," he said, orange hair messed as if he slept funny, a scar crossing his cheek. "Hey, dude, don't you dare play another dirty trick on me, you hear?" He caressed the hilt of his sword.

"I did respect your life, didn't I?" I winked at him.

"That you did, but here's looking at you, dude." With two fingers, he pointed at his eyes, then at me.

Ryanne swatted his arm. "Behave, Lhotto. He's a friend."

Lhotto snorted, but his stance relaxed, and he even smiled at me. Now that was a bloody first: all these fae creatures not attempting to kill me since Pretty Boy found us. We followed Lhotto down a hallway that ran between the main building and the eastern wing. My body tensed with every step. I didn't expect a trap—the oath I gave last night protected me as well as them. Yet, the sole idea of being trapped here at their whim made my blood boil.

Ryanne kept stumbling, her exhaustion not over, and shivers crossed her body.

"Are you well?" I asked, worried that the trick she did with Edward had longer effects.

"I'm dizzy. I . . . like I ate too much, too fast, and now . . . I don't know. My *préachta* is acting weird." She gave me a worried look.

"Weird how?"

"Unstable. Cuidi warned me about this."

"We'll sort it out."

The stone-walled room where we arrived was warm and full of light. A few chairs and a couch were scattered near the large windows where Cuidigtheach and Pretty Boy stood.

"Cheerio, dude." Lhotto thumped my back and closed the door after him.

I scowled at the door. Why would he thump my back if we weren't friends? It served no purpose.

"Welcome," Cuidigtheach said, spreading olive hands to the side.

I folded my arms over my chest. "Why am I here?"

"Yeah," Ryanne said, "why are we back? Oh . . ." She shook her head as if coming out from a stupor.

Sensing her confusion and knowing her *préachta* was playing tricks on her, I pulled her to my side.

Pretty Boy gave me a hard look.

"Annoyed, fae?" I said, enjoying his discomfort.

To my surprise, he smiled back. "Not in the least. And you, pirate? Does it still hurt where I wounded you?"

"Actually, no." I patted my side. "Healed pretty well."

Thanks to Ryanne and the fae-spirit.

The door opened. A dark-skinned fae entered the room, her curly hair like molted bronze down to her waist, blue eyes as clear as a glacier-fed lake. Her white, plain gown did a poor job of concealing her dazzling beauty and regal posture.

She must be Tuiren, the third Eadrom, a fae I'd never seen before, albeit I couldn't mistake the wave of fae power she wore like a silk dress.

All three Eadrom united here was not good news for me.

Cuidigtheach and Pretty Boy mirrored the small bow of the head Tuiren gave them, while Ryanne sank her knee to the floor, despite her tiredness. I folded my arms across my chest.

"Please," Tuiren said in a singing voice. "Arise."

My beast tried to emerge like the kraken when it breaks the surface, unsettled by so many powerful fae who could beat me to a pulp. For once, I agreed with it, sick of them playing us like bloody puppets.

"Why the hell was I brought here?" It was high time for the queenies to explain what the spirit didn't.

"Behave, pirate." Pretty Boy took a menacing step toward me.

Tuiren lifted a hand. "I am not displeased by his question. He certainly is entitled. Please, what troubles you?"

"Why the hell did this fae"—I nodded at Pretty Boy—"have to skewer me? You could have asked nicely."

"You needed to die so you could live," Tuiren said. "Pain was essential to achieve the goal."

"*My* pain. *Your* goal."

"Yes, he was too hurt," Ryanne snapped. She pushed away from me, then staggered.

Tuiren smiled as though I was a bloody child she needed to reassure.

"I'm okay; I'm okay," Ryanne mumbled when I reached out for her.

Lady Cuidigtheach slid to her side and pulled her to an embrace while she whispered words I couldn't fathom. A wave of cold fae power hit me, mixed with the scents of roses and pine. Ryanne sighed, then stood up straighter, visibly better.

"You forget I'm no fae." For me there was only a vowel difference between fae and foe. They ought to know that. "Hell if I bend to you. I'd rather be blasted into oblivion."

Tuiren cocked her head, curls brushing her bronzed shoulder. "Is that what you think of us? That Fé Erie holds the coin to manipulate you?"

"Perhaps the part where she bet on my life is what upsets me. What do you call that? A disinterested gesture?" I bared my teeth in a smile.

"Watch your manners, pirate," Pretty Boy said. The threat was present in the way the dryshite's fingers tightened around the hilt of his sword. The same one that had pierced me.

"The coin is part of a potent spell," Cuidightheach said. "Your kin cannot kill you without it. If they do, the spell will be undone. Thus the power, not having a proper vessel, will disperse. Your Alpha wants to make sure your power goes to him. You know that."

I reluctantly nodded. "I'm surprised you know about this."

"This is recent news for us. Your death helped uncover many secrets."

"With Fé Erie's possession of the coin, nobody can take it," Tuiren said. "Think of her as a Leprechaun who would guard your gold."

"I want it back." What did these fae think, manipulating Ryanne and me like that?

"You know why you want it, Aodhán?" Tuiren asked.

"It's mine," I snarled.

"Yours? Or Anord's?" Tuiren asked, her gaze unwavering. "Part of you belongs to Chaos, and part belongs to Life. Who are you really, Aodhán?"

Both forces struggled within me. As they had from the beginning. My fists clenched tighter. "My name is Doyle, not Aodhán."

She removed a gold ring from her index finger and held it at eye level. "What do you feel?"

The golden chain in Minho's neck. The two golden coins Edward flashed before my eyes. I'd been too worried both times to notice the lack of allure. I didn't feel the urge, the desire to own it. It didn't pull me as before.

"Nothing," I said, unclenching my fists.

"Naturally." Tuiren threw it at me. I caught it without looking. "You don't have your trigger anymore."

"So that's why," Ryanne mused. "Without the coin, your gold lust is gone and Anord can't control you." She looked up at me, hope in her eyes.

It pained me to disappoint her. Anord might not be able to control me, but the beast still could. A task I was yet to master.

I played with the ring between my fingers. Just metal. Couldn't compare it to Ryanne's soft touch.

"Why aren't the others created like Edward and me?"

"The spell Anord used then," Cuidightheach answered, "is not an easy one since it feeds upon Tír na Vraoichta and balances with the human realm. When he tried the second time, he failed, and he destroyed that creature."

Did he? So many unknown facts about our kin.

The Lady continued, "Since he didn't have that same energy for the rest of the bradaís, he had to borrow power—"

"Steal," Tuiren snarled.

"—from other powerful beings in the realm of darkness, Tír na Vraoichta, where he's from."

"Kara's Odin," Ryanne said quietly.

Aye. Kara had an affinity for Odin. Had she been created with energy from Odin? Sergei from Baba Yaga? It made sense. Anord created us in places of power.

"You were supposed to be like the firstborn Edward," Tuiren addressed me, "even darker. Anord's apex creation. You can kill the Alpha. He must be obliterated."

Ryanne had been right. They were playing with us like chess pieces. And the Morrigan's crows could peck my eyes for eternity if I shared my plans to kill Edward with them. That was for Kara and Sergei.

I snickered. "Kill him yourself. You have proven you know how. Send Pretty Boy for your deed."

"Alas, we cannot. The Alpha's Name is unbeknownst to Fé Erie, like the rest of your kin's. You saw Anord's mistake by creating you where the connection of Tír D'aois to the human world waxes strong. As soon as he placed a foot in Éire, his presence was no longer obscure to Fé Erie."

"Éire?" Ryanne asked, confused.

"That's Ireland's original name," I explained.

Tuiren continued as if we hadn't spoken. "It is within you that the touch of fae has interacted and inhibited your abomination to some extent. Your hand shall be the one that pierces his own abomination."

The beast.

Anord had told me I was defective. Now I knew why. I was part fae. Bloody hell. No wonder Aghna's touch had changed me.

Most likely Anord had thought sending me off the cliff with the fae-spirit involved would have been the end of me. Anord had not need to destroy me once he realized I was under his command. I furrowed my brow. What would happen when I put a foot outside?

Aye, my back was turned to the bradaís' path, and Anord had failed in his attempt to obliterate me to the void.

Thanks to the fae. I scowled.

"You want me to kill Edward, but if you don't know his Name, then there's no way to terminate him."

I locked eyes with Ryanne while I spoke, hoping she understood my silent message to not say a thing about how we both fought Edward. Her lips twitched, slightly enough for no one to notice unless they were watching her. But all eyes were on me. Grand.

"That is your path," Tuiren said. "You have a connection with Anord, and you have a connection with us. You are our bridge now. You must find the way to use both to know his Name and terminate him. He is our biggest foe."

The hell with that. The path was what they dictated for me as a lackey. My beast roared and thumped against its *préachta* prison. With pleasure, I would remove both *dorcha* and *préachta*, be my own man. Feel the peace I had back in the cave where both were quiet. The peace I felt in that flickering moment when I was created.

Feel. What Edward was after.

"How did you kill the other two bradaís?" Ryanne asked.

"I beg your pardon?" Tuiren exclaimed.

"Two died?" Pretty Boy asked at the same time.

Only the Lady of the taigh remained quiet, though her obsidian gaze didn't leave me.

"Wait a minute. This guy," I pointed at Pretty Boy, "was the one to 'kill' me. Didn't any of you Eadrom kill the others?"

"No," Tuiren answered. "We were unaware bradaís could be killed. Not until Fé Erie share the news of your own demise."

"Edward lied then," Ryanne said to me.

"No surprise then," I seethed.

Edward had killed his own kin.

"Then Fé Erie was testing me," Ryanne said, thoughtful. "When Peter wounded Titus."

"She expected you to show compassion," Cuidigtheach said. "You showed love, which exceeded our expectations."

Compassion. The reason why they needed humans to do their dirty deeds. Without it, humans wouldn't have approached us.

Ryanne would have never approached me.

"And now Titus has an advantage over Edward," Ryanne said.

"I wouldn't call it an advantage not to die at his hands," I said, dryly. "They're still after my hide."

Regretting my outburst, I gave her an apologetic smile.

"By the troll's bridge, it's more than any bradaí has ever had," Tuiren said. "And you shall have another. Gallchobhair will help you in your quest."

"Hell, no!"

Pretty Boy grinned. "You need someone to watch you, pirate, so you don't stray from the path."

Like a bloody, deadly babysitter. Grand.

"Your Alpha must be destroyed—we cannot do anything more with him alive. If he finds out about the plan, it'll be more difficult. He shouldn't expect it."

"And after the Alpha is dead, we can get rid of the others," Pretty Boy said, mouth twisted in a snarl.

"You're talking about my kin," I said, raising my hand. "To exterminate *them*." Hell if I'd help them, Edward or not. Once they did, who would stop them from eliminating *me*?

"You *are* an aberration," he said. "You were never meant to exist."

"Whatever, Pretty Boy, but it's my kin. I won't be a part of this. Go ahead and crush me."

"Fear not, Titus. It shant be all of you," Tuiren said.

"The rest can be transformed," Cuidightheach said. "If not like you, at least to remove their coins for them to begin to be themselves and not mindless murderers. We'll give them the option. If they accept, they'll go through the same as you. If not . . ." She left the sentence incomplete, but it was clear. If they refused, they would die.

It wasn't only the gold coin. The beast still intruded in our perceptions. The nádhúrtha's words came to mind.

Do not let it control you when she's not by your side.

Yet, if what they said was true, that with my beast and the touch of fae I'd be able to get Edward's Name, then converting the others wouldn't be as hard. Ideas swirled in my head, the golden coins of each one shining within my reach. Their power at my fingertips. I shifted, uncomfortable, a knot forming in my shoulders.

Tuiren continued, "Once the Alpha disappears, Aodhán will approach every bradaí to offer redemption. Those who don't accept the change shall be eliminated."

And that was why I was needed. My kin would never allow a fae to approach them. I would become a pet. No, I'd always been one. I was just trading one master for another. My nails dug deep into my palm.

"Not everyone will want it," Pretty Boy said. "There are some who enjoy torturing."

"Bloody right. Some are already rotten to the core." Like Minho.

An image of Ryanne at Minho's hands weakened my knees. If Sergei hadn't taken care of Minho . . . Bile rose in my throat just to imagine what could happen.

"What's my part in this?" Ryanne asked.

"You will remain here for some time," Tuiren answered, "while you learn to manage your fae power."

"No! I haven't gone through all of this just to be swept aside." She glanced at Cuidigtheach. "My job isn't done, my Lady."

"You would be in extreme danger with him. It cannot be so," Tuiren said.

"Could there be a way?" Ryanne insisted.

"No," Cuidightheach said. "This endeavor might take years and years. Remember what we talked about."

"But I can help him!"

I crossed my arms, hoping she would stop, or my newly formed plan would go to hell.

"As certain as the stars shine upon the lake," Tuiren said, "you would be used by his enemies to reach him."

Peter said to Ryanne, "You aren't fit to fight against them, not yet. This is not within your reach."

Her eyes blazed in sudden anger. She opened her mouth to retort, but I pressed a finger to her lips.

"Cuidigtheach and Tuiren speak the truth. The danger will be greater and there's *nothing* you can do. Your touch of fae isn't *enough* against us bradaís."

Her eyes flashed briefly with comprehension, then she lowered her gaze and covered her face in her hands. A half-hearted sob escaped from her lips. Grand.

"Give me three days with Ryanne before I leave." Enough for my plan.

"Granted."

With another sob, Ryanne stormed out of the room. I refrained my smile and lowered my gaze, feinting a concerned expression. The fae didn't understand misdirection. Perfect.

FORTY-SEVEN

Ryanne

After I stormed out from the room, I slowly wandered around the halls of the taigh. Cuidi's embrace had helped to stabilize me.

The alabaster floor had beautiful amber designs of faerie beings placed here and there. I studied them at my leisure with the excuse that I had to keep my head down in case I met a fae and our little theater was discovered. I wondered why Titus hadn't wanted me to talk about how I helped to thwart Edward's intent. Or why he didn't even mention it.

Bricius zoomed and hovered near me. "How did it go?"

"Not good, Bug. They want me out of the way." I lowered my voice. "But I'm not taking it."

He grinned. "I knew you wouldn't, no, no, no. Can I tell you a secret?"

I raised my eyebrows. "Another? How many have you been hiding?"

He flew next to me and spoke quietly. "My Lady was expecting you to run away, when she told you you had to stay."

"What?"

"Sssh! Lower your voice! You're a *bean* now."

"Bann?"

"Woman. Fae who aren't *cailín* anymore need not to follow all rules. They need to find their own footing."

I sighed. "That sounds like young adults in my world."

"Yes, yes, yes," he said, "it's important they go on their own quests and follow their hearts."

Follow your heart. Huh.

Préachta whirled in that erratic way it'd been doing, and I staggered.

"Oh!" Bricius's wings perked up. "She's calling you. Go, go, go."

The door on the left of the corridor throbbed with a gentle green light, and without hesitation, I walked inside. Fé Erie stood in the middle of the otherwise empty room. She approached me with a graceful gait, and I made a move to sink to my knee when her long, thin fingers rested on my chin, preventing me from kneeling.

"Do you know why I brought you here in the first place?" she asked with a young and cheerful tone.

"You wanted me to save Titus. From the beginning," I said, mesmerized by the fire-red curls dancing around her face, moving with their own music.

"That is only the stone that triggers the landslide." She reached out and cupped my cheek.

Hot and cold mingled over my skin at her touch, and a strong juniper and mint smell hit me. I couldn't take my eyes off her, drinking her ageless beauty like a thirsty child.

With a gentle spin like a dancer, she went to a balcony overlooking the forest beyond the walls. There was this harmony in her, like her body was attuned to the energies around, like every part of her belonged to the surroundings.

Or maybe the surroundings belonged to her.

Comfortably, like talking with a friend, I leaned beside her. "Why did you choose me? And how did you know I'd save him?"

She laughed, and the entire forest vibrated as if a fresh rain had fallen. "Bricius chose you, hence I accepted his decision. He knew you would be compassionate and receptive. Nonetheless, I observed you to make sure those qualities held. You were receptive when we gave you the gift: you went through the portal to where Bricius waited. You showed your compassion when you diminished the suffering of the bradaí when he was a prisoner and when you accepted to save him."

"But I took too long to accept your gift."

"Long? No. Just a sigh. Many humans spend their entire lives bent on seeing just one thing. You opened to us, and you accepted us, making my power grow within you." Her thin, pale hands lifted as if they held a giant ball between them. "You are like a flower opening to the sun, shy and curious."

She began to change from solid to translucent as if her cells were part of the air.

"Trust thyself on the changes to come." Her tri-toned voiced echoed all around and wind picked up, sweeping my hair.

The last thing I saw were her bright eyes.

I told Bricius everything she'd said. And even described what I did to Edward. His eyes grew big, and his jaw slacked.

"But hush!" I hissed. "Not a word, you hear?"

He grinned. "You are indeed *bean* now."

Titus appeared from the other side of the corridor. With a few long strides, he reached my side. "Is there a place where we can talk in private?"

He eyed Bricius, who slumped his shoulders, mumbling something about not being wanted anymore while flying away.

I wanted to tell him that yes, he was loved, but there were times I needed privacy.

"The south garden."

Holding hands, we headed to the covered passageway that took us to the southern section of the taigh and into the garden. The odd anemone-like plants puffed their yellowish vapors.

"I saw one of those apelings here," I said, pointing at the plants. "How did you send them? I never understood their purpose in that skirmish."

"Zorkar sent them. Homkar's older brother," he clarified. "They were our ears to know if the fae took you out, so we could be prepared. Tricky thing to do—I still have no idea how Zorkar gained their help."

A gravel path surrounded the lakeshore, and we walked along it for some time until we reached the cluster of pines near the eastern side. Titus stopped and closed his eyes, arms outstretched.

Could I do the same? I focused on my surroundings, the smell of pine, juniper, and a hint of mint hitting my nose. I pushed farther and whispers reached my ears.

Faraway whispers, one upon the other, with no discerning words. The beings inside the wall.

"No one's near," Titus said.

No one, but what about those invisible beings? My gaze reached beyond toward the black stone wall, and a tingling spread through my arms.

"Let's sit."

He pointed at the nearest tree. The grass was soft, comfortable. Birds chirped nearby and overgrown squirrels scurried about. Otherwise, all was quiet and serene.

"I've been thinking," Titus said. "What we did with Edward, with our connection, shows something can be done. That was quite a feat, *ashtore*."

"You didn't tell them that."

He kissed the bridge of my nose. "You noticed. Now we're in danger in the human world. Minho discovered a way to travel, evidently working with someone from Tír D'aois. And we can't stay here since your friends want us to split."

"Your ship isn't an option if Edward can find you so easily."

"Aye, we're in danger at sea as well. We have just one option."

"Quintus. But he was impossible to find."

Titus gave me that adorable, crooked smile of his. "*Ashtore*, you weren't thinking this was going to be a stroll on deck, were you? This is an impossible quest."

"I know a thing or two about impossible quests." I pressed a hand to his chest. "We still need to activate your spark."

He sighed in exasperation but didn't say no, which was a start.

"I need . . . *We* need to make sure Kara and Sergei are okay. But Edward will be expecting that. Homkar and I have some safety spots. We'll look for him first and task him to check on them. Now, *dorcha* didn't work against Edward. *Préachta* is the key, but we need to practice before facing Edward again. Enhance what we have together."

"I like that, but do you have an idea of how to get his Name? Tuiren wasn't explicit in how to use both your beast and the fae-power."

"Have they ever been explicit with you?" He arched an eyebrow.

I shook my head, smiling.

"That's their way."

"They're just giving you the ingredients," I said, "and you have to figure out what to do with them."

"That's the fae. Giving orders like some bloody general hidden far away from the battle."

"And Quintus might be able to hide us from them?"

"For sure," Titus said. "Remember that your dimension, Tír na Donna, is nádhúrthas territory. And he's a Master of Shadows. If someone can, it's him."

"But, how to find him? We weren't successful."

"We only tried for a few hours. I spent months trying to find him back then, but I'm sure it'll only take us a few weeks. We need to be patient and stealthy enough so no one can find us in the meantime."

The idea of being able to help, to increase our connection with the fae-power, made me fidget in place. I couldn't wait to get out of here and look for Quintus. Could we defeat Edward on our own?

How my *préachta* entwined with Titus's. How Edward stumbled back.

The barren land. What had that been? It'd been just for a second, but I needed to find out more.

We sat in silence, watching the soft breeze swirl over the grass as if invisible beings caressed the top of the blades. Or maybe there *were* invisible beings.

"Are you sure we're alone?" I whispered. "I feel something."

He closed his eyes and took a deep breath, then nodded. "Not physical beings. Spirits. This place is odd."

"It's wonderful," I breathed. "I'm going to miss it."

"I told Tuiren I wanted to cherish every single minute with you." He chuckled. "I want to wait until midnight in case they're suspicious."

Despite his good humor, something had changed. It was subtle— sadness peeked behind his cheerful facade. He grabbed a blade of grass and twirled it between his fingers.

What could change his mood? It wasn't the fae or the escape. Then I recalled the only thing he hadn't wanted to talk about.

"Titus. What did Amriel show you?"

He lowered his gaze to the blade of grass. "He showed me what I had done. He showed me the suffering I've caused, the trail of destruction I've left behind me." He glanced up, eyes the color of a storming sea. "Everything I've done. All the consequences of my actions. One after another went through my head."

I pulled his head onto my lap, gently stroking him, and he trembled. For some time, I rocked him until he calmed down.

Titus sat, and our gazes locked. He tucked a lock of hair behind my ear, brushing my cheek with his fingertips.

His lips eagerly sought mine, his hands tangling in my hair as he kissed me with the passion of the storm raging inside him. His intensity awakened my own desires, and soon we rolled over the grass, our arms and legs entwined until he was on top of me.

"Wait, we're in a public place," I said, breathlessly.

"Don't worry, *ashtore*. The queenie faerie gave instructions to leave us alone. There's no one around," he said hoarsely.

I swatted his arm playfully. "Show some respect."

"Let's focus on more important matters." He nibbled at my lower lip while his hand slid beneath my skirt.

Sun rays filtered through the branches above, a warm breeze circling us. Desire flashed in his steel-colored eyes, a different storm brewing behind.

"Let's," I said, unable to conceal my mirth.

He chuckled against my lips. The laughter from the depths of my belly drowned with his kisses. We melted into one another, hungrily seeking each other's mouths. I poured my feelings into the kiss, printing the same intensity in every touch, in every breath. My love for him bolted like a capall at full speed, wanting to find him.

I didn't want to let go, didn't want to stop touching him.

My chest burst with raw energy, a cold that didn't freeze but empowered me. *Préachta* spread through my arms, my legs, my head, my lips. I felt light as a pixie yet strong as a fae. I could feel Titus— something wakened from slumber inside him, aware of the energy I was transmitting through my kiss.

He yearned for it—I knew for certain. He grabbed my shoulders, like a drowning man reaching for that coveted gulp of air.

Our *préachta* wrapped us, made us part of it in a crazy dance, melting my being with his.

We kept on kissing, kept on touching each other as if we were afraid to stop and break the connection between us.

Radiant energy condensed in the pit of my belly. Like a small supernova, it began to grow, to expand, covering my body with white, pure energy. It throbbed, condensed, and swirled within me until it was too much, too bright to contain.

It held its breath as if waiting for my decision, to let it explode inside me or let it out. It was so beautiful, so pure, so marvelous that I wanted to keep it.

But it wasn't meant for me.

I broke the embrace and sat. Titus followed suit.

I pushed the white energy out of me. Toward Titus. With my hands and with my mouth, I transmitted it to him. And like a thirsty child, he drank it, clung to it, demanded it. It covered him as it did me, traveled through him, and expanded outside us, covering us.

Shakingly, I broke the kiss. I leaned my head on his chest, his arms squeezing me. Under my cheek, the accelerated beat of his heart thumped. I gasped.

A beat.

Of his heart.

FORTY-EIGHT

Titus

Ryanne jerked away from the embrace and pointed at my chest. "You-you-you had no beat . . . no heart."

"I . . ." I looked down at my chest in confusion.

The heart—Hell! I had one—pounded hard, stealing my breath away.

The annoying new addition drew attention to itself like a brat, weakening my being. And yet, the sensation was sweet, powerful, as though I was able to conquer anything with her at my side.

Ryanne straddled me, placing both hands on my chest. There it was, the beating of a heart. I shut my eyes and grabbed her elbows.

The new addition beat at full steam, connecting with my nervous system, with veins that didn't need it before. At her touch, the heart turned to it hungrily, connecting us, searching for her rhythm. And slowly, the heartbeat engaged hers until both beat in unison for a few seconds, then the thing inside changed to its own rhythm.

Behind the heartbeat, lay a small ball of condensed energy. Pure. It expanded tentatively as if not sure how to do so. Morrigan's crows, was that the spark? It was—it was exactly like the one I saw when I cut Minho's connection to his fae essence. What I saw with Aghna.

"You're right," I breathed. "There's something in there. Something . . . pure."

A dark energy interposed as a monster lurking in the shadows. It throbbed like a thick, oily splotch, its tendrils reaching out to me.

The beast.

"I feel your beast," she said, brow furrowed and hands pressed to my chest as though she wanted to rip it away.

"Aye, it won't go away. Do you think . . .?" For the first time, hope swelled within me. If she could activate it and made the beast go away . . .

"We will," she said, determined. "I love you."

"I don't know what that is, Ryanne. I don't understand."

"That's okay; I do." She took my hand and placed it on her chest. "I love you," she repeated, smiling.

Energy erupted from her chest into the heart, making it throb in confusion.

"I love you."

Again the heart pounded in confusion.

She placed her hand on my chest, and the energy tingled through our arms and hands.

"I love you," she said with such energy, the heart reacted, jumping.

"I . . . This is confusing. I don't know," I stammered.

She removed her hand and gave me space. I didn't like that.

"Do it again."

"You can say it if you want."

"Words mean nothing to me. But I like it when you say it."

"Want to try?"

I nodded. I was never shy of trying new things, and I'd do it for her.

Our hands rested over each other's hearts, our gazes locked. I glanced at the trees, taking courage.

"I love you." The words sounded hollow, meaningless. As if I was a child reciting something in a language unknown to me.

She encouraged me with her eyes.

"I love you." Now it was as if someone threw a rag doll to the floor, not caring. But I was determined to learn.

"I love you." The words reminded me of old disused machinery, dusty, that once had a purpose, but it'd been forgotten.

Dust dropped from the machine when I repeated the words, revealing something that could have once been a shining object. The heart leaped as if remembering something distant, something that it once wanted, but couldn't remember.

Like a child seeing something for the first time, something wonderful but still I didn't know what it was, I repeated the words once more. The machinery took its first squeaks, moving slowly like it needed oil.

"I love you." With a loud sound that almost left us deaf, the machinery started, prepped with her love, the heart filled with light as if it had been covered with black blankets that now fell away.

At the renewal of the words, my voice conveyed elation for the first time, the heart pumping the intense feeling to every corner of my being.

My heart.

"I love you."

I sought her mouth and made her mine under the intensity of our emotions, throbbing with unusual strength under our skin.

Energy flowed from our centers doing a circuit between the two of us, nothing standing between us, without shadows, without fear. Only this moment mattered, only sentiments flowed.

This time, our lovemaking was magical, different. Her kiss, her touch, her scent overpowered me. She repeated the words over and over again, whispering them with such contentment my eyes watered.

I never knew I could feel like that. I was bloody grateful I could.

The silhouette of her bare shoulder stood out with the whiteness of the sheet, barely illuminated by the moonlight. I ran my finger over her skin, hardly touching her. We'd returned to her room after the experience in the gardens.

I noted the slow breathing of her breast, the gentle curve of her lips lifting from time to time. The way her hair fell over her skin. I ran its soft strands through my fingers, inhaling her flowery scent. I brought her close to me.

Ryanne heaved a sigh of protest but leaned her head on my chest, hugging me, the warmth of her body against mine. Her face reflected the peace she projected. I was stunned, watching her. What if Edward guessed my moves? Could I protect her?

Aye, I would. Her energy was evolving, and so was mine. Together, we could be stronger.

I shook her gently. "Ryanne, wake up, come on."

She rubbed her eyes. "Did I fall sleep?"

"Let's go," I said with a hint of urgency. I couldn't wait to get out of here. "Get dressed."

I picked up her clothes, handing them to her. She dressed and tied her hair in a ponytail.

"Ready," she said.

I stroked my beard. "I think a shave and a haircut are in order. Have you ever wondered how you'd look as a blonde?"

She wrinkled her nose, trying to contain the laughter that loomed on her lips. "But before we go looking for Homkar, or do extreme makeovers, we need to go somewhere first."

"Where?"

"I need to see my parents. And I want you to meet them."

My jaw dropped. "What?"

She leaned her body against mine, playing with my shirt button. "If we're going to disappear, I want to say goodbye. And I want them to meet you."

"They'll look for us there. It's not a good idea."

"After we find Quintus, then?"

It was the least I could do if I was about to take her into a maelstrom. "Very well, a *quick* visit and not before finding Quintus."

She gave me a quick peck on my cheek. "Thank you."

"Don't thank me yet. Hold on," I said as I hugged her waist, just like when I took her away. Only this time, Ryanne had a huge smile stitched on her face. Not able to resist, I kissed her, feeling for the first time I was doing the right thing.

Sepia splashed in my vision and sounds muffled. She and I, laughing and embracing, not a worry in the world. Nothing seemed to rattle us. We looked content.

We separated, stumbling back. She looked at me, agape. So did I.

"Titus! I had a vision of us!"

"I saw it too."

She blinked.

And then, we laughed. I pulled her back to me, hugging tightly. I exhaled, relieved.

"So, we're right."

"Yes," she whispered.

"Come on, *acushla*."

"What did you call me?"

"Another Irish endearment. It feels right. Now, this might feel a little weird."

"And that's different from what we've done how?"

Chuckling, I called the Shadow and merged with it. The silvery illumination disappeared, turning our world to tones of sepia and blurred forms. Clasping her hand, we glided down the stairs to ground level.

At every step, my senses were on high alert to catch any sign of fae —but all was clear. We dashed toward the wall encompassing the taigh, her hand clasped in mine.

"Everything's going to be fine, *acushla*."

Acushla. How fitting.

Vein of my heart.

Epilogue

FÉ ERIE

Fé Erie watched the bradaí escaping with the human, the Shadow covering their tracks. *That was not planned*, she thought. For a moment, she paused, uncertain. Should she let them go or not? The human turned her head toward her and smiled without fear. Energy throbbed in her, in synch with her surroundings. In synch with the bradaí next to her.

Fé Erie decided then and raised her hand, isolating them from Cuidightheach's attention. They had made their decision, and she would abide by it.

Now, there was another task to be done, thus she lifted her arms above her head. Her mind conjured a blackthorn tree. She visualized the spiky thickets, bare branches punctuated by cruel spikes. The one she had in mind was a particular bare blackthorn that never blossomed.

The surrounding energy sizzled like a pooka dashing through the fields at night when the creature shapeshifts into a dark, sleek horse with a long, wild flowing mane and luminescent golden eyes.

She vanished and then materialized before the gaping mouth of a cave embedded on a rocky mound, darkness as thick as tar threatening to swallow any daring creature foolish enough to prowl nearby. The blackthorn grew to one side, its branches reaching out to her as if begging to be uprooted from this desolated land. An old black dragon perched atop the cave. It bowed its head to her and flapped its enormous wings, spanning as large as the mound itself.

The lair of the Erlking.

And there the Erlking was, standing next to the blackthorn and dwarfing the two giant dire wolves resting at either side of him, heads hidden beneath their paws as though afraid to meet her eye.

Proud as the dragon, the Erlking stood immobile. A thick gray beard covered half of his scarred face and hung to his chest. A cape draped around his broad shoulders, brushing the rocky soil, a cape made of dead leaves and bound together by the will of its master.

"You knew I was coming," she said.

The Erlking bowed his head. "Indeed, Mother. What do you desire?"

His eyes sparkled with mischief. He was untamed, like the pooka, and forever would he be. Lady Cuidightheach had been right. It was folly to involve him, but alas, it must be done.

"It is about the bradaís."

"Ah." He clicked his tongue. "Interesting creatures. I would love nothing more than to have them in my *Wilde Jagd*." There was a ring in his voice, a meaning behind his words she could not discern. Her power had its limits.

"I'm sure they have joined your Hunt already. It is also about a peculiar human."

"Your pet."

"No. A human blessed with my power."

"Your pet." His lips twitched.

"That is of no relevance." She glanced at the gaping darkness behind him. "I believe you have in your dungeons someone who does not belong here."

"I captured him. He's mine," the Erlking snarled.

"By the energies that bind all dimensions together, yes, he is. You played by the rules. May I see him?"

The Erlking gave a short bark of laughter. "Absolutely, Mother, absolutely. But beware. He's not a tame creature. He's no one's pet."

"Like you." She smiled benignly, not unlike a mother to her troublesome child.

The Erlking grinned back and waved a hand toward the lair's entrance. Darkness of a different nature than the Erlking lurked behind the trees that bordered the rugged landscape. A different tingle on her skin. Unfamiliar and untamed like the Erlking, yet she found it hard to discern.

"You know who she is," the Erlking said while he walked deeper into his lair, hands clasped behind his back.

Fé Erie cocked a fiery eyebrow but opted to follow the Erlking. The matter that brought her to his lair was more urgent than the strange fae.

She stepped into the bowels of the lair of the most dangerous creature in Tír D'aois, who had managed to capture the most dangerous creature from Tír na Donna—the land of humans.

Someone who could tip the balance. To whose side? That was to be seen.

Join the Cursed Dragon Ship Newsletter

Want more just like this one? Sign up for our newsletter so you don't miss out on the adventure. You'll get:

- A free book for signing up
- Advanced notice of new releases
- First word of books on sale
- Opportunities for free books
- Most up-to-date information on author appearances.

We're busy and know you are too. We won't send more than one newsletter a month.

Register below.

Plea from the Author

Dear reader,

From all the wonderful stories out there, you chose *Touch of Faete*. For that, I am forever grateful.

Could I ask you one last favor? Please leave a review on Amazon and/or Goodreads and say what you liked, what you didn't like, or whatever else you'd like to say. It can be as brief as you like. Reviews are the air we writers breathe.

Without your help, other readers might never meet Titus and Ryanne!

If you're interested in being first in line to learn more about the fae and the bradaís, join my newsletter (https://ligiadewit.eo.page/bd8xf) and get a free short story.

Thank you for your support,

Ligia de Wit

Acknowledgments

I remember, before embarking on this daunting journey known as writing, questioning why authors might need an entire year to pen their next book. I mean, come on, they already have it all in writing, don't they? I also harbored the notion of writers toiling away in isolation, typing their stories in solitude.

Writing a book proved to be much more challenging than I had ever imagined.

But it hasn't need to be a lonely path.

When I penned the first draft of the *Bradais Pledge*, I was fortunate to receive invaluable feedback from fellow writing peers. They helped me refine my ideas and propelled me towards crafting a story that readers could truly relish. They held me accountable and, at times, gave my writing a good, well-deserved thrashing, but they also showered me with encouragement.

These writers helped me believe in Titus and Ryanne. They made me believe that there would be someone out there who would find joy in reading their story. Although I couldn't possibly express my gratitude to all of those writers here, there are two special ones. These two writers not only served as my critique partners but also evolved into close friends: Jesse Sprague and Tracy Leonard.

Jesse and Tracy have walked alongside me through the path to publishing since I first shared that initial draft with our online critique group. They provided unwavering encouragement and unshakable belief in me. Titus has always been Jesse's favorite, while Tracy had a soft spot for Ryanne and Peter. They both chided me for procrastinating with the story and not putting it out there. And they were right, by the way. At the time, I didn't feel ready.

But Titus and Ryanne were ready, ready to share their tale of high seas and fae lands with the world, and they found their way into the right hands, those of Cursed Dragon Ship Publishing.

And this is where my next gratitude lays.

When I first submitted *Burden of Faete* to my editor, Kelly Lynn Colby, I was certain she would love it just as it was. And she did. But that didn't stop her from brandishing her formidable "Big Editor Stick" and delivering a stern rebuke. Ouch!

I protested, "Hey, I thought you loved it!" She calmly responded, "Why yes, but . . ."

As I delved into her comments, my initial indignation gave way to a begrudging recognition that she had a point. A very good point.

I embarked on the revisions, and as I did, it dawned on me like a thunderbolt. She was absolutely right! My fingers tingled with excitement, and my mind buzzed with a torrent of fresh ideas as I rewrote several scenes. Of course! Why hadn't I thought of this earlier?

This, precisely, is why editors exist—to push you beyond your comfort zone, to challenge you, and to illuminate new possibilities.

Her comments upon receiving the second version were "Ligia, this is frigging amazing." Those words are the ones every author eagerly anticipates.

Well, almost. Reviews, after all, hold the supreme place in my writing heart!

Speaking of hearts, I simply can't express enough gratitude to my wonderful family. Your support and patience as I delve into my adventures mean the world to me. Your love and encouragement are the very essence of what I cherish most.

Lastly, this acknowledgment section wouldn't be complete without a heartfelt thank you to amazing copyeditor and proofreader, Sara. Her comprehensive feedback and explanations about why she changed a word is invaluable. I'm learning so much from such talented people at Cursed Dragon Ship Publishing.

You all help me to be a better writer.

About the Author

Ligia de Wit is a quirky bilingual writer, residing in Mexico City. An eternal romantic who's loved fairy tales and swashbuckling stories all her life, she blends both with fun language and a hefty sprinkle of romance while she's at it. Her stories are full of personality with endearing characters.

You can find her short stories with Palamades Publishing, Backchannel Magazine, and WordCrafter.

When not concocting stories, she works at a global leading distributor company. Chat with her at ligiadewit.com.

f facebook.com/ligiadewit
X x.com/LigiadeWit
O instagram.com/ligiadewitauthor